bright college years, with pleasure rife,
the shortest, gladdest years of life;
how swiftly are ye gliding by!
oh, why doth time so quickly fly?
the seasons come, the seasons go,
the earth is green or white with snow,
but time and change shall naught avail
to break the friendships formed at Yale.

—Yale alma mater, first stanza

bright
college
years

(*or*, if that's not life)

by andrew pessin

OPEN
BOOKS

Published by Open Books

For G., my D., from your J.

praise for *bright college years*

"*Bright College Years* is a wistful trip in a time machine, back to those college years so filled with fun, friendship, and heartache. Travel there with Pessin to a Yale of the early 80s, when a handful of friends thought ever-so-briefly they owned the world."

—Scott Johnston, Yale '82,
author of Amazon bestseller, *Campusland*

"Although times change, key truths about the college experience remain the same. *Bright College Years* is witty and lighthearted in just the right measures, yet undaunted by the inevitable bleaker moments one faces during those metamorphic years—reminding us that those bleak moments are often the most transformational. Philosophical probing meets the nostalgia of memory, and you will relish the journey back to your own formative days as you immerse yourself in it."

—Lauren Williamson,
Connecticut College '23

"This delightful novel brought me right back to campus, to those simultaneously halcyon and turbulent days, with that delicious mixture of nostalgia, promise, and regret, when changing the world was as urgently pressing as whether your football team beat their football team. Fortunately ours usually beat theirs."

—Richard Landes, Harvard alum,
author of *Could the Whole World Be Wrong?*

"This funny, moving, deeply philosophical novel captures the spirit of Yale, moving seamlessly between past and present and illuminating both. 1980s Yale comes alive as these endearing characters navigate their studies, friendships, relationships and, ultimately, their future—and our own."

—Courtney Sender, Yale '10,
author of *In Other Lifetimes All I've Lost Comes Back to Me*

"Bravo! *Bright College Years* is a clever, humorous, touching, and thought-provoking story that perfectly captures the essence of college life. It beautifully portrays that period of time and how it shapes one's future. It's both nostalgic and timeless."

—Steven Skybell, Yale '84,
Tevye in the Yiddish *Fiddler*, www.stevenskybell.com

"Andrew Pessin's uproarious and touching novel centers around a group of semi-kindred spirits attending Yale University in the early 1980s that calls itself the 'Meatheads' and lives by the motto emblazoned on the door of one of its members: FASTER LOUDER HIGHER MORE. The Meatheads are a rowdy, reckless, and big-hearted group of boozers, stoners, and prospectors for love who also excel in the classroom, head up school organizations, attend Allen Ginsberg readings and Gloria Steinem lectures, debate the merits of Erich Segal's prose, argue over world events, and the possibility of nuclear holocaust, as well as the privilege of going to Yale when their increasingly hefty tuitions might be used for a greater cause. Pessin's story, however, is more than a *Rules of Attraction* redux. Pessin has imbued his novel with an air of poignancy, an ineluctability, a word the characters use throughout. Reading *Bright College Years*, one has the sense that the timeless and comforting rhythms of life at Yale as an undergrad, the shortest, gladdest years of life, the unlikely friendships forged, the sins committed and forgiven, are set to end, and when they do, the Meatheads are blindsided by the beautiful and heart-wrenching realization that the trajectory of their lives will never be the same."

—James Campbell, Yale '84,
author of *The Final Frontiersman* and *Braving It*

"Andrew Pessin has written the rarest of novels: a witty page-turner that's also philosophically astute. Brimming with well-drawn characters and a spot-on evocation of New Haven and college life in the early 1980s, the book will make you laugh and think. Enjoyable and serious, this novel is a delight."

—Eric Adler, University of Maryland

"'How bright will seem through memory's haze, those happy golden bygone days': Nailed it! *Bright College Years* is smart, funny, sweet, bittersweet, heartwarming, heartbreaking, and most of all meaningful—everything college typically is, in short, as well as the life in the 'real world' that then follows. A perfect mix of sentimentality, profundity, and college hijinks, with great insight as to how we all go from who we were to who we are."

—Scott Smilen, Yale '84

"*Bright College Years* is about many things, really, but most of all about friendship, which is really at the heart of the college experience. You'll feel yourself hanging out with this gang as they form the relationships that carry on, that in many ways determine our trajectories through life; you'll feel a part of their bonding experiences, the fun and the challenges and the heartbreak that make us who we are, the individuals we become through our connections with other people. 'If that's not life,' as the subtitle has it, indeed."

—Jeffrey Oppenheim, Princeton Alum

"A vision of what higher education could be, once was, perhaps could be again, a mix between the classroom and real relationships, with raw honesty, in the pursuit of 'full frontal truth'—and a lot of fun at the same time. You'll enjoy this book."

—William Jacobson, Cornell University

"Hilarious, moving, richly-written, thought-provoking and replete with wisdom seeping through the narrative, it felt almost like Pessin had had my own college experience, as what he described was fantastically familiar. The novel captures what it's like to look back on one's college years from a more mature perspective, to remove the rose-tinted glasses of nostalgia and remember it as it was—and somehow reconcile who we've become with who we once were. A must read."

—Adam Kligfeld, Columbia '95

preamble

After Jude's murder, after the federal agents had finished clearing out The Advance, after the shock of the violence had begun to dissipate, your mind wandered back to the early days, to the beginning, trying to make sense of it all. Sorting through the decades, the morass of memories, going back to the source, to the Maggie affair and the rest, going over everything. He was fascinated by Anne Sexton but what was that worm poem about? He was maybe a little intense but, what, crazy? We live life forward but can only understand it backwards, they say, yet you also don't want to project something onto the past that wasn't really there. Sometimes a cigar is just a cigar, after all, except when it isn't. Something Swill might have said, puffing on one. Not a bad guy, but what a repulsive habit.

And so you endeavor to find a clue, to follow the trail, like taking a stroll through a wood and coming across a solitary butterfly, watching it flit randomly to and fro and realizing that the back and forth is actually going somewhere. So you follow and it flits and it leads you deeper into the wood. You are in unfamiliar territory now but you feel you are supposed to be here, so you carry on. One more turn, one more bend, and then perhaps you come into the clearing ...

The dart came from behind him, whizzed right by his left ear.

Startled, he turned, looked. The place was dark, crowded, loud. No possibility of identifying its source, even as another dart now whizzed by his right ear.

"What the f—" he muttered, ducking, pushing off Black as he moved down the row. Black gave him the finger as he pushed through the crowded row, stumbling. His heart pounding he made it to the aisle, turned around again, looked.

The hall was packed. Nobody clearly aiming for him, at him.

Yet somebody clearly was.

Maybe it wasn't meant for him. It was so crowded, it could have been meant for someone else. He was feeling paranoid, that's it, all this talk of assassination.

Right. He felt his own weapon, in the holster he had bought, as another dart whizzed over his shoulder. He felt it, just maybe, touching his hair as it went by. Maybe he should get a haircut, present a smaller target. *Think about that later*, he thought, instinctively ducking, turning on his heel, crouching as he headed down the aisle toward the stage with the massive organ. For a moment he thought the organ looked like an enormous tree with all its branches pointed straight upward, its many arms raised, praising the heavens maybe.

He would *not* meet his end tonight.

He got to the bottom, to the front row. The English Beat had finished their short set, Jeff had had to admit to Black that they were not terrible, and now The Pretenders were on, opening with their hit song, "Precious." Chrissie Hynde was just now singing the lyric the gang had argued about over dinner, in which (Jeff was sure) she was going to use her, her, her *vagination*, and hearing a hot woman in her tight black tights singing about using her vagination was possibly the hottest thing he had ever heard.

But he would have to get aroused about that later.

He first had to preserve his life now.

He slinked along the front row, to the side. Another quick look around and at first all he saw was everybody singing along and dancing.

Then he saw his assassin.

Striding down the aisle toward him, calmly, confidently. Sure of his mission, not a care in the world. Openly bearing his weapon, reloading casually, his burning eyes, his killer's eyes, locked on Jeff through those little round glasses.

Was that a gentle cruel smile on his murderous face?

His heart in his throat Jeff turned, started running.

He got to the end of the row, saw the door to the side of the stage. So different from a regular concert, no security here, no bouncers, like those beefy guys who'd almost thrown him out of Toad's Place the other night just because of the little "puking incident" in the bathroom there. He had made it *to* the bathroom at least, for crying out loud. Jeff was proud he'd matched Eli to the fifth Alabama Slammer, appreciated that Eli even helped hold his hair back as he vomited in the stall just as Steppenwolf was launching into "Born to be Wild" upstairs. True, would have been nice if he'd managed to vomit into the toilet rather than next to it, but you can't have everything. How Eli held all that liquor, skinny as he was, was a marvel. Many generations of whisky drinkers for his forebears, he said. Also marvelous was his ability, with just a few words to the beefy bouncers, to let them stay in the club.

Jeff went through the door, closed it behind him, noting with dismay that he couldn't lock it. It was dark back here, a narrow corridor with some closed doors off it. Storage rooms maybe, offices, running through, feeling his way through, trying all the door handles, all locked. He could hear the music from the stage but surprisingly muted, good soundproofing here.

No one would hear him scream.

He heard the door at the end of the hall behind him open.

He'd paid ten bucks for this concert. The two tickets. He would *not* die here tonight.

Not during the opening song at any rate.

He could hear the footsteps approaching him, that steady, confident, homicidal pace, as he started running along the corridor, which seemed to stretch around behind the stage. He was behind the organ now, he could see the massive pipes stretching up to the ceiling. A funny contrast, the President, Bart as they affectionally called him, had spoken to the entire new freshman class in this hall just a few weeks before, the convocation including a brief organ concert where these pipes had belted out some Baroque masterpiece. He'd sat then with Ren who was a fan of interminably long 19th century novels and could tell you everything you really didn't want to know about Victor Hugo, including about the silent film version of *Hunchback of Notre Dame* that was shown in this hall too along with a live organ score. Ren who had declined to come tonight because he was already underway writing his own interminably long novel which he said was going to be about everything, hence the length. That sunny convocation afternoon seemed long ago, as it was now dark and late and oh so hot Chrissie Hynde was singing about her vagination on the other side of the organ, and his assassin was approaching.

"Oh Jeff-Jeff," the murderer was sing-songing. "Where *are* you? ..."

Jeff picked up his step, continued around the semi-circle corridor, trying to unsnap his damn holster as he ran. He'd gotten one that had a strap because he'd seen too many stupid old Western films where the cowboys dramatically unsnapped their weapons and he thought it looked cooler. He was obviously thinking of himself more as an assassinator than an assassinee, hadn't thought that he might need to withdraw his weapon quickly in self-defense. And whoever designed this strap, it actually required two hands to unlatch it, which he tried to do as he stumbled along the dark corridor toward the lighted opening at the end.

"Oh Jeff-Jeff," his murderer cooed immediately behind him. "I have something for you ..."

Was that the click of the weapon cocking?

Jeff jumped through the opening, finally releasing his weapon, gripping it, glad he'd loaded it at least before holstering it. As he came through he tripped on something, some wiring on the floor, and stumbled onto the stage. The music was so loud, the lights were so bright, he felt blinded, the stumble felt almost slow motion, cartoonish, like that scene in *Modern Times* where Charlie Chaplin teeters and totters on roller skates along the edge of the second-floor overhang, but finally the stumble ended and Jeff hit the ground, the floor of the stage. He found himself on his back, looking up, almost directly up, into the vagination of oh so hot Chrissie Hynde who as the consummate professional kept on singing as members of the stage crew—pretty beefy themselves—crept out to deal with the intrusion. His weapon, where was it, he had dropped it during the stumble. Frantically he reached around, was just feeling it when he managed to pull his eyes off Chrissie Hynde's private area and looked up, directly, into the murderous eyes of his murderer.

"Oh Jeff-Jeff," his murderer cooed, pointing the weapon at him, smiling that cruel smile of the slayer upon the about to be slain.

Jeff saw the finger pull, heard the click, could swear he heard the whiz of the dart as it fired through the air and landed directly on his heart.

"You dead," Jude whistled as the beefy crewman tackled him.

part 1
freshman year

=====

fall

1.
faster louder higher more

Those first weeks September what a memory, at the time it seemed forever but in retrospect it all went by so fast. As you look back now you almost don't recognize yourself, can barely pick yourself out of that crowd. You were a poor planner, saw dozens of classes during shopping period not one of which you ended up taking. You made loads of mistakes in your desperate attempt to make friends, woo women (still "girls"), and distance yourself from whoever you had fossilized into by the end of high school. Your first credit card was for the Yale Co-Op and you somehow spent $200 your first time in the store, mostly on items with the word "Yale" on it. Were you possibly unaware that you, ultimately you, were going to pay that bill? Everything dumb you did at least once, except trying to pick up Dean Large's wife—that one you tried twice.

"What?" Jeffrey said to Debra, his de facto psychologist, many years later. "She was way younger than the Dean. I thought she was like a senior."

"But twice?"

"I didn't believe her the first time."

No, you don't really recognize yourself when you look back. In fact, literally: you recently pulled out your old Freshman Facebook to show to Debra and, flipping through it, saw all those dated high school yearbook photos and then, for those who had failed to meet the summer deadline, including you, that generic George Orwell photo with the dapper mustache. Fitting, for the

9

Class of 1984, that the substitute photo would be of the man who wrote that book. Fitting, too, as you flipped through the Facebook, that pretty much every member of the gang except for Beamie was represented by Orwell.

You had a nice look at high school Beamie, beaming that smile, that loser.

Orwell was actually everywhere, in every speech including President Bart's at convocation, on posters tacked all over campus announcing meetings, events, parties, clubs, and of course the showing you attended of the 1956 film adaptation of *1984*, and on class swag. There was even a class t-shirt with Orwell's face on it distributed at freshman orientation on the Old Campus quadrangle, you with your sieve of a memory were somehow the only one of the gang who remembered it and it was sweet vindication when, after everyone doubted you at the 20th and 25th reunions, you finally dug yours out of a box in the garage and showed up with it for the 30th.

Jude—in what turned out to be the second to last time you would see him—was not impressed. "I still deny it," he said in that authoritative tone of his that could have you doubting your own lying eyes.

It was hardly surprising, then, that there were plenty of Orwells that first Halloween night mingling among the ghosts, witches, and monsters all crawling along dark moonless Grove Street as they approached the ancient cemetery entrance. People took costumes seriously here, with makeup and engineering. There was a two-headed creature whose heads were so indistinguishable in their lifelike movements that it was hard to tell which was the true head. A vampire whose fangs squirted what might have been actual blood; a werewolf more lupine than *homo sapiens*; and a witch somehow perched above a moving platform as if flying her broom. All right the motor could be a little quieter but the kid was only a sophomore.

"I've heard that the witch's broom was actually used for masturbating," Beamie noted.

So nicknamed because of his beaming (if loserly) smile, the lovable loser, as he liked to think of himself, was second-guessing having come along. He didn't like taking time from studying but at least had made it clear he would depart after the cemetery run, despite their pointing out that his chances of getting laid were much higher at any one of tonight's parties than it was studying applied math in the library stacks.

"There's any number of things wrong with that statement," Swill answered, thinking of Beamie more as loser and less as lovable. He was costumed, as he explained, as Churchill, Freud, and both Marx's (Karl and Groucho) simultaneously, meaning that he was just puffing on a fat cigar.

"Like what?"

"Like first of all, there are no actual witches. So there are no witches' brooms. Second, if you're talking about the women accused of being witches—"

"How the fuck?" Tayvon interrupted, whose chances of *not* getting laid tonight were comparable to Beamie's chances *of* getting laid. This was especially impressive given that he was dressed as President Carter less than a week before the man's humiliating electoral defeat. He was referring to the humanoid figure walking on its hands toward them, its legs swaying wildly in the air, with glowing red eyes in its upside-down head just above the ground, and emitting low growling noises.

"That is impressive," Croc said in his gentle giant tone. Giant indeed: by width, bulk, and weight the largest player on the football team, his teammates liked to rate the size of people's asses on a scale of one-to-Croc. ("That's a good one," Ren had said on first hearing this, recording it in his notebook for use in his novel.) Gentle, too, since aside from voraciously crushing opposing quarterbacks Croc wouldn't hurt a fly. In fact while most of his teammates were prone to aggression after drinking, three or four beers in Croc would more likely find him reciting some poetry and maybe weeping.

"Almost as good as that guy, man," Eli said, wearing a butler uniform, having borrowed it from his. He was pointing across the street where someone was somehow dressed up as South African Apartheid.

"You can't really compare them," Swill said, in his usual contrary mood tonight.

"Why not?" Eli asked.

"Visual versus conceptual. Like apples and oranges."

11

"Maybe, but quality transcends category. And apples and oranges are both fruit."

"Yeah, but—"

"Enough jabber," Tayvon interrupted again, arriving at the cemetery entrance. "Anyone know where the hell Walter Camp is in there?"

The stone temple gate rose before them with "THE DEAD SHALL BE RAISED" chiseled above their heads, a slightly odd thing for a cemetery manager to inscribe, when you think about it, because that would put him out of a job.

"I *said*, enough jabber," Tayvon repeated more urgently when the debate about the inscription began. "Let's head in. See if we can find Ig."

Ignacio had said he would meet them there, once he heard there would be tequila.

The tomb of Walter Camp had been settled on after a healthy argument at Commons dinner. Once it was realized that Abraham Pierson—namesake of their own residential college, Pierson—was not buried at Grove, there were surprisingly strong feelings on behalf of both Ezra Stiles and Timothy Dwight that could not be reconciled. Zar, good for maybe 7-10 words per meal, used them to advocate for Josiah Willard Gibbs but received no support and in protest declined to come. The girls—women—expressed no interest whatever in getting drunk in the graveyard, except for Maggie who was game for anything. Croc's timing was good. By the time he suggested football pioneer Walter Camp everyone was sick of the whole debate and happy to resolve it.

Maggie was indeed game for anything.

"It doesn't matter what we do," she would say, "as long as we do it together."

Maggie was also responsible for what had already become the gang's slogan—"Everybody in, nobody out"—as well as therefore the ensuing debates about whether that should apply even to losers like Beamie.

"Especially to Beamie," Maggie insisted, "because he's *our* loser."

Just a few weeks into their first year and she was already charmingly possessive about the people who had been randomly assigned to the nearby suites in Lawrance Hall, the freshman dorm for Pierson College. No surprise then that people were drawn to her like butterflies to nectar, earthworms to soil, or leprechauns to rainbows according to the preferred metaphors of Jeff, Jude, and Black respectively. Along the way she had collected countless friends from her prestigious boarding school in Maine, from back home in Woods Hole, from her many soccer teammates from teams stretching back to elementary school. She was also the most beautiful creature who ever had walked the earth, at least according to Jeff, who in endless soliloquys to Black in their shared bedroom supported the claim with detailed analyses of her long black hair, her shining dark eyes with perfect eyelashes, and certain remarks about her tall, lithe, soccer-fit body that are better left in the dorm.

Black did his best to drown these out by covering his ears and humming the Supremes' "You Can't Hurry Love," only occasionally chiming in to remind Jeff, "You don't have a chance, El Jefe. That Magdalena is a treasure. You're not worthy to carry her trash to the bin, man."

"What's the job below carrying trash? I'll do that."

"Oh, man, you gotta have some dignity. You got a better chance with her if you have some self-respect."

"Yeah? Like how?"

Black contemplated a moment. "I take it back, man. That shit has sailed."

"You mean the Lisa episode." Jeff's transparent attempt to get to Maggie via "studying together" with her roommate Lisa—they were both in a Russian history freshman seminar, Lisa because she would go on to become a journalist covering matters Soviet and Russian and Jeff because he was late in selecting his courses and this was the only thing still open—had ended in humiliation when Lisa arched her nasty left eyebrow in dismissive scorn and said, "This is a transparent attempt to get to Maggie via me."

"Forgot about that!" Black snorted. "Good times. No, man, I meant the loverboy serenade."

Jeff cringed. He was a modestly accomplished guitarist and pianist who in addition to playing Grateful Dead and Neil Young songs had begun writing his own. The first week of the semester, in a deeply choreographed maneuver, he'd casually strolled over to Maggie's room playing his guitar, waving his long hair, all prepared with his "Oh I was just walking by and thought I'd say hi" speech, only for her door to be opened by the captain of the men's lacrosse team who just laughed in his face, as Black did when Jeff reported the story immediately afterward.

Black was still laughing. "Man, that one is gold. But don't give up, man. You have the name *El Jefe* to live up to."

"Thanks for the vote of confidence, man," Jeff said, looking for his lighter to fire up a doob. "That means a lot to me."

"Oh, I got no confidence, man. You're not even worthy to bring the trash to the guy who takes it to the bin. But it's so damn entertaining to watch you try."

If only Jeff had known at the time that Maggie wasn't in her room when he knocked, and that the lacrosse team captain was actually there hitting on Lisa, who decided in that moment that his laughter at Jeff's sweet gesture was really boorish, and whose telling of the incident to Maggie afterward put Jeff on Maggie's radar in a new way. Fun-loving Maggie's radar, who may have been game for the graveyard, but unfortunately none of the other girls in her suite—women—were as adventurous as she.

There was Lisa, already writing a weekly opinion column for the *Yale Daily News* in which she cast aspersions on her generation's lifestyle choices, who referred to herself as Maggie's conscience as she cast aspersions on Maggie's lifestyle choices, and who just couldn't see the appeal of getting drunk in the graveyard with those little boys. There was Jasmine who was obsessed with her cello and with Black, Black who for reasons unknown (for she was a great beauty) resisted her advances, and who was performing in the orchestra's Halloween Concert—Saint-Saëns' *Danse Macabre*—which precluded getting smashed beforehand. And there was quiet Isabela, who always had her Nikon taking photos but who rarely spoke, who hung out with them but always seemed uncomfortable. She would meet them all at the Pierson Inferno later but the graveyard idea was just too icky for her taste.

Maggie was game, but did she really want to be the only girl among those little boys?

Happily, her totally cool English literature professor came up with an alternative that afternoon, when he invited the entire class to his house for an early evening Halloween party. A young, newly minted Ph.D., tall, almost gaunt, with long hippie hair, Dr. Taslitz Fester, or Doc, as he insisted his little freshbirds call him, had a Ken Kesey vibe as he led them through subversive readings of the great texts of Western literature—not that they, as little freshbirds, could appreciate those readings as such.

"I'm actually a professor of theory, not literature, and certainly not 'English,'" he had told them on the first day, speaking quickly. "God, no!"

"But what exactly is 'theory,' Doc?" asked that annoying girl who would go on to talk incessantly in class and never really say anything.

"Only everything," Doc answered, illuminating nothing.

The subversive readings were part of his mission of subverting Western civilization itself, he explained over the first weeks of classes; an urgent task, as its internal contradictions were rotting it from the inside out. Indeed, signs of its demise were evident right at Yale, where efforts to end the major in Western Civilization were nearly ready to bear fruit. He peered at them through his yellow-tinted glasses, you know he was handsome, in a subversive way. He could see they had understood not a word, how could they, they were so young, so naïve.

"At any rate, my little freshbirds," he continued with a smile, "here is something more digestible for you. As you are aware, there is talk of raising the state's legal age for alcohol consumption to nineteen next year. The dying establishment is fighting back by coming for your freedoms and so, in a small act of resistance, I invite you all to my house tonight. Bring comrades as you wish. Costumes—clothes, for that matter—optional. My plan," he pushed his glasses back up his nose, "is to show you how it's done."

"Give it a rest, El Jefe, I'm telling you man," Black said in their room, putting the finishing touches on his Little Richard hairdo. "You got no chance."

"I don't know," Jeff said, admiring his own multicolored clown wig in the mirror, "I think I have a chance."

"You don't think she thinks you're stalking her?"

Jeff had been attending Maggie's home soccer games, cheering her on—well not just her, he didn't want it to be *too* obvious so he cheered all the girls on, but *especially* her.

"It's not impossible," he answered, as Maggie *had* said with some alarm, "What are you doing here?" a couple of times, but had apparently been satisfied with his "I've always loved women's soccer" response. "But it's part of the plan. I'm getting her used to seeing me around."

What he didn't mention was that the plan seemed to be making progress. Maggie had stuck around after the last game to talk to him and they had talked for a while, long enough for that gorgeous sweat to stop glistening on her skin, long enough where they got beyond the phase where Jeff just made a lot of jokes, really talked actually. She had issues, it turned out, some family issues, some extended family issues, and that only made her that much more desirable.

I adore you, Jeff said to her in his mind as she spoke, watching her untie her ponytail and letting her long black hair drop.

"It was a little like being interviewed," Maggie told Lisa, whose eyebrow was deeply skeptical. Maggie was now brushing that long black hair with the antique brush her grandmother had bequeathed her. "But then I started to realize how good the questions were. Like, insightful. And the more he listened to my answers, the more I wanted to tell him. I felt like he was unraveling me."

"Oooh, the Unraveller," Lisa echoed.

"Make fun if you want."

"Oh I will."

But Black knew not of Jeff's unravelling, and persisted. "I just don't see it, man. It's a mismatch."

"How so?"

"She's a treasure, that one."

"What, I'm not?" Jeff said, gesturing at himself.

"Don't you see yourself, man? You're a clown."

"What? It's a cool wig."

"I don't mean the wig, man."

"Fuck you, man. She actually invited me to the party."

"She invited everyone. Everyone in, nobody out."

"Okay, maybe everyone. But she didn't object when I was the only one who said sure."

"Maybe she was just being nice."

"Of course she was being nice. She's like the nicest person in the world. But why not me? Seriously?"

"Seriously? How about those oversized shades you're wearing, that flannel shirt, Mr. Lumberjack, those cords you probably pulled out of the local dump, man? And that's leaving out the wig."

Jeff sighed. "I'm dressed for warmth. Practical."

"Shit, man. *That* is the problem."

"I think she likes me. She laughs at my jokes."

"Just feeling sorry for you, man. I mean, seriously, the kid who was the first one killed during the campus Assassin game? Out of like 600 players? That takes skill."

"My luck to draw Jude from the start. He did eventually win the thing, you know."

"Yeah, man. That dude is cutthroat. Those eyes."

"What about his eyes?" Jeff adjusted the wig again, pulled it down lower so that it met his shades.

"The whole boring into your soul thing, man. But still, about Assassin. You—"

"I know, I know," Jeff interrupted. Black had been mocking him mercilessly for weeping on the stage, in front of some 2,500 concertgoers, after having been assassinated.

"Speaking of the devil-man?"

"In the city."

"Yeah?"

"Went to go mock some high school friends seeing the Dead at Radio City. 'The Deceased.'" The latter was Jude's derogatory way of referring to the band.

"Yeah, well at least he's right about that," Black scowled, repulsed by his roommate's taste in music. He especially despised that whiny hippie shit, and had only agreed to go to the Pretenders because Jeff paid for his ticket. "Hey," he checked his watch, with a laugh, "you better get your ass moving, man. Your humiliation awaits."

Jeff took one more look in the mirror, looking quintessentially 1980 without of course realizing it at the time. "I'm ready, man. And you really have to give the Dead some credit. At least they're better than that Motown shit you listen to all the—"

Black had Jeff up against the wall, his forearm against Jeff's throat, before Jeff could finish that statement. At that very same moment a man *in* black had his forearm up against Beamie's throat, against the Walter Camp tombstone in the cemetery, though in this case there was also a knife involved.

Prior to this point the guys had conquered the autumn night chill by finishing the first bottle of tequila and were now on the second. Ignacio was serenading them with "All Out of Love," which, like every song he attempted to sing in his atonal rasp, came out sounding like a sea shanty. Beamie sat silently, thinking both that he should be returning to the library and that he couldn't believe how badly Ig was butchering that song. Croc was also silent, sitting under the large elm hovering over them in the dark like a giant umbrella, thinking about the poet Joyce Kilmer. Eli was calculating approximately how much his net worth had grown in the minutes since Ig began rasping, which made it at least more endurable. Swill and Tayvon were just approaching fisticuffs debating the relative merits of studying literature versus philosophy when a figure emerged from behind that lovely elm, dressed entirely in black, including a ski mask.

"Put your fucking hands up, motherfuckers, or somebody gets cut!" He was brandishing a knife, though in the dark it was hard to see.

"Dude, awesome costume," Ignacio said.

"I like the ski hat on top of the facemask," Tayvon concurred. "Good touch."

"Seriously, dude," Swill puffed his cigar, "you nailed the urban criminal look. Totally New Haven."

"I'm fucking serious, motherfuckers!" the man stomped his foot.

"Even the 'motherfuckers' thing works," Croc nodded. "But, man, don't you have a coat? It's chilly out here."

"Fuck you!" the unfortunately coatless man said, glancing around, sizing them up as well as he could given the dark—Croc was the size of an elephant, Ig was a burly hockey player not to mention holding a bottle as a potential weapon, Tayvon was tall and lean and clearly fit, and between Swill and Beamie the latter was clearly the bigger loser—Eli had already slipped away, to protect his investment in himself—so the man stepped over, pushed his forearm against Beamie's throat against the tombstone, and brought the knife close to his throat. "Motherfuckers give me your money or this boy gets cut!"

"Guys?" Beamie squeaked with fear, and an arm, in his throat.

Totally New Haven indeed, though not merely New Haven—where already early in the academic year there had been several robberies and assaults of students—but many urban centers. Although it was common to blame President Carter for these problems, in fact his record against crime was impressive, as he had tried to emphasize in his campaign. The problem was that that was overshadowed by the Iran affair. It was hard to project a tough image when Khomeini had been daily making you look like a pussy for a year now. All that made it all the more mysterious why any Yale students, just four days before that embarrassing election, would choose to dress like Jimmy Carter this Halloween, including one of the sixteen in Maggie's English literature—theory—class now sucking back shots of rum jello.

Maggie was bewitching, of course, in her little witch outfit, with the witch hat and green makeup. Jeff managed somehow to maintain his cool when she opened her door, even while Lisa cast that supercilious eyebrow at him from behind her.

"This'll be better than the cemetery," Jeff said nervously as she stepped out of her suite.

"*Anything* would be better than the cemetery," Maggie answered bewitchingly. "I'm even glad we're going the opposite direction. Doc lives up Whalley."

"Lisa didn't want to come?" Jeff hid his gratitude as they exited the High Street gate out of the Old Campus.

Maggie laughed. "She said it would be too exhausting casting ironic glances all night long. She wanted to save them for the Inferno."

"Almost as exhausting as being on the receiving end," Jeff laughed, walking quickly to keep pace with Maggie's brisk step. "And Jasmine, Isabela?"

"Concert with the symphony, and who knows." As they walked Maggie shared her feelings about Isabela, guided by Jeff's questions. She liked her a lot and was eager to learn some photography from her, but couldn't quite figure the girl out.

"And so this guy is pretty cool?" Jeff was saying as they approached the house, lit up festively on the dark night.

"Oh my God, totally. He has a sign on his office door that says, 'Sit Long, Talk Much.' I mean, how cool is that?"

"Yeah. I imagine most professors prefer we say as little as possible and get the hell out."

The house was small and was packed, with people smoking cigarettes and with paraphernalia: posters and busts of radical figures mostly unfamiliar to freshbirds, commemorations of civil rights milestones, anti-war posters and the like. Also packing the house were miles of bookshelves, including an entire case in the foyer filled with Doc's own recent book, *A Pretty Nice Rooster to be Around.*

"That's his memoir," Maggie explained as they entered.

"Isn't he a little young for a memoir?" Jeff asked.

"It's revolutionary. It's a forward-looking memoir."

"What does that mean?"

"About everything that is going to happen to him. That he is going to accomplish. His life's project. Which is awesome."

"And which is?"

"Get this. He is studying, he says, a filmmaker from the future. A man who will revolutionize film, and theory, and thereby change everything about everything."

"How do you study a filmmaker from the future? That doesn't even make sense."

"*Obviously,*" Maggie laughed, "by characterizing that person as completely as possible, then identifying the conditions that will bring someone fitting that characterization into being, and then bringing about those conditions. He already has a name for the guy. It's Charlie K—"

"Stop," Jeff interrupted, "I must warn you that I haven't understood a word of this."

"Either have we! But we're only little freshbirds. Come, let me introduce—"

But Maggie got interrupted by some friends coming over to greet her, and then a couple more, which of course involved smiles and laughter and hugging. Jeff felt a bit like a clown tagging along beside her, wondering if they were going to spend the whole evening in the foyer.

"That's him?" Jeff finally asked loudly in her ear, to be heard.

"Right, sorry," Maggie nodded. "Let's go meet him."

Doc was seated on his sofa surrounded by his acolytes, all of whom were smoking, and he was firing away on his favorite topics. "Irony is the fundamental tone of the universe," he stated with an air of *I am so sorry to state something so obvious*. "Everything is self-referential," he continued, his eyes darting behind his yellow-tinted glasses, "including the assertion that everything is self-referential," and "everybody is everybody," he added, amplifying that with a defense of what theorists referred to as B-time, illustrated by the subversive reading the class had just done of Heinlein's time travel short story, "By His Bootstraps." The man was nothing if not memorable, which made it all the more shocking that Jeffrey would fail to remember him when they crossed paths again some four decades later. True, four decades is a long time; and by that time Doc was long removed from Yale, rounder and balder, and prone rather to howl than to speak.

Well that was not an issue now, as he fired away. He didn't even break his monologue when Maggie approached the crowded sofa with Jeff, but smiled at her and gestured her toward the side of the room while drawing out Heinlein's influence on John Lennon, whose famous lyric—about his and your and everyone's being identical to an *Odobenus rosmarus*—somehow reflected the point.

"Are these the famous rum jello shots?" Maggie asked her two friends in charge of dispensing the dixie cups from the tray, after they had finished hugging her. "Awesome!" She grabbed two and offered one to Jeff.

"Thanks," he said accepting it. "You ready?"

"I was born ready! Over the lips, over the gums, look out tummy, here it comes!"

"Down the hatch!" Jeff exclaimed as they sucked them back in unison, loving the sweet burning sensation as it went down.

"Awesome!" Maggie exclaimed, then grabbed two more shots and also grabbed his hand with hers and pulled him. "Come on, you've got to meet Chastity and Temperance!"

Fixated by the warm pressure of Maggie's hand in his, Jeff would later mention to Jude—Black had made it clear he was done on this subject for now—that he felt like every cell of his hand was holding hands with every cell of Maggie's hand.

Jude, who seemed about the only person immune to Maggie's charms, only nodded and said, "You are the man, Jeff-Jeff."

"Chastity and Temperance?" Jeff said, his hands' cells welling up with love for Maggie's hands' cells. "They don't sound like much fun."

"Ha! They're identical twins. Their father is a minister and names all his kids like that. Hey guys!" Maggie called out. "Meet my friend Jeff!"

Jeff had a lot of thoughts and sensations swirling all at once. First, that shot of rum jello had warmed him all over. Then, the fact that Chastity and Temperance were drunk giggling Farrah Fawcett-Majors's dressed in identical red skimpy one-piece bathing suits who wanted to run their many feminine fingers through his clown hair made him even warmer. And finally that Maggie had not released his hand made him start to sweat in his lumberjack shirt and cords.

And she called him "my friend."

I am El Jefe, he thought, his heart pounding.

The rum jello tray had been refilled, Maggie had finished hugging everyone, and finally brought him to meet Doc. Jeff really wasn't interested in meeting the man because every second looking at someone else was a second lost from looking at Maggie, though there *were* several involuntary glances at Chastity and Temperance who were successfully pursuing licentiousness and insobriety (and who later would pursue both, together, with Tayvon about twenty minutes after he removed his shirt at the Pierson Inferno). Maggie and Jeff snuggled into the sofa, or more precisely, Maggie snuggled in next to Doc while Jeff snuggled in next to Maggie. Jeff felt the first little pang of, well, jealousy, especially when Doc passed his cigarette to Maggie to have a drag. No, that made no sense, he thought. She couldn't be into this skinny weirdo, she just thought he was cool, and that's why she was hanging on his every word, but anyway, who could be cooler than *El Jefe*?

"You can make these with grain alcohol, too," Doc was explaining as he led the toast with rum jello shots. "Dangerous, of course, because it's tasteless. But rule number one if you hope to be somebody in this world: you must learn to live with danger."

Speaking of living with danger, Beamie, when confronted with the same, had promptly wet himself. Happily that was known only to himself, as it was dark and nobody could see the warm, then cold, stain spreading on his pants. That happiness only lasted a moment, however, because for some reason he felt the need to inform everybody.

"Oh Jesus I peed myself," he moaned, squeaking it out since the mugger still had his forearm against Beamie's throat, and immediately regretted it.

"Oh man, loser," Swill exclaimed, "you are *never* getting laid, once this gets out."

"Hey, we don't have to tell anyone," Croc offered, feeling sentimental.

"Oh, but we must!" Ignacio insisted with his guffaw, a loving guffaw so infectious that even the mugger, who they had all sort of forgotten about, suppressed a snort himself.

"Motherfuckers," the mugger said again, collecting himself. "What's it going to be?"

"He may be a loser," Swill proffered. "But we probably should do something."

"Maybe we should just cut our losses," Tayvon counterproposed. "The rest of us can get away easy."

"Yeah," Swill said. "Four out of five of us make it out of here. Pretty good percentage. Wait a second. Where the hell is Eli?"

"Assholes!" Ig guffawed affectionately. "Everybody in, nobody out, remember?"

"Beamie is a nobody," Swill observed.

"What?" Ig asked.

"Nobody out. I'm just saying."

"Right, so we include him."

"No. 'Nobody out.' Like a pun. He's a 'nobody.' So he's out."

"That's just stupid. You're—"

"Motherfuckers!" the mugger shouted. He pushed the knife into contact with Beamie's neck, who groaned in terror and, thankfully, thankfully, restrained his bowel.

"Dude, really?" Croc said, rising to his feet. The mugger had noticed Croc was big, but given the dark, and that he was seated, had no idea just how big until the figure started rising and kept going. "Is that how you want to this to go down?"

"I still can't get over the ass on that dude," Tayvon whispered to Swill.

"How is that even possible," Swill concurred, puffing.

"It's a Christmas miracle," Ig chimed in, also referring to Croc's already wearing Christmas sweaters four weeks before Thanksgiving.

Perhaps they should have taken the situation more seriously. After all, though he lacked a coat the man had a knife, sharp enough to do some serious damage to their friend's neck. And the man was desperate: suffice to say he had grown up in circumstances less advantageous than theirs, which produced a less than ideal set of values and desires in him, which led to some poor choices—there are no bad people, just bad choices Jude might insist—which led to the desperate grabbing of a knife to point against the throats of some snotty rich college students. He'd seen the group rolling into the cemetery and thought that the dark and isolation gave him the advantage, yet another poor choice. Man that snotty rich college boy was enormous, he was thinking as he started thinking about his exit strategy, but as it turned out it wasn't the enormous boy he had to be worried about.

He was just absorbing the gargantuan size of the boy's buttocks when he was slammed from behind to the ground, the knife in his hand flying forward and missing Tayvon's creamy mocha cheek by less than an inch.

"Aieeeeee!" came the simultaneous screams—from the mugger, hitting the ground face first, and from Thorn, who had appeared from behind the tombstone and taken the man down, loving every second of it, and from Ignacio, who loved it all even more. Thorn would surely have learned the sneaky from-behind tackle from his father had he ever met the man. What he had got from him was only his father's strange left eye condition: it was unable to blink autonomously, so he had to blink it manually, with his finger. The stranger part was that Thorn had inherited this condition despite its not being genetic: his father had acquired it from some nerve damage suffered under never-disclosed circumstances.

As impressive as the sneaky tackle was Thorn's ability to play rugby even with many broken bones, but we'll come to that later.

Speaking of broken bones, the mugger's face did not win its contest with the nearly frozen ground. If it weren't for the light cold drizzle that had begun to fall, softening the ground, the mugger's face would have met something like concrete. (Or at least so the doctor said to Thorn and Tayvon at the Emergency Room where they escorted the poor fellow afterward, as they were paying the bill. "A rugby code thing," Thorn explained, leaving some cash in an envelope for the man, while Tayvon left the man his coat.) On the plus side, for the mugger, Thorn's tackle had obviated Croc's plan to flip him over and sit on him.

One more plus: Beamie's bowel held. His dignity, however, did not. When he later tried to counter the relentless mockery of his friends over his released bladder by pointing out, in contrast, the withheld bowel, somehow it only increased the mockery.

Speaking of mockery, Black's, it turned out, was misplaced.

Across campus Maggie and Jeff had lost track of the time and lost count of the rum jello shots. They found their way back down Whalley Avenue, Maggie's bewitching green makeup dripping in the drizzle down her bewitching cheeks. They thought about stopping at the York Street Wawa but then realized they were already past it, which was hilarious, so they were laughing, his arm was around her shoulders, she was leaning into him, or just too drunk to stand up, or maybe he was leaning into her too drunk to stand up. They stumbled down Library Walk between Jonathan Edwards and Branford Colleges, laughing, leaning, keeping each other up. You don't make the best decisions when you are drunk, who could deny that, there was the lamppost outside Jonathan Edwards, Jeff suddenly broke away from her and leaned against it instead, and started singing in a deep throaty voice, eager to begin Maggie's journey into Tom Waits as soon as possible, something called "Jitterbug Boy." What was he thinking, breaking away from her even for a second, how many weeks had he worked to get to this point, to have Maggie, *Maggie*, leaning against him like this, under his arm? After her last soccer game she had shared with him that she had an "eensy-weensy" fear of abandonment issue, her father had left the family for a few years when she was little, and here Jeff was abandoning her an eensy-weensy bit to scratch out a Tom impression where let's face it if you don't have the original you just don't do it?

Had he just abandoned the incredible trajectory he was on, he suddenly thought with his heart sinking, for a stupid lamppost?

In his impairment, however, Jeff had forgotten that Maggie had matched him shot for shot, and so rather than run the opposite way from this goofy long-haired guy in the clown wig now swinging from the lamppost and crooning "Singin' in the Rain" in that strange throaty voice—as any sane, or sober, person would have—she found it all quite charming, and the way he had listened to her talk about her difficult older brother whose challenges with what today we would call autism had nearly broken her family apart, you know Maggie was a positive person who mostly kept her issues to herself but this goofy clown singing and dancing for her had kind of opened her up and that felt, well, nice.

One more bad, drunken decision: When Maggie leaned in close to him against the lamppost Jeff found himself hesitating, they were outside, in public, there were people around, was he really saying, "Are we sure this is a good idea?"

"What?"

"There's, like, all these people—"

"Don't think so much, friend," Maggie laughed.

"Yeah?"

"Yes!"

And with that they were laughing, they were laughing, with God knows who else around them during this wild Halloween night, the ghosts the goblins the Orwells the ghouls, and then somehow, impossibly, inconceivably, her perfect lips were on his.

They never made it to the Inferno.

The next day Ignacio gave him an enthusiastic fist bump, exclaiming, "El Jefe! El hombre!"

"Come on, spit it out," Lisa urged Maggie the next day too, trying to squeeze the details out of her in order to better pass judgment on them.

"These lips are sealed," Maggie said, making the zipper gesture.

"That's not what I heard," Lisa shook her head.

Speaking of Ignacio, that Halloween night was also another first: the first of his nights in the New Haven jail, his home, he would say with a guffaw, away from home away from home.

No one could keep pace with the man in the alcohol department. No one had even realized, with the drama in the cemetery, that he had finished the second bottle of tequila himself. Even more legendary was his ability to remain unaffected by the consumption of alcohol. Put differently, you couldn't tell the difference in his behavior drunk or sober, which more reflected poorly on his being sober than well on his being drunk. No doubt this was helped by his size. Though no Croc, he *was* 6'4" and 260 pounds, at that time all muscle, and would have been one of the finest right-wingers in the Ivy League—were it not for two things. First, he was from Central America somewhere, not exactly the mecca of ice hockey so he had a clear disadvantage from the start. Second, becoming good at something requires hard work, and hard work, as Ig would put it with a guffaw, was hard work. "Who wants to lift weights?" he would say when skipping another "mandatory" session. "They're so heavy." And you know, he was just too fun-loving to work too hard. "Life is short, asshole!" he would proclaim, using the slur in an affectionate way while launching into some activity that was well suited, in fact, to shorten one's life. Those activities typically occurred between 2:00 and 5:00 AM, and would not be complete unless they were very loud and produced at least a few angry students yelling out their dorm windows, "Shut the fuck up, asshole!"

The slur there was less affectionate.

But you know, you couldn't stay mad at him: just one guffaw from him, the way his entire face cracked up with laughter, and you were saying "You are such an asshole" while feeling nothing but love for the man.

What he could do, on the ice, was skate fast and handle the puck well; what he couldn't do was both at the same time. He was also the master of penalties, having perfected the arts both of getting away with them and drawing them on the other side with masterly flops. The coach had been using him primarily as a distraction on the ice during pre-season practices so far. Ig seemed very happy all the time; it was only in that occasional vulnerable moment, usually with Maggie, whom he adored, that he might slip a remark to the effect that he hoped he would get some actual playing time once the season started.

Until then he would have to live by the two mottos emblazoned on the door of the bedroom he shared with Tayvon, in the suite with Jude and Swill: FASTER LOUDER HIGHER MORE and TOO MUCH.

On this particular Halloween night Ignacio checked most of those boxes by getting hold of a motorcycle. One wouldn't like to say he stole it, though the police seemed to like saying it. But that was just one, of several, reasons to haul his ass off to jail that evening, including the fact that he was riding the bike around the Pierson courtyard outside the Inferno at 1:45 AM buck naked rasping off key at the top of his lungs. For someone from Central America he sure seemed impervious to the New England autumn night chill. Somehow he had convinced Zar to join him on the bike, somehow tearing Zar away from the mammoth problem he had ironically skipped the Inferno for, that of creating a mathematical model of fire, whatever that meant. Zar was surely as guilty as Ignacio, riding behind him, holding on for dear life with his arms locked around Ig's washboard abs, but got off scot-free from the episode.

"Maybe it was because he at least had some clothes on," Eli said as some of the gang debriefed in the Pierson courtyard afterward, outside, as the Inferno was dying down.

"Did you get a load of that sac?" Swill said.

"Every furrow," Ren said, who had already produced a detailed sketch of Ig's infamously large testicle sac in his notebook.

"You guys are disgusting," Maya said, who had recently begun hanging out with them for some reason.

"Hey, man," Black objected, "we're not the ones with that sac."

"I'm with Maya," Jasmine said, who was actually wondering, at that moment, what Black's sac might look like.

Also at that moment Tayvon was tearing off his shirt inside the Inferno for his Mick Jagger impression, obligatory because they were playing the Stones' new single "Emotional Rescue." After leaving the Emergency Room he had led the way to the Inferno, reminding them to stay focused on his own motto: "Either we be laid, boys, or we be crawlin'."

As was usually the case, Tayvon would be laid and the rest of them be crawling.

At that same moment Chastity and Temperance looked at Tayvon, then looked at each other, then back to Tayvon and began their approach.

Isabela had just changed the film in her Nikon and snapped photos of every step.

=====

2.

i never knew taupe

Bladderball.

The greatest achievement of Western civilization, or the demise thereof?

Such a fine line.

These otherwise bright college students would assemble on the Old Campus on a crisp fall morning, in teams composed from the twelve residential colleges, this year the day before the Princeton game. At 11:00 AM sharp an enormous inflatable ball—the "bladderball"—would be rolled through Phelps Gate. At the whistle the teams would fight for possession of the ball, following no rules and using any means whatever. These being bright college students, the primary goal was to be clever. One year the Jonathan Edwards team brought in a huge fishing gaff, which seemed very clever until the thing popped the ball, thus producing the chants of "J.E. sucks!" to join the hoary classics of "Durfee Sucks!" and "Harvard sucks!" (Clever though they were, they were still college students.) These new freshmen, just two months into their Piersonhood, had already been regaled with Pierson College's greatest moment three years earlier: the renting of a helicopter to fly over and drop leaflets demanding surrender.

The gang resolved to live up to their predecessors.

There were three keys: Planning, Preparation, and Focus.

As for Planning, Jude took charge after he had pushed his own scheme to victory over the competitors. These latter included the planting of explosives (Thorn), poisoning the food in the other colleges' dining halls (Ignacio), and releasing greased piglets to cause havoc (Swill), which Jude refuted by invoking their risks of danger, death, and cruelty to animals respectively. Instead he proposed something simpler, safer, and cruel only to the animals who deserved it: chain the gates of the other colleges shut to prevent their teams from making it to the Old Campus venue. Maggie, who freshman year was the only one with a car, did the driving to area hardware stores to acquire the heavy-duty chains. Only one minor mishap, when she gently sideswiped a mailbox. ("It's allowed," she insisted with a giggle.) They had Isabela go in to make the purchases, because no one would suspect quiet Isabela of being up to no good. Eli sprung for the chains; he was good that way, particularly when no good was to be up to.

Preparation Phase I started the night before the event.

Jeff rapped on the dorm door four times, paused, then slowly rapped another twenty times.

"What the fuck—" Black started to say.

"Shh, I can't lose count," Jeff interrupted, continuing until he'd completed the twenty.

What he would never get around to explaining, because they would first be busy with their transaction, then be busy getting stoned, then entirely forget, was that four and twenty was some sort of code for weed and that the guy to whom they'd been referred required it as a code knock. Black also never got around to complaining about how irritating those twenty knocks were, though he would, near dawn, re-enter his harangue about how irritating the guy himself was, starting with his referring to himself, in the third person, as "the Guy."

"Are you the guy?" Jeff asked when the door opened.

"I am the Guy," said the Guy, bowing gently. He was tall, thin, with a scruffy beard and hair even longer than Jeff's, and wearing a Dead t-shirt under a tattered open bathrobe.

"Where are your pants, man?" Black grumbled, averting his eyes from the mangy briefs.

"Temporarily misplaced," the Guy said with equanimity, because he said everything with equanimity. "Now what can the Guy do you for, gentlemen?"

They entered the room. Lit with soft blue light bulbs, there was drug paraphernalia everywhere, Dead concert posters on the walls, sandalwood incense burning, and a bootleg tape of some Dead show playing on the stereo.

"This is …?" Jeff said, nodding to gesture to the music.

"February 18, 1971," the Guy answered.

Jeff had a sharp intake of breath. "No way!"

"Way," the Guy answered with equanimity.

"What?" Black asked, as all that whiny hippie shit sounded the same to him.

"Only the best 'Dark Star' ever, man. Capitol Theater, Port Chester NY. Segues into a middling 'Wharf Rat' though, which is why it's not so well known."

"No way," Jeff shook his head.

Black shook his own head. "What have you got for us, man?"

"Ah, yes. I assume it's smoke you're looking for?" The Guy swung open a display cabinet, revealing a half-dozen deep shelves with plastic baggies of different varieties and quantities of weed. "Happily you have arrived early this fine evening and the Guy is quite flush with options."

Indeed, 12:45 AM was early, and this evening was fine, a balmy 45 degrees for a mid-November night.

"You're like a convenience store, man," Jeff noted, studying the weed baggies with their color-coded typed labels beneath. He was focusing on the red labels, as gold and silver were out of their price range. "Open all hours, got everything you need."

"Yeah but without the hot dogs," Black added.

"I have hot dogs," the Guy said. "You want?"

"Naah," Jeff said. "We'll take this … And, um, what have you got in the way of some, you know, accelerants?"

"Ah. Only these." The Guy opened another cabinet to reveal another half-dozen shelves with little labeled bottles of sundry delicacies. Fortunately the Guy was a walking pharmaceutical encyclopedia and led them through the differences between the reds, the blues, the purples, the taupes, some of which were uppers, some downers, and some just weaved in and out.

"You *are* the Guy," Jeff said admiringly.

The Guy bowed gently.

"What the hell is 'taupe'?" Black asked, his limited Crayola experience having never been privileged to contain that color. "Is that something—" he peered suspiciously at Jeff and the Guy—"White people know about?"

31

Jeff briefly peered back. Black was a mystery to him. The man did not reveal much about himself, not even his first name, much less anything about his upbringing beyond being from Chicago. He had started anew at Yale after a year at an odd little school out west called Nevergreen. "Totally crazy there, man," was all he would say about it, though Jeff was able to glean, from occasional comments, that Black had gone there on a basketball scholarship despite the facts that (a) the school did not offer competitive sports and (b) Black did not play basketball. "I'm Black," was how he introduced himself when he arrived as Jeff's roommate in their Lawrance freshman suite. This was pretty confusing because, in addition to lacking a first name, Black was, indeed, Black.

Jeff turned back to the Guy. "Oh, and, um, any chance for a copy of this tape?" he asked, tilting his head toward the cassette player as they concluded their transaction.

"Ten bucks," the Guy nodded, opening another cabinet stocked with cassettes. "You sure you don't want a hot dog? I've got kraut too."

"We're good, man," Black said.

"Then the Guy bids you adieu," the Guy bowed graciously. "Come any time."

"I never knew taupe, man," Black said meditatively as they made their way back to Lawrance, thinking about the many implications of that fact.

Come any time they did, throughout that semester and the next. Zar would come too when he needed to restock his own accelerants. True, you wouldn't usually associate laconicness with a pill-popping speedster. But then again the fact that he could go four days without eating while solving problems Nobel laureates didn't even know existed made a little more sense.

Speaking of speed, that brings us to Preparation Phase II, the morning of the big event itself.

This involved first ingesting some magenta pills to give them the energy to hit the other colleges with their chains, then some quick heavy drinking to release the inhibitions to facilitate the task. This they did in Ren's livingroom since he had the new Cars album *Panorama*, which some wanted to listen to in preparation for the Cars concert that night at the New Haven Coliseum. The little guy was thrilled to have them there, the inevitable trashing of the room notwithstanding.

"What happened to your other roommate?" Tayvon asked on noting that Ren and his remaining roommate, a strange fellow named Fregoli, both had singles.

"You mean Steven Skybell?" Ren asked, grabbing a shot of the cheap Scotch that was going around. "Yeah, he moved off campus. Like the second week of the semester."

"What? You think he didn't like us?" Beamie asked.

"Smart guy," Ig said with a guffaw. "Only took him a week to figure out we were trouble."

Actually it had only taken Skybell a day to figure out they were trouble, but several days to effect the departure—a smart move that led to his terrific career in the theater at Yale and afterwards, but that is for another story. In any case Preparation Phase II began at 8:00 AM sharp, the plan being to drink for two hours then fan out in teams to lock the gates of the colleges.

What was the third key again? Right—Focus.

Swill got worked up again about the greased piglet idea, insisting on it for next year, and who put bossy boss dictator Jude in charge anyway. This led to a debate over the virtues and vices of autocracies versus aristocracies versus democracies, you know Hitler offered an incisive critique of democracy in *Mein Kampf* which led to a discussion of whether you should even read a person like that, which in turn led to a debate over the virtues and vices of mob behavior, you know the mob could be dangerous but some things needed a mob, like the French Revolution with all its bloody excess that played a key role in spreading the ideals of the American Revolution across Europe, or at least so argued Ignacio who, in those brief moments before he caught himself, could deeply impress with his historical knowledge. Really it was a matter of where one stood on Western civilization itself, Maya suggested, no fan of it herself in being the child of Indian immigrants who had lived under its colonial thumb, though Eli had a thing or two to say in its defense. "Of course you would," Maya countered sharply, "Mr. Elihu Yale the 14th or 15th"—there was uncertainty over the precise sequence of Eli's descent, as well as the exact percentage of the university his family actually owned—which brought up the oppressive patriarchy in question as well. "Man's inhumanity to man," Jasmine summarized a few moments later, which Ren promptly recorded in his notebook for his novel, which would be partly about the demise of Western civilization and also, partly, about Jasmine, whom he was romantically pursuing in his mind. "Gimme Some Slack" was playing when Lisa, who had joined them despite disapproving of everything they did, began ranting about feudalism which Jeff, in that seminar with her, realized he should probably be familiar with, which in turn led him to stop rubbing Maggie's shoulders and look at his watch, which is how they all realized that the Bladderball competition was surely over by now, with the only certainty being that the Pierson team, some fifteen of whom were crammed into this room, had not won.

"I am the people—the mob—the crowd—the mass," Croc was muttering, his eyes moist. "I was wondering what all that commotion outside was about."

"Right-o," Ig said philosophically, "But I think we made ourselves a nice little memory right here anyway."

"And it doesn't matter what we do, friends," Maggie reminded them, pulling Jeff's hands back on her shoulders, "as long as we do it together."

Jude nodded. "Well, we have got three more Bladderballs. We shall do it next year."

He was wrong on both counts.

And they never did get to use all those heavy chains, though Jude found other uses for them decades later in the period leading up to his murder.

=====

3.

barreling toward meltdown

The brilliant glare somehow only caught the guys' eyes.

"What am I seeing?" Tayvon whispered.

"I will never wash these eyeballs again," Swill whispered.

"You said that last time," Beamie snorted in a whisper.

"Still haven't washed them, loser," Swill whispered back.

"No man shall see that face and live," Black whispered.

"The Queen," Ig whispered.

If you haven't figured it out, whispering was required in the presence of the divine figure who had just appeared in Commons, entering the serving line with her tray. Even the way she bore the three-cheese macaroni on her tray was sublime.

Magina, incredibly, was her name, whose similarity to "vagina" could not for one moment be put from mind, and she *was* divine. As divinity, she was purity; and as purity, she could not be touched, or even approached, by any man, and frankly not even looked at. This response to her was apparently universal, so unfortunately, for Magina, despite being exquisitely beautiful, her luscious curvy body an exemplar of the Eternal Feminine (so noted Tayvon), not to mention being a wonderful kind soul, no guy ever asked her out or really even spoke to her. Not to mention her difficulty making female friends, who mostly couldn't fathom being friendly with someone who instantly made them look so much less attractive.

"You guys are animals," Maggie had said when they voted against her proposal to invite Magina to join them at meals. To be fair to the guys, Magina's presence at their table would have completely destroyed their ability to act in any remotely normal way.

"You guys are animals," Maya said now, after Alexandra had hastily gathered up her tray and disappeared from their table

35

pretty much forever. Totally understandable, given that in the middle of her disquisition on the disrespect of women on this campus the guys had begun whispering about this bosomy babe across the dining hall.

"No opinion," Jeff said to Maggie in her room later when she, having noticed his silence at the lunch table, asked him whether he felt about Magina the way all the other guys felt.

"No opinion? Really?"

"I mean, obviously, she's not unattractive. And maybe I would have felt a little more like them during my dark period. You know, B.M."

"Before Maggie?"

"Exactly."

"You are so full of shit, mister B.M."

"Good one!"

"It was. But lucky for you, your being full of shit, mister," Maggie leaned in to kiss him (God is young fresh love nauseating), "will get you everywhere."

Actually there were several things that helped get Jeff everywhere, including being a good listener who constantly gave her good backrubs and wrote pretty songs on the guitar and piano. Although you know it had already been three weeks and he hadn't yet written one for her. "What is the deal with that, mister?" Maggie queried, not fully assuaged by his protestations that her name was hard to rhyme: Baggy? Haggy? Faggie? But you know that when she was crying because of her brother's latest outrage and the strains it created on her parents' marriage and Jeff just listened and rubbed her back for a long time, well all that really helped get him everywhere too, that night, and then again on a sofa in Winthrop House at Harvard, belonging to Maggie's high school friend Ilona, where they were staying for their first Harvard-Yale football game, aka The Game.

What a glorious season it had been!

Croc was a monster, the team was monstrous, and they headed into the final game of the season with a 7-2 record, 5-1 within the Ivy conference. The Crimson, their nemesis, was formidable again this season, also 7-2 but only 4-2 within the conference, so a Yale victory in The Game would earn the Ivy title. The world was falling apart in any number of ways, most recently in Ronald

Reagan's electoral victory (seen as an unmitigated disaster across the institution), but nothing was more important than how your hormonally bloated boys would fare against the other side's hormonally bloated boys on the gridiron on that fall, forties but biting wind, afternoon.

"I don't get it. They're just a bunch of oafs on a field," Beamie said at Naples Pizza over pitchers of cheap beer. "I don't see why it matters."

"God is it painful to talk to you," Swill puffed on his cigar.

"You don't have to be so mean about it, Swill," Tayvon said, still irritated with him over their earlier debate over the merits of "ketchup" v. "catsup."

"Doesn't he?" Ig said with a loving guffaw, sitting before his own pitcher.

"Don't I?" Swill concurred. "Just a 'bunch of oafs on a field'?"

"Sorry, I'm with Beamie on this one," Lisa cast her eyebrow at Swill.

"Really," Beamie asked, not minding the insults because it meant he was part of the gang, "what else is there beyond the oafs?"

Swill sighed and puffed. "Only everything. They represent you and me, for starters. They represent their institutions. Their institutions represent the country. It is literally Yale battling Harvard down there. It is literally America battling, I don't know, the Soviet Union, Communist China down there. Hell, it is literally Earth battling Martians. I would say when those boys take the field it is pretty much the future course of history, of humanity, that is at stake. 'Oafs'! Have a little imagination, will you?"

"You're misusing the word 'literally,'" Lisa noted, unimpressed.

"I was using it metaphorically," Swill answered with a puff.

"Can 'literal' even be used metaphorically?" Tayvon asked.

Whatever it was doing battle on that field, literally or metaphorically, what a weekend!

Maggie and Jeff took the train with the gang up to Cambridge Friday afternoon. They had contemplated driving but Jeff felt uncomfortable with Maggie's habit of, you know, hitting things. ("Come on," Maggie would say, "I almost never hit *moving* things.") They attended the watch party in the Winthrop Common Room to learn who had shot J.R. on *Dallas*, and after smoking weed and after Ilona had *finally* retired to her room and Maggie had assured him a couple of times "It's allowed!" they did the deed on her sofa, which was when they also hatched the scheme to have sex on sofas at all eight Ivy League schools.

"Ack!" Maggie said when Jeff acquiesced to the scheme. "We should have gone to the Dartmouth game! My friend Allison is there."

"Well, there's always junior year."

There was a little hesitation, nearly imperceptible unless you were looking for it, but it was there. Things had been going really great in the—oh my, had it only been just over three weeks?—but was he already suggesting they would still be together two years hence?

"Or we can just take a road trip some weekend," Jeff added quickly to fill the awkward gap, finding himself suddenly wondering if Maggie were going to enter his remark into that little diary of hers she was always scribbling in.

Crisis averted, a few hours sleep on the uncomfortably narrow sofa, a few good morning bong hits to start the day, and it was Game Time. The details don't really matter but Croc's massive ass showed up in all its glory, shutting down the Crimson offense. Yale won 14-0 and clinched the title and as importantly Harvard did not. That evening Maggie and Jeff spent with Ilona downing Scorpion Bowls at the Hong Kong restaurant in Harvard Square, the former celebrating and the latter drowning her sorrows. Then it was time to stumble back to her room in Winthrop, take a few good night bong hits, and once Ilona had *finally* retired to her room Maggie and Jeff hatched the new scheme to have sex twice on sofas on every Ivy League campus.

But ah, young love, little freshbirds. It was a nuclear furnace, blasting with heat, barreling toward meltdown.

=====

4.
they killed him, man

There were many distractions heading into the end of the semester.

There were end of term assignments, and final exams, to be thinking about. Arguably more important there was a massive earthquake in Italy leaving thousands dead; Isabela, apparently Italian, spearheaded a relief drive for survivors, managing even to squeeze some dollars out of Ig (who himself normally relied on the largesse of non-acquaintances, as Jeff put it, parodying *A Streetcar Named Desire* that had recently screened at the Yale Film Society). "Happy to help," he told her, giving her a good, kind look, she really was quite pretty, but she just said thank you quickly and looked away.

"You think she was intimidated by my big sac?" he asked the guys when relaying the story.

"Tell me you had your clothes on," Jude said.

"Some."

Swill was irritating everyone with his monologues about how massively computers were going to impact the future—you could see how they might be useful for business but really, for most people, what use would they be? "Seriously," he insisted almost daily at Commons, "we're all going to have computers. Every last one of us. It's going to change everything."

"Bleh," Tayvon demurred at what he saw as a dark dystopia. Everybody's favorite Luddite preferred longhand to the typewriter, in-person conversation to the telephone, and felt, frankly, that the jury was still out on the horseless carriage.

Most immediately, New Haven crime continued to encroach when another student was raped, this time in a Yale parking lot. Maya called for a girl's night out to discuss the situation—sorry, women's night out—and Yale's dismissive attitude toward women in general.

On that dreary, drizzly, freezing-rain Monday evening in December, most of the guys headed off to the Payne Whitney gym for their occasional game of basketball while the nascent Pierson chapter of the National Organization of Women assembled at Fitzwilly's on Elm Street. A pretty, magical ambience: a lovely room with soft lighting, ferns and other greenery, light jazz on the speakers, the sweet aroma of delicious cooking, and the sangria, in bottomless pitchers, leading to things said that might not otherwise be said, that might even be regretted in being said, but that were all part of the incalculably beautiful tapestry of human relationships.

Present were Maya, Maggie, Jasmine, Lisa, Isabela, and F. Scott. (F. Scott was technically a guy but had recently left that designation behind, along with her place in her parents' will.) There were pitchers of sangria, some excellent salads, and some serious discussion about Yale's policies with respect to women; then there were more pitchers of sangria and the conversation moved on to these women's policies with respect to men.

"Okay, give me your slips of paper," Maggie said, reaching out her black knit cap to collect them. "Isabela, don't hold out on me."

"I don't know," Isabela said uncomfortably.

"Come on, Isabela," Maggie said gently. "You need to say 'yes' more."

There was a moment's pause, everyone gazing at her, supportively.

"Okay," Isabela smiled shyly as she dropped her slip into the cap. "'Yes more.'"

"Awesome!" Maggie said excitedly. "Let's see the results."

The question was which of the guys in their group they most wanted to "do." Not a question several of the girls present would normally answer publicly, but recall the sangria.

Maggie pulled out the first slip. "Tayvon!" she proclaimed, to the surprise of no one. And the next: "Tayvon!" And the next, the next, and the next: "Tayvon!" That left one slip in the hat. The women all looked around at each other.

"It's like Ellery Queen," Jasmine said, "waiting to reveal who the killer is."

"Everybody in, apparently," Maggie smiled. "Anybody out?" She pulled out the final slip and smiled. "Well what do you know. El Jefe!"

"Of course you'd stand by your boy," Lisa said.

"It wasn't me!" Maggie laughed.

There was another silence as they processed this new information.

"It's like Ellery Queen——" Jasmine started to say again.

"Oh honeys it was me," F. Scott confessed. "What? He's cute. That long messy hair of his. Those silly sunglasses. And you say he plays guitar?"

"He does," Maggie said, not quite sure how she felt about this. But then again, she had listed Tayvon so who was she to have some feelings? "I'm trying to get him to write me a song but he says my name is too hard to rhyme."

"F. Scott, hot," F. Scott offered. "Love knot. Jackpot. Why not. I'm just saying. When you are done with him honey, you send him my way."

"What do I get in return?" Maggie said with a laugh.

"Tayvon?" Maya chimed in, to much laughter, the Tayvon of such creamy mocha skin, Jeff should write a song about that, Tayvon's creamy skin, dreamy, steamy, seamy, man the thing practically wrote itself, they laughed, wish he would see me, laughter, team me, some uncomfortable laughter, then suddenly Isabela, of all people, blurted "ream me," and the laughter stopped sharp—too far.

Later Maggie wanted to share the conversation with Jeff, but then again, maybe not a good idea, so she just wrote about it in her diary. Came out of nowhere, didn't it, Isabela saying that, but you know, the drinking, *in vino veritas* sort of thing. And what a fun night it had been to that point, everyone was into it. Even stodgy Lisa, even she acknowledged Tayvon's many masculine virtues; Jasmine taking a break from her pointless fixation on Black to do the same; Maya, well she was currently engaged in a cross-cultural, intergenerational, and international dispute with her parents who had engaged her to some young man in India she had never met, so her interest in Tayvon was the next move in that dispute; and then there was Isabela, gentle Isabela, her blouses buttoned to the neck, a thin gold chain around her neck but whatever was hanging on it obscured by her blouse, even her roommate Jasmine had never seen her undress, and then suddenly blurting out that harsh phrase …

Isabela, it became obvious instantly, was a virgin.

She may only have been eighteen, but in 1980 at Yale, among

women a full generation into liberation, this was an embarrassing revelation. And while she was surely not alone in this status, she was alone in so obviously revealing it, and certainly in feeling the deep complex shame about it. The conversation continued but never recovered. The sangria was wearing off, the energy was dissipating, and the girls were distracted, Maggie, in particular, by thinking about how to help her friend. Tayvon; the guys had their silly Magina thing, but they had Tayvon, the man *was* like a dream, but you know, maybe that was a little overkill, to imagine him solving the problem of inexperienced Isabela, and anyway, you know, it would be a little unfair, they all sort of, you know, wanted him … Maggie found herself, after all these thoughts, feeling both a little guilty and rather missing her guy.

She got to Jeff's suite around 11:00 PM. She was feeling melancholy, a little nostalgic, even, though for what exactly she couldn't say. "I got you a brownie," she said when Jeff opened the door, handing him the package, and taking off her little black coat and hat. Fortunately Black was out, Zar was off with his pads and pencils working on his model of fire, Beamie was still in the library.

Her beautiful black hair was messed up from the cap but that was all right, Jeff thought: he loved brushing it with her grandmother's brush, which he had good reason to believe would be happening shortly. "I got you something too," he said, leading her to the sofa then picking up the guitar he had been noodling with. "It's just a few pieces, I haven't figured out how to put them together yet. And no, I'm not yet up to the words."

He strummed and hummed softly, the gentle major seventh chords.

"That's really pretty," Maggie said, feeling a little emotional as she heard the first stages of the first song anyone had ever written for her.

"Thanks," Jeff finished, leaned the guitar against the wall, then reached over the arm of the sofa. "I also got you this." He handed her the bong that he'd been hitting while working on the melody, waiting for her arrival.

She smiled, took a hit, held it, looked at him. "How about some Beatles tonight? Maybe early Beatles?" She thought that would hit her mood perfectly, the sweetness, the innocence, the sense of nostalgia.

"Coming right up," Jeff said, heading over to the milk crates holding his LPs. "Maybe *Meet The Beatles*? I would, after all, enjoy grasping your metacarpals?"

"What?"

"I think those are the bones of your hand."

She smiled, nodded. "The King of Corny."

It was perfect. A wintry night outside but warm inside, in Jeff's bedroom. He had put on the single blue light bulb for when they smoked weed, the Four were being Fab, they were doing a little snuggling. As the song "Hold Me Tight" came on Jeff smiled and began to hold her tight, and they were just starting some light smooching on his bed when Black totally ignored the tie Jeff had tied to the doorknob and barged right in.

"Hey!" Jeff exclaimed, bolting upright. "A little busy, here, man!"

"Shit, man," Black exhaled, out of breath, since he had just run up the five flights of stairs after he heard on the radio the news that he knew his roommate would want to know. "They killed him, man. They killed him."

"What? Who?" Jeff and Maggie said simultaneously.

"Your man. Lennon. They killed John Lennon."

Their first semester was over.

=====

spring

5.

you meatheads

The first Sunday night in February, emerging from a bitter cold snap. It was Fregoli, of all people, who acquired the secret information. He had this strange habit, a kind of tic, he would tent his fingers then start flapping them against each other, making a slapping noise. For some reason he had started doing this, a few nights earlier—around 1:30 AM—standing in the cold in front of the Skull and Bones tomb on High Street. As luck would have it, several members of the secret society were just returning from their winter retreat at their private island. The Bonesmen were initially perturbed to find this strange fellow outside their tomb— they suspected the dickwads of Scroll and Key of being up to something—but then they noticed his flapping fingers and, in the dark, mistook it for one of their many secret gestures.

"I think that's for the first or second cousin of a Bones alum," said the captain of this year's championship football team.

"Yeah, I think that's the once removed variation," concurred the Editor-in-Chief of the *Yale Daily News*.

"Let's see what he wants," said the pitch pipe for the Whiffen-poofs, Yale's premier senior male a cappella group.

They attempted what many had attempted before: to have a coherent conversation with Fregoli. Allegedly the kid was brilliant but he was obscure, tending to speak in platitudes which might, on analysis, be kernels of insight. So when the football captain asked him one of the secret Bones questions, Fregoli replied in a tone of great seriousness, something about not cutting the roots of a plant. No, that wasn't the traditional response but, after three days of "retreat" it sort of made sense to them. And then when the Whiffenpoof asked another secret question—one making reference to Yale's alma mater—Fregoli responded with equal seriousness by remarking on the natural cycle of the four seasons. Well, that was good enough for them, who, in having been away for the past three days obviously hadn't seen *Being There* at the Yale Film Society two nights earlier, which Fregoli was vaguely paraphrasing. So they were happy to inform Fregoli that the Bones were sponsoring the first Feb Club party of the year this coming Sunday night, and that he should be there. They even wrote the information down for him because he hadn't stopped flapping his fingers.

Sharing this information instantly catapulted Fregoli from the periphery of the friend group to its center, at least temporarily. This was precious intelligence: Feb Club was a tradition at Yale, where a party was hosted every night of the most depressing month in a different location each night. You had to know a guy who knew a guy to get to one of the parties, but then you were in, as each night's party would announce the location of the next night.

"You are the man," more than one of the gang said to him, clapping him on the back, for his brief period of being the man. Fregoli soaked it in, loving it, even though he then forgot all about it and failed to show up when the gang assembled in his livingroom to pregame the party, and thus returned to the periphery.

En masse the gang headed out on this cool February night to find the spacious room in the Saybrook steam tunnel hosting the inaugural Feb Club party of the year. En masse they would soon return in a mix of embarrassment and rage and hilarity and maybe just a little annoyed with Fregoli, whose intelligence had left out one key bit of information.

"Whoa, whoa," said the very large senior managing the door, behind which could be heard loud music and much hubbub. "No large groups."

"We're not a large group," Swill answered, speaking for the group.

"You're obviously a large group."

"No, bonehead, we are a collection of individuals," Swill puffed his cigar.

The senior, who was a Bonesman and sure Swill had used the slur deliberately, started to close the door on them.

"Come on, Thaddeus," Thorn pushed forward to address his rugby teammate. "It's me. These are my pals."

"Yeah, come on, Thaddeus," Swill continued to poke while Jude elbowed him in the stomach to egg him on. Though Jude himself did not drink, he took great pleasure in observing the pals drink themselves silly.

"Yeah, come on, Thaddeus," Tayvon echoed, while Jude elbowed *him* in the stomach.

"Thorn, man, you know I love you," Thaddeus said, pulling Thorn in to give him a chest-to-chest embrace. "I could overlook the group thing, maybe. But—"

"What group thing, bonehead?" Swill protested.

"Yeah, what group thing, bonehead?" Ig echoed with a guffaw.

Thaddeus was not pleased. "Look you meatheads," he turned to them with the air of a future U.S. Vice-President who was not accustomed to insubordination, "one more word and I'll turn your heads into actual meat. I was about to tell you that no freshmen are allowed to Feb Club unless escorted by a senior. No exceptions. Now make like a banana and split before I have you banned from next year too." He turned back to Thorn. "Sorry, man, you know I love you."

There was much discussion on the return to Lawrance, first on his use of the "make like a banana" trope and what that indicated about a Yale education or maybe just the battered brains of rugby players—no offense Thorn, we love you man—which led back to the idea of "meatheads," whether brains qualify as "meat," and then whether the girls were also meatheads—a surprisingly vexed question with many angles, about which the girls had much to say—and, well, if they got nothing else out of it, they at least now had themselves the delightful nickname of meatheads.

Oh, and they got one more thing.

We don't need your rotten party.

We'll just throw our own rotten party.

(For the record the Yale Film Society would show the *Treasure of the Sierra Madre*, from which this line is inspired, the following year.)

=====

6.

a mostly one-sided conversation with a cactus

There would be much to boast of, of their time at Yale. Academic achievements, a few. Zar obviously, but there would also be Jude's work in chemistry, and Jeff's; Swill's work on "the interweb," which would become the internet; F. Scott's art; and, spoiler alert, Ig would turn out all right too. There were boast-worthy extracurriculars as well: Jasmine's cello, Lisa's journalism, Eli's investment club that soon was generating returns sufficient to cover the club's Mory's bills. There were plenty of good deeds too, such as Maya's work with immigrants, Jeff's playing guitar at local nursing homes, Black's classroom volunteering with underprivileged children, and especially Jude, who, already disturbed by their collective privilege in a city beset by poverty and crime, got so outraged over the recent news that the term bill was to pass a whopping ten grand next year that he resolved to do *something*.

Oh, and Maggie's actually saving someone's life.

Above all that, there was that party.

The Dens of Sin and Iniquity.

Saturday night, Feb 7, 1981, a day that must live in infamy, Ignacio the history major insisted, a history major who seemed to know more about North America than the Central America he allegedly hailed from. The party was thrown by the fifth-floor denizens of Lawrance Hall, Entrance C: Jeff's suite, with Black, Beamie, and Zar, along with the suite across the landing, housing Ignacio, Tayvon, Jude, and Swill. Party-goers ascended the five flights to arrive at the keg on the landing. On the wall above the keg was a sign with an arrow pointing left, to Ignacio et al's suite, under the word, "Sin," and a sign with an arrow pointing right, to Jeff's suite, under the word "Iniquity." It was in Sin that you could find your way, through the smoky colored lights and loud music, through the many bodies dancing in the packed livingroom, to the plentiful supply of rum jello shots.

It was also in Sin that Jude was encouraging Beamie to make a move. The fellow had that great smile, after all, if he just maybe learned to comb his hair or something. "She wants you," Jude shouted into Beamie's ear, over Springsteen's "Born to Run." "That one in black."

There was an attractive girl in black who had been looking their way (although in fact at Jude).

"Out of my league," Beamie shouted back.

"If that is your criterion then you are doomed," Jude shouted back. "Just go for it. Statistically it is not impossible." Here he was referring to the Law of Large Numbers: as long as there was a non-zero possibility of attracting someone, then with enough efforts it should eventually pay off.

Surely it was not *zero*?

Beamie, who'd had enough jello shots to this point that he could be persuaded, headed over. He approached the girl through the crowd of dancing bodies but then kept walking past her, circled around through the crowd again, and returned to Jude.

"What the fuck?" Jude shouted.

"She rejected me," Beamie shouted back.

"But you did not even talk to her!"

"She pre-rejected me."

"What? What does that even mean?"

"She rejected me with her peripheral vision," Beamie explained.

He was often struck how, when he was walking on the street or at the library or anywhere, no passing girl would even cast a glance at him as if they had already determined out of the corner of their eye that he wasn't worth even a full glance. He would have marveled at the phenomenon if it weren't so excruciatingly, and recurrently, painful.

"Oh," Jude shouted. "I would have figured you have a better shot with the peripheral vision."

"Yeah, thanks," he shouted and slinked off in search of a jello shot that wouldn't reject him.

It was in Sin that Lisa had parked herself in a corner, sitting on top of the ratty old sofa Jeff and Black bought for nine dollars from Goodwill, casting ironic glances at everybody, including at Tayvon doing his shirtless Mick Jagger to Aerosmith's "Get It Up" who was looking at Lisa looking sort of hot all aloof on that sofa over there in the smoky colored lights. Isabela snapped a great photo catching Lisa's eyebrow, and more than a few photos of Tayvon's moves. Ignacio unfortunately couldn't make the party, despite its occurring in his suite, because the hockey team was away in New Hampshire.

It was in Sin, too, that F. Scott made her first move on Jeff.

So much for waiting for Maggie to be done with him, but Maggie had disappeared for a long while leaving Jeff deliciously unprotected. (Turns out she was busy consoling Beamie in the bathroom, who was taking the earlier pre-rejection pretty hard.) Inspired by Queen's "Don't Stop Me Now" F. Scott sidled up to Jeff, who was engaged in a shouting match with Swill that had started as an argument about pizza, evolved into one about metaphysics, then returned to pizza. Black whizzed by at one point: he had glimpsed Jasmine entering the room and was making a beeline for the rear door of the suite.

"You are wrong," Swill puffed his cigar, flatly rejecting Jeff's position on anchovies with a many-puff-long rant that soon morphed into some predictions about the future of technology. While he was ranting he didn't quite notice that first Jeff, and then F. Scott, slipped away, which would have been fine with him anyway because he had plenty to say and still like three inches left on the cigar. Tom Petty's "Don't Do Me Like That" was blasting when F. Scott cornered Jeff at the rum jello table, where he was refilling the trays from the fridge.

She put out her cigarette in one of the overflowing ashtrays.

"Hey," she said, approaching him.

"Hey," he answered, instinctively taking a step back.

She stared into his eyes, evaluating, she prided herself on her ability to read people. Jeff's eyes, or what you could see of them under the long curly bangs when he wasn't wearing his shades, were soft, kind, inviting, in addition to looking rather stoned. "Any chance you, um, want to slip back to my room for a minute?"

"What?" Jeff said, either unsure he had heard correctly or unable to process it.

"I'd like to show you something."

"What?"

"I said I'd like to show you something."

"No," Jeff said, whose thoughts had gone to some dark places he was ashamed to admit, "I meant what did you want to show me."

"Just come and see." She beckoned him toward the front door of the suite, which led to Entryway B, where her room was. With some massaging of her medical history she had been assigned to a female suite, where she got the single bedroom and her suitemates, Maya and Samilla, shared the double. (Samilla steered clear of the meatheads freshman year suspecting they were all racists, though would get sucked in by them next year.)

"Um," Jeff stammered.

"Don't say anything. Just come."

You had to feel for F. Scott in that moment. Hard enough to be a girl—a woman—in that world. Even harder to be a boy who was a girl in that world. What courage it must have taken to put herself out there like that. Jeff was totally fine with all that, or at least he told himself so. But he had a lot going on right now, including wondering where Maggie had been for the last hour, he had seen her dancing with Tayvon early on and look Tayvon was a good guy but he was Tayvon, and it was now three hours into the party so Tayvon was surely off being Tayvon by this point, and where was Maggie?

Jeff finally found his words. "Uh, uh, um."

"It's all right, honey," F. Scott withdrew, regretfully. "Another time."

She had really put herself out there, she thought as she retreated, and, okay, approaching another girl's boyfriend was really not cool. But she prided herself on reading people, and Maggie was great but she and Jeff just weren't a good fit, she thought, Maggie was fun-loving and all smiles and Jeff obviously adored her but he also had a deeper edge, a darker edge, maybe. Heavier. And an insecurity, vulnerability. You could hear it in his music, she had several times heard him playing on passing his suite door. And with those eyes, those kind gentle eyes beneath the curly bangs, F. Scott knew, just knew, that he would get it, that if she showed him her room, he would get it, and he would get *her*.

If all that was Sin, well, then you could just imagine Iniquity, across the hall.

Darker, smokier, the music less loud but more sultry. It was in fact to Iniquity that Jude showed up some time later with Cassius. Cassius was the homeless man who always wore a shower cap for some reason and spent most of his time soliciting quarters on Broadway. Jude, who'd given up on Beamie for the night but couldn't give up his disgust over Yale's privilege, had gone out for some cold air and clarity of vision on this winter's night and after giving the poor freezing fellow a dollar realized he could get him some warmth and some food at the party, where pizzas were about to be delivered. Jude was of course entirely sober; Cassius was sober enough to realize that this was not perhaps the best of ideas but hungry enough to say fuck it that's this weirdo's problem. Jude's heart was surely in the right place, all agreed the next day, if perhaps not his head.

Jeff and Maggie didn't witness the episode. Having found each other at last they had made their way back to Maggie's room for a goodnight bong and for Jeff to play for her the song he'd finally finished for her, a little melody called "The Beginning" but, alas, without her name in it. Jeff strummed softly because Jasmine and Isabela were asleep in the bedroom next door. Lisa was nowhere to be found. (She was at that moment casting ironic glances at Tayvon who was removing her clothes.) Jeff and Maggie only heard about the episode the next afternoon, at brunch at Commons, from Ren who apparently was there—nobody had noticed him, it was dark—taking notes for his novel. Beamie had not gotten laid; Tayvon had; Zar had been seen with his legal pads all night long, trying to crack fire; okay not exactly breaking news. The police had come when Jude got into a fight with another one of Thorn's rugby buddies who found Cassius's lack of hygiene offensive; Eli had bailed Jude out and the two had spent the night at the Anchor Bar along with Ig who had returned late and upset from his game—he'd had three minutes of ice time but the one time the puck came his way he had tripped on it—Ig guzzling the one-dollar drafts that Eli was springing for while Eli sipped from the two-hundred-year-old Scotch they kept behind the bar just for his family, with Jude trying to clarify his vision by understanding exactly what was the problem with bringing a homeless person to a Yale party.

"Probably still there," Ren said, checking his notes, explaining their absence from the brunch.

And Fregoli? Maybe it *was* time to start worrying about Fregoli. While the police were dragging away Jude and Thorn's buddy and Cassius, he was seen engaged in an intense mostly one-sided conversation with the cactus in the livingroom.

=====

7.
where in the lord's name are your pants

The mist had begun to thicken, it felt almost like they were in 19th century London, walking home late one night through alleys and old buildings and fog while Big Ben tolled the hour. No, not London, Jeff thought, but Whitechapel, "Imagine," he said, leading the way through the mist, "wandering streets like these, on nights like these, returning home from the theatre—" he emphasized the word, *thee-ah-ter*—"your cloak pulled tight, faraway horses clomping on distant cobblestone, maybe dreaming a little, when suddenly Jack the Ripper could leap out of some dark crevice and stab you in the heart! If that isn't life in a nutshell," Jeff concluded triumphantly, "then what is?"

"Whoa, lighten up there, asshole," Ignacio responded with a guffaw.

"That is me lightened up," Jeff said echoing the guffaw, because how could you not?

And with that they had arrived at the rear gate of Branford College. They went through, found the thick wooden door, and began their ascent of Harkness Tower.

Attached to Branford but overlooking the Old Campus, Harkness was at some twenty stories the tallest building on campus, a Gothic masterpiece studded with so many magnificent gargoyles— Jeff was using Jude's adjective *magnificent* a lot lately—that it eventually led to Jeff's declaring an art history major in addition to chemistry and pre-med. Most importantly it featured a magnificent carillon—there it was again—rung twice daily by members of the Carillon Guild, one of Yale's most prestigious student groups, at least according to its members.

"Zounds! Are *you* a loser!" Beamie had snorted at Jeff in the fall on briefly emerging from the library, for he considered the carilloneurs to be even lower on the social ladder than himself.

"Ha ha ha!" Black exploded with laughter when Jeff mentioned he was auditioning for the Guild, though he might also have been laughing in joy at the song "Celebration" just then tearing up the charts. With such responses Jeff wisely chose not to share with anyone the hazing rituals the Guild members put him through, except of course for Maggie, who thought that reciting Monty Python's "Knights Who Say Ni!" routine in Pig Latin was sort of cute.

"Joining the Guild," Jeffrey observed years later, to Debra, "was one of the best things I've ever done, ranking just beneath quitting drugs, itself just beneath doing drugs in the first place. When I played, *I* controlled the life blood of the campus, *I* created the atmosphere, it was all those Gothic buildings and *me*. At a place like Yale the atmosphere is no trivial thing, it's central to the whole experience. And I got to create that soundtrack. The Tower became a monument to my strength. From any spot on campus I could point at it and say, 'See that? Mine.'"

"And did you ever see anyone," Debra sipped her coffee, "about these delusions of grandeur of yours?"

"Well, I've got you now," he smiled. "Anyway, Ig, the one who—"

"Naked motorcycle riding, bit of a drinking problem, drinker of ketchup, Mr. 'Do it again, Iggy, do it again!'? Called everyone 'asshole' as a term of endearment?" Debra, who as a psychologist was greatly aided by having a memory like a trap, referenced some of Jeffrey's earlier stories about the man. "Adored Maggie's inclination to encourage people by saying, 'It's allowed,'" which he then abused mercilessly?"

"That would be the one. But also—"

"—the heart of gold, who would give you the shirt off his back, if he possessed one."

"You're frightening me."

"Sorry. Carry on."

"Right. So one night I brought him up the Tower during a huge storm. Or more accurately, he demanded I bring him up during the storm. 'It's allowed,' he insisted over my objections. 'There are no rules.' We were at a Tuesday Night Club party in Pierson, it was probably one of the first of those we went to, you know, as freshmen we didn't yet live in Pierson itself. The party had just started when Ignacio got gripped by the idea and there was no letting go. We grabbed a tray of jello shots on the way out—everybody was making them then—and headed up the Tower. It was terrifying. Once you climbed the internal stairs up to the room with the playing mechanism you would head out this door and be standing on a platform beneath the huge structure of the carillon itself. It hung by long steel cables from the thick stone columns rising up some five or six stories tall from the four corners of this platform. Those columns were the entire external structure of the Tower at that point, the rest of it, completely open. Wide open. You're essentially outdoors. From that spot a metal circular staircase wound fully exposed to the elements alongside the bells, to another platform. Basically you're on this flimsy staircase, climbing up, outdoors, like twelve or fifteen stories off the ground. You got close-up views of some of the gargoyliest gargoyles you could imagine. The final steps on the staircase took you through a square opening onto a flat, rectangular platform. Then you were on top of the Tower, the highest point on campus. And yes, we would sometimes go up there to get high, at the highest point on campus. *Obviously*."

"It's a little hard to connect you to that guy," Debra shook her head. "And your hair was shoulder length, then, too."

"I was cool once, sort of."

"I *said*, it's a little hard to connect you to that guy," Debra smiled. "So, what happened?"

"Right. Ignacio and I weren't really that close at that time. I mean, we were in the same group, we were all meatheads, but I was mostly with Maggie, and buddies with Black, and I was like, you know, a little afraid of him. That whole 'There are no rules' thing, and the 'TOO MUCH' slogan, not exactly my speed. But there we were climbing those little winding metal stairs outdoors, two hundred feet up, in the driving rain, the whipping winds, it was an actual, honest to God, thunderstorm. 'El Jefe, man,' he shouted at me, above the howling wind, 'we're climbing a fucking lightning rod in a fucking lightning storm!' And suddenly that thought was the funniest thought in the world, and stupid as we were, or maybe just stoned—"

"I thought you said you were drinking jello shots."

"You say that as if that excludes also being stoned."

"Ah! I forgot who we were talking about here. You were saying, 'El Jefe'?"

"Right. Climbing that lightning rod, amid bolts of lightning, we started laughing, or rather Ig started laughing and once he started, that enormous belly-busting guffaw got everyone laughing with him, and then I was laughing. We weren't afraid because somehow we belonged there, right then, right there. I jumped ahead of him onto the upper platform and in the pouring rain jumped right into my favorite Yoga pose—"

"Yoga?"

"Did I mention I was in college? Maggie always dragged me to things. But anyway, there I was, standing in that pose, in the driving rain, my arms raised but elbows bent and hands pointed down, like the raised wings of a bird, or maybe of a butterfly about to fly—that's right, it was called "The Butterfly," I had the raised wings and one knee elevated as if about to take a giant step, a leap, a launch, in what felt like the center of the universe, beneath this awesome backdrop of jagged lightning bolts, and I can still see the ecstatic look on Ig's face as he climbed up onto the platform and saw me poised and ready to take flight!" Jeffrey paused, smiled. "That was the moment we became friends in our own right. I just loved him, in that moment."

"Let me guess. He climbed up onto the platform and took his clothes off."

"Wait. Did I tell you this already?"

"No. But so far every story about him involves him taking his clothes off."

"I think it was the whole Central America thing. He was always hot. Did I mention he wore shorts all winter long?"

"Every campus has one. Next question and it's an important one. I want you to think long and hard about it before you answer."

"What?"

"Why are you telling me this whole story again?"

"Right," Jeffrey scratched his chin. "Let me finish."

So Ignacio took off his clothes up there, standing in the lightning and pouring rain on top of the world, and from the joyous force of his personality, of *Señor* "It's Allowed," combined with the weed and the jello shots and all the energy and perhaps stupidity that comes from being an absurdly privileged eighteen-year-old college student, Jeff's clothes were soon off as well. Ig started "singing"—"Imagine," which after Lennon's murder became Iggy's anthem, and then some Gordon Lightfoot—to be honest you could hardly tell the melodies apart the awful way he sang them, but the spirit was pure, the same spirit that determined that, standing on top of the world naked in the rain, they really ought to spend the entire night up there, don't you think, asshole?

"Really?" Jeff said, who found it all perfectly jolly but was also aware that it was a freezing rain and the middle of the night and he didn't have any clothes on.

"What, you're cold? Don't be a puss, man."

"I am not a puss, man."

"Of course you are not a puss. You are El Jefe, *amigo*."

"El Jefe *is* kind of freezing his ass off here, though."

"What? It's balmy."

"You're a freak, man."

"Life is short, asshole. What could you possibly be doing right now that would be better?"

This was now nearly five months into Jeff's relationship with Maggie, when the sex had declined from the "constant" phase to the merely "often" phase, but it had been a little while and they were pretty due, which was the obvious answer to Ignacio's question.

"Yeah, man, I get it," Ignacio said, Ignacio who as a good-looking studly athlete of solid muscle seemed to score at least off the ice pretty well, as he had been seen leaving more than one party with some clearly interested co-ed. "But let's face it. You're going to have that anyway later, while this—" here he gestured to the platform, the dripping heavens (the rain had slowed), the world around them, and then to himself—"this is a one-shot, make-a-memory deal." He paused a moment then added, as a confirmation of his deep warm feelings for his friend, "Asshole."

Ignacio was big on those one-shot make-a-memory deals, the meatheads would become aware, as despite sometimes leaving parties with a co-ed he didn't ever seem to generate an actual relationship. "Love 'em and leave 'em," he might say when pressed, especially to Maggie who saw through the bravado and realized what an insecure person he was underneath. Naturally a guffaw followed upon saying this, but she couldn't help hearing it as a diversionary tactic.

Still, you couldn't argue with that, Jeff thought—Ig's point about one-shot memory deals. Then again he had already had enough tonight to have a damn good memory and he was, in fact, freezing his ass off, so they began their descent back down the Tower. Ignacio, already recovered from his disappointment, was singing on the way down, though in protest he did refuse to put his clothes back on. He also insisted that Jeff tinkle a few bells as they passed the carillon mechanism on the way down.

"Are you crazy?" Jeff protested, it being already almost midnight and this would be, well, *not* allowed.

"Come on, asshole, you are El Jefe!" Ig guffawed. "Don't poop the party."

That use of Maggie's expression hit home. But even if it hadn't, who could look at the butt-naked Ignacio, with that big grin and bigger personality, and say no?

So Jeff relented, and, after a moment's deliberation, played the opening from Saint-Saëns' *Danse Macabre* that he had heard Jasmine practicing so many times and seemed the perfect soundtrack to a drizzly dreary Tuesday night. Ig was loving it, soaking it in; that look on his face itself soaking into Jeff's memory, to be permanently retained despite his notorious sieve.

"Come on, let's go," Jeff suddenly said, snapping out of it and realizing quite smartly, for someone legally incapacitated, that they should probably leave before the New Haven Police department got to the Tower. They did get to the bottom before the police but not before the dog-walking Master of Branford College. He was an otherwise lovely British professor who taught art history and fortunately did not recognize Jeff from the large lecture class that Jeff had signed up for because (a) Maggie was also taking it and (b) the gargoyles.

The Master also called the carillon a "harmonica" for some reason.

"I say," he said, standing there in his hat and overcoat, his little dog sniffing Jeff's feet, "you're jolly lucky I haven't called the police. I heard you tinkering with the harmonica up there, that is right out of bounds."

"So sorry, sir," Jeff mumbled, "I'm in the Carillon Guild," he dangled his keys, "I didn't realize how late it was." Only later did it occur to him how ridiculous that—was it an excuse?—sounded.

"And you, my good man," the Master's attention had turned toward Ignacio, "Where in the Lord's name are your pants?"

"Temporarily misplaced," Jeff heard Ignacio saying with pronounced earnestness, realizing that Ig was quoting the Guy about the missing pants because Jeff had told Ig the story which made Jeff feel very close to Ig, and then Jeff was thinking it was also odd of the Master to ask after only the pants when Ignacio was entirely naked, in fact he hadn't even bothered taking his clothes down from the Tower with him which really was the funniest thought in the world, and with that they were off, guffawing, heading back to Lawrance to share their exploits with the meatheads on this now early dreary hey it was the first of April morning. They crossed High Street and had just gone through the iron gates to enter the Old Campus when they noticed all the commotion at Welch Hall.

The rest was a bit of blur, Jeffrey told Debra.

He could recall vague images of Ig's muscular naked body being slammed into the mud by a half-dozen Secret Service agents, could Ig have been guffawing while being tackled into the mud, as if it were the most hilarious thing in the world? Almost surely. Had Ig mouthed off at them in some way? Jeff couldn't remember but almost surely as well.

Or maybe it was his sheer brazen nakedness. "I think it perfectly obvious," Ig said with a guffaw at the following week's Tuesday Night Club, "that my raw masculinity threatened the agents. Those big guys with their scary 'guns' and intimidating 'shades' simply felt very small when confronted by my enormous sac." But hey, no hard feelings, and no he said to Swill who was urging him to sue the ass off the federal government, "They were just doing their job, asshole, and a pretty fine job it was, all considered."

Was he merely being philosophical? Was he imagining the Secret Service as a possible future career path for himself? Maybe he even enjoyed the body slam? In any case they *were* just doing their job and couldn't be blamed for thinking that a large naked man appearing out of the dark and mouthing off at them might be up to something. They were highly trained professionals but these were highly unusual circumstances: it isn't every day there's an attempted assassination of a sitting President by a deranged fellow obsessed with a young actress, and it wasn't at all clear that the fellow was working alone, and maybe it wasn't only President Reagan he (or they) were targeting but the young actress herself, and when your job is to secure the freshman dorm where that actress is living and a large naked man comes barreling out of the dark and drizzly night what else would *you* do but tackle him into the muddy ground and haul his naked ass off to jail?

"*That's* why you are telling me this story!" Debra exclaimed. "Jodie Foster!" Debra had recently learned that the actress had attended Yale in the early 1980s and asked Jeffrey if he knew her there. "You do realize that in the course of this elaborate saga you haven't actually answered my question?"

"That may be," Jeffrey answered, "but in so doing I have answered two far more interesting questions."

"Those being?"

"'Can you tell me another story involving Ignacio getting naked and hauled off to jail?' And 'Would it kill you to include a famous actress, the attempted assassination of a President, and being tackled into the mud by Secret Service agents?'"

"Fine," Debra smiled, sipping the coffee which, unsipped during the saga, had grown cold. "All that said, I remain curious whether you knew her at Yale?"

In fact he did, Jeffrey finally answered: Jodie was friends with one of Maggie's friends, because everybody was friends either with Maggie or with one of Maggie's friends, which was in fact how this conversation with Debra had started. She had seen something on *The Jon Stewart Show* about the "Kevin Bacon" game, which got Debra and Jeffrey trying to figure out the "Bacon number" of various actors, which is how Jodie Foster came up, and Debra had read that Jodie Foster attended Yale in the early 1980s and did Jeffrey happen to know her then? In fact he did, thanks to everybody's low "Maggie number," which since he was dating her meant everybody had a much lower "El Jefe" number, too. So yes he knew Jodie, had hung out with her on several occasions, he remembered being starstruck a little but also wondering why anyone should ever be starstruck. She was just another human being like himself after all—albeit more famous, more successful, and better-looking—but in the end she was, as Jude would put it, a sack of meat and molecules just as he was, and they would both end up as worm food though perhaps she would be feeding higher class worms.

=====

8.
that sh-t is deeper than you think

Freshman year was more than three-quarters through.

Beamie continued not to attract females with his early declaration of a major in applied mathematics. Swill continued to annoy everyone with his absurd claim that soon everyone would have their own PCD.

"And what is a 'PCD'?" Tayvon asked wearily at lunch at Commons.

"Personal Computing Device," Swill explained with an enthusiasm inversely proportional to that of his audience. "And just a few years after a critical mass of PCDs is achieved, everyone will be connected via a gigantic interweb so you'll be able to communicate instantaneously with someone in, say, Siberia."

"About what?" Tayvon asked.

Swill snorted. "You could start with 'Good morning,' and 'How are you?' And then move on to how amazing it is that you are able to communicate."

"Wouldn't there be a language barrier?" Ignacio asked, wiping his lips after a chug from the ketchup bottle.

"Instantaneous translation too, *obviously*," Swill sighed. "I cannot believe I hang out with you Neanderthals."

"Fun fact," Jude chimed in, pointing his index finger. "Neanderthals actually interbred with modern *homo sapiens*."

"That would explain a lot," Lisa said. "Like Thorn."

"Good one!" Thorn chortled, always appreciating a clever remark even if at his expense. No self-esteem worries there: this was the man who played the last rugby match of the season with three broken bones because he would not let his teammates down, and who would later earn a medal as a Navy Seal for saving the lives of a dozen men while having even more broken bones.

"Hey, friend, you all right?" Maggie asked, having noticed Tayvon yawning during the meal, even when Swill wasn't pontificating.

"Yeah, yeah, fine," he yawned again.

Because he had taken several college literature classes in high school Tayvon was enrolled in an upper-level seminar on romance novels in which he was one of only two male students, the other one being gay, along with eleven female juniors and seniors. Suffice to say he was *very* busy that semester, not least because he also actually read every book on the ambitious syllabus.

Lisa was gazing at him, weighing the pros and cons of pursuing a second conquest of the man in light of the stiff competition, not to mention her time-consuming responsibilities as Assistant Managing Editor of the *Yale Daily News*, a position rarely held by a freshman. She was so focused she didn't notice Ren gazing at her, rather uncannily reading her mind and entering it all into his notebook.

Maggie turned to Maya, who as a vegetarian had taken only two slices of cheese on a hamburger role and a small green salad. "What's the latest with Doc?"

"Doc," Maya said dreamily.

Though her interests were in pre-law she had signed up for a class with Doc on Maggie's recommendation. Ostensibly the class was about an obscure 17th-century philosopher named Ignoratio P. Elenchi but in reality it was about everything except him, as it was nearing the end of the term and the man's name hadn't come up once. "A thing is most thoroughly grasped by grasping what it is not," Doc explained when a student inquired about this. Ren, doing some close work with Doc—who had now worked out the role his new protégé would play in his long-term project of bringing about his future filmmaker—sat next to Maya, taking notes for his novel and forming his own long-term project of seducing Maya. This he would pursue by never speaking to her.

Maya, sitting next to him at the table, was oblivious to all this, wondering rather about possibly pursuing Doc himself. Isabela happened to snap a photo capturing Ren and Maya next to each other, each with dreamy expressions.

"I think it's allowed," Maggie had affirmed recently when she and Maya had bumped into each other at the Beinecke Library. "Literally. You know, Dean Large?"

The Beinecke Rare Book & Manuscript Library was an architectural gem, across from Commons and Woolsey Hall with which it shared a plaza. Architecture student Isabela, who spoke so little and often seemed so melancholy, would have waxed eloquently and happily about this building if she weren't so painfully shy: a box within a box, the precious materials housed inside a six-story glass-enclosed tower of book stacks, itself within a building whose "windows" were translucent marble panels an inch and a quarter thick. The best part was the legend about what would happen in case of a fire: to extinguish the flames the oxygen would instantly be sucked out of the interior box, much the way it was from the room whenever Beamie attempted a joke or Swill began to pontificate.

Maya was there to examine the original manuscript of Baillet's biography of Descartes, *The Irrationalist*, which had some references to the obscure Elenchi; Maggie to find for her art history paper some original examples of "Wound Man," a medieval trope in anatomy and surgical texts from the 15th-17th centuries. These were explicit depictions of the many types of wounds and injuries a person could suffer: you'd have a picture of a man inserted into whom was an assortment of arrows, swords, knives, the occasional axe, or even a dog or snake or scorpion biting the poor fellow's leg or feet.

"Now if that isn't life in essence," Jeff had whispered to Maggie when the professor showed some slides on the screen, "then what is?"

"You should try to be more of an optimist," Maggie whispered back.

"That *was* me being an optimist."

"It's his brilliance," Maya said, on bumping into Maggie in Beinecke.

"It's hot," Maggie concurred.

"Everything is connected to everything. Everybody is everybody."

"Everyone stars in their own biopic."

"Irony is the fundamental tone of the universe."

"The conclusion is implicit in the premises," Maggie said, by this

point both Maggie and Maya were laughing because they both rec-
ognized all these ideas even though they had taken different classes
with Doc, which suggested that whatever he was teaching he just
taught the same ideas, his ideas, ideas that in connecting everyone
and everything were very sexy ideas, ideas that were inspiring Ren
to have sexy ideas about Maya, who was having those ideas about
Doc, who, frankly, was having those ideas about himself.

Back at the Commons table Jasmine was casting only the brief-
ish of glances toward Black. Fortunately her interest in him had
started to wane, for two reasons. First, she was all in on her music
studies. Taking two advanced theory classes this semester, practicing three hours daily, plus rehearsals now that she'd already made
Second Cello in the Yale Symphony Orchestra all kept her very
busy. And second, Black had started dating Sugar, with whom he
was sitting at the end of the table.

'*Sugar*'? Jasmine had thought incredulously on first hearing
the news.

"Hey baby," Black was murmuring to Sugar as he fed her his
cheeseburger.

"Hey baby," Sugar murmured back as she fed him *her*
cheeseburger.

Give me a break, Jasmine thought, thinking she might actually
be sick. Happily, however, she didn't have to put up with Sugar
long. It was over at pretty much the same time everyone in the
gang independently reached the conclusion that they liked Black
a lot better when he was single.

"What happened?" Eli asked at another meal in Commons a few
days later. He had asked whether Black and Sugar were planning
to make them all vomit again soon and received the reply that they
had split up.

"Not really my type," Black answered.

"Was it because she was a 'she'?" Ig asked quickly then guffawed.

"That's assuming she *was* a 'she,'" Maggie added, the only one of the
girls occasionally willing to descend into the lower meathead realm.

"Just wasn't my type," Black answered quietly as everyone
breathed a sigh of relief.

More Black's type, of course, was Earth, Wind & Fire, whose
album *Faces* was tearing up the charts and had finally dislodged

Michael's *Off the Wall* from Black's record player. He would only break from *Faces* to play the group's single "September," which was simply the greatest song that would ever be written, though of course this was still before Michael's *Thriller*. Jeff and Black got along fabulously except with respect to their squabbles over who could play his records when, given their shared bedroom. True that situation got easier once Jeff started spending more time in Maggie's room—lately they'd started playing cribbage regularly, that was sort of sweet—although that only exacerbated the simmering music conflict between Maggie and Lisa, the latter of whom liked early Soviet worker's songs and disliked the Dead almost as much as Black.

"The 'Grateful Dead'?" Black would say skeptically, passing the bong. "What the hell is that supposed to mean?"

"It's like Egyptian folklore," Jeff exhaled. "The dead person bestows blessings on the people who took care of him when he was dying. Something like that. But really Mr. Earth, Gas, & Fire, I wouldn't talk."

"Fuck you, man, Maurice is a genius." Black knew the band on a first-name basis, and would start chanting their names as a relaxation mantra whenever Jeff was blasting that whiny hippie shit: Maurice, Verdine, Leslie, Wad, Yackov ... "It has to do with horoscopy. The zodiac constellation displays an original property of oxidative combustion and phenological properties related to soil and oxygen." Black had no idea what that meant, but it was on the album cover and by this point he was too stoned really to care. "So there you have it."

"That doesn't make a lick of sense," said Lisa, weighing in despite having only observer status when they smoked weed. "First of all, why change 'air' to 'wind'? And second, the classical elements were earth, air, fire, and water. So why leave out water?"

"It's obvious why water was left out, man," Black said, taking the bong back.

"Why is that?"

"It didn't belong."

To this Jeff and Black both cracked up for reasons entirely invisible to Lisa, who only sighed, remembering the well-known rule that non-stoned persons should not participate in stoners' conversations. At least, she thought, this conversation was marginally more bearable than the heated one, a few days earlier, about the quality of the lyrics of the two groups.

"What the hell," Black had groaned, taking the bong, "transitivity is like a mathematical property. It has *nothing* to do with the fall of night, much less diamonds. Are you shitting me, man?"

"At least it pretends to mean something," Jeff released the deeply held smoke from his lungs. "Unlike 'doobie-doo,' or whatever the hell they're saying, which doesn't mean anything no matter how many times they repeat it."

"That shit is deeper than you think, El Jefe."

"Big step up from 'Uh Huh Yeah,'" Jeff concurred, marveling to himself that after these months of rooming with Black he could actually name the second single from The Salty Peppers, which he also now unfortunately knew was the predecessor band to Earth, Gas, & Fire.

Zar had also been present at these debates, saying little but thinking much. The first thoughts might be ordinary thoughts: how excited he was that once they moved into Pierson itself next year their rooms would have fireplaces. Then on to less ordinary thoughts, about fire, this mathematical model eluding him so long, he wasn't used to that; this was a tough nut to crack, an earthnut, he thought. And listening to these two argue, thinking about earth, then wind and fire, the overlooked water. The idea of elements: atoms, literally "uncuttables" from the Greek, the irony that what today were called *atoms* weren't actually "atoms" as they were divisible into smaller particles. Then again perhaps Aristotle was not entirely off the mark in identifying "elements," as really those could be any fundamental categories, so fundamental there would be nothing more fundamental in terms of which they could be understood. But now—as Zar moved on to Zar thoughts—he realized he was going after the whole fire model entirely wrong, that it was earth as a fundamental category he should be modeling instead. In fact the calculations from his geophysics class would probably be the right place for him to start.

From the outside Zar was just another meathead staring into space.

Jude and Zar had started hanging out quite a bit by this point, partly because of their shared interest in science, partly because can anyone ever really explain why some people like to hang out with other people? They got in the habit of taking walks in the Grove Street Cemetery, where they didn't say a word, each silently thinking his own deep thoughts in the company of the eternally silent. That was how it came to pass, some seventeen months later, in the fall of junior year, that it was Zar who reported back that Jude had spent their most recent stroll fiddling with a Tylenol bottle. Now normally this would not be noteworthy, but this happened right after the Chicago Tylenol murders had made the pain killer a people killer. Seven people had died from capsules laced with potassium cyanide—which, coincidentally, Jude had been synthesizing in his Independent Study that semester.

"Okay that is a little weird," Jeff said when Zar reported this at the Pierson dining table.

"Telling you, man, don't trust that dude," Black said. "Those staring eyes."

"You're paranoid, my friend," Maggie laughed.

"That doesn't mean I'm wrong. Man, you just look stupid when you do that."

Jeff had been trying to imitate Jude's penetrating stare. "Sorry."

To be clear, nobody was accusing Jude of involvement in the Tylenol affair. Although Jude *was* from Chicago, too, now that they thought about it. And had been there over the summer.

Fall of junior year was also the period where the academic competition between Jeff and Jude was at its peak. That semester they were both taking physical chemistry and vying for the top spot. Sophomore year they had taken organic chemistry and tied for first in the class, both semesters.

"Fuck, man," Jeff said to Jude when the results were released at fall semester's end. "If I hadn't been stoned a third of the time I would have kicked your ass."

"Not sure that is possible, Jeff-Jeff," Jude answered, always marveling at the stoner brain's contortions, "considering that we both earned 100%."

"If I weren't so stoned right now I would be able to explain. But even so," Jeff took another hit from the bong he had fashioned out of equipment filched from the organic chemistry lab, "the fact that I earned 100% mostly stoned clearly indicates my victory over you."

Jude didn't bother to mention that he had scored his own

100% despite not having cracked the three-inch-thick textbook even once.

Back in freshman year they were in general chemistry together but there they were tied with numerous other mostly pre-med nerds with 100% averages. They also briefly developed a staring competition thing, but Jeff quickly conceded that one because damn the devil-man's beady little eyeballs (Black's phrase) were savage. There was a, what might you call it, a bantering competition, too, though you got the sense something deeper was going on. The topic could be almost anything. Maggie at one point was trying to convince Jeff, at a Commons brunch with the gang, to try sailing with her that spring afternoon. Jeff promptly reeled off a half-dozen reasons not to, including his morbid fear of large bodies of water.

"You're no fun, mister," Maggie pouted. "You really should say 'yes' more."

And off the debate went, with Jeff taking the negative on the proposition "One should say 'yes' more" and Jude slipping in to take the affirmative. Suffice to say, in this case, that Jeff ended up going sailing with Maggie once he realized he was arguing his way into Jude going with her instead. The only thing Jeff truly ended up affirming that day, unfortunately, was his morbid fear of large bodies of water.

Jeff's and Jude's differing attitudes toward mind-alteration also skewed this playing field as well as provided much material for it. What started out as good-natured teasing freshman year about their different relationship to drugs—Jude's principled abstinence in the name of "clarity of vision" versus Jeff's principled consumption, also in the name of "clarity of vision"—seemed to get harder, darker, more bitter as they progressed into the upperclass years, a kind of tug-of-war where the combatants' bloodied hands were tangled up in the ropes as they pulled for their lives.

You got the sense that only one of them would come out alive from this.

In a sense, only one of them did.

=====

9.
you think cool thoughts

Their year as freshbirds was coming to an end.

There was some campus excitement as the year wound down. Rustication returned as an official disciplinary measure, a fact that would become quite relevant to them senior year. There was controversy over the term bill officially rising to the exorbitant amount of $10,340 per year. There was some good news, too: the winning design for the Vietnam Veterans Memorial in Washington D.C. was announced as that of Yale senior Maya Lin, and the surviving Beatles reunited for a memorial song about their murdered colleague, "All Those Years Ago."

The idea of a paean to a murdered friend; very moving.

As for the meatheads, well, it had been a memorable year.

Ignacio didn't score a goal but did make the most of his ice time zipping around and confusing opposing players into committing penalties. The lovable loser Beamie had failed to even get a date, though somehow maintained that beaming smile anyway. After breaking his brain unsuccessfully on fire Zar more or less cracked the model of earth almost immediately, once he grasped that the thingamajig was an inverse form of the whatsit and recalculated using his fire equations. Jude's Cassius endeavor had failed but had deepened his concern both for the problem (the immediate needs of those homeless) and for its roots (the social conditions that create homelessness). Maya not only managed to escape the shackles of her parental engagement, but then snared a paid summer internship in D.C. to help all the women in the country escape their shackles by advocating for the extended ratification deadline for the Equal Rights Amendment. F. Scott's portfolio of freshman work also got her a choice summer spot for painting at an artist's colony, even as she was realizing her artist heart was really elsewhere.

There were just a few things to wrap up; most importantly, a birthday to celebrate.

Pierson College threw an annual courtyard bash celebrating the birthday of Abraham Pierson, the 17th century minister who co-founded the Collegiate School that would become, with the beneficence of Eli's great-great-great-etc grandfather Elihu Yale, Yale College. That no one knew anything about Abe made it easier to accept that his birthday always somehow landed on the last day of classes each year. Indeed after Jude's murder, after the federal agents had cleared out The Advance, after the shock of the violence had begun to dissipate, your mind wandered back to the early days, to the beginning, to the Assassin game, to Halloween, to Bladderball, to the Dens of Sin and Iniquity, to your chemistry competition, to Maggie, and to that late afternoon in late April, heading over with Black to Pierson for Abe's birthday bash by way of a detour to Naples Pizza.

Jeff and Black were just cutting through Cross Campus when they beheld the curious sight. Thanks to Maggie's obsession with European popular culture Jeff had "Making Your Mind Up," that horrific Eurovision song, burrowed into his head, and was ranting about it again to Black when he became aware, first, that the weather was absolutely perfect—sunny, dry, 73 degrees—second, that the angle of sunlight on the majestic elm dominating the Cross Campus courtyard created a complex pattern of reflections across the tree's leafy canopy, and third, that sitting on the bench across the courtyard, in a pose reminiscent of *The Thinker*, was Jude gazing intently, unbrokenly, through his little round glasses, at the tree.

"What's he doing," Jeff whispered to Black.

"Making his mind up about something, maybe," Black answered.

"Hilarious. But really."

"I'm way too stoned to care, man. I'm heading over. Be cool."

Watching Jude not blinking Jeff engaged in an undeclared staring contest with him. Long moments passed; Jude did not blink, unless he blinked in the very same instant when Jeff finally did. Nor did he move, at least that Jeff could see: his legs bent at the knee, the right arm bent at the elbow resting on the left thigh, the narrow face resting on the back of the bent right hand, and the unblinking eyes gazing through the glasses at the tree in front of him.

Maybe he should join him on the bench?

Abe's birthday would be going for several hours, and it was a perfect spring day. And it actually was a pretty cool tree, now that he was looking at it. That thick strong vertical trunk. The branches opening out like welcoming arms to the sun, the air. Almost open in prayer, even, to the gods above. Entreating. Beseeching. The new spring leaves shimmering green, the promise of a new life, a future. He had probably passed this tree a hundred times during freshman year without looking at it once. He now noticed the handfuls of other people, mostly students, many with Yale caps or sweatshirts or backpacks, walking past, crossing through Cross Campus, not noticing the tree either.

Clarity of vision, Jeff thought.

"Fun fact," Jude had pointed his index finger a few weeks earlier near the red sunset maple tree in the Pierson courtyard. "The term 'tree hugger' was first coined in 1730, when 294 men and 69 women of the Bishnois branch of Hinduism held on to the trees in their village in order to prevent them from being used to build a palace."

"Good for them," Jeff nodded at the time.

"Not exactly. They were murdered by the foresters cutting down the trees."

Now if that isn't life, Jeff thought now, remembering that moment, gazing at his friend gazing, thinking about his friend thinking.

"You are such a pessimist, mister," Maggie had said recently, or maybe complained.

"It's true," Jeff admitted. "I *wish* my glass were half-empty. It's two-thirds empty, and leaking."

"That is not entirely unfunny," Jude had remarked when Jeff told him of the quip afterward, a real compliment from the fellow. It was so late, he'd had that spat with Maggie and was heading back to his room in the middle of the night when he'd found Jude sitting on the stairs in the Lawrance stairwell. They'd gotten to talking and at some point—in fact it was 3:06 A.M. exactly, Jeff looked at his watch—Jude was monologuing that the world is designed, you see, to produce creatures who can appreciate its design. That we fit it, or that it fits us, two sides of the same coin: like we who breathe in oxygen and breathe out carbon dioxide and the tree that breathes in our carbon dioxide and breathes out our oxygen. The system was designed for *all of us*, not just human beings, by passing resources around we all get to live, us, the trees, the animals, the bugs, the earthworms. And by our living, the things, the resources, the inanimate things, all become meaningful, have a function, a purpose. Every individual thing has its role, this moment, this conversation, this sentence. What you see as waste, Jeff-Jeff, he had said, is actually abundance, and opportunity. The world is not made worse because some beings enjoy less goodness than others, or because some parts do not make sense to us, or even because of the calamities, but rather more beautiful by the magnificent variety of beings and experiences it contains. It is a self-ordering order, you see, the impersonal impersonating the personal. It is circles made of smaller circles made of still smaller circles, all the way down, and betterness throughout. And that, little Jeff-Jeff, Jude had sucked in a dramatic breath as if sucking it all in, everything, all of it, is clarity of vision.

Jeff remembered all that, watching his friend gazing at the tree, thinking, as he had at the time but had not said, *you think cool thoughts.*

Come on, he thought to himself now, taking one last glance at his friend then taking off in the direction of Pierson. There was a birthday to celebrate.

There was a bit more ahead. Reading period, final exams. While moving out, Jeff chatting with everybody's favorite homeless person, Brother John, and telling him to go help himself to the good stuff these comfortable Yalies left behind in their rooms as trash. The fantastic weekend gathering of the meatheads at Eli's family's summer house, complete with private beach, on Penzance Road in Woods Hole, and yes the *obvious* "Pirates of Penzance" jokes. (For those paying attention, Maggie's family's Woods Hole house just a few miles away—their only house—was, shall we say, on the other side of the tracks.) Convincing Beamie to come watch the Islanders grow their dynasty against the North Stars in the Stanley Cup Final. And then a weekend working at the Yale reunions, great money to provide a great experience for alums

71

to relive their college days and reconnect with their old chums. Sobering moments to look at these fogeys and realize that you, too, will soon enough be them.

Then the meatheads dispersed, and year one was in the books.

Have a summer one and all,
We'll meet back here in the fall

part 2
sophomore year

=====

fall

1.

maybe love does require apologizing

In the fall semester celebrity author Erich Segal was teaching at Yale.

Debra, whose insights into people were more sophisticated than anyone else's Jeffrey knew, had a cynical fascination with the phenomenon of celebrity. So in another conversation some years after the Jodie Foster one the name Erich Segal arose. Googling, they were both surprised to learn that in addition to having written, in *Love Story*, the *New York Times* number one top-selling work of fiction in 1970 as well as the screenplay for the number one movie of the same name, Segal also had a writing credit for the Beatles' movie *Yellow Submarine*.

"I must have known that then," Jeffrey said.

"It must be difficult for you, remembering so little of your past," Debra chided him.

"It must be difficult for *you*, remembering so much of my past."

"Difficult for *you* that I remember so much of your past. But that's why—"

"—you're paid the big bucks," Jeffrey sighed. "I know."

Welcome back, you're a sophomore …

Or a "sophbore," as Doc put it in the class that Ren and Jasmine were taking this semester on Baillet's autobiography. ("It's amazing," Ren answered Maggie's question early on, "Baillet finally finds his long-lost sister!" Also amazing was Jasmine, he thought, hatching a plan to seduce her by ignoring her entirely.)

The biggest change, of course, was that they were now all living in Pierson College itself. Designed in the "Georgian Revival" style (as Isabela would tell you if only she weren't so shy), its architectural highlights included: (i) the Pierson Tower with its four clock-faced sides, (ii) the Lower Courtyard (neé Slave Quarters), the separate small courtyard home to the half-dozen most coveted rooms that yearly went to seniors, including the Tuesday Night Club room, and (iii) the Pierson Courtyard, the green central space within the main quadrangle, site of wiffleball, bocce, bonfires, a red sunset maple, Abe's birthday, general hanging out, and, as we shall see, the seeing of what no man had seen before. There was also its spectacular dining hall: bright and airy with its very high ceilings, enormous clerestory windows above their heads letting in so much glorious light, clean white wood-paneled walls, and long wooden tables and black wood college chairs—a truly splendid space in which to sit long and talk much.

Overseeing it all, Master Harold and his wife Mistress Lucille, whose house in the corner of the courtyard was home to gatherings intellectual and social, including the occasional V.I.P. coming through for a Master's Tea. If there were adults overseeing the students, at least theoretically, it would be they. (Though strictly speaking *loco parentis* was *not* part of their job description, Black would point out testily, and correctly, in their defense when the question might arise, for example during reunions, of where the hell were the adults back then?)

If the Master and Mistress oversaw, then running beneath them all were the steam tunnels, which not only connected all of Pierson but also connected to the adjacent Davenport College and which, rumor had it, connected to the rest of the university if you only knew where the secret doors and passages were.

"Fun fact," Jude would say, pointing his index finger, "typically some 90% of the mass of a fungus lives under the ground. That happy little mushroom you see poking up in the grass is just the tip of the mycelium. I am telling you. It is all subterranean."

Well maybe not all, but plenty *was* subterranean in Pierson: the squash court where Jeff sometimes played his new guitar for the awesome acoustics (his previous one stolen when he inadvertently left it behind in Lawrance Hall), the music practice rooms where Jasmine practiced her cello, the *ad hoc* galleries where F. Scott installed her installations, and the Buttery, the student-run snack bar where the meatheads would often congregate after hours and continue their dining hall arguments about Russian literature, the new game paintball (discovery of which may have been the start of Jude's fascination with weapons), the future for "videophones," fungi, and celebrity author Erich Segal.

"Still, I will *not,* I repeat, will *not* yield on the asininity of love exempting you from having to apologize," Tayvon insisted over an eggloaf, at the start of a several-meals-long rant against Segal's *Love Story*, "I don't care how famous the dude is."

We needn't reproduce the subsequent debate about the relationship between love and apologizing, which obviously involved deep dives into what constitutes love and what constitutes an apology, etc. This was in fact an ongoing topic that semester as almost all of them signed up for one of Segal's classes, dividing between "The Classical Tradition in Comedy" and "The Classical Tradition in Tragedy," with Ren signing up for both. Nor were they alone: each class enrolled more than 100 students.

"I'll grant you he can lecture," Tayvon did concede, as the man *was* pretty electrifying in the classroom. But even more electrifying was his announcement, on the first day, of the "Term Paper Challenge": the course required only a term paper and a final exam, but if you submitted the term paper by an earlier deadline of Friday, November 13—Princeton weekend—and received an A or A-, the paper grade would serve as your final grade and you'd be exempt from the final exam.

Thus did Erich Segal dominate the fall of their sophomore year.

Many discussions—at the dining hall table, at Tuesday Night Club, in the common room outside the dining hall where Jeff might tinker on the baby grand piano, in the courtyard—about love and apologies, about how someone so smart could write such schmaltzy tripe as *Love Story*, about how such tripe could become a bestseller and what that said about America, Americans, and the future of humanity.

"Seriously," Tayvon continued late one night over greasy cheeseburgers at the Buttery, after reading aloud a sentence about the sound that snow makes. "That's a sentence a high school freshman would write in a creative writing class. And get a bad grade."

"Unless the assignment," Lisa pointed out, "were 'try to sound deep and meaningful while demonstrating you are neither.' Solid 'A'!"

Thorn grunted either in agreement or in pain as he attempted to raise his cheeseburger to his mouth using his right arm, attached to his dislocated shoulder.

"Oh, and here's a good one," Jeff said. Despite not being in the class he was thumbing through the book, taking a break from cribbage with Maggie, and read a line about falling in love being like falling off a precipice.

"Cue the strings," Swill said. "Big swells."

"I just vomited in my mouth a little," Tayvon announced. "Ren, you getting this down?"

Ren, scribbling, nodded.

"Oh, oh," Maggie moaned, then quoted a line about shedding tears in the arms of one's lover. "Why exactly is *that* so vomitacious?"

"Overly dramatic," Lisa said.

"Like, oh my God can you believe she had never wept in front of him!" Samilla weighed in.

"Like, oh my God, like in his arms!" Eli laughed, even though one of his father's companies had made a killing in the film of *Love Story*.

"Maybe the whole thing is meant to be ironic," Jeff suggested. "Like he's actually making fun of such prose, and of people who take it seriously. Maybe he's making a commentary about the state of the American soul." This comment struck him as very deep, either because it was or because he and Maggie had smoked a doob before coming down to the Buttery.

"There is something seriously wrong with you people," Ig finally weighed in, having waited in order to finish his own double cheeseburger. "I think the book is beautiful. And it made me fucking cry like a baby. I mean, and I mean seriously, what *can* you say about a beautiful young girl who passes away?"

The others stared at him, not quite expecting that the man whose primary ambition in life, beyond scoring a goal, was producing long unbroken turds (last week's 13-incher was so far his record), would have an affinity for schmaltzy literary tripe. But then again, Maya pointed out, that literary tripe was a kind of long unbroken turd, and anyway, in retrospect, the clues were there. The love of easy listening, his penchant for emitting sounds resembling Lennon's "Imagine," the way he wept at the budding romance of Luke and Laura on *General Hospital*, and, finally, his infectious gut-busting guffaw that, when it pulled you into its orbit, made you feel the warmth and love of a man whose heart was as weighty as his turds.

"Need a Kleenex there, big fella?" Jude said. Jude, like Jeff, was in neither Segal class, preferring, rather, to kick Jeff's ass in organic chemistry.

"Yeah," Ig answered, "to wipe your carcass from the floor after I crush you, little man."

This tough guy remark got a little laugh from the meatheads, no one realizing that Ig meant it seriously. He was actually loving the Segal class. Erich was brilliant, dynamic, hilarious, his wise eyes darting confidently behind those adorably nerdy oversized goggle glasses, his delicate facial features exuding intellectual might. If these insensitive assholes couldn't appreciate the sound that snow makes, so much the worse for them.

Thus Ig added a new goal to his time at Yale, in addition to scoring *a* goal: he was going to shine in "The Classical Tradition of Comedy." Despite his heavy hockey schedule, and heavier drinking schedule, he actually began buckling down. In fact, "Anyone seen Ig tonight?" was heard on more than one occasion at a Tuesday Night Club, as he might instead be found somewhere else doing the assigned readings. He finally found out where this "Sterling Library" was that he had been hearing about, made his snack runs to the subterranean area leading to the Cross Campus Library modest and short, even discovered the famous Linonia and Brothers Reading Room hidden away in Sterling and, between the naps (inescapable given the plush leather chairs, ottomans, and soft lighting), got that reading done.

"No way I use that room," Maya declared on a run to Park Street Sub, behind Pierson.

"Why not?" Jasmine asked.

Maya finished cutting the veggie sub they were going to split five ways. "Bad history. Only opened to women in 1963, and even that was considered scandalous. Hundreds of male students signed a petition condemning it. One veritable asswipe of an undergrad claimed the women would sit in those chairs in an 'undignified way.' Can you imagine?"

"I'd be happy to sit on his head in an undignified way," Lisa noted.

"Yeah, it does have the feel of a gentleman's club, doesn't it," Jasmine said, taking her fifth of the sandwich and passing fifths to F. Scott and Isabela. "You sort of expect to sit there smoking cigars."

At the indirect reference to Swill they all simultaneously shuddered.

"Wait one sec," Isabela said after the shudder had ceased. "Let's get a photo."

Not every photo has to be special to be meaningful, you know. Looking back it was sometimes those ordinary snapshots of the most mundane moments, the trip to Park Street, the brushing of teeth at adjacent sinks, Ig snoozing in the L&B Room, that really captured the place.

It was soon all mapped out in his head.

He found a great topic: examining the relationship between Brecht's *Threepenny Opera* and its original inspiration, the 18th-century *The Beggars' Opera* by John Gay. What *wasn't* to like about *Threepenny*, and any theater piece based on something by a man named Gay had to be good. Not to mention the song "Mack the Knife," which briefly displaced "Imagine" in his repertoire, until the catastrophe. And how satisfying was it to see Tayvon's eyes widen when Ig informed him that the original idea for *Beggar's Opera* came from Jonathan Swift, who wrote to Alexander Pope in 1716, asking "What think you, of a Newgate pastoral among the thieves and whores there?" (Newgate was London's central prison; Ig looked it up). Such names as Swift and Pope were supposed to come from Tayvon's creamy lips—simply delicious. And wow, that the Yale Musical Theater was producing *Threepenny* that semester—you know, fellow Piersonite Steven Skybell would be a first-rate Mack—all of that was icing on the cake, which Ig was only too happy to consume then lick his fingers.

Ig actually giggled out loud in the L&B Room more than once, before settling into the comfy chair for a satisfying nap.

=====

2.
women's studies

The meatheads were all very busy that semester, leading up to the November 13 Term Paper Challenge deadline. So much so that they didn't even bother with Bladderball that year. Already jaded a bit, as sophbores, maybe, with the been there, done that?

"But the piglets!" Swill insisted, puffing furiously.

"Next year," others assured him, falsely.

Jeff finally finished his summer's project of reading, on Ren's suggestion, all the major 19th century Russian novels. Zar was consumed with developing a new model of gases, after his summer as a fire lookout on Desolation Peak attempting to return to the fire model had instead revealed the parallels between fire and tornado vortices. Tayvon got some of the guys to contribute their Sundays to building houses for the new organization Habitat for Humanity.

Black continued his campaign against the devil-man.

"Those eyes, man," he said at a meal when the man wasn't present. "Peering at you and all from behind those little round glasses."

"What are they supposed to do?" Swill asked.

"Maybe stay out of your soul?"

"Lay off Jude already, man," Jeff said. "Trust me. He's cool." Maggie squeezed his leg under the table. This was most welcome since, as they hit their first anniversary, the sex had declined to the merely "occasional" phase.

Black scoffed. "I don't trust you either, J.-man. You aren't worried about his new obsession with mass casualties, and the like? Like, all I said was 'How you doin', devil-man?' and he went on for twenty minutes about that collapsed walkway in Kansas City. A hundred casualties or something. I swear he could name every one, man."

Speaking of casualties, the Yale football team was producing many through another incredible season, crushing its opponents. So far undefeated, their win streak grew with Croc's increasing ass, itself aided by the new machine in the Payne Whitney weight room custom-designed to turn all his gluteus muscles into maxima.

There was also progress on another front: Despite the frequency decline Maggie and Jeff checked off sofas at Columbia and Cornell belonging to her high school friends Dana and Kerry respectively. A scheduling quirk made this possible, as Maggie's soccer schedule happened to be free on those two key weekends.

"The gods are clearly favoring us," Jeff said to her after checking off Cornell.

"Thank you Eros and Aphrodite," Maggie snuggled into him, showing off what she had learned as a member of the Comedy Cohort.

The female meatheads had plenty going on as well. Maya was President of the campus chapter of N.O.W, organizing events. There was the celebration of Sandra Day O'Connor being seated as the first female justice on the Supreme Court. There was the Take Back the Night march to protest violence against women—almost 1,500 women participated, and a few men, mostly hoping to get laid—and the talk by Gloria Steinem, held in Ezra Stiles College to a large crowd (also mostly women, with a few guys hoping to get laid), and finally the talk by Betty Friedan in Harkness Hall which had a higher percentage of men because word had got out that you could get laid.

And let's not forget the celebration of the new Women's Studies major, approved by the faculty on November 5. "I'm already majoring in Women's Studies," Tayvon said more than once, with a sultry glance at Lisa. He truly appreciated that she was totally fine with merely having a spot in his rotation. What never crossed his mind was that he too merely had a spot in *hers*.

Not everyone was so successful in that discipline however.

"Damn, this might be another case for Jude," Samilla observed, in the livingroom of the double she shared with F. Scott. She had by now become an official member of the meatheads. There weren't any initiation ceremonies or anything—though that had been discussed—but by regularly joining the gang at the dining hall she was clearly throwing her lot in.

"What changed?" Maggie had asked Samilla at another Park Street Sub run a few nights earlier, receiving the veggie sub that would be shared five ways.

"Change of scenery, that's all," Samilla left out that she had grown interested in scenery that included Black.

"Why do *any* of us hang out with those animals?" Maya asked, grabbing Tabs from the case.

"Seriously," Jasmine said.

"You most of all, Maya, honey," F. Scott observed, "with all your 'women's liberation.' I would think you would run for the hills."

"You'd think, wouldn't you," Maya said contemplatively as she distributed the Tabs.

"Well I think they're fun," Maggie jumped in as she began carving the sub. "They're immature, and they sometimes cross the line, but they're fun."

"If I were dating Jeff, honey, I'm sure I'd agree," F. Scott said with a laugh that Maggie did not entirely share.

"Of course," Jasmine added, "a couple of them are pretty hot."

Tayvon, obviously; but you know Thorn and Ig were athletic studs, Jude had this magnetic intensity, Zar had this dark brooding thing, Jasmine and Samilla were keen on Black, and at least Maggie and F. Scott found something appealing about Jeff.

"Yeah," Maya said, adding a dab of mayo to her fifth. "The hotness has its appeal. But not so much fun, I think. More like rubbernecking. It's horrifying, but I can't tear myself away. By the way, where's Lisa tonight?"

Lisa was off at that moment not rubbernecking, just necking, with Tayvon.

"Start with a haircut," Maggie said now back in Samilla's living-room. "That's what Jude did with Brother John."

Brother John was the local homeless man Jude had taken under his wing for this semester's rehabilitation project after last year's Cassius debacle. Brother John generally occupied the corners around Broadway, York, and Elm, soliciting you to spare a dime or some time with his cheerful toothless smile, and if you chose the latter would regale you with literally incredible tales of his previous life as a person with a domicile. Jude spared both dimes and time and often engaged with him. No, he didn't quite believe

Brother John's stories, but was determined to help the man. After all, he felt responsible for at least part of the man's current plight.

"It wasn't even you who did it, man," Black said to Jude when he first learned that Jude was enabling yet another deadbeat. "The J.-man should be the one undertaking this harebrained scheme."

It was Jeff who had directed Brother John, at the end of last year, to help himself to whatever had been left behind in the dorms. Well that turned out to include the guitar Jeff had forgotten, and by the time Jeff realized that and went back the guitar, and Brother John, were long gone. Jeff obviously was not going to press charges, but the New Haven Police insisted on doing that for him. Jude happened to see Brother John being hauled off and when he later bumped into the distraught Jeff, got the full story and jumped into action. Paid for the lawyer, got the charges dismissed, and now that school had resumed had gotten the man some temporary shelter and a haircut. The next step was to construct an actual resumé out of those incredible bits and maybe get the man a job.

"Yeah, well, we are all Yalies, man," Jude replied to Black cryptically, ending the conversation.

"Haircut, check," Lisa answered Maggie in the livingroom. "The appointment's tomorrow at the salon."

"Clothes?" Samilla asked. "We're not going to let him dress like *that*."

"Check," Maggie said. "We're heading to J. Press this afternoon."

"Budget?" Jasmine asked.

"Two hundred," Maggie answered. Twenty-five provided by him, seventy-five from the female meatheads, and Eli doubling the pot.

"And you'll shower? And wash your hair?" Jasmine said, finally addressing him directly.

"Check, and check," Beamie nodded, sitting there with a beaming smile.

He deeply appreciated that the females had taken him on.

Things are really starting to go my way, he thought.

First, he had arrived at Cutler's Record Shop at 2:00 AM the night before the tickets went on sale, which meant he was one of only the few people who scored tickets to the Rolling Stones' Hartford shows before they ran out after twenty minutes. The tickets for the second show went to Tayvon, who had also paid him to get on line so early. Then the real miracle occurred: the not entirely uncute girl in his statistics class had agreed to go with him to the first show. Admittedly she was a bit of a loser as he was, but (a) she was a girl, and (b) she had said yes. Maggie had volunteered to lend him her little red Spirit for his—yes, he could say the word—his date.

The Beamer had a date!

Beamie, who always smiled anyway, smiled at the thought.

And a date was of course the first step toward, you know. He felt good about his chances: after all, she was a girl and she had said yes so far. Plus—speaking of statistics—if he kept putting himself out there, eventually, even if only randomly, he was bound to succeed. He'd been to the O'Connor party, the Steinem talk, the Take Back the Night march, all with no luck. So maybe Monday night would be the charm. With luck maybe he wouldn't have to go to the Friedan talk in a few weeks!

"Well if the man has finally got a date for a rock concert," Jeff said to Maggie and Black over a doob when he heard the news, ready to do his part, "we'll need to get him some supplies."

"Where are your pants, man?" Black grumbled again that night when the Guy opened the door in his open bathrobe. It was 1:30 A.M.

"Pants are The Man's way to subdue the masses," the Guy answered with equanimity, letting them in.

"May 8, 1977," Jeff promptly identified the music playing as they entered the softly-blue-lit room. "Yes! Cornell University. Has the best 'Dancing in the Street' ever."

"Ten percent discount for either setlist, my man," the Guy said, not yet impressed.

"Second set," Jeff answered immediately. "Scarlet-Fire, Prophet, St. Stephen," he hesitated. "Not Fade Away. One more. Ack!"

"Encore?"

"Saturday Night," Jeff answered.

"The Guy will give it to you. You missed Morning Dew."

"Ah! Of course."

"There is something seriously wrong with you guys," Black observed.

Beamie just smiled silently, soaking it in.

"Listen, gentlemen," the Guy said after he had weighed some silver label on the scale on the coffee table (the guys were springing for Beamie and wanted to do it right). "You ready to take the leap? Just got a fresh shipment in. Direct from La Chorrera."

"Are we supposed to know what that means, man?" Black said.

"Stomping grounds of my man McKenna. They say this grows where butterflies leave their droppings."

"Are we supposed to know what *that* means, man?" Black said in irritation.

"Do butterflies even have droppings?" Beamie asked, finally able to speak.

"Have a gander," the Guy swung open his fridge to reveal shelves of baggies filled with dried bluish-green fungi.

There was a long silence as the best 'Dancing in the Street' ever came on and they stared at the shrooms.

Some of Maggie's Woods Hole friends had done shrooms over the summer and raved about them. Maggie wanted to try them but Jeff was, well, Jeff. "Live a little, mister," she had tried to encourage him, "It's allowed."

"Strictly speaking, in this case, it isn't," he had replied. "Maybe at some point, okay?"

"I'm good, man," Black said.

Beamie shook his head.

Not tonight. There were other priorities.

"Nine bucks for the tape?" Jeff asked instead.

=====

3.

a *rashomon* kind of thing

What a weekend that was.

Yale football visited Cornell and notched another victory toward an undefeated season while Maggie and Jeff notched that additional sofa. Staying behind, however, were Beamie—nervous about his Monday night date and throwing himself into statistics—and Ig, who was using this final week before the Term Paper Challenge deadline to go all in on his paper for Erich.

The more he threw himself into it, the more he appreciated Brecht's genius. Ig attended the *Threepenny* production not only the opening night but the three remaining nights as well. That Skybell fellow was fucking *talented*, handsome as hell and could sing and dance and act like no tomorrow, to the point that Ig decided to spend less time with the meatheads and get to know other amazing Piersonites like Steven.

"That was cute," Jeffrey told Debra years later, "as if he weren't a meathead through and through. Though one does wonder, if the catastrophe hadn't happened, might he have left us then for the theater crowd?"

These changes that Erich wrought in him, it was almost enough to change your conception of Ignacio from—whatever—to that of a serious student, especially compared to the other meatheads who failed to see Erich's massive appeal. It was hard to square it all: where was the man who chugged ketchup, whose endearing "assholes" even seemed to be vanishing?

"Maybe it's a *Night of the Living Dead* scenario," Tayvon suggested, as the film had just been shown over Halloween. "Like he was eaten and replaced by somebody else?"

"No," Jeff proposed, "more a *Rashomon* kind of thing." That film had also recently screened, Jeff had gone alone because he could persuade no one, including Maggie, averse to subtitles, to join him.

"What?" the others who had refused to go responded. They then tuned out his detailed analysis of how different subjective perspectives can anchor to one objective reality and how that reflected their own experiences as meatheads.

For the record the meatheads also wanted to meet the Term Paper Challenge. But meatheads will be meatheads, so they went and had their weekend at Cornell, and then there was Beamie's big date on Monday they all needed to prepare for, and Tuesday Night Club. When the Friday deadline arrived Ignacio was the only one to meet it, and oh did he meet it in a whole-assed way.

The assignment was a modest ten-page double-spaced paper.

He submitted thirty-nine double-spaced pages with detailed endnotes, plus a three-page single-spaced bibliography. A masterpiece, of that he had no doubt, and he knew that Phil, the graduate student Teaching Assistant, would admire it so much he would pass it on to Erich to appreciate as well. And Erich would call him in to talk about the paper ...

Who *are* you, some of the gang might have wondered if they weren't busy recovering from Cornell and preparing for the trip to Princeton. And oh well, guess we didn't meet the Term Paper Challenge. Will just get the paper in next week by the regular deadline.

C'est la vie, now let's go Bulldogs!

But we get ahead of ourselves.

First, feeling much less *c'est la vie*-ish was Beamie, as his date approached.

=====

4.

it will not always be like this

At least he had help.

Tayvon, the man of letters and the Luddite, was all in on technology on this one. "Can't we wire him up or something?" he suggested at one point the week before. "A microphone so we can hear, and some kind of thing in his ear so I can guide him? A la *Cyrano de Bergerac*?"

They couldn't do that, but could do other things. The women got him groomed and dressed. The men offered him plenty of advice, especially Tayvon, whose advice turned out not useful because when you are Tayvon with your creamy mocha skin you merely need bat your lashes and you're in. Jeff might have been a better source of advice except that he had so totally lucked out in

Maggie that he'd forgotten how difficult it was for normal guys like him to get women.

Black was most helpful. "You work with what you got, man," he offered with a pat on Beamie's back. "And what you got is a million-dollar smile. So beam that smile and just don't stop, man."

Beamie practiced the smile, a bit awkward staged like that; maybe just three-quarter-million dollars.

"There you go," Black said, his work here done.

The consensus was reached that, given Beamie's challenges in the looks and, frankly, personality departments, the best strategy would be to get her very stoned. That would maximize his chances of some action at the concert, in turn maximizing his chances of some action back at the room. To the objection that he couldn't get too stoned because he had the hour drive back to campus in Maggie's car came the reply that it wasn't him who needed to get stoned but the girl. To the objection that she might not want to get stoned came a long debate about whether consent to drugs was necessary given her consent to going to a concert where obviously there would be lots of drugs. Zar, Beamie's roommate, would sleep in the library that night, per usual, thus vacating the room in case the miracle should happen.

The gang assembled in his livingroom for a final pep talk before walking him to Maggie's Spirit, which she'd parked behind the college with the right rear wheel up on the curb. There was much laughter at the look on Beamie's face when he saw they had decorated the car like a newlywed car, with streamers and the words sprayed on the rear window, "Newly Laid." More laughter at his relief when they removed the streamers and wiped the window and sent him off to pick up his date with cheers and whistles. Ig was not there, off in the L&B room writing his magnum opus. His plan was to finish by Wednesday, which would give him two days to type the whole thing up and submit it by Friday.

Beamie dove right in, at least if you don't count the hour of small talk in the car about boring theorems in statistics. "Would you like a hit?" he asked Janet, having pulled out a joint as soon as the lights went down for the Garland Jeffreys opening act.

"Just say no!" Janet exclaimed oddly, looking at him in horror, her panicked eyes peeking through her long straight bangs.

As it turned out, she was in her Aspergery-world a strict rules follower and no rule had been more ground into her from an early age than that of saying no to drugs. Her parents had made her repeat the phrase, "Just say no," every morning at breakfast throughout high school, which is why it popped out when she was confronted with Beamie's drugs—a year before, incidentally, the First Lady would roll out her own "Just say no" campaign.

Abort! Abort! Beamie thought frantically, withdrawing the proffered joint.

What the hell was he supposed to do? There was no plan B. They should have wired him up, as Tayvon suggested, Tayvon would know what to do. Or better, Maggie guiding him. He was good at mathematics, at crunching numbers, but spontaneity, thinking on his feet, appealed to him about as much as that joint appealed to his date. What would Maggie do? "Everybody in, nobody out," she would say, but wait, that wasn't helpful here. Or "It's allowed." *What's* allowed? Making a complete jackass out of himself?

"Suit yourself," he heard himself say, then watched himself pull out his lighter, light the joint, and take a deep puff. What the hell was he doing? He was trying to refute his loserness by showing off the joint, when in fact he was only confirming that loserness given how uncontrollably he was now coughing from the hit. "What?" he heard himself say to her through the coughs as he saw the continued look of horror on her face, "It's allowed."

"This is your brain on drugs!" Janet exclaimed, oddly, having in that moment the fried-egg-in-a-pan inspiration for the ad campaign she would produce several years after graduation for the Partnership for a Drug-Free America.

"Everybody out! Nobody in!" Beamie exclaimed back in a panic.

"And why do you keep smiling like that?" Janet asked with confusion joining her horror. "It's kind of weird."

Suffice to say that Beamie was so discombobulated from this dreadful start that he chain-smoked the three joints the gang had given him all during the opening act, that stupid smile on his face the whole time, quarter-million-dollar tops.

"You fell *asleep*?" Tayvon asked incredulously much later that night, when several of them wandered by his room to see how it had gone.

"Yeah," Beamie said embarrassedly, his eyes watery and red, from the smoking he hoped they would all think.

"You missed the whole show?" Maggie asked gently.

"Not all of it. I caught the last part of 'Satisfaction' as the encore."

"More apropos," Swill puffed on his cigar, "it's called '(Can't Get No) Satisfaction.'"

"Yeah," Beamie acknowledged. In fact this was a lie. He had only woken up at the final encore, a playing of "The Star-Spangled Banner," and thus had succeeded in going to a Stones concert and not hearing a single Stones song.

"And the girl?" Black asked, impressed how this fellow could keep taking loserness to new levels.

"She," Beamie said, then felt a smile coming on, because he smiled when he was nervous or uncomfortable or just utterly defeated, "was making out with the girl sitting next to her." Janet may have said no to drugs, but apparently said yes to some lesbian suck-face.

"You fucking turned her lesbo, man!" Black exclaimed, as the man had done it yet again. "You are a fucking gem, man!"

"I suppose I am, man," Beamie said, with a smile, realizing that Maggie was gently rubbing his shoulder and thinking what a lucky guy Jeff was. It was Maggie who came back to check on him the next afternoon, who managed to get through that smile, who hugged him when he started to weep.

"I know they all laugh at me," he said through the tears.

"No, Sam," she said, "they're just playing with you."

"No, I know what they think. And you know I pretend it doesn't hurt, but it does. I'm a real human being, with real feelings, you know?"

"Of course," she hugged him again.

"I just want a girl to look at me, just once," he was really weeping, "It's like I'm invisible. Why won't they even look at me?"

There had been a girl in high school, it turned out, you can't tell anyone this, he said, they'd dated a few weeks, and he took her to the junior prom, and then back at his house it was actually happening, it was incredible, they were starting to do it, and his mother walked in on them, just opened the door to his room and walked on in to put away the underwear of his she had just laundered, and it was the most humiliating moment of his life, and the girl never spoke to him again, and no girl had even glanced at him since, they rejected him with their peripheral vision, you can't tell anyone this …

Maggie hugged him while he wept on her shoulder.

"Just a glance," he wept, "just a glance."

"It'll happen, Sam," she said after a few minutes, "It'll happen when it's ready."

"You can't know that."

"I can, and I do," she said. "I promise you."

You know that just as every cell of your body expresses your DNA in all those different ways, every moment of your life reflects every other moment in the collection of moments that is you. The person you are now foreshadows the person you will become, and reflects the person you were.

You may not perceive it at the time, but you may know that it is true.

And you may know that it will not always be like this.

Maggie would wait a few days for some healing, then start thinking about how to get him back in the saddle.

She never did tell anyone his secret.

=====

5.

more like a brick

Ig missed this whole episode, but it was worth it.

He got his masterpiece in on time, a pleasure only magnified by the fact that his peers, several of whom thought themselves academically superior to him, failed to do so. How he would enjoy relaxing while they studied away for the final exam in the course! His paper in, off they all went to Princeton to celebrate their team's march toward their undefeated season.

Well, not all: in a significant but not insurmountable blow to Maggie's and Jeff's sofa campaign, the scheduling gods had given her a soccer game that precluded her going. The women's soccer team was having a mediocre season and now this. "Well, there's always senior year," Maggie said in a nod to that awkward moment last year when Jeff said something similar about Dartmouth. But this time it wasn't awkward because of course they would be together senior year, and then check off—if the gods returned to favor—what should by then be the final box, on Maggie's friend Mairav's sofa.

As for the others, there was much wonderful partying that weekend, to be sure. Ig, ebullient, even scored not a goal but his first New Jersey arrest for some lovely disorderly conduct. But the first sign that things were not to be as copacetic as anticipated was the devastating loss to the Tigers, who didn't even have a winning record.

The Elis fell 35-31 for their first loss of the season.

Well, there was still the Harvard game to look forward to, next weekend. But first, for Ig, two things would darken that week after Princeton.

First Erich—how could he—announced on Monday that given the small number of students who had met the Term Paper Challenge deadline, he was extending that deadline a week. You didn't need anywhere near the impassioned sense of injustice that Ig had to understand how unjust this decision was.

"You know," Jeffrey said to Debra years later when reminiscing about Ig, who by that point had disappeared from everybody's radar, "Segal was a guy whose main claim to fame was prose about the sound of snow. Maybe a sophisticated sense of justice should not have been expected of such a person."

Then, to add insult to injury, Ig's Teaching Assistant, "I've got a stick up my ass" Phil, a bearded thick-eyeglassed classics graduate student, returned Ig's graded masterpiece.

"B" was written in red ink atop the cover page.

Which meant that despite meeting the original deadline of the Term Paper Challenge, the paper had failed to earn the grade to meet the challenge.

There was no additional red ink on the forty-two typed pages, a fact explained by the only red ink on the cover page: "This paper exceeds the assigned page limit by thirty-two pages. Your violating the instructions frees me from the obligation of providing further commentary."

"Phil," Ig tried to say evenly when he went to meet with him, "Do you have a fucking stick up your ass?"

"I must insist you address me as 'Professor,'" Phil said, reddening behind his beard and glasses and indirectly answering Ig's question.

"My apologies. Professor, do you have a fucking stick up your ass?"

"Really, I shan't be spoken to in such language."

"Fine. Do you have a fucking stick up your rectum then?"

Phil held his ground, staring at him silently with the patience of a man long habituated to the stick in his rectum.

Ig sighed. "I honestly don't understand what the problem is, Professor."

"It is very straightforward. You exceeded the page limit by thirty-two pages. What could be clearer?"

"That's not at all clear. And anyway I exceeded it by only twenty-nine pages. Three of those pages were bibliography."

"The page limits were inclusive of bibliography. Not to mention that you single-spaced the bibliography."

"So?"

"The double-spaced instruction included the bibliography."

"Eureka!" Ig exclaimed.

"Pardon?"

"I think it's more like a brick."

"Pardon?"

"What's up your ass. Phil."

What was perhaps most remarkable about this conversation was that Ig somehow managed, after this, not only *not* to smash Phil's face into the wall but to steer the conversation back toward the actual content and thus merits of his work, and, even more so, to convince Phil to re-read the paper and reconsider the grade.

Phil did so, and returned the paper the next day regraded to a B+.

"Fucking shit fuck and damn," Ig muttered, trying not to care that his meathead friends were all just now finishing up their term papers and about to submit them, still eligible for the Challenge.

It was time to raise the stakes.

To speak with Erich.

=====

6.
a truly impressive piece of work

Ignacio was not the nervous type. Not nervous speeding around the ice contesting with burly men. Not nervous confronting powerful policemen corralling him to the ground and slapping cuffs on him. Not nervous stripping off his clothes and riding motorcycles in public.

But he was sweating bullets in Erich's office.

"So what brings you here, my friend," the celebrity author said, gazing at him through those 1970s goggle glasses that he hadn't quite realized were on their way out of style, although Ig did have to admit that the fellow somehow pulled off the look.

"Yeah," Ig said, trying to get his footing, "It's just that, uh, the T.A. and I don't exactly see eye to eye on my paper."

"Which T.A.?"

"Phil. Uh, Philip."

Segal nodded. That was a good sign. If Erich knew Phil then he would know about the brick in Phil's bowel, and that should work to Ig's favor. "Pass it here, would you?"

Ig obliged, willing his hand not to shake as he did so.

"It is rather bulky, no?" Segal said, taking it.

"I put a lot of work into it, Professor."

"I can see that," Segal flipped through the pages. "Well, Ignacio—did I pronounce that properly?"

"Perfectly, Professor," Ig answered, admiring Erich all the more.

"Well, then. I'd be delighted to have a look."

Erich would give it a look.

Erich would read the whole thing, would see what Phil could not see, and everything would be all right.

Harvard game, The Game, here we come.

It would be—it was—a massive blast.

Well, the night before was a real downer. Some poor fresh-man died the night before the game, collapsing in the Wright Hall courtyard on the Old Campus. The word on the street was alcohol and mauves, those little pills that might, just might, implicate the Guy, so in addition to the tragedy of the death there was also the shadow of those implications cast over the weekend.

But nothing a little dominating 28-0 shutout win over the Beantown Bastards couldn't fix. Or at least mitigate, a little.

Or dampen, slightly.

At least if you weren't the poor fellow's family or immediate friends.

This delightful destruction sealed Yale's share of the Ivy League crown. Ig was right there at the front of the mob tearing down the goalposts, with unmitigated gusto. A weekend of fantastic par-tying, then everybody disappeared for Thanksgiving break, then they returned to classes on the Monday, for the homestretch of the semester, and, in the case of The Classical Traditions in Tragedy and Comedy, to see whether they met the Term Paper Challenge. Erich's beautiful lecture had concluded and students were gath-ered around their T.A.s to receive their papers and then, inevitably, to compare how they had done.

The Comedy Cohort did great.

Meeting the Term Paper Challenge: Maggie (A-), Lisa (A), Jas-mine (A-), Eli (A), Tayvon (A), Ren (A), Fregoli (A—Fregoli's T.A. thought Fregoli was a modern Delphic Oracle, thus that the word salad he submitted was worthy of the top grade), Samilla (A-), Isabela (A), and even Thorn (A-), who, it turned out, had a keen aesthetic sense.

Ig eagerly received his regraded paper, to see, in Erich's black ink, that he had crossed out Phil's stinking B+.

And replaced it with his own stinking B.

Erich had lowered Ig's grade.

It was the lowest moment in Ig's time at Yale, even lower than his senior year rustication which would at least have some redeem-ing qualities.

True, there had been low moments in his mysteriously obscure past prior to college, and there would be others in the years after when he would disappear into another mysterious obscurity before dying early on them. But it was hard to imagine anything lower than sitting in that auditorium, come final exam, with only seven other students out of the two hundred who had taken Tragedy or Comedy with that prick Segal, an auditorium where the heat was not working and even Ig, who wore shorts all winter long, felt the hair on his legs standing on edge and his fingers growing numb as he took the exam.

But it wasn't so much the physical as the spiritual discomfort, in particular that of being the only meathead taking an exam he hadn't prepared for because all along he was going to meet the Term Paper Challenge. Ig was the man with the enormous guffaw but also with the enormous heart, who didn't merely rasp out "Imagine" but who sometimes might weep at its vision of a worldwide brotherhood. As he scribbled out the best answers he could he felt "Imagine"-worthy tears forming, tears he imagined dripping down his cheeks and freezing in that gloomy, unheated room.

"It's just so fucking unfair," he had raged to Maggie, who had come to check on him before the exam. "Why fucking me? Why always fucking me?"

"I know, I know," she affirmed, "It's so unfair." She herself had just thrown her paper together the few days before submission, and was as astonished—and outraged—at her own A – as at Ig's B.

"Fuck," he continued, his fists clenched, "It's like I always get the short end of the stick, Mags. Even *after* I pull it out of Fuckface Phil's ass."

Maggie would have laughed if it were appropriate. But she also realized that Ig was hinting at something, that this wasn't only about Fuckface Phil. "You know," she said, "there are a lot of people here who love you."

Ig just looked at her with that face, that sad face, that angry face, that really handsome face that deserved a much different outcome than he'd gotten from that fuckface.

He had pretty much that same face on sitting there in that nearly empty freezing auditorium making up answers when he heard a rustling in the back.

He turned around to see Maggie sliding into the seat behind him.

"I brought you this, friend," she whispered, pulling from her bag a thermos of her famous pepperminty hot chocolate.

Yeah that was a salty tear or two on that face of his when, after the proctoring T.A. chased her from the room, he returned, at least a little invigorated, to the fucking exam. Another salty tear or two when he got back to his room afterward to find his 42-page masterpiece on his bed, marked up in red ink with the many comments of substantive critique and good deal of praise that ought to have been there, with a solid A underlined twice at the end, signed, "In admiration for a truly impressive piece of work, your pal, Tayvon."

And then he unwrapped the box on his desk to discover an old brick smeared with chocolate pudding and the note, from Jeff, "Got it out of his ass," which replaced the tears with hearty, gut-wrenchingly hearty, guffaws.

=====

7.

the moral failures of capitalism for $500, art

It was just a dorm room, but that didn't limit Croc's imagination when it came to Christmas.

The gentle giant's greatest pleasure, true, was in physical violence; he was never more happy than when he was tackling, or being tackled by, another large body. He and Thorn thus made terrific roommates, their courtyard wrestling matches, attracting crowds, surprisingly even: what Thorn lacked in ass he compensated for in a pain tolerance that now enabled him to sling back drinks despite both arms being *in* slings from rotator cuff injuries. Their Christmas spirit was also even, and thus the chilly and dark December 5:00 PM in the Pierson courtyard was a study in contrast outside the warm and bright dorm room adorned with laurel and wreaths and twinkling lights, with a huge bejeweled Christmas tree in the corner and with Zar on the floor tending to the roaring fire. You don't need to be told that the radio component of the stereo was tuned to Christmas tunes.

Croc you will always be Mr. Christmas for me ... The gang was there, everybody in, nobody out. People dressed nicely, Isabela snapping photos, even Master Harold and Mistress Lucille popped by for a drink and for some photos, the former wearing his Christmas toupée and the latter, clearly, wondering what evil she had done in her past life to merit living among college students.

Well, not everybody was in. Fregoli wasn't there. True, even when he was there he wasn't all there, but this time he also wasn't there physically.

"Even him. Even that crazy fucker Fregoli made the Term Paper Challenge. How is that fucking possible?" Ig muttered, already well underway toward drinking TOO MUCH. This was still a few days before the final exam he would take practically alone. Maggie was there rubbing his arm while Jeff went over for more beers.

"Hey, be nice," Croc gently reproached him as he mingled through, refilling eggnogs. "It's Christmas season, man. The time of our Lord."

"Where is Fregoli, anyway?" Emre asked, being generally out of the loop (and out of our story) because of the long hours he spent in the library. A few minutes after his question was answered he would abscond without a drink back to the library.

"Society has failed the poor kid," Samilla answered, who had cemented her meathead status by cementing a spot not in Black's rotation but, as it turned out, in Tayvon's. "He's locked up in the cuckoo house."

Having gone back home to Portland for Thanksgiving Break, Fregoli, she explained, had collapsed after playing a new video game called *Polybius* at a local video arcade. The fact that he had been playing it for twenty-eight consecutive hours and downing can after can of Coke didn't stop the rumor from instantly sprouting that the federal government was attempting mind control of the nation's youth by means of video games. When after a maybe thirty-second intake interview it was determined that Fregoli had more than a couple screws loose and he had been carted away for further evaluation, that only fueled the rumor. Most remarkable was how fast and far these rumors spread, even before Swill's interweb would take reckless rumor-spreading to wonderful new levels.

Ren feverishly jotted every detail down in his notebook, having been wondering why his roommate hadn't returned after break. "*Polybius*! Really?!" he said to Doc, running out there immediately after this conversation. "What were the chances? That couldn't possibly be an accident."

"Of course it couldn't," Doc reminded him, "because there are no accidents."

Indeed no protégé of Doc's, no one who had studied Baillet's biography of Descartes and Baillet's own autobiography could overlook the essential role of Polybius in those stories. It could not possibly be a coincidence that Polybius was the name of the video game in question.

Ren suddenly stopped on the walk back from Doc's, feeling a chill.

Doc must have some role in all this, he realized.

If there are no coincidences.

Swill was at that moment standing by the Christmas tree, the bottle of Glenfiddich that Eli had brought in one hand and a glass in the other, arguing with Maya about the thick Cuban cigar Eli had also brought. Maya was opposed to smoking in general and in favor of the embargo in particular, so there was little she approved of about Swill as you can imagine, starting with his looks—there was something about that face of his, that disgusting cigar always sticking out of it, that drove her crazy—continuing on to his behavior, then his worldview, and eventually all the way to his interweb. (The latter, she would insist at the 25th reunion, had as its main accomplishment that most people now spent eight to ten hours a day watching funny cat videos.) She didn't mind the Christmas tree, however, and had acceded to him his role, in that morning's outing with Croc and Isabela, in selecting the tree from a nearby farm.

"Go big or go home," Swill was saying, deliberately puffing the smoke from his cigar in Maya's face because there was something so scintillating about irritating her. "And I emphasize the 'go big' part of that. I think that would go a long way toward fixing not just that one but pretty much a lot of her problems."

"I can't decide if that is more offensive or disgusting," Maya replied, referring both to what Swill had said and the fact that he had winked at her after saying it.

"Hopefully equally both."

"You think of women as vessels for your own sexual fantasies. And of women's sexuality as a kind of currency. To be bartered, exchanged."

"It's not?"

"That's not funny."

"*Au contraire, mon frère*," Swill objected after gargling a swig of the scotch. "It's hysterical."

Maya was fuming now. That word was one of her major peeves. Derived from the Greek word for the womb, reinforced by that misogynist Freud, the implication was that women were irrational, out of control. Given that Swill was one of her other major peeves, she was feeling herself getting—well, hysterical.

"The trifecta," Maya declared.

"What?"

"Actionable, too," Maya explained.

"I *said*, what?"

"Not just offensive and disgusting."

"What is?"

"Everything you say. Everything you do. You, period."

Maya, who loved her weekly session with Lisa cataloging Swill's offenses, couldn't wait to share this one. Though the line wasn't straight, this was how Swill's and Maya's conversation initially about (a) whether the fact that Croc had invited Isabela to go tree-hunting with them meant that they might start dating and then about (b) what Isabela "needed" because her virginity was approaching the point of absurdity eventually led years later to (c) Lisa taking a break from her Pulitzer-winning reporting on Soviet and Russian matters to her Pulitzer-winning reporting on the #MeToo movement and then, the following year, on the scandalous nomination of fellow alum Brett Kavanaugh.

It was around that moment that the commotion was heard outside. Many of them went to check it out, including Swill who was not that interested in Maya's views on mandatory chemical castration.

Thorn and Ig were getting into it on the hard frozen ground of the courtyard. Loud swears, sharp breaths of foggy air, body-slamming, the works.

"Hey! Break it up!" Croc exclaimed, pulling Thorn off Ig, unsure whether he was more upset at the violation of the Christmas spirit or that there was body-slamming going on without him.

"Ow!" Thorn exclaimed, as Croc had pulled him by his rotator cuffs. Somehow he had gotten the better of Ig—no slouch himself—despite fighting with both arms in slings. Then again, this was the man who would later save another dozen squadmates' lives in Iraq even absent one of the arms now merely inhibited by a little rotator cuff problem.

Then again, again, God knows just how much Ig had been drinking to this point. Not to mention, as Jasmine swore later at Rudy's Bar, to F. Scott, Lisa, and Isabella—by that point Maggie was off with Jeff, Samilla off with Tayvon, and Maya off researching chemical castration—that she saw tears in Ig's eyes.

No one ever did find out what this fight was about, or why its consequences would linger all the way to graduation and beyond, except possibly Maggie—and she wasn't talking.

Back in Croc's room F. Scott was taking advantage of the court-yard commotion to corner Jeff just under the mistletoe hanging over the doorway. She had him up against the doorframe, was gazing into his eyes, reading him, her evergreen-glossed lips soft and moist.

"Hey," she said, her lips pursed.

"Hey," he answered back, backing into the doorframe.

"I wanted to ask you something."

"Oh. Um," Jeff answered eloquently, feeling the heat of Zar's nearby fire.

"Can I show you something?" she said, licking her lips.

"Um. Uh."

"Just come back to my room and see. I think you'll like it." She figured Samilla would be with Tayvon and they'd have the room to themselves. "It would mean a lot to me."

"Um," Jeff's mind was working furiously. What was all the commotion outside, where the hell was Maggie, and would it kill Zar to maybe set fire to the room as a distraction?

"Fun fact," Jude interrupted, popping back inside after the fight in the courtyard was broken up. "Mistletoe is actually a parasite. Instead of rooting itself in the ground it roots itself into tree branches, from which it steals water and nutrients. That it can grow even in the depth of winter no doubt contributes to its use as a symbol of fertility and therefore to the tradition of kissing under it."

"Why are you talking about mistletoe?" F. Scott asked, unaware they were standing under some.

Jeff took advantage of Jude's arrival to slip away in search of Maggie, who lately had been spending a little too much time and energy on Ig, in his opinion, including now tending to him outside.

"Hey," he said to Eli outside, "F. Scott wants to talk to you. By the doorframe."

But by the time Eli got back inside F. Scott had gone, with Lisa, Jasmine, and Isabela, to Rudy's—which would be pleasantly devoid of meatheads since they were all at Croc's Christmas party—to complain about the meatheads. Still at Croc's were Jude, Black, and Zar, who had taken a break from tending the fire because he'd had a breakthrough in modeling heat absorption in gases and wanted to run it past Jude, who'd had enough chemistry to maybe appreciate it. But unfortunately Zar couldn't break through the heated argument Jude and Black were having. Ren was there taking notes, back from Doc's with his own breakthrough about how to fit Doc and Polybius into the Christmas party scene in his novel.

"Why don't you *land*, devil-man!" Black was saying to Jude as Eli approached.

"If you do not have ideals to start with," Jude replied, if irritated then suppressing it, "then what, I ask you, is the point? Ah, exhibit A," he added as Eli joined them.

"What'd I miss?" Eli asked.

"Ren, you want to read it back?" Jude said.

Ren flipped through his notes. "Okay, let's see. Jude told an anecdote about a child drowning in a shallow pond. You come by, you have the ability to save him, but you would maybe ruin your new shoes. Are you morally obligated to save the child? That's where it started."

"What a stupid question," Eli said. "Obviously not."

"That's what Black said," Ren said, still flipping. "And they were off."

"So," Jude dove back in, "Exhibit A here. 'The Moral Failures of Capitalism for $500, Art.' Who is Eli Yale the 12th or 13th or 15th?" Jude, a fan of fun facts, was obviously a fan of *The All-New Jeopardy!*

"I'm sure that is very clever," Eli said with the poise of someone who acted like he owned the place, because he usually did.

"The argument is simple," Jude said with the poise of someone who acted like he was right, because he usually was. "If you can prevent some great harm at the cost only of some much lesser harm to yourself, you should. Obviously a child drowning in a pond is a great harm, and your getting wet—"

"Doesn't it depend on who the child is?" Eli interrupted.

"That's what I'm talking about, man," Black had made the same response a moment earlier.

"—and your getting wet is a minor harm," Jude ignored them. "But it does not stop there. The argument generalizes. Look at you with your J. Press clothes, your Yale blue blazer, your account at Mory's. And your 'rooms' at the Taft—" here Jude referred to the floor of the elegant hotel Eli had moved into upon its renovation—"because a simple dorm room would never suffice for Eli the 10th or 16th."

"No, it wouldn't. What is your point?"

"He fucking earned it, devil-man." Black hesitated. "Well, his father."

Jude was not impressed. "There are people starving in Cambodia for example. They are predicting imminent and massive famine in Ethiopia, too. The money you spend on these superfluities could literally feed people and save lives. Hundreds of lives. Yet there you are, relaxing, sipping from your monogrammed snifter—" Eli brought his own alcohol, and glassware, to parties—"essentially watching a child drown in a pond."

"The insult to me I don't mind," Eli answered unmoved, "not that you actually know anything about me. Or my family for that matter. But I'll have you know this is a Rémy Martin XO cognac that was custom distilled for my family by my Eton chum, Rémy Martin the 15th or 16th. This spectacular beverage is, frankly, one of humankind's greatest achievements. It trumps your hypothetical drowning child."

"Thank you," Jude said.

"For what?"

"For making my point even more clearly than I did."

"Elihu here is too easy a target," Black interjected. "My beef is with everything up to the point of our goddamn American gentry. Little man?"

Ren flipped through his notes. "Buying a pair of shoes. Going to the movies. Going to college in general. To Yale in particular." Rumors had been circulating that Yale's term bill was to break eleven grand the following year. Eleven grand could feed an awful lot of those Cambodian and Ethiopian children. Could any serious person defend spending that much money for a college education while letting maybe hundreds of children *die*? And while you're at it, that five or six bucks they each spent on tickets and popcorn seeing *Halloween II* last month? That was enough money to feed a starving child for months. You might as well munch popcorn wearing your new sneakers while you watch a bunch of children drown.

"'You are a terrible fucking person for going to the movies. For buying a pair of sneakers,'" Ren finished with a direct quote from Jude. "'And for going to Yale.'"

"You don't have to apologize for your success, devil-man," Black insisted. "You don't have to feel guilty for earning a new pair of shoes, or a college degree. You should be fucking proud of those things, man. The problems lie elsewhere."

Jude just stared at him through those little round glasses, then turned to stare at Eli. "And you?"

"I am sure that is all compelling, and I would like to subscribe to your newsletter," Eli answered after a relaxed sip from his snifter. "But just think of how many lives you could have saved instead of wasting time on this conversation. Anyway, I need to go over there now."

"There" was over toward Lisa, who had returned from Rudy's. Turns out that she had gone there looking for Tayvon and was now back here doing the same. After Eli had polished off his chum's bottle she was looking very appealing to him, so Eli didn't stick around to hear Black's rejoinders, to see Zar disappear when Thorn came in looking for speed because with the Guy laying low after that freshman died Zar needed all of his stash for himself, or to learn about Jude's scheme to move Brother John, about to be kicked out of his temporary shelter, into Jude's own room over the Christmas break. But this was no loss to him because it turned out that Lisa was just realizing that she *wasn't* okay merely being part of Tayvon's rotation, and as she watched Eli approach she was thinking that on this long, dark, and cold night there were worse things than slipping between the silk sheets with the richest person she was ever likely to meet.

Years later, when doing the research into Eli's Russian dealings that would earn her first Pulitzer and his first stint behind bars, she also discovered that the man ran a secret network of philanthropists, personally funded sixty percent of New Haven's social services budget, and in fact was paying not only for Fregoli's psychiatric care but also anonymously paying Ig's tuition. That gave her a certain amount of regret in exposing his other, less exemplary dealings.

The next afternoon after the Christmas party, at approximately the same time that Lisa was regretting her decision-making of the night before, a female law student was sexually assaulted in her office at the *Yale Law Review*.

Have yourself a very merry Christmas indeed.

=====

spring

8.
oh my lord

You need not be an artist or architect to feel the irony that Yale's Art and Architecture Building seemed worthy of neither discipline. Could the ugliest most poorly designed building on campus really house those two august departments and their studios, classrooms, galleries? Not ironically but literally the beast was designed in the Brutalist style, with jarring concrete heaps haphazardly piled together. The interior was equally jarring, emotionally, with thirty-seven different levels strewn across its nine floors. As for its functionality, the first words that came to mind were dark, cramped, moist, and cold. Another word was moat, one of which was, for some reason, built around the outside conjuring two things: the medieval period (speaking of dark, cramped, moist, and cold), and water (such as that which regularly seeped into the ground floors). On the plus side, its graduate students were motivated to finish and get out as quickly as possible.

Two such graduate students were there on Tuesday, January 12, the second day of classes of the spring semester, in the Art Library, which, to better illuminate its dreary décor, at least had some windows. What those windows revealed was a bright winter morning; what those windows let in were drafts of frigid single-digit air, starting with a reading of zero degrees at 8:00 AM on the thermometer someone had installed in the moat outside.

One of the students, Frederick, arrived to study around 10:00 AM, or so he would inform the responding officers, after indulging in a fried donut breakfast at the Yankee Doodle. He had so indulged because if all went well he would be out of this hellhole by semester's end and move someplace warm. That is what he was thinking as he sat down nearest the least drafty window, after glancing at the three-degree reading on the thermometer. He had a good morning, all bundled there in his cute new winter hat and mittens, blissfully unaware of what was lying maybe twenty feet from him.

Licentia, the second student, arrived an hour later. Oddly she too had stopped for breakfast at the Yankee Doodle, including three cups of that acidic black coffee. She said hello to Frederick, with whom she had once flirted for maybe three seconds until it became apparent he didn't swing that way, then made the customary glance at the thermometer outside.

"A balmy seven degrees!" Licentia started to say, but then stopped short. "What—is that a ...?" Her first thought was that it was an installation: students were known for prank installations in the moat, like last Halloween's zombie display. In fact several decades later her youngest daughter, Mahlia, would have a thing for prank installations at that funky college she attended in the Northwest, but that's a story for another time. For the moment Licentia was not sure what she was looking at, it was hard to make out what it was, there was, well, a pile, some parts.

Frederick came over to have a look.

"Oh my Lord," he exclaimed, and promptly fainted.

That was a human body out there.

=====

9.
life continues, until it ends

You're immortal, when you're young. You're especially immortal when you are a snobby college student, you have excelled at everything to this point and now the path to success and happiness lies open before you. But then you go and drink too much, maybe combine the alcohol with some colorful pills, and then you're no different from any other adolescent whose brain is not yet completely developed and now won't ever be.

Or you plunge seventy feet into an ice-lined moat, with nobody to hear your screams.

Nobody really knew what had happened.

She was a junior in Silliman.

Her pocketbook was found on the ledge of a seventh-floor window. Do people bring their pocketbook when they are planning to jump off a building? She studied Japanese, had plans to travel there over the summer. People with plans don't jump off buildings, do they? She lived in one of the rooms in Silliman that had been broken into over the break. Upsetting, yes, but is that a reason to plunge seventy feet into a moat? You didn't know what was worse: was it deliberate or an accident? But who casually hangs out on a seventh-floor ledge, in single digit weather, with overnight winds of 15-20 mph, God knows what the windchill would be up there? Who would open that window, if it were closed? Or if it had been left open maybe she had gone to close it—but closing it didn't require putting your pocketbook on the ledge, leaning out ... A few days later it was reported that the window didn't close properly, a fact maybe for the lawyers to haggle over but that didn't answer any questions.

"I just can't believe it," Maggie muttered many times over those days, brushing her hair to self-soothe.

"It's dreadful, it's dreadful," Jeff might answer as they consoled each other, he sometimes helping with her hair-brushing. Though they didn't know the girl they had both, as prospective art history majors, spent time in that building. And the darkroom there— Maggie took an introductory photography course in the fall and Isabela had given her a tutorial on the facilities, so Maggie and Jeff were in talks about having sex in there some time. (Never happened.) It was just so weird, this place they knew so well, being the scene of something so shocking.

"I just can't believe it," Maggie muttered many times over those days.

But Isabela wasn't interested in the endless speculation, because she knew. Well, not *knew*—as a fellow architecture student she knew the girl, not well, but nevertheless she knew, in her gut, it all made sense to her.

How she played the scene over and over in her mind in the weeks and months ahead. Just picturing it. Forming the resolution. Torturing herself about it, over days, or weeks. A huge gap between the decision and the execution, a gap filled by hesitating, revisiting, working out consequences, filled by fear and dread alternating with certainty and conviction. Isabela could easily fill in the gaps in what was being reported, what was known. Forming the resolution, and executing it. Entering the building. It wasn't known when exactly. She had entered the building the day before, was seen in the Art Library at some point during the day. Some asked whether someone planning to jump would bother studying en route but Isabela understood what a stupid question that was.

Life continues, until it ends.

She entered the building the day before and was not seen leaving it.

She would find a quiet place to hide. That was easy, in that monstrosity with its thirty-seven levels, its misshapen rooms and corridors, its nooks and crannies. She would be considerate. She would find a time and a place so there would be no witnesses. Of course there would be later witnesses, but that was unavoidable. She would feel terrible for whoever found her after but infinitely worse for anyone who witnessed it happen. She would find a quiet place to hide and to wait and to think, once the resolution is reached, truly reached, no more analysis and hesitation maybe just a bit of fear but no not really fear, she would wait and think a little, clarity of vision, she liked that expression, she would have achieved clarity of vision. And then it would be time, time to emerge from the hiding spot, all is quiet, all is dark, the last decision is the easiest, that window on the seventh floor, that window was loose, it didn't lock properly, as badly designed as the rest of the building, with weird angles and corners and nothing fit, like the world, with *its* weird angles and corners, and nothing fit, nothing fit ... like her ... maybe walking, maybe creeping, maybe even running, yes, to run, to sprint to that loose window and push it open and pause just that one long second and then out ...

=====

10.
i'm really sorry that i called you a f-cking f-ckhead

Death was much in the air in this period, whether metaphorically or hurtling through it or resulting from it. That Silliman junior. The next day a plane crashed into the Potomac river, killing seventy-eight. A short while after that an oil rig sank in a nasty storm off the coast of Newfoundland, taking eighty-four with it. The report came in confirming that the freshman who died prior to The Game had combined barbituates and alcohol, and the Guy had disappeared from campus until the nasty storm outside his door subsided.

The new semester was off to a rough start, but really it was just continuing a streak that started earlier. Over the Christmas break there was a rash of break-ins in several colleges. This was a no-brainer for the thieves, aware that the living quarters of these privileged citizens would be unpopulated for several weeks. The fact that there were so many potential thieves—the New Haven economy as depressed as the temperatures—meant that the stereos and televisions and jewelry were there for the taking. One such thief was unsuccessful, however, for his attempt to break into a room in Pierson, Jude's and Swill's room, was foiled—not by the campus police, but by Brother John who was living in that room over the break, thanks to Jude having given him the room key as well as a small pile of cash to feed himself.

Brother John had just emerged from the shower—he was developing a real taste for showers, now that he had access to one—when he came upon the fellow climbing in through the first-floor window he had just broken. Now as Brother John would explain to anyone, he believed that if a brother doesn't have principles he truly has nothing, and while he himself may not have had anything other than the shopping bag with his junk, he did at least have principles. He begged and borrowed but would not steal, nor condone stealing. Brother John also was filled only with love, and thus said with genuine warmth and affection, "My brother, this hurts me more than it hurts you," as he clobbered the fellow over the head with a poker from the fireplace.

"Oh, my," he added when the fellow collapsed and didn't move. "It may have hurt you more."

This put him in a delicate position, he realized, being stark naked in a Yalie's dorm room holding a bloody poker over an unmoving body with a puddle of blood forming around its head.

But a brother without principles has nothing. He hesitated only a moment to reflect on his good fortune, to be sound in mind and body, to be clean and warm and in this lovely room, before walking over to the telephone on the stained coffee table. He placed the handset to his ear and mouth, squeezed his index finger into the nine hole and dialed the number more typically dialed about him than by him, effectively ending the good fortune he had just been appreciating.

Of metaphorical deaths, there were several to report.

There was the death of one of the great corporations, as AT&T, which provided the phone service that led to Brother John's undoing, divested itself of some subdivisions. And if that death was due to overregulation (by Eli's reckoning), there was also the death *of* some regulations, in Connecticut at any rate, concerning alcohol. Tayvon, who had begun working at Quality Wine Shop, could explain the details using words such as wholesale, price controls, and the Distilled Spirits Council of America, but it boiled down to one useful fact: the price of booze was to decline. Say hello to Blatz, Molson Red Label, and the ever-popular Carling Black Label Tall Boy bar bottles. "Cheap beer," Swill observed, ordering a keg of Stroh's for the first Tuesday Night Club on their return to campus, the night before the junior's body was found in the moat, "goes well with an expensive education." Swill was flexible that way, as he found expensive Scotch also went well with that education.

And then there was the death, we are sad to report, of the Black-Jeff bromance, though they did not use that word until one of Black's later weddings, when it had achieved popularity. When they joked about it during the tenth reunion they called it their mutual man crush.

"You were a definite himbo, my brother," Jeffrey said under the tent in the Davenport courtyard, parodying the *Seinfeld* expression for a masculine bimbo.

"Past tense, J.?" Black answered. "Listen, my brother, I still got it."

Unlike that of the poor fellow on Jude's floor the death of the bromance was both drawn out and eventually reversible. Although dining hall analysis by assorted meatheads identified many precipitating factors, in the final analysis three or four were decisive.

"Fuck you, man!" Jeff exclaimed, flushed. "Never happened."

"Fuck *you*, J.-man!" Black retorted. "I know what I heard."

"Mind your own fucking business!"

"Keep your fucking business to yourself and I will!"

"What are you, some kind of pervert? Get your own, man."

"What are you, some kind of exhibitionist? And I got my own, man."

Not exactly the intellectual debate you might expect at a fine university, but then again the topic didn't exactly merit as such. Black insisted that Maggie and Jeff were, well, on the noisy side when they engaged in their, you know, snuggling, and claimed that he could hear, through the bedroom door, through the fucking walls, man,

Maggie's squealing eventually culminating in Jeff's very revolting groan. Jeff wanted to deny it but let's face it—that *was* the noise they usually did make, and really, who doesn't? The tipping point was that, last night, Black claimed, he had overheard Jeff's very revolting groan followed by his exclaiming, "I … am … *El … Jefe!*"

"Well, I *was*, man," Jeffrey sort of conceded under the Davenport tent.

"True dat," Black conceded too, because after all, any man lucky enough to be loving and loved by that Magdalena was a true *jefe*.

But back in the day, well, it surely would annoy anyone to be subjected to such aural abuse even on an occasional basis, especially when added to the ongoing irritation over their irreconcilable music tastes. It was bad enough having to hear them boning in there without also having to hear that shit they liked to bone to.

The fall of sophomore year was particularly stressful. The new Earth, Wind & Fire LP *Raise!* dropped in November, but the single "Let's Groove" had been dominating the charts since September. Black's efforts to play that single repeatedly were contested by their attempts to repeatedly play the new Police album, *Ghosts in the Machine*. On the plus side that decreased the amount of whiny hippie shit Black had to endure, but only by substituting the whiny shrill Police shit. Black got so frustrated at one point that he bought several long extension cords at the Co-op, ran them down into the steam tunnels, then moved his stereo down there with a sleeping bag. He found a comfortable nook that F. Scott had decorated on a whim, installing purple lights to illuminate a mural she had painted on one wall. It was lovely, that mural, Black thought, a mural of the very spot in the steam tunnels where the mural was, including the mural, as he gazed at it for the two days he lived down there playing the new Jacksons album repeatedly. He only opted to depart his new digs when what he was pretty sure was a mouse scurried over his feet in the middle of the night. Jeff and Maggie's squealing was bad, but rodent squealing—followed by his own—was worse.

A possible third factor in the decline of the bromance was the fact that Black, as he had put it, had "got his own." Whatever he had going on, though, he kept it discreet.

"Come on, man, tell," Jeff would plead when they weren't

fighting about everything else.

"J.-man, I do not kiss and tell," Black answered.

"So don't tell me about the kissing. What else you been doing?"

"Let me just put it this way, man. Unlike certain cretins who know nothing about music, she wants to be with me when I put on 'I Wanna Be With You.'" Here Black was referring to the second single from *Raise!*, newly dropped.

That remark quickly led the conversation south. By the time Black had shouted "Fuck you, man!" and headed out to the Co-op to go buy extension cords, Jeff had only extracted the information that he was dating some townie named Honey he had met at a club.

"Now you know the truth," Black had admitted sheepishly, in fact lying through his teeth.

"Now you *really* know the truth," Black said twelve years later, under the Davenport tent, when he finally divulged the actual truth about his fling with Piper, the Morse freshman who was rebelling against everything her father stood for, except his money, by dating a Black guy.

"You the man," Jeffrey acknowledged on hearing this.

"Always was," Black sighed nostalgically.

"I'm really sorry that I called you a fucking fuckhead."

"Good times, my brother, good times."

And the final straw?

"Are you—and he—out of your fucking minds, man?" Black exclaimed on hearing, first, of Jude's plan to house Brother John over the Christmas break and then of Jeff's support of that plan. "Are you high?"

"As a matter of fact I am," Jeff answered, "but that has nothing to do with it."

"Absolutely no fucking way," Black immediately quashed Jeff's proposal, in his ongoing competition with Jude, that he and Black find their own homeless person to house over the break.

"Come on, man. Sister Susan will barely take up any space. She's just got that one shopping bag."

Black shook his head. "I can't decide. Either you have your head up your ass or you have shit for brains. Help a brother out."

"Fine," Jeff harrumphed. "So I suppose that's a no for the fund to support Brother John then?"

"No, it's a *fucking* no. There are social services in place for these people. That's what fucking taxes are for, man." Black hesitated. "I know what your problem is."

"Yeah?"

"It's that whiny hippie shit. It's like that amoeba that eats your brain from the inside out."

"Total non sequitur," Jeff scoffed. "Jude doesn't even listen to 'the Deceased' and it's his plan."

"Fine. Then maybe there's some contagious brain disease."

"Yeah. It's called 'compassion.' You should try to get infected."

"Fuck you, I have more compassion in my little finger than you have in your whole body, man." This was not true; the amounts were about equal. "You actually have no concept of what true compassion is. But it's not about compassion, man."

"Yeah? Then what?"

Black sighed. "Fuck, man. First there are rules—"

"Made to be broken."

"You looking forward to explaining to your Daddy-o that you've been expelled?"

"Not entirely," Jeff conceded. "But—compassion, man."

"Look, J.-man," Black took on the same tone he took when he was about to lecture you on the history of Motown, also serious business. "If you want compassion then you must address the system. Starting with the economy. Improve the schools, introduce competition, starting with elementary. Give people what they need to become independent, self-sustaining, contributors rather than takers, man. That is true compassion. Enabling the deadbeat will only support whatever bad habits got him into the situation in the first place. I have nothing against Brother John personally but I guarantee that if the devil-man puts him up over the break there will be trouble. Honestly the plan is so harebrained that I'd put ten bucks down that somebody even winds up dead."

"I guess you were right," Jeff conceded as he forked over the ten dollars, not immediately, not for many months, but when they were over the worst of it.

But for now—with roommates hearing your sexual cries, with incompatible tastes in music, with the social justice argument devolving into nasty personal attacks, by the time the *Raise!* single

"I've Had Enough" dropped in January, Black had had enough. Maggie's efforts to mediate—"Everybody in? Isn't viewpoint diversity wonderful? Unconditional love? Agree to disagree?"—were about as successful as her attempts to mediate the mysterious tension between Thorn and Ig, only succeeding in getting all parties annoyed with her.

And so Black found himself some off-campus digs and disappeared from their story for a while.

=====

11.
it's pretty nice to have some friends

With Black gone Jeff and Maggie had his suite to themselves. Many pleasant nights smoking a bone and watching *All in the Family* reruns on Jeff's little black-and-white TV, playing cribbage, and of course the, you know, snuggling which, now that they could do it any time, they weren't exactly doing so often.

Meanwhile Jude remained unimpressed with Black's arguments.

"Clarity of vision dispenses with those masturbatory exercises in rationalization," he whispered to Jeff during an organic chemistry lecture.

"Compassion cannot be institutionalized," he had yelled to Black in the steam tunnels, over the blasting Jacksons, when he'd gone down there to check out the arrangement. Seeing the ambiance that F. Scott created down there in fact gave Jude some ideas, and his fascination with the subterranean tunnels had begun.

"Of course you have to address the system," he yelled at Jeff over the noise at Rudy's, packed as always when the men's hockey team arrived after a game, not to mention with the Rangers game on the TV over the bar, "but by the time you can do that who knows how many individuals will have died?"

"I think we are going to get him off," Jude shared at the dining hall table over dinner, having spent most of the day in court. Jeff supported Jude's work on behalf of Brother John, not least because Jude had missed several organic chemistry lectures along the way. "The judge seems inclined to dismiss the case."

"And what about getting you off for hosting him?" Maya asked, who was volunteering at a New Haven legal aid clinic for the homeless and had helped Jude locate the attorney.

"Are you offering?" Swill, Tayvon, and Eli all said simultaneously, the synchronicity also startling them simultaneously so that none of them laughed at their own literally sophomoric humor.

Ren got the exchange down in his notebook. Isabela snapped a photo of Ren's scribbling.

"Such meatheads," Lisa cast her scornful left eyebrow at them, though she did not leave the table.

"Just probation," Jude answered, glad he had only thought, and not said, *Are you offering?* "At least three steps away from rustication. Master Harold went easy on me."

"Yeah," Ig snickered, flushing, "I heard he goes easy on guys."

"Unlike Mistress Lucille," Tayvon said, going for a high five, "I heard she comes down hard."

Lisa and Maya shook their heads, wondering if it were too late to transfer into literally any other college.

"Hey," Ig stood up. "Gotta go. It's almost game time."

"Which means it's pregame time," Thorn added, standing up and blinking his eye.

The meatheads finished their meatloaf and headed over to Croc's room for some pregame Tall Boys. Croc had the biggest fridge, so his room was ground zero for gatherings even when, as tonight, he wasn't there. The detritus from their Superbowl party five days earlier only improved the atmosphere, which, combined with the Tall Boys and with their debate about President Reagan's economic recovery plan, meant they were late to the Whale—surely the coolest building on campus, designed by the many-vowelled architect Eero Saarinen, and home to the hockey rink.

They missed the first period of the game, but no matter. Ig looked great out there during the second and third periods as the team crushed Princeton 7-4. Lots of goals, though none by their hero. At one point he did manage a shot, which in the gang's imagination occurred in slow motion, allowing exclamations of excitement.

"He got a shot!" one of them exclaimed.

"It's heading toward the goal!" another exclaimed.

"It's going in!" a couple of others exclaimed.

"FUCK!" the entire gang exclaimed when the shot did beat the goalie, but not the crossbar, and ricocheted away.

"That so was a shot on goal," Tayvon yelled over the noise at Rudy's after the game, including over the Rangers game on the television.

"Counts for me, friend," Maggie said, squeezing Ig's arm, Ig who knew perfectly well that though this was his first successful shot *toward* the goal, in hitting the post it did not count as a shot *on* goal.

"Still, the assist," Lisa yelled, who disliked Rudy's—loud, the smell of beer, the sticky floor, the little boys—but usually came along after the home games. Plus, she needed a break: she was taking Leonhard's History of the Soviet Union class, which, with some 771 students, was the biggest class that semester. With that enrollment they had to increase the number of sections. Though she was only a sophomore Prof Leonhard had picked her out of the crowd—with a word from her T.A.—to make her a T.A. leading a section in her own right. Suffice to say, she was one busy woman that semester, which was probably good because there was less time to resent Samilla's lately hogging Tayvon.

"You're nice, Lise," Ig yelled back, "but strictly speaking that doesn't count either." Ig had skated so fast around one of the Princeton defenders that the poor fellow fell down and lost the puck, which had then been scooped up by one of Ig's teammates and deposited in the net.

"Counts for me," she'd shouted back, and Ig did have to admit that, though still smarting from the Erich affair and still short of his first shot, much less goal, it was pretty nice to have some friends.

=====

12.
the dishroom is the mushroom of the civilized world

Roaring flames licking the middle-of-the-night sky, Harkness Tower, the tallest building on campus, visible for miles around, an enormous torch lighting the night sky to the soundtrack of sirens and alarms, from every direction, surely the world was coming to an end, an end by fire. Fire, the great destroyer, the disorderer, the destruction of order, combustion, oxidation, air, put out by water, reducing all to ashes, to dust, to the earth whence all came. Fire, heat, hot, passion, lovemaking, sex, noise, squealing, groaning, death. Fire, water, steam, steam tunnels, tunnels, underground, beneath the earth, earth, worms, Ignoratio, Doc. Everything is connected to everything, Doc said, everybody to everybody, everybody *is* everybody, everybody in nobody out ... the unity behind diversity ... the syzygy (look it up) ...

Those in the know could not be blamed for thinking the Harkness Fire was not unrelated to the cosmic syzygy (look it up!) that heralded the end of the world, and Jude was in the know, and that's what Jude was thinking, thinking or conspiricizing, to understand is to connect the dots and to conspiricize is to connect the dots, what's the difference, all dots should be connected, there can't be random dots, which was the dot that would lead to the dot that led to the vicious murder so many years later ...

Jude got a job in the dining hall.

He didn't need a job, though nobody knew that. He was a public school kid of modest background, no reason to suspect he had any means, and indeed this would be a matter of interest to the investigators decades later. The fact was that he wanted the job, and may have been the only college student who ever actively wanted to be a "dishdog" washing dishes. But how could they not? There was the aesthetics of it, the hot water, the soap, the steam, but more than that was the order of it. To load the dirty dishes and silverware into the racks, to put the racks on the belt, to run them through the machine. To create clean from filth. To create order from disorder. To return the now clean dishes and silverware to their shelves and trays, ready to serve again. The transition, the return, the ongoing cycle, the circles made of circles.

"It is a well-oiled machine," Jude would try to explain at a Tuesday Night Club.

"What, the dish machine?" that night's victim would respond.

"The whole operation." The goal was to develop an organic process out of inorganic materials. Like a well-designed ecosystem, a well-designed dishroom, a well-oiled machine, was itself a cog in an even larger machine. Dishroom, mushroom, shrooms, mycelium threads, mycorrhizal network, interconnected, underneath, the structure underneath, subterranean, the domain of *Lumbricus terrestris*, and beneath it all, in the center of it all, was the humble dishdog.

"Infrastructure," Jude might explain at Rudy's, shouting over the Islanders game, "is the key to everything." If you were unable to escape the conversation he would explain that to operate the dishroom one needed the personnel, the managers, the workers, who in turn must be paid by the institution, which required students to pay tuition, which required a fully functioning society to produce those students, one which understood that its own future required it to train the next generation. It takes not just a village but a society, an ecosystem, a globe. And then he would explain that the dishroom was essential to the dining hall, itself essential to the institution which trained the next generation who would be essential to the future of humanity, the same humanity which just might reach its end in the cataclysmic syzygy (*look it up!*) expected on March 10.

"The dishroom," Jude might explain to Jasmine in the Pierson courtyard, Jasmine who—though she would become as famous as Yo-Yo Ma (whom she would meet when he performed at Woolsey Hall just two days before the Harkness fire)—was still just a cellist, and therefore didn't really follow the details, but it didn't matter because what attracted her was his magnetism and his eyes that penetrated into the infrastructure of your soul, "the dishroom is the mushroom, the earthworm," he would explain, "of the civilized world, the center of it all, when you think about it."

Jude's gaze momentarily diverted from Jasmine's soul to her gold drop earrings with their alabaster pearls, pearls which (fun fact!) are formed when an irritant penetrates the mollusk, gold which (fun fact!) is formed by nuclear fusion in a star that then explodes and scatters the element across the universe until it finds its way to planets such as earth, the planets just then making their way to their syzygic rendezvous that would herald the end of the same earth …

But he also noticed that those pearls looked really beautiful next to Jasmine's bistered skin, and that Jasmine herself was really beautiful, and her cello-playing quite sublime, almost as sublime as a well-oiled dishroom.

=====

13.
the world coming to an end, by fire

"Beamie? Sam?" Maggie said to Jeff after *All in the Family* had ended and instead of beginning the sexual activity that Jeff had been hoping for (it had been a while) before he entirely bungled everything. "Are you high?"

"I am," Jeff answered, as she well knew because they had smoked the bone together, "but that's not relevant."

"He was upset. He just wanted to pick my brain."

"That needed a lunch? Out?"

Maggie looked at him with, well, that look. "I didn't think about it. He just asked to meet there. It was lunchtime. I was hungry."

"I don't know," Jeff said, aware that he was digging himself into a hole but unable to stop. Later on as he did this more frequently Maggie would say things like, *Why don't you keep digging because I can still see the top of your head.* "It's like our place. One of our favorite places."

"Every place we go to is like 'our favorite place' for you," Maggie said, maybe a little more softly. A couple days earlier he'd had a similar response when Maggie had gone to Louis' Lunch with Jasmine, who wanted to process her nascent relationship with Jude.

"Yeah, but you know."

Wow, eloquent response, El Jefe.

Bet that one will end up in her damn diary.

In fact the Educated Burgher on Broadway really *was* one of their favorite places, not least because Spiro the proprietor adored Maggie and always brought them a free dessert. Jeff had passed by the restaurant after picking up Lou Reed's new album, *Blue Mask*, at Cutler's, and glanced in the window to see Maggie and Beamie huddled over cheeseburghers (as they were called).

"Wow, eloquent response, mister," Maggie said, a little more softly, thinking about entering this episode into her diary before resetting and going on to update him on poor Beamie's latest debacle.

On her recommendation he'd signed up for a Tai Chi class at the gym to try to meet women, and seemed to have hit pay dirt. *Finally saw a woman, he met her at the gym,* a really cute freshman from Trumbull, God was she sexy in her sweats, he *couldn't stop thinking about the moves she could do with him.* When Maggie didn't stop him there he told her about one exercise the class did where they partnered up, and he got the woman, and they had to face each other and push their palms against each other, one pushed and the other resisted minimally, gradually yielding but not entirely yielding, and then that person pushed back and the other gradually yielded but not entirely yielded, then repeat, and sure there was some yin-yang thing going on but basically they were making love through their palms and it was like every cell of his body was making love with every cell of her body.

"Too much information?" Beamie asked when he saw the look on Maggie's face.

Maggie nodded.

Well anyway the point was there was obvious chemistry between them and so Beamie was hopeful there might soon be some physics as well, so *at last he summoned up the courage, asked her to a double bill.*

"And what debacle ensued?" Jeff asked, trying not to smile at Beamie's expense because he knew that Maggie disapproved of mocking others, but let's face it Beamie's loserness was downright hilarious, particularly when you were stoned.

"Well, he asked her out."

"And?"

"She said she had plans that night."

"And?"

Maggie took a deep breath, because Beamie had totally *not* followed her strategic advice. "He asked her out for the next night instead. She also had plans."

"Please no."

"Yes. He asked her out for the following night. She had a lot of work to do."

"He didn't."

"Yes he did. He kept going. He asked her out for the next night."

"You're killing me."

"Right. Finally instead of saying no she just asked him if there weren't any other Tai Chi classes he might transfer into."

This one was so cringeworthy that Jeff no longer felt the need to crack up, despite the weed. This was good because had he cracked up that would have severed any possibility of sexual activity because Maggie truly ached for Beamie. She did admit he was rather a, you know, the L-word, but that fact, she insisted, didn't mean that his feelings didn't matter, although Jeff was pretty sure it meant exactly that by definition. Still, Jeff had a better chance of getting laid by sympathy for Beamie than by mockery so he was smart enough not to say anything. And the next phase of their evening did get off to a good start, what with lighting up another bone, watching some of the *Twilight Zone* rerun, a little bit of snuggling, but then, dammit, how do things like this happen.

"You seem particularly interested, I don't know," Jeff found himself saying, the top of his head just dipping below Maggie's visibility.

Was Maggie flushing, a little uncomfortable? "I am interested, of course. Why wouldn't I be? But *particularly* interested? What does that mean?"

Yes, what does that mean, El Jefe?

They'd just been talking about Beamie so why wouldn't they be talking about the latest Pierson coupling, *intramurals at their best* as they liked to say, and now that Jude and Jasmine were dating then *really* intramurals because it was intra-meathead. And it was a *particularly* interesting coupling, after all, since they seemed like such opposites and nobody had seen it coming.

"Retracted," Jeff said in a too-late attempt at humor, mocking the *Petrocelli* reruns they also watched, maybe the stupidest courtroom show ever.

"No," Maggie resisted, because maybe you could legally retract your objection but let's face it everybody heard it, "what does that mean? Like how do you quantify interest? How much is too much interest? 'Particular' interest?"

Damn those were good questions, El Jefe.

Was he maybe connecting dots that ought not to be connected?

Or inventing dots that weren't even there?

"Jasmine is my friend," Maggie said, thank God moving on from her questions, "why wouldn't I be interested in who she is dating?"

"Of course, of course," Jeff said, it was *Jasmine's* welfare she was interested in, *particularly* interested in, not Jude's. Maybe his endless competition with Jude was getting the better of him. "Hey look," he exclaimed with relief at the diversion, "*Petrocelli's* on!"

But not even that stupid show could erase his stupid behavior, and the damage was done. They watched for a while, then rolled over back-to-back to go to sleep. Finding their positions, finding their spots, everyone has their spot, if you could three-dimensionally X-ray Pierson College you would find most people in their spots at that hour, the little boxes that were suites had littler boxes that were bedrooms and in each bedroom was one or two or three people, not everyone was in their spot, some people were in other spots, or others' spots, or en route to those spots, but everyone was in some spot. Also en route to their spots, their designated spots, were the nine planets, on the move, each moving independently yet with a date with destiny, with syzygy, they were aligning into order ...

Also at that moment Zar was sliding the cubes on the last row of the Rubik's Magic Cube into *their* designated places. This was not play, however, but homework. He and Beamie were taking Prof. Howe's Davenport College Seminar on the Cube, which was a mathematics class about something called group theory. Zar first solved some problem in group theory then applied what he had done to the Cube, and solved the Cube.

"Really?" Beamie had said to him earlier that evening, immediately after the seminar.

Not one to waste a word, Zar just nodded.

"It doesn't seem fair. I try everything to get laid, and you get laid without trying."

Zar just shrugged. It wasn't really a big deal. He and Caroline, also in the class, had met in her room two nights earlier to work through the problem set together. The work got a little intense and soon transformed into flirting.

"The quotient group," she'd whispered, the little vixen.

"G modulo N," Zar replied breathlessly and before they knew it the deed was done and they were back on the problem set.

And while that deed was being done it just so happened that Jeff went in search of Zar to ask him something about chemistry. Jeff was trying to keep pace with Jude in organic but the mathematical parts were challenging and when you've got a future Nobel laureate in your friend group you take advantage. He approached Zar's and Beamie's room with his offering—some orange accelerants from a new source—and, as was custom, went in without knocking. Seeing Zar's bedroom empty he was just turning to leave when he heard something from the bathroom.

"What the …" Jeff started to say, thinking at first that Art Garfunkel was in there singing "Bridge Over Troubled Water."

It was Beamie singing in the shower.

"It was, I don't know," Jeff reported back to Maggie shortly after, "magnificent? Who knew the bugger had it in him?"

"That's great," Maggie said with sincere pleasure.

"Kind of had that choir boy thing going on, but like the opposite of grating. Maybe more, I don't know, angelic?"

"That's just so great. I'd love to hear it."

"Absolutely not," Beamie turned bright red when Maggie asked him the next day. Not wanting to be pushy, she let it slide—for now.

Meanwhile at exactly the same moment that Zar was sliding that last piece of the Magic Cube into place and realizing that the mathematics of the cube's solution was also relevant to the model of gases he was working on, directly below him, in the steam tunnel, in the game room, alongside the *Frogger* and the *Donkey Kong*, Ig was reaching the eleventh screen of *Pac-Man*, his personal best. Why exactly is this game so intense, Ig might have wondered if the game weren't so all-consumingly intense. It wasn't real, it was all in the mind, being chased by the ghosts whom someone had named Inky, Blinky, Pinky and Clyde, and what exactly made these creatures "ghosts" anyway beyond someone simply labeling them as such? There was no safe space here, no assigned place, you were always on the move, the place you needed to be was always over there, you could never quite get there ...

Sort of like the planets, always on the move, always where they had to be at the one moment and elsewhere at the next, until their March 10 rendezvous.

So are we, Jude was thinking.

As sacks of meat and molecules our bodies simply followed the laws of physics, of chemistry, of biology, and his place, toward which he was hurtling, was in the chemistry and the biology. Lisa's place, meanwhile, was in that Soviet Union class, her sack of meat and molecules already laying the foundations that would bring her to her first Pulitzer. The second largest class that term was Spence's Modern Chinese History, which Samilla, Eli, Ig, and Swill were all taking, each for their own reasons and with their own eventual destinations, while the third largest was Brodhead's 19th Century American Literature, about those long-winded novels Tayvon was now absorbing on Ren's recommendation. There was a reason these classes were so popular: the professors, each master orators, each able to spray many dots on the blackboard like stars in the heavens and then connect them, one by one, into constellations, into galaxies ... order from disorder, an order obscured by the messy day to day, the daily distractions, the chores and catastrophes, the injustices, but perceivable on reflection, in the quiet of a dark night, in the calm of a deep mind, where clarity of vision could be found. Jude could not understand why his friends were into drugs and drinking, Jeff, in particular. Jeff had the potential, the spark. Jeff had glimpsed that something was up, that nothing was an accident, but then would cloud his vision with his extracurriculars. Tragic, and ironic: the drugs prevented him from seeing that he should dispense with the drugs.

Irony, the fundamental tone of a universe that resists our endeavors to understand it.

Speaking of Jeff and his extracurriculars, it was cold outside but toasty warm in the room where he and Maggie had somehow recovered from their earlier cul-de-sac. They couldn't get to sleep in that little bed so had gotten up, enjoyed a small doob and then before long were enjoying everybody's favorite extracurricular, doing their thing, the thing that would soon culminate in an 8.7-second groan at a pitch of 77.8 Hz and a volume of 84.3 decibels roughly matching that of a small revving motorcycle, similar to the one that Iggy had some ten minutes earlier parked in the courtyard.

You might ask how we know about the specs of that groan.

Iggy had parked the bike, come up the stairs and let himself into Jeff's room in search of some of the weed usually lying around there.

"Didn't it bother you that he'd just come in and take your stuff?" Debra asked Jeffrey years later, when he was relating this story.

"No, not really. Iggy was the most selfless person you could ever meet, and brought that out in all of us. Whatever he had, was yours, and so whatever was yours, was his. Of course generally he had nothing so what you were sharing was yours, but with that big guffaw of his somehow it didn't matter."

Iggy didn't discover any weed in the livingroom but something much much better.

As soon as he entered he heard the squealing.

He had a moment of discomfort; he adored Maggie, and he would never do anything, nothing, *nada*, to hurt her or humiliate her.

But Jesus listen to that!

Either she was a sexual monstress, or Jeff, the man, was a sexual maestro, or Jesus maybe both. The Monstress and the Maestro. Somebody should make a movie he thought, finding himself thinking of Jeff in a rather entirely new light.

That's when he saw the cassette recorder.

There it was, on the floor next to the guitar that Jeff had laid down after playing the latest song he had written for Maggie. Jeff had by this point written several dozen songs, of which, he liked to say, at least three or four were not bad. Whatever their objective quality they were good enough for Maggie, who found him very sexy when he played, the way his hands, his gentle hands, moved, the right hand strumming, the left fingering the strings. Very sexy even though, of the three songs he had written for her, he still hadn't managed to work her name in.

Well there was the cassette recorder on which Jeff recorded his songs for posterity, and this song he was now playing, on his girlfriend, talk about preserving for posterity. Iggy looked at the recorder, saw that the cassette in there was at about the halfway point. For a moment, a microsecond, he thought he really shouldn't do this, and then in the next microsecond he understood that he must, because sometimes, after all, you need to make your memories, and this was a memory that badly needed making.

"Come to papa, my little ones," he whispered affectionately, with nothing but love for his friends in his heart as he crept toward the bedroom door and then, just before Maggie emitted the squeal of all squeals, had the enormous good fortune to press "record."

"There *is* an Asshole," he whispered using his preferred term for the deity, thanking the Great Asshole for granting him the favor of capturing this squeal, and the next seventeen seconds of squealing, as well as Jeff's fantastic groan. It was all so beautiful Iggy wasn't even disappointed that Jeff left out the "I am *El Jefe*!" that Black had told absolutely everyone, including random strangers, about.

As for the scientific measurements, those came some fifteen minutes later, when Iggy ran guffawing over to Thorn's and Croc's room to share his treasure, because what was his was everyone's, and this tape definitely belonged to everyone. Croc, who when he wasn't crushing running backs liked to crush some Jim Croce on the ukulele, had a device to measure pitch; Zar, in his work on sound as part of his work on air, had something to measure decibels; and Ren, who was nailing the description of the ecstatic smile on Ig's face into his notebook, had a stopwatch. It was quite amazing how something under thirty seconds of length could, when repeated and repeated, fill the next several hours.

"That's my boy," Black said when he heard the tape in Tayvon's room a couple days later. Now that he was no longer directly subjected to these sounds he could better appreciate the artistry involved in producing them, and anyway, if Magdalena, that treasure, was happy, then he was happy, and damn she sounded pretty happy.

"Zounds!" Beamie exclaimed, alarmed, when he heard the tape in Ren's room. "Are you sure he isn't hurting her?"

"Pretty sure," pretty much everyone else laughed.

"I'm jealous," Samilla said when she heard the tape, when the meatheads finally couldn't keep it just to the guys any longer, and figured she was the safest female.

"I know, right," Black said, who had brought it to her room once the male meatheads gave the approval.

Awesome as it was, this tape too had its place and time. As the meatheads were easily distractable, it wasn't all that long before other things came to occupy their attention, such as the dismissal of the case against Brother John.

"Thank you, my brother, thank you, my sister," Brother John said to everyone at the table, shaking hands as he went, when Jude brought him to lunch at the Pierson Dining Hall. Jude had also bought him some fresh clothes on his release from jail and paid for a month's lodging at the YMCA. Everyone at the table shook his hand back, even though they had had nothing whatever to do with the affair.

"I'm not sure this is a good idea," Swill whispered to Jude.

"I am not sure you would recognize a good idea if you ever had one," Jude whispered back, then turned to John, who was just sitting at the table with his laden tray. "Eat up, my brother, we have a long day ahead of us." Jude had scheduled appointments with a rehab clinic and an employment training service for the afternoon.

But everything hurtles on, in its place en route to its next place, and all things, good and bad, come to an end. The planets were just eight days from their world-ending alignment: that massive gravitational pull would trigger sunspots and solar winds, increase the Earth's rotation, produce natural catastrophes, jiggle the San Andreas, the end of it all. It was building motion by motion, but the climax was still eight days away, and apart from Jude, the only one seriously concerned about this—he had hoarded toilet paper and canned food in a steel lockbox in his closet—the others carried on their little lives as if the end of it all were *not* a mere week away.

One other thing also coming to an end at this time: Maggie's not knowing about the tape.

It was approximately 3:30 in the morning and Tayvon was in the Pierson College Library reading *Moby Dick* for Brodhead. He was distracted, as he was experiencing some new feelings. He had been dating only Samilla and Lisa for some time by this point and *wanted to carry on*. In fact he could almost say *he didn't want anyone else*. Well, maybe not entirely, but his other desires had been infrequent and easily extinguished. He couldn't make sense of this. Was something wrong with him? He was falling behind in his classes, what with these strange new feelings, and so he'd come up here to study tonight. The library in the tower had two levels, and Tayvon had lugged that thick book all the way up to the upper level, to isolate himself. Thus that's where he was, alternating between a page or two of Melville and a thought or two of Samilla, and one or two of Lisa, when he could hear the footsteps coming from down below. Tap tap tap, they exclaimed, for they were definitely exclaiming. Tap tap tap, more urgently. You might think that by this point in their relationships they could distinguish each others' footsteps but that wouldn't be true.

But these taps, these angry harsh taps that clearly exclaimed *I pity the person toward whom I am tapping*—that was definitely Maggie.

The woman was upon him.

"Where is it?" she demanded.

"What?" Tayvon responded, eyes blinking.

"*Where is it?*"

"Where is what?" Tayvon knew perfectly well what she was referring to but needed time to formulate a plan.

"The tape."

"The tape?"

"The tape!"

"What tape?"

Tayvon generally had a way with words. He was a serious student of literature, he would go on to become a much beloved teacher of literature at a prestigious private school, and of course it didn't hurt that he was a looker, but ultimately, in the end, it was his way with words, his gentle voice with its tenor tone, that he was to be known for—but all he had working for him now were a couple of "what"s and a case of echolalia.

Maggie's eyes burned into his.

She really was beautiful when her dark eyes glowed red like that.

"The tape of me and Jeff fucking!"

She exclaimed this so loudly—to the great hilarity of the meat-heads soon after and even herself an adequate number of years later—that she could be heard by the several Piersonites studying on the lower level of the library.

Later Tayvon would knock himself for not being just slightly quicker and responding, "*Which* tape of you and Jeff fucking?"

"Oh, *that* tape," he said instead, blinking furiously.

The power of the syzygy was growing, you could feel it if you paid close attention. Maybe not consciously but it was in the air, in the shadows, in the interstices, it was affecting people, the way you feel ill at ease, it was similar to the feeling you had in *Pac-Man* in that one instant when you hadn't quite processed that you were no longer hunting and it hits you that you are now the hunted. That was the feeling Zar was having at the moment that Tayvon was answering Maggie, because he was down there in the game room staring at *Pac-Man* and thinking about air, getting close but not quite there, so close but not there, but then, the way of the world, the distraction came, the tide turned, in this case in the form of sirens, the many alarm-sirens ringing all through the campus.

The world was coming to an end, Jude was sure of it, hearing the sirens.

The power of the syzygy, Iggy also could feel it because he had been feeling it for a long time really.

"It isn't me, Al," he would say to the arresting officer later that night, whom he knew on a first-name basis by this time, "It's much bigger than me."

The same Iggy who had crept into Jeff's room in search of weed and thus produced the tape whose role in our story was just then hurtling towards it end, like the nine planets hurtling towards their cosmic rendezvous, had earlier that same evening crept again into Jeff's room and this time found some weed and also Jeff's Harkness Tower key. It was a bulky key annoying to carry so Jeff left it in his livingroom on its giant skull key ring.

"When cosmic forces pull you," Ig told Al, "are you going to resist?"

Jeff's weed and Harkness key and the power of the planets all pointed to the same end, that Ig must smoke that weed up on Jeff's special place, because after all what was Jeff's was his. And you couldn't blame him, Al, it was not in his control, it was logically ineluctable, with the information available and the cognitive processes in play. It was pretty chilly outside, March in New Haven, there was a barrel up there on the scaffolding filled with construction waste (the Tower was under renovation), and Ig had his trusty Bic lighter—okay Jeff's lighter, so his—and what could it possibly hurt to make a small toasty fire in the barrel?

"It was out of my hands, Al," Ig concluded.

He had to.

We all have to, because forces beyond our control control us, as Jude could demonstrate by means of biology and chemistry and in this case, some astrophysics and cosmology.

In a sense, then, you could say the syzygy caused the fire.

Though in a truer, more immediate sense, it was Iggy.

"But does it really matter *who* exactly caused it, Al?" Iggy suggested in a penultimate-ditch effort to avoid charges.

Apparently, according to the New Haven Police Department, it did.

"Agree to disagree?" Ig uttered in the last-ditch effort as they locked the cell door with him on the other side.

Roaring flames, licking the four-in-the-morning sky, Harkness Tower, the tallest building on campus, visible for miles around, an enormous torch lighting the night sky, to the soundtrack of sirens from every direction, surely the world was coming to an end, an end by fire ... The tallest building on campus could be seen from everywhere including from the Pierson courtyard where they all gathered, Zar, distracted from air and redirected to fire, Tayvon, distracted from Maggie's fiery eyes, Maggie for the moment distracted from the second most humiliating thing that would ever happen to her, Jeff, distracted from his failed quest to get Maggie to agree not to erase that tape, Jude watching it all confirm that the world was coming to an end, they all stood there as one in the chilly March morning watching the world as they knew it go up in flames.

=====

14.

paranoia

There was zero media coverage of the syzygic end of the world.

"Maybe," Swill said to Jude when the latter complained, "that's because it didn't happen."

"Maybe it did happen," Jude answered, "in ways not manifest to reptilian brains such as your own. Only in time will people understand." Many years later, after the murder, Jeffrey would come back to this remark, feeling that it might be the answer to some key question they hadn't yet formulated.

There was also minimal coverage of the fire on the Harkness Tower scaffolding which was really little more than a small fire in a construction barrel quickly put out.

The world may not have ended but surely something was afoot.

The Sony Walkman hit campus that spring, just in time to play the infamous tape that was now safely back in Jeff's possession for erasing. The fad was so big that Lisa—now Editor-in-Chief-Elect of the *Yale Daily News*, normally reserved for juniors—assigned a reporter to cover the craze. Luscious Piersonite Magina was quoted in the article—someone finally spoke to her, they found a gay freshman male reporter somehow blind to her divinity—as affirming the sound quality was "exquisite."

"'Exquisite,'" several of the meatheads sighed.

"Animals," Maya muttered again. She had become friendly with Magina and learned that the universal male disregard of the poor woman left her feeling there must be something really wrong with her. It was small consolation when Maya reminded her that the disregard was due to their finding her divine.

"Still alone on Saturday nights," she said sadly.

Maggie got one.

Jasmine got one.

Beamie got one because he thought it might make him cooler; that was funny.

Jeff borrowed Maggie's Walkman constantly and would return it to her cued up to the Tom Waits song he at that moment thought it most imperative she should know. Somehow, though, she found Tom less sublime than he did—a fact he found as incomprehensible as it was annoying—so she finally made him get his own.

Even Brother John got one, once he started raking in the wages from the job Jude got for him.

It was a stroke of genius. John's greatest skill was apparent the first moment you met him: he was a people person who loved, just loved, to chat. And what do people love to do while chatting? Drink coffee. There was this guy Nico with a coffee and donut cart whose business was as anemic as his brew. Jude, with his dining hall connections, helped him first improve his brew then introduced him to Brother John, whose job it became to chat passersby up—what he would do anyway—and lure them into having a cup of coffee while they chatted. Throw in three more fine ideas—location, location, location—and now they were bringing in big bucks—not Eli big bucks but Nico big bucks and John enormous bucks—selling donuts and coffee to carb-and-caffeine-starved college students who had slept through breakfast.

"For you, compliments of the house, my brother," Brother John would say as he handed Jude a Boston Creme thrice weekly, when Jude stopped by the cart's morning location en route to organic chemistry.

"What about me?" Jeff would ask in mock offense.

"Two bits, my brother. You think we're made of money?"

"With Thorn?" Jeff asked Maggie some weeks later, speaking of Nico's coffee cart, doing his best to sound merely curious and not jealous.

"Are you jealous about Thorn now?" Maggie asked, doing her best to sound merely curious and not annoyed.

"I'm merely curious," Jeff insisted not very convincingly.

Was he out of line in feeling those little feelings of jealousy? Earlier that afternoon he'd seen Maggie engaged in some intimate pow-wow with Thorn outside the Payne Whitney gym, on one of the benches near Nico's cart's afternoon location. Thorn was a fine specimen of masculinity, you know, with that chiseled jaw and the short sharply groomed hair. You could see why he would become literally the poster boy for the Navy Seals after graduating.

"You're spying on me now?" Maggie was no longer pretending she wasn't annoyed.

"No! The gang was heading to the gym to play some basketball."

Fine. The whole thing was perfectly innocent, Maggie protested. "I wanted to speak to him about Ig. About whatever the hell is going on between them. I love them both to death and it just kills me that there's so much tension between them."

That much was credible, and Jeff actually loved Maggie's desire that all the people she loved should also love each other. He wisely decided not to mention how intimate the conversation looked, the huddled heads, the whispering—and was it really necessary that they share that single chocolate glazed?

"And?" Jeff said instead.

"Didn't budge. Claimed there was nothing."

"Do you believe him?"

"Not in the slightest. But if he doesn't want to talk to me, that's fine. I'll be here when he's ready."

For the record, this was the first time Maggie lied to Jeff.

In fact Thorn had opened up to Maggie—there was something intimate about sharing that donut, combined with his predilection for tall, lithe dark-haired female athletes—thus burdening her with information she would need some time to process, as well as keep from her boyfriend.

Meanwhile there were other things to be upset about, for all of them, and whatever problems there were between Thorn and Ig, or between Maggie and Jeff, were barely a mound of legumes in the shitshow that was humanity (as Jeff would parody *Casablanca*, recently shown at the Yale Film Society).

It was confirmed that next year's term bill would break the stunning figure of $11,500, which caused even Eli to hesitate momentarily before purchasing an additional floor of the Taft Hotel. Worse still, the other Spiro in town, owner of Bulldog Pizza, sold the restaurant and moved away to pursue family interests. Even though Jeff admitted the pizza there was mediocre—especially in a town famous for pizza, with Pepe's and Sally's—he would miss the incomprehensible Greek accent on the phone and the long discourses on how great America was ("This is freedom! I can make egg pizzas, heart-shaped pizzas, shamrock pizzas! God bless America!"). Worse still, news came out of the Connecticut State Senate that they were indeed finally raising the drinking age to nineteen, effective over the summer.

"Nooooooo!" could be heard the collective cry of college students across the state.

Could you blame them if it seemed to them, a little, like their mound of legumes was crumbling, like their world was coming to an end? The syzygy was maybe a bust—at least that's what the government wanted you to believe—but something *was* happening here, in New Haven, on this early April afternoon.

"But what, exactly?" Jeff thought, who felt it but couldn't articulate it as he listened to Creedence Clearwater Revival on Maggie's Walkman because Iggy had taken his. Despite being stoned an awful lot at that time Jeff did remember clearly where he was when what really did feel like the end of the world began.

"Check out the fuzz over there," Samilla said to Tayvon, holding his hand with one hand and pointing with the other at the police officer. She was glad for the distraction because the conversation was getting heavy, Tayvon suddenly seeming unable to understand English as she explained to him that her feelings for him were waning. She too would remember clearly saying, at that moment, "Watch him pull his gun on that innocent Black man, just because he is Afro-American."

"You saying I must be wary?" Brother John said skeptically to the officer, who had pulled his gun on the fellow suspecting him of peddling donuts without a license. Nico, thrilled with John's work and profits, had gone to the bank to see about a loan for a second donut cart, maybe to put John in charge of it. Now why on earth would it occur to Nico to leave his license with John for the short while he would be gone, Brother John attempted to explain to the officer. This interaction was about to become ugly because Brother John was a man of principles, and his principles did not take kindly to having a weapon drawn on him without cause.

"I believe we need to stop," Jasmine had said to Jude on the bench beside Nico's cart a while earlier, expecting, correctly, that Jude would be relieved she was ending their brief affair because he really wasn't into it and was too much of a wuss to end it himself. The affair *was* interfering with his clarity of vision, but he really did hate to hurt people.

"Listen, children, do you hear that?" the fourth-grade teacher said who was leading her little flock on the annual field trip to the Yale campus. They were just crossing the street after getting donuts when that first gust of wind came and the temperature instantly plunged. The simultaneously plummeting barometric pressure generated a mournful howling sound, one that could chill your soul the way the freezing wind chilled your body, the kind of sound someone like Tayvon might make when for the first time in his life his heart was, inconceivably, being broken.

"Hey, look!" Thorn said to no one in particular, bending over to examine the tiny little bird twitching under that little bush. "What's going down here," he said, "little fella?" He got on his knees, reached in to pick up the little fella, noticed the injured wing. "Shh," Thorn comforted the bird, who had been blown out of the nest above by that strange sharp gust of wind and was shivering from the suddenly freezing temperature—it was April for crying out loud what was up with this Arctic plunge?—and of course the little fella was not comforted but scared out of his mind when the human being picked him up and uttered sounds that constituted the phrase, "It's okay, little fella, I got you." This phrase would become Thorn's trademark, as he uttered it every time he rescued a squadmate in combat and added to his pile of medals.

Thorn would always remember that little bird.

Everyone was worried about acid rain, but nobody saw *this* coming.

Very little could penetrate Zar's concentration, but that thunder, produced by dramatic bolts of lightning, got through. He had been studying in one of the cozy nooks in the Pierson steam tunnels. There were now several such nooks because Jude, after seeing F. Scott's original, had convinced her to create more, and this because "subterranean" was now a metaphor for a whole way of being. Well those two claps of thunder got down to that nook under the ground, and shook Zar from his Zar-thoughts. He made his way up and would always remember coming out into the courtyard as the first heavy wet slabs of snow began smacking his face, as he tried to make sense of the conflicting sensations of massive wind gusts, lightning and thunder, and what already seemed like a mountain of snow being dumped from the heavens.

He had thought so deeply about fire and earth, he had made great progress this year on his model of air, but as the frozen mounds descended upon him he realized he'd given no attention to the role that water played in, well, everything.

"Paranoia," Jude was explaining to Maggie in the dining hall. They had lingered after lunch as everyone else peeled away, caught up initially in the "Walkmans" versus "Walkmen" debate, then the question of when a mound of legumes becomes a mountain of legumes, then moving on to other weighty matters. "It begins when you try to make sense of things, to connect dots, to find the unity behind diversity. It creeps in with each connection you make. It is born in fear, of the unknown, of the lack of control, that is why it is often connected to the feeling that if you step out of line the men will come and take you away. But it is also the first step toward truth, and that is why it is essential for the advance—"

That was the moment those first thunderclaps exploded and they realized that the bright sunlight streaming through the high windows had disappeared and the world had turned nearly black outside.

It was an "adverse weather event," the government said, an extratropical cyclone maybe; "extreme" weather, unforeseeable. Had the evaporimeters malfunctioned? Who exactly had screwed up, mistaking as frontolysis what instead was frontogenesis? And this business about "unforeseeable." Where was it, before it was pounding upon them? Did it just materialize *ex nihilo*? But how could anything, much less something so enormous, come from absolutely nothing? But if it came from something, from somewhere, where was it and why was it unforeseen?

Everybody was worried about pesticides, about hazardous wastes, about nuclear holocaust, but was it possible to believe they could just *miss* the deadly combination of snow and lightning, of fire and ice, and two feet of snow on a spring day with wind gusts of 70 mph as the temperatures plummeted?

Paranoia indeed, Jude thought to himself many years later, at the start of the chain of events that culminated in his murder: for fun he had decided to look up a little meteorological history, got himself online to confirm what he remembered so clearly, he remembered being in the dining hall with Maggie when it began, but when he entered New Haven CT and April 6, 1982 he was returned a report that there had been zero precipitation that day.

The world may not have ended that day either, but something did, and it went all the way to the top.

=====

15.
embrace the irritation

It's not all about you, little Jeff-Jeff, though you may perhaps be forgiven for thinking it was.

You were the one to go see Beckett's *Not I* at Branford College, by yourself, the night before the last day of classes. Maggie made fun of you, and the mockery had that little harsh edge because she was maybe a little upset since you had just told her about your plans for the program in Florence for next spring. "Are you crazy?" Swill said when you described the play—a disembodied mouth monologuing about something that may or may not have happened. Tayvon might have gone with him but since Samilla had dumped him had been acting weird lately and thrown himself into a long-winded paper about Joyce. Lisa was busy with her own long-winded project of explaining to Tayvon the concept of monogamy. Jasmine had rehearsal, Maya was helping the attorney defending Brother John for his alleged assault on the police officer, and Samilla declined saying she really had no interest in seeing her nemesis, Naomi Wolf, even if she *was* starring as a gaping blabbing mouth.

And Jude had subjected him to a lecture on his new favorite

139

topic, inspired by his course with Doc this semester. "Coleworts and Caterpillars" was ostensibly about an unpublished manuscript by an obscure academic named Theodore Gale about that even more obscure 17th-century philosopher Ignoratio P. Elenchi, but in reality was about the idea that everything is connected to everything and everybody is everybody.

"Infrastructure is everything, little Jeff-Jeff," Jude said in that tone he adopted when in this mode. "Like the fine threads of mycelium beneath the ground supporting the fungus above. The wigglings of the earthworm that aerate the soil. Those secret non-sticky threads through the web that allow the spider to glide while its prey gets trapped. The physical plant that enables the institution, the hospital, the corporation, the university—the mind—to function. It is what you cannot see that underlies what you can. Infrastructure," the stock boy that Jude would soon become added, "is the linchpin of dining services: no system, no stock, nothing to cook, no food, everybody dies. No infrastructure, no structure."

"I would like to subscribe to your newsletter," Jeff said, backing away slowly, "but right now I'm late to the show. And by the way, I really hate when you call me that."

"What?"

"'Little Jeff-Jeff.' You know, I'm actually taller than you."

Jude shook his head in disbelief. "Have you learned nothing, little Jeff-Jeff?" Meaning thereby that—*obviously*—you never reveal your vulnerabilities to your enemy, who will now exploit them mercilessly.

Not I was pretty amazing, thought Jeff, Naomi's performance, and particularly the staging—the infrastructure: the blackened stage with the darkly dressed Auditor barely visible stage left, the powerful spotlight illuminating Naomi's blabbing red lips and white teeth. Reminded him of the tenebrism of his favorite artist, Caravaggio, the 16th-17th century Italian whose mastery of light and dark inspired the Baroque period in general and Jeff, in particular, to study his work in Florence next spring.

"The way he would transfix his subject in bright shafts of light amidst darkening shadows," Jeffrey explained years later to Debra, who had foolishly revealed she enjoyed the way he talked about art, "to express crucial moments and scenes, often of violent struggles, torture, death. Light and dark as the ultimate symbols, the ultimate violence, Caravaggio himself led the life he depicted, sheer creative brilliance mixed with disputes, brawls, manslaughter, murder." How could you not love a man who "unintentionally" murdered his opponent after a disputed game of *pallacorda*? "Something like tennis," Jeffrey explained, "and meanwhile this same man could then channel his misfitness, out-of-placeness, into paintings so profoundly expressing the human condition."

"Take 'The Beheading of Saint John the Baptist,' for example," Jeff said to Samilla at the Buttery after *Not I* in a way that might have been flirtatious if he weren't so thoroughly irritated by her constant insistence that White people were responsible for every awful thing ever, from the Holocaust to the Bay City Rollers. "You could hardly imagine a more dramatic, painful moment. Yet that scene, that act of evil, is lit by the light, while the background, the physical context of it all, the infrastructure, is in the dark."

"Infrastructure?" Samilla asked, sipping her chocolate shake.

"Sorry, been talking to Jude too much. The point is: so much evil, spotlight. But then, to the left, half-shadowed, the old woman looking on, her hands holding her head, in horror. But not just horror. Compassion. Helpless compassion." Jeff suddenly felt a wave of emotion. "Shouldn't she be covering her eyes? But no, she needed to see, to witness. She had to hold her head up. That is it. The helpless compassion. The human condition."

"Thank you for sharing," Samilla said, backing away with her milkshake, "but right now I have to return to the regular world."

Never mind Samilla, Jeff thought, shaking his head, that wasn't the main point. That point was the thought that the old woman in Caravaggio's painting reminded him of the Auditor in *Not I*, the woman was there to see and the Auditor was there to hear, to hear while the Mouth tried to make sense of it all, the Auditor heard and occasionally made gestures of—helpless compassion—but mostly just *listened*.

Don't we all need an Auditor?

Would be nice if Maggie were interested in these thoughts, but her interest in art was mostly in pretty paintings of flowers.

"Caravaggio was a tortured soul," Jeff was explaining to Iggy a few minutes later, who had appeared for his nightly cheeseburgers and sat next to him. "Rumors about his sexuality. Had female lovers, for sure, but also probably male lovers, maybe tried to hide them, got into brawls about them. Would hire prostitutes for models, male and female, fall in love or lust with them. You can imagine how intimate that relationship is, artist and model."

"Yeah?" Ig said after swallowing a large bite of cheeseburger, genuinely interested, but also understanding that comedy might have to trump the curiosity. "Tell me more."

Jeff didn't need the encouragement. "The female lovers might have been cover. Imagine having to suppress your identity, your true longings, to conform to oppressive social norms. That tension, the passions suppressed in the dark bursting out in disguised forms into light, no wonder he was the master of chiaroscuro. It all makes sense."

What a powerful moment.

Jeff pausing in this moment of insight, compassion, for this tortured figure from four centuries earlier, locking eyes with Ig, thinking to himself that Ig too struck him as a tortured soul, a beautiful soul but there was something in his public persona, the commitment to comedy, his guffaw was infectious but it was also off-putting, he could be so evasive, like this whole thing with Thorn, like there was some secret he didn't want anyone to approach—

Ig's tortured eyes were locked with Jeff's.

This moment was so close, his pal Jeff, El Jefe, was so close.

Iggy held that locked gaze for just those few moments then released one of his trademark belches, a bad boy of a belch, one filled with the stink of partly digested cheeseburger and maybe the first hints of diabetes.

"I still got it," he guffawed, but not I, Not I, the Mouth kept saying, it didn't happen to me, none of it, but of course all of it is happening, to all of us. Lying face down on the grass, a picnic with Maggie last summer on the grass at Tanglewood. At a supermarket, where we acquire food, the stock boy, the dining hall. Sitting on a mound in Croker's Acre, that one was hard to work in but just because you didn't see the connection didn't mean there wasn't one, you couldn't expect to grasp everything now could you? That time in court, Brother John in court, Caravaggio in court, on trial, *The Trial*, Tayvon held forth about Kafka the other day in the dining hall, damn ever since Samilla dumped him he had become a real scholar, Jeff-Jeff would like to subscribe to *his* newsletter, as did Lisa, who was maybe beginning to crack his nut. Whatever it was that happened to her in that field in April is the essence, start telling, there is an Auditor, there must be an Auditor, how could you go on unless you believed there was an Auditor? That time in court, that field in April, the courtyard in April, the Pierson courtyard in April, the blizzard in April … The blooming buzzing confusion, the buzzing in the skull, were they connected, did they click … Click click click click click …

"Coming through," Jude appeared in the tunnel from the direction of the squash court. The clicking noise was made by the surveyor's wheel he was pushing, also known as a hodometer, waywiser, or perambulator he would be happy to inform you whether or not you asked.

"Fun fact," he said, sitting down to join them. "The surveyor's wheel—also known as a hodometer, etc—was introduced in the 17th century, but a major upgrade in the 19th century introduced this little fellow here." He pointed at the doohickey where the grooved thingie locked with the thingamajig, driving the wheel. "These two elements are called a 'worm screw' and a 'worm gear.' The unit as a whole is called a 'worm.'"

"That *is* a fun fact," Jeff said with genuine enthusiasm as Ig tried to gather another belch but realized, with disappointment, that the recent masterpiece had left him depleted.

"I am telling you, children," Jude continued, "the worm is the key to everything. Digging away quietly beneath the ground, making all of this possible. There is a reason that Darwin's last book was about the worm. Listen to this poem." He cleared his throat and launched into something they could make absolutely no sense of.

"Is that by Darwin?" Jeff asked.

"Was Darwin a poet?" Jude asked annoyed as if they should know.

"Was that poetry?" both Jeff and Ig said and laughed.

"Honestly I do not know why I talk to you people sometimes. It is by Anne Sexton."

"And who is that?" Jeff asked.

"Killed herself."

Both Jeff and Iggy shuddered. "Right-o," Ig said, "but the

question was who she was, not how she died."

"In this case that is the most pertinent fact about her."

"Fine," Jeff moved on. "So what are you doing with that thing, anyway?"

"Ah," Jude said, getting up to order a veggie sub but then getting distracted at the counter and not coming back to explain. Working the counter was their classmate Charlie, that weird kid who mostly kept to himself. Jude had a fascination with him, initially because of his last name—"Morphogen," which Jude seemed to think was also the key to everything—but also because of God knows whatever it was they talked about.

What Jude was doing with the contraption, it turned out, was measuring the steam tunnels. As to why he was measuring the steam tunnels they wouldn't find out for a few more days, the final days, as classes were coming to an end, reading period was soon to begin, and their sophomore year was hurtling toward its end.

The end of the academic year was always intense, packed with assignments, wrappings up, grand conclusions, culminating performances. Prof. Vann Woodward won the Pulitzer for his book on the Civil War, but that was nothing compared to the civil war newly brewing between Samilla and Black. This latter began during their public argument at the Afro-American Cultural Center after the talk by Kwame Toure, then spilled over into the Pierson Dining Hall over the next several meals, and only reached its initial reconciliation during some massive armistice sex at Black's off-campus digs.

Zar made great progress in these final days.

After a days-long session where he consumed nothing but amphetamines he got his model of air, of gases, near completion. There *was* that weird parallel with his geophysics model from freshman year though: it all worked except for one little tiny piece, a dangler, a rough corner, it needed a little smoothing, that's all, he could still treat the theory as more or less complete, but God was that another irritant, the kind of irritant that maybe eventually would produce a pearl (Jude tried to encourage him) once Zar's mollusk mind worked it over some more. Zar, finally ready to eat something, had come along to the new pizza joint Jeff found downtown during one of his new-pizza forays. Now Zar, who had developed nearly complete models of both earth and air and who understood better than anyone that, in the end, everything must fit, nodded.

"This is no accident, mollusk man," Jude continued. "Those two little irritants are going to be connected. And once you see the connection, you shall have your pearl. Until then, embrace the irritation."

To embrace the irritation …

Maybe *that* is the human condition, what it's all about, Jeff-Jeff. But of course it's stressful to live with irritation, when the end of the academic year is upon you, with the assignments, the speakers, the summer planning. Oh once you've gotten through it there will be the gathering at Eli's Penzance house, that wonderful weekend on that wonderful beach, sneaking away to watch the Islanders grow their dynasty against the Canucks, and then you'll work at the reunions again, and then it will be summer. But until then the pressure was building, the last day of classes was here, there was Pierson's birthday to celebrate in the courtyard, but to get there you had to relieve the pressure, the growing steam pressure, it was necessary to blow off that steam …

How could something you knew was perfectly safe be somehow so terrifying?

The pitch dark.

The familiar made unfamiliar.

The crowds, the screams in the darkness.

The running, somehow the sheer physical action of running that made your heart pump and your lungs expand and your adrenaline flow, merely by putting your body into flight mode that impacted your mind into thinking you were in flight, if you were in flight then you were in danger, you were running from danger in the dark and the screams you were screaming, if you were screaming you must be in terror. You ran through the steam tunnel packed with others running in the dark, nearly pitch dark, there was a thin glowing stripe on the floor you could follow, luminescent, Jude had mapped out and measured the tunnels, F. Scott had designed the luminescent strip, together they had laid out the path. You descended into the steam tunnel at entryway D, you went left, you followed the strip around and under the college, or you followed the masses of people ahead of you in the dark, they had installed decibel meters at key points that glowed their readings as you passed them in the dark, the instructions were clear: run and scream and run and scream, these were no longer the steam tunnels but the blow-off-steam tunnels, you blew off steam as you ran and screamed in the dark then followed the strips up the stairs, through entryway C, you emerged from the depths and the dark into the light, the light of a beautiful early spring day, it was Friday April 23 and classes were over and it was Abraham's birthday and it was a bright afternoon with a balmy 65 degrees at the end of your sophomore year and you can finally stop screaming and celebrate ...

Have a summer one and all,
And we'll meet back here in the fall

part 3
junior year

=====

fall

1.

the bubble

It was a rough summer, for the world.

The Falklands War ended, but not before some thousand people had died. A Louisiana plane crash killed 154. In Japan rain and mudslides washed away roads and bridges killing some 300. Maybe Jeff was onto something that afternoon at the fishmonger's at Penzance, where he and Maggie were housesitting. He was waiting to order some salmon and watching the lobster tank, the lobsters with bound claws all crawling on top of one another, each trying to get to the top of the heap, to get out of the death trap that was the tank.

"Now if that isn't us," he said to the woman in front of him.

"Pardon?" she said, then turned back and ordered a dozen for her weekend guests.

Welcome back, you're a junior ...

Or *junior*, as Doc put it, with a cynical emphasis on the word to reinforce the wretched status the former sophbores might wrongly think they had left behind. "And as for the *juniors*," he peered at them through his yellow lenses on day one of his upper-level class, "Nevergreen or Never Green?", "you might want to bring your tweezers. Things are going to get stressful in here." Doc had just been discussing trichotillomania, whose sufferers feel compelled to pluck out their hair when stressed. Black, taking the class because of its focus on that wacked out college where he had wasted a year, found this condition hilarious. Lisa was to the

149

contrary horrified, while Ren was too busy realizing that Lisa was the perfect woman to form an opinion. Perhaps Lisa might have noticed Ren's subsequent ignoring of her if she weren't so busy *not* ignoring Tayvon, who by this point had also realized that Lisa was the perfect woman and he therefore needed no other.

Fun fact, for those at home: Mike Brady, paradigm papa on *The Brady Bunch*, had hooked up with Mickey Lubitch and sired the Boy in the Plastic Bubble, in the 1976 television movie of that name. Man is it uncomfortable today to see a man so obviously gay play a paradigm papa pretending he is something other than what God made him (although Ig's "gay-Mike-Brady" routine *was* a memory-maker). And while the movie itself was a disaster, we do have to thank it for one thing: the expression "being in the bubble" and its cognates.

And so it was a rough summer for the world, but summers end, and it was time to return to The Bubble for junior year. Upperclassmen (and women!) now, it was time to get serious. The Bubble it may have been, but the real world was pressing hard, like a nail, trying to penetrate.

=====

2.

they've got your back

This was going to be Beamie's year.

"That one," Horace whispered, suggesting that Beamie's first target of the new year might be the ungainly Pierson sophomore who had wandered into Tuesday Night Club. Horace was the sophomore Tayvon, minus the class.

"Really?" Beamie said, appreciating the team effort for his quest but trying to conceal his disappointment in the details.

"Just trying to increase your odds, buddy," Horace explained, "to ever so slightly more than zero."

Swill, chewing his gum furiously, shuddered at the thought of Beamie and the sophomore together. Normally he would also have emitted a cigar puff but he had given up that unpleasant habit and replaced it with another, the furious chewing of gum. In this case it was a Swedish nicotine gum awaiting FDA approval, obtained via one of the Russian pharmaceuticals Eli or his father owned. It turned out Swill had feelings: Maya's remark to him last Christmas—"There's something about your face with that long burning phallus sticking out of it"—had really sunk in.

Nonstarter, as it turned out: by the time Beamie screwed up enough courage even to look in the sophomore's direction she had pre-pre-rejected him and made her escape.

Things needless to say went differently for Tayvon, speaking of. "*Habba-do-gaggedy*," he had exclaimed on arriving on campus, "tonight, my friends, and every night!" In this way he declared both his ambition for the year and some spanking new vernacular for it. He had spent the summer in Philadelphia working with disabled kids and there discovered the radio personality (today "shock jock"), the Greaseman. Grease told outrageous stories about his many adventures with his *Latin loop-de-lou*, with whom he liked to engage in *habba-do-gaggedy*, using his *manly hydraulics* to get her to make all the noise she normally made as they traveled to *Shangri-La*, tonight, my friends, and every night! (At the fifteenth reunion the gang would debate whether the term *gobble-do-gee* was Greaseman lingo for oral sex or just their own Grease-inspired creation; nobody could remember.)

"It's just stupid," Jasmine said at brunch the next Sunday morning.

"Juvenile," Samilla agreed.

"Demeaning," Lisa concurred, though of two minds about the issue. The way these guys talked about women and sex *was* stupid, juvenile, and demeaning, yet there was something awfully hot about the term *gobble-do-gee*.

"They're gross," Isabela said, who had resolved to put herself out there more this year. That albatross of a virginity of hers was making it impossible for her to function normally, much less as a meathead. If she *was* a meathead, that is; she hardly felt part of this group, but she was part of no other. Well, maybe slaying the albatross would help, though she clearly hadn't thought that through. Calling all the guys of your acquaintance gross, no matter how accurate, was probably not the best way to attract one.

"What's going on?" Jeff yelled to Black a few days later over the blasting strains of the first major college party of the semester, a Morse Motown night. The state drinking age now nineteen, they had to be carded before gaining entry—how annoying.

"That is some serious brick house," Black yelled back. His off-campus arrangement hadn't worked out—he wouldn't elaborate—and as Jeff had roomed with Beamie he had been stashed back in a suite with Ren and Fregoli, who was also back. ("The looney bin," as he referred to it.) No longer roommates, Jeff and Black began to rekindle their friendship, beginning with Jeff's peace offering to hang with him at his biggest night of the year. (Samilla had refused to come due to the White capitalist exploitation of the Motown artists, debate over which had produced a short-lived moment of their not being on speaking terms, which typically preceeded a journey to *Shangri-La*.)

"What is?" Jeff yelled, a little distracted by his annoyance with Maggie who had also declined to come because she was so annoying.

"That is," Black pointed to a large African-American senior, though why he pointed her out was not clear. Maybe it was because he liked the term "brick house," because it reminded him of houses, and thus of housing policy, and thus of Samilla who had such heinous opinions about housing policy. Trying to understand how or why that aggravation with her got his hydraulics going so was enough to put someone in the looney bin.

Speaking of housing, there were some developments for Brother John.

On the plus side, he'd received merely probation for his altercation with the police officer and the city managed to place him in a decent residential facility. On the plus side, too, he was feeling so good over the summer, what with the roof over his head and the daily coffee cart crowd, that he made a major life decision. "I'll trust myself," he said to himself, cheerfully, on the first day he went cold turkey on his meds.

Jeff, meanwhile, ruminating over Maggie, could only generate the following response to Black's remark, "Brunette and brunet, eh, buddy?" In so doing he managed to both praise and mock the recently released single by Paul and Stevie that both Jeff and Black both despised and loved.

"You know it, J.-man," Black said, but his former roommate had wandered off in pursuit of beer. *Either we be laid or we be crawlin'*, Jeff thought as he showed his hand-stamp at the bar for the warm foamy stuff that passed for beer. *Or maybe both*, he thought, if annoying Maggie would stop being annoyed with him for his being annoyed with her. By this point, nearly two years in, the sex had declined to the "maybe tomorrow?" phase, as she had said again last night. Well, it was tomorrow, and she had declined to come.

"Hullay," Fregoli said, having materialized next to him at the bar.

It was freaky how Fregoli did that, materializing out of nowhere.

"Hey welcome back," Jeff said warmly enough, or rather yelled over the Temptations' "Ain't Too Proud to Beg." "I heard you were back on campus. How are you doing?"

"Fantabulous," Fregoli said, and meant it too.

But if Jeff were inclined to pursue the conversation he was immediately distracted. Twins Chastity and Temperance were dancing past him barely wearing little red minidresses, followed closely by Eli who was either chasing or being lured, followed closely by Beamie who was trying to keep up without spilling the three beers he was carrying because Eli had told him to get the beer and he maybe would assist Beamie in obtaining one of those fine fillies. (For the record, not a chance.)

Running behind Beamie was Ren, his ears flapping, scribbling in his notebook.

Would be nice if Maggie were here, Jeff thought, turning away to see that Fregoli had evaporated as quickly as he had materialized.

As Stevie Wonder's "Signed, Sealed, Delivered" came on there was some hubbub in the center of the dance floor. Jeff pushed through the crowd, it was a warm early September evening, steaming with all the dancing bodies in there, God he'd forgotten how hot those twins were and damn, Eli. They had installed a strobe light and disco ball in the Morse dining hall, and the combination of warm beer and steaming bodies and hot twins and loud music and flashing lights was making him dizzy.

But he pushed through and came to the middle of the floor, where a circle had formed. He knew some of the folks, well not knew, those faces were familiar from classes, from intramurals between the colleges (Jeff was captain of Pierson's duckpin bowling team). Then there were the strangers' faces, the people that populate your campus and provide anonymity and possibility. A lot of them were here tonight, and a circle had formed around Croc and the woman he was dating, the goalie of the women's ice hockey team who was a brick house herself. That she could bust some moves on the dance floor was no surprise, given the moves she could bust on the ice.

But Croc?

They had this synchronized thing going on, as she did this and he did this, and she did that and he did that, and damn they were smooth.

"I remember it as if it were yesterday," Jeffrey said to Debra many years later.

"You generally can't remember what happened yesterday."

"Then I remember it better than yesterday," Jeffrey said, as did everyone who was there.

Croc busted some move but in so doing busted a muscle. He dropped to the ground clutching his rear and emitted a howl, *a howl*, that Jeffrey could still do a fair rendition of, much to Debra's dismay. That howl was heard throughout the entire Yale campus that night and throughout the football season, and into the following season. The mighty Croc had struck out—and been struck from the roster.

"You okay, big guy?" Maggie asked him, visiting him at the hospital the next day.

"Maggie," the big guy blubbered. "I let everybody down."

"The team will be fine, Croc," she assured him, stroking his arm. "They've got your back."

She was wrong.

=====

3.
why did that sound so ominous

Even with Croc out of action most of the gang made the trip up for the game at Brown a few days later, to watch their team's shameful defeat by the university named, as they enthusiastically chanted at the game, after the color of shit.

Taking the sting off, if only slightly, was their gathering afterward at the famous Crook Point Bascule Bridge. This poignant symbol of urban decay was an abandoned, rusting railroad drawbridge, left eternally in the open position to allow boats passage up the Seekonk River. Ig directed them there, as he'd had a rendezvous at the isolated spot the night before—"What? What kind of rendezvous?" Tayvon asked with a nod to the structure, which, undeniably, resembled an enormous erect Black phallus—"A perfectly wholesome one," Ig answered with a guffaw, "I was purchasing some weed." Apparently true, because on the evening after the game he did demonstrate, possibly for the first time, that what was his was theirs. The weed was relaxing, which was good because the sight of him climbing that monster would otherwise have been nerve-racking.

"Making a memory, people," Ig called down as he scampered up. "It would also make a memory," Jeff observed, "if he fell and died." "You shush," Maggie shushed him.

Also taking the sting off the defeat, at least for Maggie and Jeff, was that with their accommodations in the livingroom of Maggie's high school friend Gaby, they could cross a Brown sofa off their list. Taking it off even more was the Dartmouth weekend, six weeks later. With Croc finally back in the lineup in a limited capacity the Elis eked out a 22-21 win while Jeff and Maggie eked out the penultimate notch on the Ivy League belt on the sofa of Maggie's friend, Allison.

155

"Only Princeton left," Jeff exhaled quietly in the darkened living-room afterwards. For those keeping score, Maggie and Jeff had made a trip to Philadelphia over the summer when they realized that her fall soccer schedule conflicted with the Penn game. Tayvon, living in a Penn dorm while getting acquainted with the Greaseman, spent that weekend in D.C. with his own *Lisa loop-de-lou* while they took care of business on his sofa. "With still three semesters to go. And one more game there, next year. I think we've got this in the bag, Mag."

Maggie snuggled into him but expressed some unusual caution. "You know," she whispered—Allison was in her bedroom a few feet away—"I don't like to count my chickens before they hatch."

Why did that sound so ominous, Jeff thought. "I don't think confidence is the same as counting chickens," he whispered back.

"I don't know. It feels like—I don't know, cockiness. And anyway—"

"What?"

She paused. "It's only two semesters."

That was a pregnant pause, Jeff thought. But there was no denying that his semester abroad in Florence was indeed looming over them.

Why did the word looming *feel so ominous?* Jeff thought.

"Maybe we should drive down to Princeton right now," he whispered.

"It's entirely out of the way," she whispered back but in the dimmest of light—Allison had a Minnie Mouse nightlight—Jeff could see she was smiling.

"Priorities, babe," he urged.

"We don't have a sofa there."

"Didn't you say one of your ten million high school friends was at Princeton?"

"I did. Mairav."

"So?"

"She transferred to Penn this year."

"Ack. Without consulting us?"

"She's selfish that way."

"You need some better friends."

"Or really just one more friend. At Princeton."

They laughed. A nice moment.

Wait, was that a sign of trouble, that you notice the nice moments?

"All right, problem solved," Jeff said, shaking off the thought about the nice moment. "Jude."

"What about Jude?" In the dim light Jeff could see she had scrunched up her brow, perhaps contemplating being incautious.

"He has a friend at Princeton. An Indian guy. He visited last year for a weekend."

"So?"

"He'll have a sofa."

"So we ask Jude to ask his friend if we can have sex on his sofa?"

Jeff hesitated. "Yes?"

The scrunch became a furrow. "And how would we get in touch with Jude? Where even is he this weekend?"

Jude had not made the trek to Hanover with the gang, having some strange theory that watching large men piling on to move a piece of animal skin was somehow less valuable than, say, pretty much any other conceivable human activity.

"Technicality," Jeff whispered gently, yielding, because this one was hard to reply to in those days before cell phones, as he also yielded to Maggie's declining his suggestion to compensate for deferring Princeton by doing a double at Dartmouth. It was late, they were not likely to sleep well on this narrow sofa, they had a three-hour drive back to New Haven tomorrow, and anyway Maggie (and also Jeff) had a boatload of work to do now that they were juniors—odd how after all those very good reasons against more *habba-do-gaggedy* Jeff remained in favor.

"Are you as committed to our sofa glory as I am," he whispered to her after her breathing had become regular, after she had already begun the night of uneasy sleep that lay ahead of them.

=====

4.

two birds one stone

It was a good year for the vernacular.

"Hullay," Jude said as he took his seat for lunch. Since being promoted to stock manager he had largely been working during meals, so this was a rare occasion.

"Hullay," Ig said as he took his seat for dinner, having just returned from New York City for reasons to be revealed.

"Hullay," even Maya said as she sat next to Ig, having accompanied him to New York for reasons to be revealed.

"Hullé," Black said with that edge in his voice, preferring the alternate spelling.

"He said 'hullay'?" Jude had asked at the last Tuesday Night Club, when Jeff had filled them in on his fleeting encounter with Fregoli at Motown Night. "Like h-u-l-l-a-y?"

"Well he didn't spell it out. He just materialized, said it, and disappeared."

"Maybe it's the Canadian thing," Tayvon suggested. "Hell-eh?"

"Is Fregoli Canadian?" Maya said.

"Is Fregoli an earthling?" Jude asked.

"Be nice, friend," Maggie insisted. "It's allowed, you know."

"I say that shit's with an accent," Black asserted. "H-u-l-l-é."

"No," Jude said.

"What do you mean, 'no'?"

"I mean opposite of yes. What kind of question is that?"

"I mean who the hell are you to just say no?"

Beamie shuddered, remembering last year's debacle with— wait, what was her name?

Jude had no problem just saying no—to drugs, and to Black.

"No," Jude just said, and left it at that.

The "hullay" spelling stuck as the word became their motto, their greeting, their shibboleth. It was, after all, some fantabulous slang, as Jude had observed before dictating its spelling. Even the women got into this one, and were the first to start stretching it.

"Hellay," Maggie said, taking the seat Maya had saved for her at another talk by Gloria Steinem.

"Hulloo," Jasmine said, joining some of the gang prior to the first Pierson Cabaret of the year.

"Hoolay," Maya said on taking her seat at breakfast or lunch or dinner.

"Huhhhh—" Samilla said, sliding in next to Black at the Alexander Haig talk they were using as foreplay, "—lay!"

"Huhhhh—" Black corrected her, "—lé," already feeling the sparks that would be flying between them after, and possibly during, Haig's talk.

"That," Jude said in the Lower Courtyard outside the next Tuesday Night Club when Samilla re-created her dramatic "hullay," "is one hella hullay."

Beamie was inspired by Jude's comment, or his fourth Tall Boy, or both. "Hul-lay," he started to sing, "hullay-ay ..." They all looked at him, simultaneously recognizing the closing melody of the Beatles' "Hello, Goodbye," realizing that the loser could sing, and grasping that he had just discovered a whole new vein.

They'd find him a woman yet.

"Hul-lay," Ig started to rasp along in that sea shanty voice.

"Hul-lay, hullay-ay," others joined in with the verbal percussion.

"Some Rundgren," Ig changed direction with that rasp, wisely identifying the tune because otherwise no one had a chance, and launched into the song, "'Hullay It's Me'..."

"How about some Doors?" Swill offered, sticking his gum on the banister to the upper story of the Lower Courtyard, and began to chant the song, "'Hullay, I Love You' ..."

"Oh I got one," Jeff began, but then stopped himself—*stopped time*, he thought to himself, weirdly.

"I was about to sing the line from the Tom song 'Martha,'" Jeffrey told Debra years later, "He's calling up an old flame from like

159

forty years before to—"

"—reminisce about their relationship," Debra smiled gently. "I know."

Jeffrey nodded. "Right, well you know, I suddenly understood that instead of 'Martha' I was going to say 'Hullay, Maggie,' like it would be out of my control, I just saw it happening, like it was predestined. Remind me to tell you about this time travel story, this guy—"

"Jeffrey, you had me read 'By His Bootstraps' a few years ago."

"Recommended by—"

"Ren, who had read it in Doc's class, freshman year."

"Damn you're good." Jeffrey shook his head.

"I am. Should I be worried about you?"

"I'm happy to call a doctor if you think I should."

"You're referring to yourself, I assume?"

"I may stink at medicine but the family rate can't be beat."

Debra shook *her* head. "Anyway, the story?"

"Right. I knew that if I tried to sing the song 'Martha' it would just come out 'Maggie.' And then had the weirdest sensation, it was like I was in the future, looking back—"

"Like from now."

"Like from now. Like I was talking to you as I am and looking back, and I was calling up Maggie years later like Tom was calling Martha, and I guess what I'm saying is that in that moment I knew my time with Maggie was limited. But weirdly I also knew that it would be all right, that betterness would come of it all. Ren was always quoting these lines from Doc, 'The conclusion is implicit in the premises,' 'Your soul manifests itself in the soul of your beloved,' and in that moment, I understood them. The thing with Maggie made me who I was, loving Maggie made me who I was, and who I was, whoever I was, would find the person I was really meant to be with, and it would be the thing with Maggie which made me the person who *that* person was meant to be with. Are you following? Tom closes with that devastating line, that unfinished thought, that memory, of course he remembers because that paved the way to his soulmate, years later, now, the real deal ..."

"Are you crying?" she offered him a tissue from the box always nearby.

"No," he said, taking it, dabbing an eye.

She smiled at him. "And you had all that in the, what, maybe two seconds it took to change your mind about singing that song?"

Jeffrey nodded.

Every moment of our lives contains every other moment of our lives.

"Hullay, once more, hullay," Beamie began to sing when he saw Jeff hesitate, with all the drama of the Neil Diamond "Hello Again" original and all the feeling of the four Tall Boys in his veins. When no one stepped in he made the decision to continue, his eyes closing as he began to croon: "Hullay, once more, hullay ..."

So the loser *really* could sing.

But seriously, Neil Diamond—the singer they all hated? Or was it loved to hate? Or was it loved to hate to love? However anyone really felt about the man's music it surely was forbidden to admire it in public. And there was Beamie doing Diamond, with feeling, his voice somehow as perfect for the bass-baritone as it had been for Garfunkel's angelic "Bridge Over Troubled Water" the year before, and clearly loving every moment of it, losing himself in the song, and—Jesus Christ, were those tears dripping down his cheeks from his closed eyes?

"Too far?" Beamie asked in a now quiet voice.

"Hyellay!" Tayvon arrived with Lisa's hand in one hand and a Tall Boy in the other, but instantly grasped, in the silence and uncomfortable faces all around, that something was happening here. "Hyellow?"

"You, Sam," Maggie said softly. "People need to hear you."

One other person among them was also weeping, with a swelling heart. Later, after the tragedy, there would be debate over who was responsible for the fatal idea, but maybe everybody was. Jasmine saw that Isabela was moved and mentioned it to Maya and Maggie, who had both noticed themselves; Maggie mentioned it to Jeff who couldn't believe his good luck in obtaining such choice gossip, then couldn't believe his bad luck in being forbidden from using that gossip in any choice way. But the fact was that that gossip ultimately couldn't be contained any more than a perfect belch could remain in Ig's gut, or the water Zar was studying could refrain from finding its level.

It was out of their hands, and really, it couldn't be more obvious. Two birds with one stone.

The loser who had gotten laid precisely once—nobody knew the story but Maggie, who hadn't told a soul, but *he* knew it, including the details he didn't share with Maggie, how his mother had walked in at the key moment on junior prom night—"Don't mind me, I'm just putting away your underwear," she had said, opening his dresser drawer—"Ma!" he'd exclaimed, rapidly losing enthusiasm if you get the drift, "I'm kinda busy here!"—"Oh, I'll just be a minute, dear," she said and had carried on, *she had carried on*—he had been laid exactly once (or maybe just a half) and had spent the subsequent three and a half years in pursuit of his second lay (or maybe completing the first). And now here was someone who was perfect for him—she was female—his requirements were minimal—she was also quite nice looking and, most of all, she was obviously a virgin herself and desperately in need of resolving that situation.

Beamie and Isabella—"We hadn't thought of it earlier," Maggie explained to the investigating officer after the tragedy, "because we were all, I don't know, like siblings"—but now it suddenly seemed not merely obvious but necessary.

But now how to bring it about?

=====

5.
how does it happen

Speaking of pseudo-sibling romantic relationships, Lisa and Tayvon, wow.

She, all had noticed, had lost her original dourness now that she was getting some. He, all had noticed, had lost the need to conquer a new woman tonight and every night. In fact both of them were as focused on their work as they were on each other. Tayvon was already sketching ideas for next year's senior thesis, while Lisa was underway on her campaign, as Editor in Chief, to turn the *Yale Daily News* into a serious rag. There was just one kink in her plan for journalistic dominance at Yale then, later, the world. This was the arrival of Anne Applebaum, a new Pierson freshman who arrived on campus along with her significant talent.

"There's room enough for both of you," Maggie tried to persuade Lisa during an emergency run to Durfee's Sweet Shoppe. Word was that a shipment of Reese's Pieces was in, and given the demand—the recent movie *E.T.* had made them popular—they had to move quick. "You don't have to sabotage her."

"Oh, my dearest Maggie, who sees the best in everyone," Lisa answered receiving the sweets that would fuel tonight's scheming, "there will be *more* room for me once she is destroyed."

In contrast to Maggie was Maya, who saw the worst in everyone, justifiably. Archaic patriarchies, oppressive labor practices, bigoted immigration policies, there was just so much nastiness and so few resources. It would not be accurate to say that she hated men, but, you know, she hated men, whom she blamed for much of it. All this made it that much more puzzling why Maya found herself with her eye on, of all people, Ignacio.

"No. Really? Ig?" Maggie said over lunch at Viva Zapatas, on the house in gratitude for Maya's helping the owners through the onerous local immigration system.

"I know, right?" Maya answered. "We're like total opposites. Woman-man, student-athlete. Indian-, wait, where is he from again?"

"Central America somewhere. I can never nail down the specific place."

"So, Indian-Central American. And, I don't know, non-partier-partier."

"How about 'classy and refined' versus, I don't know, 'Iggy'?" Maggie smiled.

"Hyellay!" Maya laughed, using the expression that included, among its many meanings, "You've nailed *that* one on the head!"

But that was only on the surface, perhaps, because there was more to him than the overt grossness. He was smarter than he let on: punctuating the antics were thoughtful comments, a keen sense of politics, and even his humor, when not that of a thirteen-year-old boy, had an intelligent edge. And of course his Segal paper, which had gotten passed around after the debacle, was really impressive, and add to the above Ig's sweetness and sensibility, and it was clear that there was more to the man than his occasionally public bowel movements.

And then there was that voice, that croak.

Was Maya alone in finding it, well, enchanting?

Yes, but you know, it only takes one.

Three-thirty in the morning, singing in the Pierson courtyard, "(What's So Funny 'Bout) Peace, Love and Understanding," the Elvis Costello cover, that song was perfect sung slow in that rasp late at night in a courtyard. Okay so it had woken her up, she thought, cracking open her window to hear better while other windows were being slammed shut. She looked out from her darkened room: Ig was sitting in the maple tree in the courtyard, had climbed up near the top, was singing to the moon. Somehow the song had segued to his favorite, envisioning world peace …

Maya would later encourage Ig to sing up on a stage, at the Pierson Cabaret.

Though the mass opposition to this idea didn't surprise her its ferocity did, and while her initiative did not obtain its aim, betterness did come of it, as we'll see. At any rate before initiating this initiative she had to crack the nut of, well, cracking his nut. She who could bring down archaic patriarchies and oppressive bigotry could not understand why Ig didn't seem to be picking up on any of her cues. You know, the lingering around him, the casual touching of his arm, the laughing at his jokes (even the juvenile ones), the standing at certain angles to emphasize her considerable breasts, her finally saying, sitting there in the maple tree with him, "Don't you want to do a little—" here she hesitated, but finally capitulated—"*habba-do-gaggedy* with me?"

"Hyellay!" Ig responded with a laugh, using the expression that included, among its many meanings, "Man I never saw *that* one coming!"

But that laugh was deflective, and the way he looked at her— was it fear? A deer in the headlights? The look of a man who, no matter how hard he tried, could not get the puck in the goal?

"Honestly," Maggie said over lunch at Gentree's, on the house in gratitude for Maya's helping their staff through the onerous local immigration system. She was struggling to help Maya without betraying any confidences. "I think he may have some self-esteem issues."

"Really?" Maya answered. "How could that be? He seems entirely comfortable in his own skin. Entirely comfortable *revealing* his skin."

They laughed, neither able to count the number of times they had seen him naked.

What Maya was wondering, instead, was whether it was just *her*.

Maya had no deficit of self-esteem herself, though if there were cracks it was with respect to her looks. Maya had seen the women Ig would sometimes slip away from parties with: they weren't the pretty types, in fact they really were the very plain type. That wasn't much competition—she hated herself thinking this way—but was she less attractive than these types? If he had a type at all; it was actually clear that Ig was not really into the women he was going with.

"I'm not really about the relationship thing," he explained to her there in the maple tree once he regained his ability to speak. "More the love 'em and leave 'em type."

"Okay," Maya said.

"What?" Ig started blinking again, back in the headlights.

"I said okay. Whoever said anything about a relationship?"

Was he sweating, on this cool early fall night?

"It doesn't happen like that," he said.

"How does it happen then?"

How *does* it happen, indeed.

It's simple: one thing leads to another, this happens then that happens, in a word, shit happens and that's pretty much all you can say—and all Doc did say, in the book he was just completing on the philosopher David Hume: Stercus Accidit, *or Unnecessary Connections*—and somehow what happened here, with Maya and Ig, sitting in a tree, t-a-l-k-i-n-g, is that one thing led to another and off they went that very morning to catch the train to New York City to observe the United Nations' first International Day of Peace. This irenic commemoration occurred three days after a massacre in a refugee camp across the globe, and prior to the massacres of millions that would occur in global military activities in the decades after.

"You've got to love the United Nations," Maya said with her sharp eye for the futility of human endeavors, watching the proceedings.

"A man can dream," Ig answered, and promptly launched into "Imagine" to underscore the point. Maya, more impressed by that "singing"—"You know you really should sing at the Cabaret," she suggested in the U.N. hallway—than by the U.N. itself, had at least to admit that a man can, after all, dream.

"Be that as it may," Maya said when Ig had finished with a deep bow, "you must admit that the United Nations is a joke, a really really bad joke."

"There is nothing funny," Ig said with a sudden sternness, "about harmony, affection, and mutual comprehension," then cracked up, that wide-grinned guffaw that came from deep within, from the diaphragm, from the sternum, from the bowel damn it, from his inner soul then spread outward. When Ig laughed like that the world laughed with him, like a virus infecting everything it came near, like the plague but without the oozing sores. When Ig laughed it sent shockwaves across the world, not unlike those threatened by the nuclear weapons some 30,000 women (including Maya) would be protesting at RAF Greenham Common just three months later, except bringing not immediate annihilation but a sweet dose of harmony, affection, and mutual comprehension.

=====

6.
it is a little hard to take you seriously in your little short shorts

"I have big fucking news," Black interrupted as he slid into his seat with his dinner tray. In fact he had some big news *about* fucking that he had no intention of sharing; this thing with Samilla had reached some interesting places, but if he wouldn't kiss and tell then he surely wouldn't do *that* and tell.

"Bigger than Johnny D's arrest for selling coke?" Eli said skeptically, the only one of them who would ever own a DeLorean, the conversation having already examined whether the sting was entrapment and whether entrapment was morally justifiable.

"Bigger than Ireland finally decriminalizing homosexuality?" Lisa said skeptically, who had earlier critiqued the initiative for being both too little (setting the age of consent for homosexual acts at twenty-one where that for heterosexual acts was seventeen) and too late (by *centuries*).

"Check and check," Black said as he examined the amorphous mass that was dinner. He would have to have *another* word with the devil-man who now seemed to be running the dining hall about how a place that cost twelve grand a year could serve such smeg as this. "Hey, you all right over there, homeboy?"

Zar had picked up and was staring at a glass of water. "No, no way," he muttered, probably not in response to Black's question.

"Black," Beamie said, "you really ought to subscribe—"

"Check it, B.-man," Black interrupted. "I have big fucking news. Aren't you all going to ask what the fuck it is?"

"What the fuck is it?" several responded wearily.

This did not include Jeff, who was brooding because something was up with Maggie, there'd been some bickering lately and she wouldn't talk about it, she was spending all this time writing in her diary, did it have to do with his pending departure—

"I'm glad you asked!" Black exclaimed, then dropped the bomb. "Michael has a new album coming. In precisely forty fucking days. Forty days and forty nights."

"How many hours would that be?" Swill snarked.

"You think I wouldn't have worked that shit out if they had announced the exact hour of release?"

"Hey assholes!" Iggy affectionately exclaimed, then launched into "ABC," joined by Tayvon who stood up, pulled off his shirt and did some Mick Jagger—which reminded everyone that it had been like forever since he'd last done that.

"That's awesome, Black," Maggie said, who'd been quiet to this point, touching his arm.

"That is awesome, man," Black looked at her hand, then looked up. "You know what this means?"

"Zounds!" Beamie said. "It means you're going to be insufferable for the next six weeks." He stood up to bus his tray and escape back to the library.

"Damn straight I'll be insufferable!" Black shouted after him as he left. "We all have work to do, people," he returned his gaze to the table. "We have to get ready."

Getting ready involved, at minimum, listening to every Michael Jackson album to date, in order, then repeat. The Motown records, starting with *Got To Be There*, which peaked at 14 in the U.S. charts, America was not yet ready for Michael, Black explained. Then there was *Ben*, that hit number 5, Black had this one on 8-track, don't get Samilla started on the phasing out of 8-tracks which she believed was due to racism. *Music & Me*, *Forever Michael*, more racism in America (Samilla said) was responsible for those only peaking at 82 and 101 respectively, one of her rare claims with which, regrettably, Black agreed. Jeff's suggestion that perhaps the albums didn't do well because they weren't, you know, good, fell on very deaf ears. Meanwhile *Off the Wall* hit number 3, because not even the rampant racism Samilla saw everywhere could withstand the greatness of Michael.

Speaking of Samilla and deaf ears, hers were when Jude said to her at one lunch, briefly emerging from the kitchen area, "Can I not just dislike Black without counting as a racist?"

Samilla just stared at him uncomprehendingly.

As she had at Black when she criticized him for not doing more for his people, and he replied, "I don't represent 'my people.' I am an individual and will believe whatever seems true to me, not whatever someone tells me that 'my people' should believe."

"Good stare," Jude commented approvingly on Samilla's.

"Her inability to understand anything except through the lens of racism is just insane," Black shared with Jeff one time, "and insanely hot. Oh my Lord what that woman does to me."

Though Black was focused on getting ready, the world did continue to turn in that interval, both inside and outside The Bubble.

Zar reported to them that Jude had been fiddling with Tylenol bottles on their Grove Street Cemetery walk, shortly after the news about the fatal Chicago tampering. As this episode came on the heels of Jude's Halloween costume—he'd arrived at President Bart's annual party as a human-sized bottle of Tylenol—well, it was a little weird. And maybe even weirder that he was handing out tablets of "candy," he insisted as he proffered the pills he had made in the lab to look like Tylenol. After Chicago he got not a single taker, unsurprisingly, although perhaps the three scantily clad runners from *Chariots of Fire* could have had a little sense of humor about it.

"People fucking died from this," one said as the three surrounded him.

"It is a little hard to take you seriously," Jude answered, "in your little short shorts."

"We'll take *you* seriously, asshole," another said, pushing him.

"I totally could have taken them," Jude insisted later at the Pierson Inferno, recounting the story. He hadn't had to test that hypothesis because at that moment Croc showed up, dressed as a Frigidaire, and simply stood next to Jude as the runners quickly resumed their race to wherever they were going.

"Okay that is a little weird," Jeff admitted when Zar told them about the cemetery walk.

"Telling you, man," Black said. "I don't trust that dude."

"You're exaggerating," Maggie said softly, always uncomfortable when they spoke ill of people.

"So, what," Jeff asked, "you think he supports poisoning people with Tylenol? The guy always talks about saving the world. He was probably working out the chemistry so he could synthesize an antidote."

Jeff wasn't sure why he was defending the fellow currently maintaining his intellectual superiority over Jeff. Physical chemistry was busting Jeff's balls, it was all he could do to keep pace with Jude who barely cracked the textbook. Maybe he was taking Jude's side because Maggie would, and it seemed imperative, lately, to connect better with her, this funk they were in with his looming departure.

Gosh, the word *looming* felt so ominous.

As it turned out, what Jeff said was true.

All of it, the search for an antidote, the saving of the world, one soul at a time. Poor Brother John, speaking of, just that afternoon

Jude had gone to check on him only to learn, from Nico, that he hadn't shown up to work for a few days. Skipping physical chemistry class—give little Jeff-Jeff a chance to keep pace—Jude went looking and finally found him, on the New Haven Green, conversing with a tree. When Jude tried to interrupt, Brother John glared at him without recognition and snapped, "Mister, can't you see I'm talking to my brother Demetrius here? Give a brother some space?"

The world kept turning around them but none of the gang was paying attention since, after "ABC," Ig had begun rasping one of the Tuesday Night Club Michael favorites, "Off the Wall." Black interspersed the grunts and hoots in all the right places, the grunts and hoots that Tayvon claimed sounded like animal noises, which Samilla claimed revealed Tayvon's racism, and the fact that Tayvon was of creamy mocha skin didn't mitigate that racism, though to be fair Samilla was the first to admit to her own White guilt because admitting that was the first step toward atonement and reparation, all of which led to many dining hall conversations that semester and some really big fucking news that Black would never share.

=====

7.
to each his own

At the very moment that Black began to grunt and hoot a gas tanker exploded in Afghanistan, killing some 170-plus in the worst way possible. Inside The Bubble three students ended up in the hospital after Friday's epic Bladderball match, with minor injuries in comparison. Neck and back injuries, but seriously, was that a reason to end the match after only thirty-five minutes? True there were loads of *really* minor injuries too, but that was normal—"That's what Bladderball is about," one student quoted in the *Yale Daily News* said, "The whole point of hundreds of people piling on is to produce a little hurt."

"And whatever happened to people taking responsibility for their own actions?" Black asked at the following Tuesday Night Club.

"Jesus, Black," Jasmine joked, "have you passed your initiation into the Yale Tories yet?"

Black blinked at her, disturbed, because Eli had *sworn* his application would be confidential.

He had also blinked, disturbed, upon reading Bart's announcement, on Monday, abolishing Bladderball for good. "It is not a matter of anger, guilt, or blame," the President released a statement. "The University has a responsibility to oversee student safety, and so we have decided to abolish the game."

"Does it, though?" Black shouted at Rudy's, where some were watching the Islanders game.

Thorn manually blinked his eye, then grunted, his way of affirming the view that individuals are responsible for their own safety decisions. This from a man who accepted the risk of bone crushing every time he stepped onto the rugby field, for the benefit of inflicting the same upon another.

"This nanny state mentality," Swill shouted after removing his cherry Charms Blow Pop from his mouth, "has got to go. There's a reason Carter lost in a landslide. It's morning in America, my friends, and Yale needs to wake up."

For the record Swill was one of those "Reagan Democrats," which led to his working for Reagan's 1984 reelection campaign. Meanwhile Maya's recent remark to him—"There's something about that face of yours with the mouth constantly chewing like a cow"—had really sunk in, so he'd dropped the nicotine gum in favor of the candy.

"Blow Pops for a blowhard," Jude commented then disappeared back into the kitchen.

"You don't think that Yale has some responsibility for those injuries?" Maggie asked at Rudy's.

"Legally, they do," Maya had studied this very issue in her "Society and Law" class.

"I'm talking morally, not legally," Black said. "This country obviously has a history of immoral laws."

"True dat," Samilla said, irritating him with her habit of imitating his expressions.

"Yale should just make everyone sign some sort of waiver," Jeff offered, moving next to Maggie at the bar. "Wouldn't that handle the legal problem, and the moral problem too?"

Black shook his head, "Totally impractical, J.-man, and worse, it misses the bigger picture. The university is not our parent. Its job is not to 'keep us safe.' Its job is to provide a neutral arena where people with different ideas can debate, hopefully en route to the goddamn truth. Some of the ideas we encounter might disturb or upset us, but that is the point. We should not be kept 'safe' from those ideas but exposed to them, grapple with them. And for that to work individuals must be allowed to make their own decisions, which includes accepting the foreseeable risks and consequences."

"You are such a racist," Samilla declared, turning them both on.

"False dat," Swill interjected, shaking his Blow Pop for emphasis. "That is the opposite of racism. It is treating everybody identically, with equal value, with equal respect. Everybody is welcomed into the arena no matter how much they may disagree with others. It is anti-racism."

"It's like us," Maggie said.

"Totally," Jeff agreed quickly, anxious because she had again spent the whole afternoon writing in her diary.

"How do you mean, Maggie?" Ig asked, gazing at her.

"All we do is sit around arguing, and we are like the biggest collection of opposites you can imagine. On the one hand we've got—" she was about to go through the gang, but then realized she couldn't do that without sounding judgmental, which would defeat her whole point—"we've got a whole range of perspectives, of values, of money, of race, but we all, you know, we're all friends, we hang out."

"Like a family," Black said.

"Like a family," Maggie repeated.

"Everybody in," Jeff said, rubbing Maggie's shoulders, feeling her tense up.

"True *dat*," Black sipped his Tall Boy. "To each doing his or her own thing. We come together around that common ground, and thus we make our way toward the goddamn truth."

"Damn you really are a Tory, aren't you," Samilla said, who couldn't believe how someone whose opinions were so revolting could be so hot. "But who was talking about ideas, and truth? What does any of that have to do with Bladderball?"

Black sighed. "Only everything, man."

Only everything, man.

=====

8.
"the girl is mine"

The days crept forward.

Everyone was busy, so much work, so many decisions, fall of junior year. Life beyond The Bubble was encroaching and you needed a plan. By this point everyone had declared a major or two, maybe a minor, and was committed to extracurriculars. These were to prepare you for the "real world," as the grown-ups called it, which would include medical school, or law school, or—why was this word so hard to say—a "job." You know, what your father had, maybe your mother too, and now you were to get too, along with a house and yard, a spouse, 1.84 kids, and a shady spot in a cemetery to deposit your sack of meat and molecules.

Jeff had made the decision to pursue medical school, which brought with it everything you need to do to get into a good medical school, starting with studying more. It didn't help that he was also preparing to take the MCAT exam over Christmas break; and that this little secret side project of his was running into complications; and it probably *would* help if he spent less time writing songs that only Maggie ever heard.

"Still not my name?" Maggie recently said, teasing, not-teasing.

"Saggy? Naggy?" Jeff protested.

173

At least he could justify his down-low visits to Yale's Art Gallery as being part of his education.

Having matured from his gargoyle and Caravaggio periods he was now obsessed with the Dutch Masters, and visited the current exhibition nearly daily to stare at Rembrandt's masterpiece, *The Anatomy Lesson of Dr. Nicolaes Tulp.* Something about this painting struck him in the soul, the little pointy beards, the soft light on the pale white faces of the doctors observing the dissection, that one guy, to Tulp's right, staring right at you with that *look.* The mastery of light, there, the chiaroscuro. His other favorite painting, De La Tour's *Dice Players*, another chiaroscuro he could stare at for hours. Of course it possibly helped that Jeff usually smoked a doob before visiting the gallery.

One time he brought Jude who even without a doob would, as Jeff correctly surmised, love the surgical details of the Rembrandt: the grayish flesh of the corpse on the table, the dead stillness of the right arm laying there, the flayed left arm ...

"Now if that isn't life," Jeff observed. "Doesn't matter who that guy was, what he achieved, who he loved. Just ends up on the anatomist's table getting flayed."

"Fun fact—" Jude started to say, raising his finger.

"I'm good," Jeff interrupted. "Oh, and would you mind signing this? Just a formality."

"You got it, Jeff-Jeff," Jude signed the non-disclosure agreement Jeff had written on a napkin to keep his art history major secret.

Jude seemed softer lately; he'd seen Brother John on the Green again, this time speaking with a half-dozen invisible people whom he was addressing by bizarre names, and for the first time in Jude's life he had no idea how to solve a problem.

Maggie was busy, too—more on that anon.

Black's insufferability grew as the Big Day grew closer.

He'd sing "The Girl is Mine" to Samilla both as foreplay and again after satisfying her, for satisfaction was surely the outcome for any girl of his once he was finished. Of course Black also sang this first single from the album, the duet with McCartney, at the dining hall, at Rudy's, in his suite, and hummed it during classes.

Jeff's opinion of the song? "It should have been Paul," is all he would say, referring to the tragic event their freshman year.

"That's not funny," Maggie said when she heard this, not appreciating the humor.

"Well it isn't his finest hour," Jeff insisted, not appreciating her not appreciating the humor.

"Man, but it is catchy," Black glanced at Maggie for her approval.

"So is the plague." Jeff waited, in vain, for one of them to say "good one!"

"I'm sure you're glad now, father of the year," Debra said many years later, "that it wasn't Paul."

"God bless the man," Jeffrey responded. "If he only knew."

What McCartney did not know was that he had just given one very challenged thirteen-year-old boy the greatest single half-hour of his unhappy life. For thirty minutes was about as long as the child could handle the loudness and crowd at Fenway Park where McCartney was performing, at a concert Jeffrey had taken him to for his birthday. But in that half-hour the boy could marvel at the fact that he was in the same space as his idol, and briefly pretend that his life was not one of impossible challenges.

Speaking of challenges, the football team had met some of those generated by Croc's limited capacity and shown signs of life. There were several wins, including over Princeton that brought the team to 4-5 on the season, with the hope, with the big Harvard game to go, of somehow pulling off a .500 season despite opening the season with three losses.

Well, this big day arrived first.

It got off to a start about as auspicious as the losing streak that opened the season.

Everyone was heading up to Cambridge, some as early as Thursday evening. That's what Jeff proposed, they were going to stay with Ilona again and she and her friends were a blast, and anyway, they'd had such success on her sofa the last time round …

"I can't," Maggie said earlier in the week.

"Why not?" Jeff was annoyed because it was just really annoying.

"I've got my huge project due right after Thanksgiving Break. I need to be in the darkroom." On Isabela's recommendation Maggie had jumped into an upper-level photography course with a massive final project.

"Aren't you working on it over break?"

"Yes, but I need every hour I can find. With the soccer season I've fallen behind."

Another disappointing soccer season was in the books, Maggie's own fine personal performance notwithstanding. Maggie still loved playing, still loved her teammates, but she was feeling the academic pressure now, as they all were. This huge project was essential for this class which was essential for the photography internship she was applying to for next summer in New York.

Junior year had gotten to Maggie too.

Jeff knew he shouldn't say what came next. "You're spending a lot of time in the darkroom lately."

"What? I just told you, it's a huge project. It takes time."

"I guess I don't understand. You have other classes too. How can you spend so much time just on this one?"

"I just have to," she said, her frustration apparent.

"Fine," Jeff yielded, his annoyance apparent.

Maggie gazed at him, softened. "We'll go up Friday afternoon, Jeff. There will—" she touched his arm, "—be sofa time."

Utterly unmentioned in *this* conversation was that asswipe Burt—rhymes with squirt, subvert, pervert, and flirt—who was in that photography class with Maggie and who was apparently the next great thing, a cross between Shabazz and Ridgers and other names Burt liked to drop that impressed Maggie but meant nothing to Jeff. Thank God at least he lived in Timothy Dwight, about as far from Pierson as you could get.

"You gotta be nicer to her, man," Black said over a bong in his livingroom, on Friday afternoon, after Maggie informed Jeff she needed another night in the darkroom. They would go up to Cambridge early tomorrow morning, she said, plenty of time before the game. It was no big deal, she said, they'd have Ilona's sofa Saturday night though she would need to get back Sunday morning to continue working.

"I *am* nice to her," Jeff took the bong. No big deal, she said. It was an enormous deal. She should be nicer to *him*!

"*Pardonnez-moi*, but accusing her of cheating on you is not very nice."

"I haven't accused her of cheating on me."

"But you're thinking it."

"Burt the fucking turt! Of course I'm thinking it."

"'Turt'? What the hell is that?"

"I was going for 'turd,' trying to force the rhyme."

Black shook his head. "You're smoking too much weed, man," he said, exhaling a bong hit.

"Or not enough, dude. Pass it fucking back."

Black obliged. "Burt may be a 'turt,' my man, but your Magdalena would never do you dishonor. But listen to me, man. You listening?"

Jeff had zoned out, was wondering why there wasn't music on, then remembering that with all the arguing about Michael or the Dead or lately he had been listening to Springsteen's *Nebraska*, wondering what had turned the Boss so dark—the phrase "your Magdalena" got through, though, he loved the way Black said her name, and the possessive there, that was nice—

Jeff nodded.

"Universal betterness will arrive," Black said, "once the album drops."

"What?"

"You listen to Michael. You fight for her. Sing it with me?"

"God, no, no," Jeff waved his arms helplessly.

"I believe you're familiar with 'The Girl is Mine,'" Black began …

"No, no, man," Jeff cut him off, parodying the song, "I'm a romantic, man, not a warrior."

"In this case man," Black said with such earnestness it was almost hilarious, "you wage war for her by romancing her, man."

"That," Jeff said in that classic stoner way, "is either the most profound thing I have ever heard or the stupidest."

"Such a fine line, man," Black nodded.

Saturday morning came, and up they went to Cambridge, filled with hope of glory on the gridiron, and, in Jeff's case, of some coochie-coochie on the couch.

The weather was adequate: cloudy, a bit windy but in the 40s, perfect for some pre-Thanksgiving football. The first sign that something was wrong was Harvard's first possession, where they steamrolled to Yale's 23-yardline, followed by their quarterback casually jogging 23 yards into the end zone. The shutout victories over Harvard of the past two years suddenly seemed very far away. This disastrous opening series was actually the highlight of the game for the Elis, as it was followed by various Yale miscues invariably followed by Harvard scores. When it was over, the Crimson—who chooses a color for a mascot, anyway?—had destroyed the hapless Yale squad, 45-7.

Jeff did not fare much better than his team.

There was obvious partying to do afterward—celebratory for Harvard, consolatory for Yale—and Ilona was popular too so there were many parties to pop in to, and Ilona's friends all adored Maggie so she was always swarmed. At various points in the evening they crossed paths with various meatheads and Maggie wanted to talk with every one of them. Wasn't that a little strange? After all she saw those people all the time, they had practically every fucking meal together, so why did she have to go talk to them just because they all happened to be in Cambridge?

"Isn't it interesting," Swill had said recently at the Buttery, "that the people you spend the most time with are the ones you have the most to talk to about? You would almost think it's the other way around."

Swill had a point, but fuck that—there was a sofa waiting for them and here was Maggie laughing, having a grand time with everybody and his brother. And Croc, really, maybe needed some consoling, but did that require a good thirty minutes at that Lowell House party?

"I really want to thank you, Maggie," Croc was saying so seriously when Jeff wandered over. "Your support means the world to me, to the whole team."

"God, we love you guys," Maggie touched his arm, did she have to touch everybody's arm when she was speaking to them?

"We just stunk this year. And today. There are no words for what happened out there today. Just humiliating."

"Those sort of *are* the words for that," Jeff was smart enough not to say, instead just nodding faux sympathetically.

"Yeah, but you're *our* stinky team," Maggie stroked Croc's arm as if they hadn't all been saying among themselves this past week that thank God the hockey season was starting on Sunday and it will be good to finally root for a not shitty team.

Where was Maggie now? She had gone off with Bira, a friend of Ilona's, to maybe score some coke from another friend in Adams, but ah, here she was back now and had brought some coke but he was anxious that it was awfully late—and wasn't she all in a rush to get back to Yale early tomorrow for her huge project? "It's only—" she said, glancing at her watch, "3:06 AM. Come on, don't poop the party again, Jeff. Say yes."

"Fine," Jeff finally yielded.

"You didn't say 'yes,' mister," she giggled.

Jeff gazed at her. "So," he said some time later, after a couple of lines, his head ringing from hours already with loud music and people talking, "maybe head back?"

"Fine," Maggie nodded reluctantly, her long dark hair swishing.

"Where's Ilona?" he thought to ask as they headed to the door.

"I don't know. I assume back in her room."

But she wasn't back in her room, nor any of her roommates, they discovered after knocking for ten minutes until someone down the hall opened the door and, annoyed at being awakened, asked if they would please stop knocking already.

"What now?" Jeff said.

"I guess we wait."

Three-fifty-five in the morning sitting in the dimly lit hallway of Winthrop House, the buzz wearing off, he was at least enjoying Maggie's head leaning on his shoulder and starting to feel sleepy when Ilona came bounding up the stairs clearly upset about something.

"Sorry, sorry, sorry," she fumbled for her key to let them in.

Damn it was late but not too late, there was the sofa, the one they had conquered two years earlier after that much happier game, and here they were now, and maybe with a little of that coke they had left they could finally move this thing along.

"Here," Maggie said, pulling out the packet of cocaine. They had brushed teeth, changed into sleepwear, it was just after four, there was all the time in the world for El Jefe to work his old magic. "I'm just going to check on Ilona."

"What?"

"She was obviously upset."

"She'll survive." That came out colder than he intended but Jesus at four in the morning after a night of partying you can't be expected to be on top of your game.

Maggie gave him that look. "She's my friend. I just want to

check on her. Why don't you get started making the lines?"

Jeff nodded and Maggie was gone into Ilona's bedroom. He could hear whispering in there, maybe some crying. Then more whispering, sounded like Maggie was doing her share of it, was it possible that Maggie was crying? Whispering and crying, that sounded like diary material, what the hell was she always writing in that diary anyway? "The Girl is Mine" popped into his head, he shook his head to banish the tune, banish the thoughts.

He wasn't sure exactly when he fell asleep, with dark thoughts settling into deep dark dreams.

=====

9.

the best day of his entire life

The hockey season began the next day, with a solid 6-3 win over Princeton.

A good start, the team winning five of the first six, and Ig looking good on the ice, though not yet scoring the long-sought goal. But never mind that, or Thanksgiving Break, Maggie spending most of it on campus working on her project.

The other big day arrived.

Black showed up to breakfast on Tuesday morning, November 30, 1982, at 6:20 AM.

He had camped out the night before outside Cutler's, arriving at two the previous afternoon to be second on line, much to his chagrin. Things got marginally better around 11:30 PM when the person first on line, freezing his fanny off, gave Black twenty bucks to buy the album for him and headed home to his warm bed. Cutler's opened early for the occasion, at 6:00 AM, with Black first on a line of maybe four dozen people. Ten minutes later, the maximum three copies of *Thriller* pressed close to his chest, he arrived at the dining hall to show off his new treasure on what would likely be the best day of his entire life.

No one was at the table at that ungodly hour except Zar, who had been scribbling on his pads all night popping pills and thinking about liquidity.

"Astounding," Zar said without looking up, probably referring to some process that would transform something into something else and thereby explain something.

Maybe Samilla was right, Black thought as he headed back to his room to wake her up and begin his record player's needle's process of wearing its way entirely through the vinyl. Maybe his friends *were* a bunch of racists.

It may have been a bust that early Tuesday morning, but the post-*Thriller* phase of his—everyone's—life had begun.

=====

10.
"get together"

Living occurs while we're distracted formulating alternative arrangements.

Or so, more or less, said the great contemporary philosopher John Winston Lennon. Well not contemporary anymore, perhaps, since his tragic murder two years earlier. But God knows how much living occurred while the meatheads were distracted arguing over whether Lennon still counted as contemporary or not.

In Jeff's case, *living* kept him so busy he almost forgot about his alternative arrangements.

We mentioned his academic load but he was also churning out songs in this period. These included serious ones such as "Another

Round," a meditation on the futility of life. There were half-serious half-silly songs, such as "Quite an Animal," also a meditation on the futility of life. Then there were the silly songs, like "God Bless Stanley H." inspired by the long hours he spent preparing for the MCAT at the Stanley H. Kaplan test prep center, filled with sopho-moric (junioric?) sexual (and possibly homophobic, we might say today) innuendo that Jeff found hilarious at the time but cringe-worthy even just a few years later.

"I just think it's kind of cringeworthy," Maggie said, explaining one evening why she didn't want to hear "God Bless Stanley H." again, at least sparing Jeff her opinion that the so-called humor in the song was actually offensive.

"Yeah but it's *my* cringeworthy song," Jeff tried to hide his dis-appointment because who was he supposed to play this for if not for his girlfriend, and by the way weren't those innuendos about homosexual sex with Stanley H. hilarious?

"What does that mean?"

"Um, you know, you always say 'Yes but he's *our* loser,' or 'You're *our* stinky team.'"

"So I should want to hear your cringeworthy song because it's yours?"

"Pretty much."

Maggie contemplated this, one of those moments that could go either way, really, a forking point that maybe determined the whole future trajectory—or so Jeff was thinking as he waited for her response. That it was taking her so long to respond—a full three or four seconds, an eternity when your whole future trajectory rides on it—was already a problem so Jeff decided to pre-empt her.

"I just wish you asked to hear me play more often," he immedi-ately wished he hadn't said.

Well this threw Maggie for a loop since she had been all pre-pared to say you're right please play me your cringey song and the maybe two-second delay had only been because she was trying to think of a witty way to say it. But now she was confronted with what was obviously a very deep feeling that her boyfriend had been keeping from her and what had begun as a fun little evening banter that might have ended in some *habba-do-gaggedy* had just turned southward.

It doesn't really matter what she eventually said because the three additional seconds it took her to process the above was enough to divert the trajectory from one possibly containing *hab-ba-do-gaggedy* to one containing Jeff up late in Black's room, doing bong hits and reflecting on the futility of life, which in turn ended up with the playing of *Thriller*—because *every* trajectory included *Thriller* in those days. And true to Black's word betterness was to be found, because by the end of the second side they were singing together, tearily, "The Lady in My Life"—each reflecting on their respective lady—and that in turn brought them so close that by 2:00 AM they had their arms around each other singing "Ebony and Ivory," really just feeling their love for each other or maybe just really being stoned.

Black was a good friend, Jeff thought.

The J.-man made it back to his room by maybe 2:30 AM, in the mood to wage war for the dang lady in his life by romancing her.

Maggie wasn't there.

There was no reason she should have been. He had been gone for hours and had possibly said, on departing, "I'm not sure when I'll be back so if you want to go back to your room that's fine." Of course it wasn't the least bit fine but that'll learn you to think a little before speaking. There was no reason she should have been there and yet her not being there hit him like a sledgehammer.

The second sledgehammer was the realization that they were running out of time.

With all this distracting life going on—academics, MCAT prep, *Thriller*, songwriting, relationships—the realization that Jeff was about to depart for a semester in Florence hit Jeff, and Maggie, as suddenly as the "Billie Jean" single hit number one on the charts.

The end of classes came and went, Croc's Christmas party and finals came and went, and as they entered Christmas break the tensions, the frictions, the disagreements, his occasional jealous suspicions (Maggie might say "frequent"), all melted away. Those things were insignificant, they were normal, they had been dating for twenty-six months and *all relationships at Yale have their ups and downs*, and in those final weeks maybe there could be more up than down?

The MCAT also came and went.

And then it was the night before.

Since Jeff's departure was a few days after spring classes began, he joined his friends on campus for those first few days. They threw him a going-away party, in Maggie's and Lisa's room. What a grand time, early in the term before any of the pressures began, everyone felt great. Ig put *The Youngbloods* album on, rasped along but was drowned out by everybody joining in, lots of arms around one another, laughing, brothers, sisters, loving each other, now, forever. Isabela snapped one of her classics, must have made copies because Jeffrey had one years later. They were all piled on and around the livingroom sofa, they were so young, arms around one another, leaning on one another, a group of friends, they were a gang, a pack, a unity of diversity, it didn't matter what they did as long as they were together. Only when you looked a little more closely, at Maggie with a big smile in the middle of the sofa, her arms around Lisa and Maya and extending even to Swill with his purple Blow Pop next to Maya, did you see that her eyes didn't quite match her smile. And then when you looked at Jeff, sitting on the floor in front of the sofa, a bit off to the side, you could maybe just see the watery eyes, and no for once it wasn't due to the weed.

=====

spring

11.

everywhere, everywhere

Everyone stars in their own biopic/There are no bit parts in your heart, Jeffrey would write as a lyric many decades later, inspired by the work of a superb writer named Andrew Postman (Pierson '83), itself inspired by the work of filmmaker Charlie Kaufman, in turn inspired by Kaufman's study of Ren's work, which was inspired not merely by Doc but, Jeffrey liked to think, by Ren's hanging around Jeff all the time who would occasionally drop such little pearls of wisdom. Jeffrey proudly played the song for Debra, who always loved to hear his music.

"Last call for passengers to Rome," the loudspeaker had announced as Jeff was whisked away from Maggie onto the plane. The card she'd given him featuring a couple embracing under a large bubble umbrella was stuffed in his pocket. The *Time* magazine she'd also given him, featuring a computer as its "Man of the Year," was not, having fallen out in the haste; shame, because Swill was quoted in it since the algorithms he had developed with his professor were already making some of his sci-fi predictions come true. The bootleg from the car, with the kick-ass June 24, 1973 Memorial Coliseum Portland "Box of Rain," was still playing in his head with that closing lyric—about being away for so long and present for so little—"Now if that isn't life then what is?" Jeff had said, also thinking that he simply could not *believe* that after months of planning he had left the little music box he'd had custom made for Maggie on her dorm room windowsill, the box which, when she opened the cover, would play "The Beginning," the first song he had written for her.

We'll leave Jeff to his own story now, one-sixth of the way around the globe.

Somehow the world went on without him.

Most of the gang had a smashing good time at a Studio 54 "Yale Ball" sponsored by Calhoun sophomore Steven Mnuchin. Smashing good time, ditto, assembling in the common room to watch the first episodes of *Fraggle Rock*, one of HBO's first original series, which fellow Piersonite Cheryl Henson's famous Muppets father had produced. Not ditto at classmate Tina Landau's brilliant Yale Dramat production of *The Woman*, because most of them (okay, the guys) were not persuaded to go by Maya, who couldn't comprehend why they weren't drawn to a contemporary feminist retelling of the Trojan War. And of course there was Motown's 25th anniversary special, which left the J.-man, away without access to a television, among the last people on earth not to know about the "moonwalk" that Michael premiered on the show.

In other news there were bushfires in Australia claiming seventy-five lives, a massacre of twenty-two hundred Bangladeshis in India, and the bombing of the U.S. Embassy in Beirut that killed sixty-three; and then there was Jude's odd recording of such events into his little notebook, in which he kept the dates and details of all incidents involving ten or more casualties.

Speaking of Jude's penchant to document things, "You'll keep an eye on her, won't you?" Jeff had said to Jude shortly before his departure.

"What does that mean, keep an eye on her?"

"Like, keep an eye on her."

"What, like stalk her? Surveil her?"

"No. Cut it out."

"Should I bug her room? Buy one of those spy pen cameras and take photos when she is not aware?"

"You know," Jeff said uncomfortably, "just make sure she's okay."

"You do not think she will be okay, Jeff-Jeff?"

His fear, of course, was that Maggie would be perfectly okay without him. "I don't know, make sure she isn't lonely." That was actually the last thing Jeff wanted, that she not feel lonely; or worse that she not feel lonely because she had plenty of company.

"What, you want me to hang out with her?"

When he put it that way Jeff realized how ridiculous it sounded. Jude and Maggie didn't get along all that well; they seemed uncomfortable in each other's presence. And Jeff really did not want Jude to start hanging out with Maggie. He only wanted to keep Maggie from hanging out with anybody else.

"You'll keep an eye on him, won't you?" Jeff said to Black in Black's room, referring to Jude, shortly before his departure.

"Anyone who tries to start up something with your dang lady," Black said, stepping to his stereo, "here's what I'll tell him." The opening riffs of "Beat It" came over the speakers.

"You, my friend," Jeff said fondly, "need some help."

"I do, J.-man. But your baby is yours, man. I'll guard her honor for you."

The world turned.

The Bubble bubbled.

"I swear she gets more beautiful every time I see her," Swill commented on Magina early in the semester, sucking on his first and only Blow-Pop of the day. (He'd begun weaning off them after Maya recently said, "There's something about those concave cheeks of yours sucking like a toothless old man.") He was part of the Pierson cohort taking Doc's class on gender and other social constructs, "Homer Was a Woman (and Her Name Wasn't 'Homer')," a cohort including Maya, Isabela, Ren, and the one who should not have been looked at.

"Holy shit!" Tayvon exclaimed, squeezing Lisa's hand under the table. "No man shall see that face and live."

"Right-o, we have to kill him," Ig said, sincerely.

"No, no!" Swill protested. "I don't look directly. I infer it from the general glow from her direction."

Beautiful lonely Magina thus went by herself, that same evening, to see the Pierson Dramat's production of the Who's musical *Tommy*. Fregoli turned out to be a talented thespian (at least when he was taking his lithium) and did a fine turn as Uncle Ernie. Watching him give his all on stage made you wonder whether everything about Fregoli was an act; really, could he have gotten into Yale, and stayed there—one looney-bin stint notwithstanding—if there weren't at least some, you know, *there* in there?

Also giving it his all that semester was Iggy.

There was the extra training, and he played his heart out, leaving everything on the ice (as they say), including a smattering of vomit after an end-to-end speedskate with the puck at the Brown game. The gang was going nuts, clapping and screaming, "Ig-gy! Ig-gy!" The gang continued to clap and scream as Iggy crumpled over and vomited. To be clear, he managed to keep most of the vomit in his mouth, swallow it down, then continue his sprint now in pursuit of the Brown player who had stolen the puck from him while he was chucking. And to his credit, *you* try keeping a cheesesteak sub down when you've sprinted all over the ice like that.

"You are a superhero," Tayvon said to Iggy after the game.

"Iron Man," Swill said, "though without the Iron Stomach."

"Good one," Ren said, writing it in his notebook.

"To be fair," Iggy answered with a guffaw, "that fucker was a full foot long. I only puked a couple inches worth, tops."

"You may have lost the puck," Maggie touched his arm, "but you won our hearts out there."

No, he didn't score a goal, that night or that season, but his theatrics on the ice sparked the team that night to end its seven-game losing streak and, with the win over Brown, commence a five-game winning streak. That extra training really paid off: he was faster and stronger, and his presence on the ice was an inspiration to his teammates. That's why he was missed so when he couldn't dress for the Harvard game, resulting in a 3-0 loss and commencing the skid of losing six out of the final seven games.

"Stomach thing," was all he shared with the coach, and with the gang. What he didn't share was that, while he could keep almost a whole cheesesteak down, even an Iron Man can't keep *two* cheesesteaks down. Only Maggie, who happened to be at Park Street getting a Tab prior to the game, saw him order the two subs. Iggy had long won her heart but that night he also broke it a little.

She added that to the other secrets she was keeping for, at this point, pretty much everybody.

Feb Club came and went. Warren Zevon came to Toad's Place and went. Poets Allen Ginsberg and Peter Orlovsky read at a Pierson Master's Tea, and Tayvon was so excited that just before the event he looked a little like Iggy before the final third of the second cheesesteak. "Orlovsky is the real deal," he had explained over an earlier brunch, sitting freshly showered next to freshly showered Lisa. "He's not only Ginsberg's partner but also a professor at the Jack Kerouac School of Disembodied Poetics."

"Say what now?" Swill said, sitting next to a freshly showered Maya who, he thought, smelled really nice, like jasmine—the fragrance, not the cellist.

"It's part of Naropa University, in Boulder. It's also part of—" here Tayvon hesitated, knowing he should quit while he was ahead— "Chögyam Trungpa Rinpoche's 100-year experiment."

There was a long silence.

"*Guh-huh!*" Jude's guttural mockery nicely expressed what everyone was thinking. (He had popped out from the kitchen to keep an eye on Maggie, per Jeff-Jeff's request.)

Black, keeping an eye on Jude, narrowed his eyes.

The devil-man was disrespectful, but that was among the lesser of his faults. He seemed to think he was smarter than anybody else, pretty arrogant with a Zar in your circle, who was at that moment swirling a spoon in his broth and thinking thoughts involving words like entropy, hydrophobia, and mean kinetic energy. Not to mention a Beamie who if he could step out of his own loserness and stop saying things like "Zounds!" might really shine. Jude made a show with his rants on morality and distributive justice and lately on animal rights—"What matters is not whether animals can reason but whether they can *feel*" was his latest nonsense—there was even talk of his making the dining hall vegetarian, God forbid!—but Black didn't trust him for a minute, he saw right through it, it was all some elaborate put-on.

And that business with Brother John.

"If it weren't all so tragic on the personal level," Black had said recently to Samilla, as foreplay, "I'd rejoice that it confirmed everything I've been saying about social welfare policy."

You normally thought of Jude as pretty damn stoic. That went with the confidence, the clarity of vision, the whole usually being right thing. But that look on his face when he came upon his brother on the Green, lying in the snow without a coat, without the coat that Jude had bought him at the start of winter, talking, raving, unintelligibly.

"Who?" Jude kneeled beside him, trying to follow the names the man was uttering. Strange names, maybe gods, or demons, they sounded vaguely familiar, if he could just make them out.

"Everywhere, everywhere," John said, his eyes darting feverishly like prey surrounded by a pack of predators.

"Fucking call 911!" Jude yelled at the passersby, gawkers, he would run for a phone himself but he was needed here, by his brother's side. Then he turned back to John, said pleadingly, "What do you see? What do you see?"

"Demetrius, my brother, wait," John said suddenly to someone he believed present, his eyes cleared up for a moment, then saw, seemed to recognize Jude. "You don't see?"

"See what?"

"Them."

"Who?"

"All of them."

"John," Jude said helplessly. "There is just me."

"I was so blind," John muttered. "They were here the whole time. I just needed to—tune in. Like a television, brother. To see them. The right channel. The right—the right—"

"Frequency?" Jude offered.

"Yes. My brother," John said peacefully but then the moment passed and he was raving again, there was nothing Jude could do but kneel there holding his hand and yes, Jude was sobbing, the stoic was sobbing, holding his brother's hand until the paramedics came and took the poor man away.

"You would think that would teach the devil-man a little humility, man," Black said when he had finished satisfying Samilla, "that while he may have a load of useless 'fun facts' stored in his devil-head maybe his little theories about everything aren't correct. But no. Instead of recognizing mental illness when that shit is screaming in his face, he says that with a little time he'll be able to explain what was going on. How arrogant can you be, really, when all you are is a glorified stock boy with a few useless facts in your head?"

That boy, Black thought as Samilla started criticizing Reagan's latest cuts on mental health services as part of another round of foreplay—the dang girl had stamina—really needed to be put in his place, preferably soon, and preferably by Black.

=====

12.
the logic of chance

Glorified stock boy!

More like *glorious* Stock *Man*!

Screw Superman, Iron Man, Batman—he was—cue the music—na na na na na na na na Stock Man!

Jude didn't know what Black's problem was, or why Black seemed to be following him around a lot lately, but the reality was that Black, in his opinion, was like a little pimple on a bigger pimple on someone's ass. Whatever, Jude couldn't bother himself with him. Jude more or less liked the gang, or most of them anyway. The whole meathead thing was interesting: each one had a few people they were close to, but then the overlaps were like Venn diagrams creating a cluster, so you ended up hanging out with people who were close to people you were close to, but weren't close to yourself.

Oh, fun fact: In addition to creating the diagrams that bore his name John Venn also wrote a book on probability called *The Logic of Chance*.

Chance, the very thing that defied logic, had its own logic.

"There are no accidents," Jude would inform everybody in his Venn when, not by chance, he would bump into them. Most would roll their eyes, Swill would argue (Swill was Swill), but so much the worse for him. That Heinlein story from that class with Doc: each incident had its place in time, each one informed the other, each one made sense of the other, whether before or after the other, and it was only the illusory passage of time that made us think events were disconnected. Life was lived in time but understood outside of time; no necessary connections within time, nothing but necessary connections outside time. You thus had to examine all events, future, past, present, before you could understand any event, past, present, future; you could not understand *anything* until you understood *everything*. Like an impressionist painting some paint splashed here, some splashed there, and eventually the panoply of interconnections emerged and it all made sense.

Nothing to chance, everything had its place, Jude thought, wandering through the walk-in pantry behind the kitchen, running his fingers along the shelves. There was little more beautiful than either a full shelf, fully stocked, or an empty shelf, about to be restocked, that turnaround, that transition, was just, well, *sublime*. Man was a machine, and nothing could happen in this place—no research, no teaching, no truth, no beauty, no friendship, no social capital, no social activism, no commitment to God (if there were one), to country, to Yale—nothing could happen here unless those machines were fueled. The dining hall was the furnace powering the institution from its core outward, from its trunk to its branches, its leaves, its fruit. The dining hall machine drove the bigger machine, that in turn drove the machines who were its meatheads, and Jude in his position as Stock Manager was the driving force of the dining hall, the spirit of that machine. The job required focus and persistence as entropy worked tirelessly to dismantle the man-made order, everything poised at every moment to break down, disintegrate. You relax your vigilance for an instant and *snap!* it's darkness and disorder, as sudden and devastating as the massacres, the bombings, the fires that even as he reflected were taking the lives of thousands.

He poked his head into the walk-in refrigerator; good, this morning's dairy delivery had already been processed.

His heart was broken by the Brother John affair, but he was at least pleased with his efforts here in charge of the stock. It was really the same battle against darkness and disorder. The system required ordering but the system created its own orderers, he was fine-tuning the universe, as the universe intended him to do. Fine-tuning the universe: a nice expression, Ren had written it down. You can't win every battle; he was just one man, but if he could not save every soul he would save as many as he could, by creating systems. The vegetarianism project was intimidating, true; he didn't yet have the power to implement that here in Pierson much less across the university. But what he *had* done here, a first step in the larger project, was to develop new systems of tracking stock. After consulting with Swill he had had installed that little box called a computer, had Swill write some programs, and he was the first Student Dining Hall Manager (his modest payroll title) to start using the Universal Product Code system.

"The future is *now*," Swill said when they turned on the system, feeling emotional both because the future *was* now and because he had just sucked his last Blow Pop and was heading into the oral unknown.

Glorified stock boy!

Glorious Stock Man—Enemy of Entropy, Destroyer of Darkness.

"Fuck, we're out of ketchup out there, devil-man," Black liked to pop behind the serving line to taunt him with an empty bottle, only to be as impressed as he was mystified when Jude would respond, "Fuck we are not, asshole," and Black would return to his table to find the replacement already in place.

Na na na na na na na na Stock Man!

=====

13.

you never find just one

Spring Break.

Two weeks for catching up on work, for working on summer job and internship applications, for being laid or crawling in South Florida or Mexico, for replenishing spirit and stock. You came back refreshed and ready to go, and if you were Iggy—in an eery portent of senior year—with a case of crabs acquired from you would not specify where. It was apparently uncomfortable despite Iggy's milking its comic potential.

"Is that asshole joking?" Thorn said to the air, because he was still not speaking directly to Ig.

"I am not, asshole," Ig said and could not help his guffaw, "my crabs are in my ass hair."

"Please, no," Tayvon said, unable to believe such a thing possible.

"Oh believe it," Ig said with a guffaw as he pulled down his drawers and mooned them to confirm that the remarkable claim was true. Well, at least the condition was not fatal, unlike that strange new disease recently affecting homosexual men.

Disinfecting ass shampoo aside, everyone came back ready for the home stretch.

But the first crab in the metaphorical ass hair appeared on the first Tuesday back and certainly put a damper on that first Tuesday Night Club. The inconceivable happened: the Guy, who had not long before re-emerged from laying low, was arrested.

"It was one of those calamitous moments," Jeffrey told Debra years later, "where everyone remembers where they were when they heard the news."

"You're not saying it was comparable to the Kennedy assassination, or the Challenger explosion, are you?"

"Not at all. It was much, much worse, for most of us."

"You realize that's really pathetic?"

"Possibly."

"Not 'possibly.' Actually." Debra shook her head. "You said 'most of us'?"

"Right. Amidst the despair on campus there was one solitary shout of joy. The brave lonely voice of clarity of vision, celebrating the vanquishing of the scourge."

Black carefully documented Jude's support for the arrest, including his sending a dozen boxes of donuts to the New Haven Police, and added it to his ever-growing list of indictments against the devil-man.

But with respect to crabs, you know, you never find just one.

Connecticut was going to raise the drinking age again.

Again!

"On the plus side they voted down raising it to twenty-one," Tayvon noted, reading the *New Haven Register* article at the dinner table that happened to quote him, as a Quality Wine employee.

"Yeah, but voted up raising it to twenty," Eli observed, having already had his assistant call his father's assistant to see who Elihu Yale the 13th or 14th owned in the state legislature.

"More power to them," Jude interjected, who had come out to survey the salad bar.

"Clarity of vision my ass," Black's eyes narrowed as Jude disappeared back into the kitchen.

"You guys are getting too worked up over this," Swill weighed in, stumbling over the words because he had developed the habit of sucking on his own tongue. "Going up to twenty, we're fine. It's the underclassmen's problem. Ah!" he added when Maya squeezed his leg hard under the table. "I mean of course we should get worked up over this. We have to look out for those behind us."

The conversational fire had been lit. What kind of world would it be if you only looked out for yourself? We who had so benefited from alcohol during college owed it to those behind us to preserve it for them. What did it matter that, when asked to specify those benefits, nobody could come up with anything specific? Try to imagine Tuesday Night Club without the booze; just another Tuesday night. The Pierson Inferno, without the heat. Carillon Guild or secret societies' initiations performed entirely sober? You would sooner join a monastery in the mountains where you fasted all day in a cement cell, like that movie *Black Narcissus* that Jeff would have seen at last week's showing if he were here. Instead it was Lisa who saw the film, though it was Tayvon who weighed in here on her behalf. She was busy elsewhere, trying to persuade the T.A. working under her in this year's Soviet History course that Anne Applebaum's outstanding term paper was actually a steaming load of horseshit.

Not even the fact that Maya had gotten Betty Friedan in the running for Class Day speaker could calm Lisa out of this campaign.

That's when the crabs really began to reproduce.

=====

14.
in the raw

Isabela observed the debate about the drinking age in silence.

She didn't really know where she stood on the issue, which was true of most things, she supposed. She had been doing some light drinking this year, to fit in better. She'd take a cup at Tuesday Night Club, nurse it all evening, a sip here or there. It tasted awful, and she didn't like the way it made her feel—maybe it was an acquired taste, but she wasn't sure she wanted to acquire it.

"Nor am I sure where I stand on whether I am, myself, a meathead," she wrote in her diary, which was to be, beside her Nikon, her best friend during her final months.

She'd heard Jude's rants on Venn diagrams, which raised the obvious question: to whom exactly was she close? Yes she hung around with this group, but was she in any of *their* Venn diagrams, or was she like, maybe, Pluto, a little dark frozen ice clump (fun fact! Jude said) hurtling alone on the periphery of the solar system? She was not in Jude's Venn, she was sure, but Jude was not in hers either: she found him intimidating, oh she saw his generous streak, but she wasn't convinced it was kindness operating there. And even if it were, those eyes, behind those glasses, shooting little laser beams into your soul when they came your way.

"My soul is none of his business," she wrote, and she thought, but did not write, that she felt almost, well, *violated*, the exactly three times Jude had glanced directly at her.

And the other boys, well, what could she say.

Jeffrey was all right: he clearly had a kind soul, and you could see he was a good listener, when people were talking he would look at them and really listen. His love for Magdalena was sweet too especially now that they had stopped touching each other all the time. If only he weren't trying so hard to be cool, with the drinking and the drugs and the silly long hair. She maybe wouldn't mind if she were in his Venn.

She was in Magdalena's Venn of course, she wrote. But then again everyone was in Magdalena's Venn. And of course *you're* in my Venn, Isabela wrote with a smile to her diary. Actually the two Venns overlapped: it was Magdalena who had suggested she keep a diary and then given her one.

"It was on sale at the Co-op," she'd said with a warm smile, handing it over. "Keeping a diary helps me process things. I think you'd get a lot out of it, Isabela."

Magdalena; she was nice.

What about Black, and Samilla? What a strange couple. They bickered constantly, yet the way they looked at each other it was obvious they were touching each other all the time, though thankfully mostly in private.

And on that subject, Tayvon.

"The man seems to be made for copulating," she had said to Jasmine freshman year, her roommate then and now suitemate, meaning it as a criticism.

"There *is* a God," Jasmine exhaled, putting her hand across her breasts.

Isabela merely frowned, already early in freshman year cementing her status as a little frozen ice clump on the periphery of the solar system. And even now that Tayvon had apparently settled into something with Lisa, their bodies just never stopped touching.

"What is it with these people and copulating?" Isabela asked her diary. What was she was missing here? She was here to study, architecture and classics, it was about the education, yet for everyone else, it seemed, it was about the copulation.

Jude would argue that, per Darwin, it *is* all about the copulation. Swill would tell you about future robot sex dolls that would allow copulation without producing hungry screaming babies. Maya would support that idea, because while she defended women's right to terminate their babies she would much prefer to avoid conceiving them in the first place. Ignacio—now there was a mystery, he was hiding something, she was sure—but he would just make some joke about his naughty bits and guffaw.

"What do you think is going on with him?" Isabela had recently asked F. Scott, following her through the steam tunnels toward her room.

She was always a little uncomfortable around F. Scott, not sure what to make of the gender thing, but F. Scott was always kind to her and was interested in architecture and her photography and Isabela wouldn't mind being in *her* Venn. They'd been chatting in the common room after dinner, that nice sophomore Ashok was playing some beautiful classical music on the baby grand and they were maybe procrastinating about end of semester assignments. They were talking about this or that, then started talking about their acquaintances, and when Ignacio came up F. Scott invited her back to her room to show her something.

"You are the first," F. Scott said with a hint of sadness, stepping aside to allow Isabela into her bedroom, "to enter my world."

Isabela glanced at her then stepped through the portal.

It was like entering another dimension.

When you entered her bedroom you were first made aware of the soft blue light bathing the space and the faint lavender incense.

Some soft music was playing, more felt than heard. And then your eye was drawn to the center of the room, to the pedestal under the white spotlight, and when Isabela's eyes caught the sculpture there she emitted an audible gasp.

"Ignacio," F. Scott announced, "in the raw. My latest."

Oh my goodness, Isabela thought but did not say, because there were no words to express what she was seeing.

F. Scott had been procrastinating on her assigned artwork by creating a masterpiece.

The body, the naked body though without the naughty bits; it had his shape, his gait, it was his body, muscular as he was but also thin and frail at the same time. The sculpture didn't go down to the feet but from the shape of it, the flow of it, you imagined he were on the ice, skating fast, skating toward something, toward the goal, but he was also skating away, escaping. It didn't go all the way down to the hands either, both the legs and arms ended in raw wires protruding from the thighs, from the upper arms. This was the wire around which the body had been shaped but there was no clay for the hands and feet, the sculpture was finished but it was the actual hands and feet that were not, that was crazy, Ignacio was a fully formed human being but somehow those unfinished wires were *him*, they captured him, he was skating away but they captured him.

And the face ...

"It sort of looks like Fregoli," Isabela whispered, recovering her breath.

"Fregoli is my model," F. Scott clearly appreciated Isabela's appreciation. "The challenge is to use his face as the basis but—"

"—capture Ignacio."

"Exactly."

It *was* Ignacio, not in any of the particular features—if you looked at the nose alone, or the eyes alone, it was Fregoli—but the face, overall, was Ignacio's, the whole emerging from the parts. It wasn't his literal face but it was *his* face, the expression, the motion of it captured by the clay, the spirit maybe: a face of joy, of bliss, of wanting to feel joy, of wanting to feel bliss, but also of pain, of one in pain, in bliss and pain at the same time. Isabela wanted to take him and hold him and comfort him, somehow, say it's all right, it's all right, it'll be all right.

"Do you have a—"

"Here you go, honey." F. Scott offered the tissue as Isabela was weeping. Feeling the gratification of her work finally being appreciated, she felt her own tears welling as well. She had been wanting to share her real work for a while but when she tried to, when she invited others to come see after giving up on Jeff, they, with all their hangups, their preconceptions, weren't interested—they made excuses—it was so unbearably painful to be invisible, to have this thing to share and not a soul with whom to share it. Wiping her own eyes F. Scott found herself wishing she were attracted to women because right now, with those tears streaming down Isabela's cheeks, Isabela was possibly the sweetest, most vulnerable creature she had ever seen.

"Don't you study—painting?" Isabela asked, looking at her.

"That's my major. This, I don't know. My sculptures are personal."

"You have others?" Isabela finally composed herself, finding herself wishing she were attracted to women because right now, with those tears gently filling F. Scott's eyes, F. Scott was possibly the sweetest, most vulnerable creature she had ever seen.

"Mmm," F. Scott nodded, then pressed some buttons on a gadget on her dresser.

The perimeter of the room had been darkened, the blue light not quite reaching there, but now the spotlight on Iggy was turned off and smaller spots illuminating several more sculptures on shelves along the wall came on.

"Black," Isabela said immediately, though again the face was Fregoli's, yet it was Black. The clay didn't distinguish the races but captured the human essence apart from the material. That same face, that same body, but angry, Black was so angry, maybe he had a right to be, about simply everything. A man alienated, that was the word, Isabela was taking Doc's course on Homer—was it even on Homer? The semester was almost over and Homer, or the woman wrongly referred to by that name, hadn't even come up—what the course was really about was the idea that everybody is everybody and therefore everybody is not entirely themselves, thus alienated from themselves. Isabela was gripped by the idea of alienation, of making strange, there was even this syndrome, Dr. Strangelove syndrome—she really needed to see that film, she missed it every year because, well, she had no one to go with, well some meat-heads went but was she a meathead?—anyway in that syndrome a person experiences their limbs as not belonging to them, as acting on their own. That was Black, his head stuffed full of ideas but unable to align the world to fit his ideas or to make his ideas fit *him* or maybe both. And to capture all that with a little chunk of clay shaped into what should have been Fregoli and a body with wires for hands and feet, unfinished, frail yet with vigor, the same clay capturing such utterly different people as Ignacio and Black …

"Wow," F. Scott touched Isabela's arm, "You're good at this, Isabela."

"Ah," Isabela was startled, not realizing she had expressed those thoughts aloud, not having any idea whatsoever what to do with the alien hand on her arm.

F. Scott, sensing that, removed her hand. "I'll go with you next time."

"What?"

"To see *Dr. Strangelove*."

Isabela looked at F. Scott's soft face in the soft blue light. *If only I were attracted to—anybody*, she would write in her diary later that evening.

Her eyes moved to the next sculpture and she stopped breath-ing. "Magdalena."

"Do it again, Isabela."

"What?"

"Your analysis."

"There are no words, Scott."

"Apparently there are, honey. You did pretty great with Black."

Isabela looked back at the sculpture and did not speak. Fregoli's face was Magdalena's face, the same body—Isabela looked closely and no, there were no little breasts added there—it was the same body and yet a woman's body. It captured her posture, her bearing, her—kindness, Magdalena was the kindest person Isabela knew, she always called you friend, and she knew you were sad even when you were concealing it. The wires for hands and feet, for her, somehow, weren't frailty but strength, the solid core beneath her soft, supple flesh. There was, how could that be, a hint of Jeffrey to the sculpture, the angle of the body, slightly leaning, leaning against Jeffrey, maybe whispering to Jeffrey, sharing her deepest fears, sharing her insecurities, maybe they were under a sheet in bed and she was leaning against him sharing and touching and unraveling. But Magdalena was strong, she was independent, she was not dependent on Jeffrey, she could lean on him but she could turn away, assert herself, run away …

"A penny for your thoughts," F. Scott whispered, not wanting to disturb that expression on Isabela's face, the gaze, was it longing— but really wanting to hear what Isabela was thinking.

Isabela shook her head, reached for another tissue. "Why do you use Fregoli as your model?" she changed the subject. "For everyone? Isn't he a little, you know—crazy?"

"Have you ever spoken to him?"

"It's hard to. He's kind of, a little, you know—crazy."

"You have to persist. There's more going on than people realize."

"Like what?"

"'There are no words,' Isabela," F. Scott smiled.

"Touché. But can't you try?"

"All right," F. Scott pursed her lips. "You know that terrific analysis of Black—of my sculpture—you just gave?"

"Yes. And thank you."

"I got that from Fregoli."

"You got that from Fregoli?"

"I got that from Fregoli. He shared his analysis of Black with me, and I turned it into a sculpture. The same for the others."

"Ignacio? Magdalena?"

"Exactly. He generates the most penetrating psychospiritual profiles of everyone he observes. All these things, I learned from Fregoli. And then I sculpt them."

"Has he profiled me?" Isabela asked, suddenly feeling cold.

It was a ridiculous question. Why would Fregoli even have noticed her, flying all alone way out there a billion of miles from the sun?

F. Scott smiled gently, an uncomfortable smile. "Yes, you too."

Isabela was tempted to ask—who would not be? Like asking the Tarot card reader who has looked at your cards …

"No, I haven't sculpted you yet, honey," F. Scott interrupted, which was not the answer to the question she was thinking—not "Have you sculpted my essence yet?" but rather "Can you tell me what my essence is?"—but did suffice as a distraction. "I've just done one more so far. I have it here, in the closet."

Isabela was relieved to change the subject. "Why in the closet? There's still room on the shelf here."

"It's just," F. Scott opened the closet, moved some stuff out of the way, retrieved the sculpture, "I'm having trouble finishing it. Not entirely my fault: Fregoli had trouble too. Said his essence was elusive. That he had materials so deeply buried he had trouble extracting them, but they were there, undeniably there. If you have any ideas, I'm happy to hear them."

She plopped the unfinished sculpture onto the shelf, adjusted the spotlight so Isabela could see.

Fregoli's face, that same body, but that smile—

"Samuel," Isabela said.

It was Beamie.

=====

15.
the hole in the shade

There were no togas and no live music, but the penultimate Tuesday Night Club of the year nevertheless bore some resemblance to the aspirational film *Animal House*, whose soundtrack was playing on the stereo. The mood was heavy—still reeling some weeks from the Guy's arrest—the drinking was heavier, and the conversation was heaviest, particularly when Black was informed that Otis Day and the Knights was not a real group. Isabela snapped a photo of his face and you'd almost think he was at a funeral, deaf to the shouts of "Chug! Chug!" going on around him.

But lest you think this chugging was that merely of animals in the house, remember that this was a place with many hoary traditions. You didn't merely drink; you turned it into a competition. Take Tang, for example, that intramural sport wherein your eight-member team sat at a long table with two eight-ounce glasses of beer before each player. On the other side of the table was the opposing team, lined up the same way. When the gavel was slammed the first player on each team had to guzzle his (or her!) glass and when the glass was returned to the table the second player had to drink. This went down the line to the eighth player, who had to drink his (or her!) two glasses consecutively before returning back up to the first player. The first team to drink all the way down and back was the winner, and got the first trip either to the bathroom to vomit or to the hospital as necessary.

Or you wrote a book.

Andy Griscom, Ben Rand, and Scott Johnston, who had honed their skills at Tuesday Night Club before graduating last year, also had literary ambitions. They had used their final year of school not merely producing stellar senior theses but also developing a book manuscript, *The Complete Book of Beer Drinking Games*. This year's seniors were giving the manuscript a test run—"It's called beta-testing," Swill informed them one evening early in the year, shortly before passing out—so the "chug!"s you just heard were actually scientific research.

Tonight they were fine-tuning the rules of Quarters, wherein you attempt to toss a quarter into the opposing player's shot glass of beer; if you succeed, he (or she!) drinks the glass. Boot Factor of three. Isabela was documenting the whole thing with her Nikon, maybe to use some of her photos for the book.

"You do realize," Debra said to Jeffrey many years later, "how outrageous this all sounds now?"

"I do," Jeffrey nodded.

"And maybe even—"

"—offensive? I do."

"And, I don't know, gross?"

"Yep."

"I can't even see you doing these things, being like that."

"I know. It's almost like the college me is a fictional person. Somehow it all seemed so fun, so cool, at the time. Vomiting was a badge of honor. You'd come out from the toilet with your arms raised, like a champion. For a while after college I would say that the most important thing I learned there was how to stick my finger down my throat when I'd drunk too much."

"And now?"

"What I could have done, or could have been," Jeffrey shook his head.

"And you lived in that room in the Lower Courtyard, and hosted the party, your senior year."

"Unreal, I know."

"You regret it now?"

"No, it's not that. I don't regret it, even though I can't defend that behavior today. I am a different person now," Jeffrey tried to work it out. "Though if I could travel back in time the person I am now would probably shake his college self and yell at him, 'Who *are* you?' and 'What, I ask you, *what* are you doing here?' You know, did I ever tell you about this time travel story…"

And what, we ask you, what was Isabela doing there? the investigating officers would interrogate them all the next day.

What kind of question was that, most responded. She sometimes came to Tuesday Night Club, they said, many Piersonites did. Our gang were regulars, and she was one of our gang.

Did she drink a lot, they asked.

What kind of question, everybody drank a lot, but that really wasn't true, was it, for Isabela, she didn't usually drink much, nursing a single cup all night long.

Did she seem upset?

She always seemed a little upset, she didn't talk a lot, had things on her mind.

What things?

Well we can't rightly say, can we, since she didn't talk much?

We'll thank you to answer politely, we are just doing our job.

Sorry, you understand *everyone* is a little upset.

Speaking of, did she seem at all more upset than usual?

No, not really, really can't say.

I'm sorry, young lady, if you need to excuse yourself?

Maggie was weeping, weeping, it was all so dreadful, why did Jeff have to be away. It wasn't anybody's fault, it wasn't their fault, though of course it was, everybody was responsible for everybody and maybe they shouldn't have pushed so hard …

How did they convince her to play Quarters, exactly?

She wanted to. She was tired of being on the outskirts all the time, taking photos, never being in any. She was watching, sipping her warm beer a little more vigorously than usual, enjoying the energy in the room, enjoyed people singing the song "Shama Lama Ding Dong" along with the stereo. If anyone else were taking photos they could have gotten a good one of Isabela at one point, well, smiling, it was kind of a smile, she was pretty when she smiled. It was Jasmine who noticed Isabela watching, creeping forward, who, when the current match ended, called her name.

"Izzy," Jasmine shouted, holding a cup of beer in her left hand and sliding her right arm around Isabela's shoulder, "your turn?"

That was nice, Isabela thought, Jasmine was always kind enough to her but the nickname, the arm around the shoulder, that felt good. And people cheering, excited that she said yes. Tayvon and Lisa took a break from dancing to come over enthusiastically and watch. Samilla was there, all smiles, where was Black, had disappeared. Ignacio guffawing, he was parodying the song playing, rasping "Hey Isabela" instead of "Hey Paula." Someone shouted at him that he should perform at the Pierson Cabaret, yeah when the Cabaret starts featuring sea shanties someone else said, Ignacio guffawed with them and kept rasping. Ren was at the side of the room scribbling notes, even he was smiling as he chronicled her taking her place on the floor for the match. Time to come in from the frozen periphery and maybe warm herself in the inner circles for a while.

Magdalena came over, leaned over. "You good, friend?" she rather shouted into Isabela's ear, over the music.

"I'm good," she nodded, taking a sip of that gross warm beer.

It was loud, but it was good, she was ready for this she was thinking as there was commotion, some excited shouting, and accompanied by an entourage of their friends Samuel was dropped into place on the floor opposite her.

"Hi," he shouted, sort of smiling at her, not entirely making eye contact, entirely fine with her.

Her heart, already beating rapidly, kicked it up a notch.

Their friends liked to call him a loser and they had been trying for almost three years now to help him copulate with someone and they had just dropped him in front of her.

I'm someone, she thought to herself.

The song "Dream Girl" came on and he was smiling at her, he was probably supposed to say something, she thought, but it was so loud, with the music, the hooting, what could he say? But that smile, that's why they called him Beamie and maybe she should too, she supposed the smile *was* a little goofy but of course she saw something they couldn't see, she had seen F. Scott's sculpture, the one that captured that smile though on Fregoli's face, she saw the sweetness in it, the tenderness of it, the sadness, his was a human soul the same as everyone else's they were all unique and yet they were all interchangeable.

The game had begun and sweet sad—Beamie—missed his first quarter toss at her shot glass and she landed hers and there were shouts of "Drink! Drink!" as Beamie obligingly downed his glass. He missed again and she hit again and there was raucous laughter and shouts of "Drink!" and she realized the game was diabolical because the person losing got drunker faster and thereby would lose even more, and she felt bad for tender sad lonely Beamie so she downed her own shot glass in sympathy. The beer was gross and maybe that broke the rules but there was laughter their glasses were refilled and Beamie missed again and this time she missed but then he missed again and she hit and he drank. She thought it was kind of gross to drink beer that a quarter has just landed in, the quarter touched by how many dirty fingers and with the metallic taste how could they stand it but that was more his problem than hers because he apparently couldn't land a quarter in an open barrel if he were standing right above it that suddenly was the funniest thing she had ever thought and she started to laugh and he was still smiling and then she felt bad for lonely Beamie and had another sympathy drink and people were shouting the song "Shout!"

The next sequence was not very clear (how could it be).

She was the victor, they were celebrating her, it was weird she had this one moment where she remembered it was a Tuesday night and she had an assignment due tomorrow on Homer not for Doc but for her classics seminar and she wasn't finished with it. But then she was basking in the celebration, the warmth of it, it was very warm in the room with all the bodies and loud music and then she was in Beamie's room somehow, she could sort of remember his asking so sweetly, "Do you want to maybe go for a walk?" and people were cheering as she said sure and they went for a walk, a stumble really, around the courtyard past the red sunset maple tree and the cool fresh air felt good at first and Beamie's hand bumped into hers, was he trying to hold her hand that was sweet and sad but then it was too chilly, it was an April evening in New Haven and she felt so exposed walking with Beamie there were people about and it was she who suggested maybe they go hang out in his room a bit. A sweet sad nervous Beamie said yes let's he actually wasn't feeling terrific, how could he be he had just been destroyed in a Boot Factor three drinking game, but here was opportunity knocking on his door no that was him knocking on his own door that was funny they had a good laugh it really was sweet and tender between them and they went on in. Jeff was abroad so Beamie had the suite to himself, it was all pretty slick, like *a three-room apartment with toaster oven and television* and he had nobody to share it with but now he had someone because Isabela was definitely someone.

There *were* people about in the courtyard, meatheads to be specific. Tayvon and Lisa and Swill had followed Beamie and Isabela out, oh they kept some respectable distance in the courtyard but when they saw the couple heading towards Beamie's room they started rounding people up.

"Genius," Iggy said when they retrieved him from the TNC room.

"Goddamn genius," Black followed along, and Samilla said do you actually have to swear so much and Black said yes I goddamn do.

"This is fantastic," Jasmine said when fetched from her own room, having left TNC before the end of the Quarters match because she really couldn't stand the coarse music. On the way she swung by the common room to pick up Maya, who liked to study there on Tuesday evenings because Ashok usually played piano at that time.

"How did you know they would go to his room?" Maggie asked Tayvon as she arrived as well.

"Easy," Tayvon answered.

"How?"

"No, because his room is easy. Easy access. First floor. It's a law of nature that drunken revelry tends toward easy access. Now shh, everybody, shh."

The buzz was buzzing, they all felt it as they piled in around the quarter-sized hole Tayvon had cut in the window shade to Beamie's bedroom window earlier that day.

"Hyellay!" Iggy muttered as he pushed in for a look, using the expression that included, among its many meanings, "My eyes cannot *believe* their good fortune!"

"Genius," Swill said, stepping back to allow Maya a glance, who couldn't decide if she was thrilled for Isabela or outraged at the patriarchy of it all.

"Goddamn genius," Black muttered again, pushing in, and reflecting on the awesome scope of the plan. Almost three years in the making, really, this team endeavor to get the loser some action, and while the Isabela angle was more recent, well it was splendid to see it unfolding according to plan. Had the air of ineluctability, really, to use that word that Tayvon slung around in formulating the plan, they were all just playing the roles they were destined to play. Tuesday Night Club, Quarters, bringing them together, the path of least resistance to his room, really they almost had no say in the matter. *At the second to last TNC Beamie, that stud*, at last, was about to *get lucky*, some *habba-do-gaggedy*, and now *through the hole in the shade* so were they all.

Tayvon pushed in again with his Instamatic, he was prepared down to the detail, he lined up its lens with the hole in the shade and captured some immortal shots they were smart enough not to mention to the investigating officers the next day.

To be clear, the women were there too: Lisa, Samilla, Jasmine, and Maya, all in favor of Isabela taking matters into her own hands but also not entirely sure that this counted as her taking matters into her own hands. There were important futures ahead for all of them, including Pulitzers and Head Counsel positions for the NAACP and international performance careers, but at the moment nothing was more important than Isabela losing her virginity and that they were all in it together.

"This is something," Samilla whispered to Jasmine, clasping her hand.

"Shh," Tayvon said.

And Maggie …

She was there, she glanced through the shade, she was glad she did and yet something was not sitting right, and she immediately pulled away.

"I really wished Jeff were there," she wrote in her diary later that night. "I was so missing him. I'm sure he would have enjoyed that as much as the other meatheads, but then he would have realized something was bothering me, and we would have talked it through, he would ask his questions and undo the knot in my thoughts, in my stomach. To make explicit what's implicit, he always says. I wished I could call him. I wish I could call him now."

But he was one-sixth of a world away, it was seven or eight in the morning there so he was probably just getting into deep sleep, and anyway the long distance calls were so expensive and there was only one phone in his dorm hallway and it was so much trouble to actually connect that that was why they had only spoken once since he left, and only briefly.

Maggie took her glance through the shade then backed away, and grabbed Tayvon's Instamatic and focused it on the meatheads jockeying for viewing position through the hole, restraining their hooting lest they disturb the activities inside. These photos were also never mentioned to the investigating officers.

It was only later, on looking at the photos, that anyone realized Jude wasn't there.

As for what was going on inside the room ...

Can't a guy and a gal get some privacy around here?

"What was that?" Isabela whispered in a panic thinking she heard some rustling right outside.

"What? Nothing," Beamie whispered back, sweating, not at *all* thinking about his mother walking into the room.

Suffice to say that by standards you might apply to Tayvon or Samilla it was an unmitigated disaster in there, but by standards you should apply to the innocent and the loser it was, with some fits and starts, a smashing success.

Eventually there was much rejoicing.

Maybe not so much rejoicing.

Everybody would know.

Isabela was sure of it.

Maybe they already did.

That rustling, she was sure she heard it, a few times.

Were they loud? It was all such a blur.

He was snoring next to her and it was kind of gross and she jumped out of the bed and got her long skirt back on and sat on his desk chair and looked at the wall and listened to the gross throaty rumblings and turned the desk light off she couldn't believe they had left the light on the whole time.

She felt sick, the drinking, the smoke from the TNC room, the smells, the snoring.

All of it.

=====

16.
where did the butterfly go

Everybody would know.

Maybe they already did.

She would walk out of here in the morning and no one would say anything but they would look at her differently. Maybe smile at her, she couldn't bear that. Even the staff in the dining hall would know, that kind woman who checked them in and smiled at Isabela, that nice woman who was always kind to her on the serving line. Isabela would go in for lunch today and they would smile at her and the woman would give her extra fries because she *knew*. The idea that the woman would smile at her and give her extra fries made her feel sick. The idea of fries, the idea of lunch, the idea of the dining hall, it all made her feel sick.

They would know.

Maybe they already did.

How she longed to be a frozen chunk of ice hurtling through the dark empty space four billion miles away.

That snoring was repulsive.

All of it.

The clock on the desk said 3:06 AM.

It was weird but she suddenly saw a butterfly, it was flapping its wings by the bedroom door, she was so tired and not feeling well and she watched the butterfly flapping by the door and saw it wanted to get out. She got up and went to the door, opened it, followed it into the livingroom, the lights were still on, and it went right to the door of the suite. What was a butterfly doing here, and now, in the middle of the night, still practically winter, she wondered as she followed it into the courtyard and toward the Pierson Tower, it was peaceful out here at this hour, quiet, no motorcycles, no sea shanties, just the silent cool night.

She followed the butterfly out the Pierson gate, headed down the Pierson Gateway, the long corridor toward York Street. As an architecture student she had much praise for this corridor. Narrow and paved with stones, lit by faux 19th-century gas lanterns, halfway down rose tall brick chimneys on either side and across from each other, like the touchdown signal from the football ref, she knew enough about football to know that. And of course looming over the corridor—Isabela turned around to glance—was the Pierson Tower with its four faces and clocks, the one facing her reading 3:11 AM. How many evenings had she trudged back down this corridor, watched over by the Pierson Tower which seemed to welcome her home, to keep her safe. There was nobody coming up the Gateway now, she didn't see anybody, she headed down and turned right on York Street without thinking about it because she didn't need to think about it because it really wasn't up to her, she headed toward that brutal monstrosity that had become her other home over the past couple of years.

It was quite chilly she realized as the wind hit her on York, realizing at the same time that she didn't have her coat, that sweet little pink coat her mother had given her before she died and was now in her closet in her room. It was in the low forties, a rather biting wind, she could almost hear Jude reciting the weather forecast in her head adding some fun meteorological fact, but it didn't matter because it wasn't far, she was already past the Yale Dramat, rubbing her arms from the chill, and she was walking past the

Wolf's Head tomb, these secret societies were creepy and she felt so out of sorts and the wind made a rustling noise, kind of like that noise, those noises, she heard earlier, earlier this night, was it just the wind, was it just the wind.

Clarity of vision. Funny to think that, just now, when so little was clear, or was it. Maybe the weather, the thought of Jude, Jude who she suddenly thought was key to everything, the center of it all. Wait, what could that mean? She rubbed her arms against the chill and had this strange thought that she was thinking about the future, that Jude would *become* the center of everything, one should pay attention to Jude. Somebody smiled at her as she approached the building, it was that sophomore sculpture student, Oren, F. Scott had mentioned him. Obviously he was a hard worker, being here at this hour, smiling at her as she approached the door, he didn't usually smile at her, maybe it was the hour, no—she realized—he *knew*, that was it, he knew, she was sure of it, because everybody knew, because she was seeing the future and maybe going a little crazy.

Oren held the door for her, he saw her enter, smiled.

What an awful building, she thought on entering. Dark, cramped, moist, cold, jarring, the hours she had spent here, emotionally jarred.

She walked past the Art Library, saw a couple of vaguely familiar people studying in there, at this hour, maybe one of them smiled at her, but she did not enter, did not enter where she had done much of her studying in the past fifteen months or so, ever since the, you know, incident. There was no reason to go in there, she was not here to study, she hadn't brought her books with her, she had that assignment due tomorrow but that was not going to happen, her knapsack, had she brought it to TNC earlier, yes, she had come from the library and planned to return, she had left her knapsack in the TNC room. Somebody would find it there, her name was on it in permanent pink marker on the inside label, somebody would collect and return it to her. People were kind, most people were kind, many people were kind. Beamie was kind, there was kindness in his smile, but it made her feel a little sick to think of it.

Her Nikon.

Where had she left that.

Quick, up these stairs, here.

She entered one of the staircases, they were located at such unintuitive places, what a fire hazard if ever there were a fire in this godforsaken building, in fact this was itself a fire stairwell in the back corner of the building, a fire escape. Onto the brown metal steps with the brown metal railing, the noisy steps, they rattled, the denizens of this building would recognize that rattle on their deathbeds. She remembered her mother in that old bed with the rail headboard, it also rattled, different rattle, same rattle. As she began her ascent she had a moment where she saw the future again, a future, that smile smiling at her. But then there were footsteps above her, a footfall, falling feet, coming down, the stairs rattling in that way and that vision evaporated and somebody, an older woman, maybe a professor, clattered down past her, saw her, smiled at her as she continued up.

She knew, too; she knew it.

"Isabela!" she heard someone call out as she arrived at the fifth-floor landing.

She liked the fifth floor, there was a walkway there that overlooked the fourth-floor senior drafting studio. It was a good concept, that junior architecture students might learn something by watching over their senior colleagues, though it always felt a little, maybe, voyeuristic to her. She preferred to work in private, obviously the work had to be shared with people, the professors, it had to stand up to critique, that was excruciating but she understood. That's why she loved the darkroom, you could usually be alone in there, not have people watching over you while you worked, peering at you while you worked, observing you, watching you, knowing, that she could not abide, what she was going to do when she was a senior she hadn't really worked out.

She came off the stairs, in search of the voice.

There was nobody on the walkway over the studio. There was nobody in the studio either. Architecture students were the night-owl type, strange that the area was empty at this hour, though she now wasn't sure exactly what hour it was—she had forgotten to put on her watch, she realized, and the building was famously spare of clocks because the last thing anyone needed to be reminded of was how many hours of their life were lost in this building, and God knows how long it had been since she came out the Pierson Gateway was it just a few minutes ago but then why did it suddenly feel like that was weeks or months or years ago?

Where did the butterfly go.

"Isabela!" the voice came more urgently, from up above somewhere.

Back onto the stairs, up she went, to the seventh floor.

She found the window, the window.

It was a fabulous view, looking over sleepy New Haven, scattered twinkling lights, the real world, mostly asleep, outside The Bubble. The lock had been fixed, and it was now closed and locked, but it was a simple mechanism to unlock the window.

Someone really hadn't thought it through, but Isabela had. She had come up here many times over the past fifteen months, to look at the view, at different times of day and night, to think, to imagine, to see the future. She had played the scene over and over in her mind, resolutions, execution. A quiet place to hide. There should be no witnesses, that would not be kind to subject anyone to that. She would have to wait. She could wait. There was all the time in the world really, once you thought about it, everybody was everybody, Homer was a woman, she would know when the time was right. Was that clarity of vision? How would you know? Unless you already had clarity of vision then your evaluation of your clarity was itself suspect. Jude had talked about this more than once, he could be very articulate, if anybody had clarity of vision it would be he, but then again, how could she trust her own judgment of his judgment? There's the rub, how could she trust her own judgment, how could she trust her own judgment?

There was no way out of oneself.

It was stuffy in here, overbearing, she could use some air.

She fiddled with the lock mechanism, it snapped open easily.

She hesitated then opened the window and felt the cool thrust of air, looking out over the sleeping world. Freshman year she had this idea for a movie, it came to her like a vision, the way she could sometimes see the future, it would be in German, it would be called *Der Himmel über Berlin*. There would be angels in it, invisible angels because angels were invisible, maybe her mother, because her mother was an angel, and they would move among all the suffering people, and they would put their hand on the shoulder of a suffering person, her mother's hand, the person wouldn't know the angel was there but there would be a moment of lightness, a moment, a lightening.

She felt that, there, lighter.

For a moment.

For a sweet passing moment.

Then she leaned out the window and looked down at the moat some seventy feet below.

=====

17.

man of the year

Jeff had missed Croc's Superbowl party, all of Feb Club, the Blow Off Steam run, Abe's birthday, a dozen or so Tuesday Night Clubs, and all the tragic drama surrounding the Isabela Incident, but he made it home in time for the annual meathead gathering at Eli's family's beach house in Woods Hole, the weekend after finals. Black surprised him (he was expecting Maggie) at Logan airport.

"J., the man, the myth, the legend," Black exclaimed, giving him an exaggerated wet kiss on the cheek, "is in da house!"

"Hyellay!" Jeff exclaimed embracing him, using the expression that included, among its many meanings, "What the hell was *that*?"

"Things are pretty gray in The Bubble right now," Black explained, "but nothing that a little thing the entire fucking world now knows as the 'moonwalk' can't lighten up."

Jeff shook his head, then looked at him in that way.

"Your lady is at the house," Black nodded gently. "With the gang. Playing hostess, the way she does. Hey," he added to change the subject, "you need some help with that?"

He was pointing at Jeff's enormous suitcase.

"If you're offering," Jeff said quietly.

"I'm not. Just curious. Follow me, J., let's get out da house!" Black took off toward the parking lot to begin the process of remembering where in the hell he parked Maggie's busted up little Spirit.

"You said things are pretty gray in The Bubble right now?" Jeff said once the swearing was done and they were underway for the two-hour drive to the Cape.

Black didn't bother with the littler things—the coming rise in the drinking age to twenty, the Guy's arrest, the disappointing hockey season, the failed effort to dissuade Iggy from doing the Pierson Cabaret next year—those could wait. He took a deep breath and filled him in on the big thing, the tragic thing, the Isabela Incident. Jeff had many questions, so many questions, most of which Black could not answer, so by the time they finally pulled up along the other cars lining the Penzance driveway he was a big mix not only of travel fatigue and jet lag but irritation, anxiety, deep tender sorrow, and did we mention the anxiety?

"The man!" "The myth!" "The legend!" were among the cries when Jeff stepped out of the back door of the house onto the deck overlooking the lawn that overlooked the private beach that overlooked Buzzard's Bay. It was a pleasant enough late afternoon in mid-May, a bit cloudy but in the sixties, a bit windy: not swimming weather but perfect barbecue weather, especially with a sweater on as the sun was just past its highest point in the sky. The reception was warm, the high fives and embraces were warmer, but it was subdued, after everything they had been through, and most of all it was incomplete, because she wasn't there.

And then there was a creaking sound as the door to the shed opened and she came out with two more lawn chairs and the friends parted and Jude stepped to the side and then there she was, there she was.

Never had he seen anything more beautiful.

Her long dark hair draped on her shoulders, recently brushed by her grandmother's brush. The early foundations of her summer tan, already in place. Those gorgeous dark eyes. Looking at him. Smiling. The bathing suit clinging to her soccer-fit body that she was optimistically wearing—the water too cold for swimming—that he optimistically hoped to be unclinging from her if they could steal away during the weekend. Maybe tonight, when most of the gang would be busy watching the Islanders advancing their dynasty against the Oilers and their evil phenom, the Great One, in the Stanley Cup Finals game.

She was smiling. At him.

Maybe, he thought, this is going to be all right.

"You forgot this," Maggie said, handing something to him.

It was the *Time* magazine quoting Swill and featuring the computer as Man of the Year.

Have a summer one and all,
We'll meet back here in the fall

part 4
senior year
fall

=====

1.

tries to smile but it's all over

Welcome back now we are seniors…

It was spontaneous. The first week of classes senior year, *my God the time just flies*, someone said there should be a photo, sure, be in the courtyard at the maple at four o'clock. Some mentioned it to others, the Venns expanded, suddenly people were arriving a little before four, and before you knew it *let's get everyone in the picture*, well not everyone but a nice sample of Pierson 1984, thirty-nine out of some hundred-plus made it, an impressive turnout in those days before social media could rustle up a crowd. Wait who should take the photo and thereby not be in it, someone asked, but just in time Daisuke showed up, who was a junior, and Japanese, so he probably was good with cameras—you could say that then—and so that problem was solved.

Blink your eyes and we're older … So there they were on that early September afternoon, several dozen young people, standing, kneeling, sitting on the grass under the maple, Pierson seniors embarking on their final year in The Bubble, this moment captured for eternity, most of the meatheads, some peripheral meatheads, some outside the meathead Venn whose names would evaporate after graduation. Smiling faces, arms around shoulders, Tayvon shirtless and with a bandana, Swill with his arm around Maya, Ig with his arm around some woman whose name he didn't know, Maggie all smiles standing in the middle, sublime Magina with an invisible cordon around her. Croc used The Photo for his annual Christmas card so that in their future soon to diverge trajectories, *wherever you might be,* everyone could trace back to this one moment, this shared eternal moment.

All those happy faces, smiling faces, the prime of youth, bright futures ahead, immortals. It was the kind of photo that really kills you after somebody in it dies, as it would some years later after Ignacio's untimely passing—he would be the first to go—and again after Jude's murder.

Happy smiling faces and there, in the rear left corner, *tries to smile, but it's all over,* was Jeff-Jeff not smiling, in fact looking miserable.

Across the world the Sri Lankan Civil War was underway, thousands dead. Flooding in Spain killing dozens. Closer to home Hurricane Alicia—such a gentle name—was anything but, killing twenty-two.

But far far worse, on the first day of classes Maggie had dumped Jeff.

=====

2.

as these things tend to go, this thing went

It was a perfect moment.

Late afternoon, late August, seventy-nine degrees, the sun on its slow descent to the watery horizon into which they were gazing, the yellows already deepening into oranges, the waters deep and calm and clear, they were sitting on the hill of this private Penzance beach, on their blanket, flip-flops off, toes in the sand, side by side, an open bottle of wine on the blanket. It had been a good summer, the Isabela Incident beginning to lift, life goes on, life was good. His not recently touched copy of Proust's *Remembrance of Things Past* was on the blanket too. A whole summer trying to read that thing and he was maybe a hundred pages in, all of which consisted, as far as he could tell, of the narrator turning over in bed. He would have some words with Tayvon when they got back, for recommending the thing.

But no matter.

This beautiful place, this easy time, they were relaxed, leaning against each other, they were feeling good.

Their perfect moment.

"It doesn't get any better than this," Jeff said, moving his right arm around Maggie's waist, his left hand holding his wine glass.

There was just the slightest hesitation before Maggie scrunched up her face and answered quizzically, "Does it?"

It was a joke, of course it was a joke, he understood that, right?

"You know," Jeff said uneasily, in one of those moments that years later you look back and see for the turning point it was, one of those branching points that determine new trajectories, the butterfly flaps and there's a hurricane or doesn't and there isn't, "You know," Jeff launched in, later replaying it in his head, "You know," he said watching himself say it again and again in that now inevitable way, it was out of his hands, "I really mean that seriously."

It really had been a nice summer, hadn't it?

Maggie spent weekdays in New York doing her photography internship and weekends at home in Woods Hole. Jeff scored a pre-med internship doing organic chemistry research at Boston University, spending most weekends with Maggie as they got reacquainted after his semester away. With Eli's family summering in Europe they had the run of Penzance and the beach, which was where Maggie caught him up on all the meathead news, including, of course, the Isabela Incident.

Isabela's freaking out like that, nobody saw that coming, maybe they should have, maybe Maggie did a little, but how awful her climbing back up to the same window that woman jumped or fell out of last year. And then Maggie, missing Jeff a little, couldn't sleep and made a middle of the night hot dog run to Wawa and happened to be returning up the Pierson Gateway as Isabela was leaving it. She immediately saw something was off, it was cold and Isabela didn't have her coat and she didn't seem to see her when Maggie smiled and said hi. Alarmed, Maggie turned around and saw her turn down York Street and then hesitated, deciding what to do. By the time she got back down the Gateway she just saw Isabela turning into the building down the street. Maggie started running, for a half-second worried how she could possibly find Isabela in that labyrinth of a building, but as she arrived it became perfectly obvious to her where Isabela was going. Maggie was glad for her soccer stamina as she dashed to the back stairwell, clattering up those stairs two at a time, making it right up to that seventh-floor window to see Isabela leaning out the window leaning forward ...

"Iz," she exclaimed, her heart in her throat, reaching out her hand.

Maggie saw Isabela freeze.

"Iz," she said again, more gently, reaching her hand to touch Isabela's shoulder. She felt Isabela shudder, she found herself thinking *please God please do not let her do this*, "Iz," she almost whispered and then Isabela pulled herself in from the window and dropped into Maggie's arms and was sobbing sobbing sobbing...

"My superhero," Jeff whispered, caressing Maggie's beautiful hair, who had resumed weeping when telling the story.

Isabela survived the story but did not survive Yale, having withdrawn the next day never to return. It would still be some time before the meatheads could joke about it, about Beamie's magic touch that either made women lesbians or drove them to seventh-floor windows.

It really had been an okay summer, hadn't it?

It was fine that they spent so much time on those weekends with her Woods Hole friends, might hang on the beach during the day, play some cribbage in the evenings. The last weekend in July Jeff met Maggie in New York where they also met up with Black and Samilla for the Diana Ross concert in Central Park. Black was taking education classes at Columbia's Teacher's College while Samilla was working at a public defense law firm, and, subletting together, the bickering (and subsequent sex) was nearly unremittent. Black was in great form that night, thrilled to see Diana, and nothing could dampen his mood, not even the ferocious thunderstorm that sent them back to their apartment soaked.

"It'll be good practice for Princeton," Jeff said when they realized it was too late to journey back to Maggie's Brooklyn sublet and when he realized she seemed under-enthusiastic about sharing the narrow sofa. The face she made in relenting also seemed a little under-enthused, he thought, for their only-one-left-to-go sofa project.

It had not been a bad summer, had it? And now his arm was around her waist as the sun settled down toward the water, her head was on his shoulders, nestling in, "You know," he said, and why shouldn't he have said it, "I really mean that seriously."

What was taking her so long to respond?

Was it Jeff's imagination that he felt her tense up?

"Mmm," she finally answered, not moving.

You could have stopped there, Jeff.

Instead you cleared your throat and said again more softly, "I really mean that seriously."

Happily, or unhappily, the time delay in responding was shorter.

"It was just a joke, Jeff," Maggie said tersely. "You understand that, right?"

Jeff, yes?

We needn't detail the ensuing discussion; suffice to say that as these things tend to go, this thing went. The sun was nearly kissing the water when Jeff said something melodramatic and she, trying to lighten the mood, said, "Well aren't you the poet, mister," and playfully poked him, adding, "You should put that in a song. With my name in it finally? Maybe?"

"Yeah," he said, and got up, maybe to go do that right now. "I'm heading in."

Jeff went back into the house, pausing only once or twice without turning around to listen for any footsteps following him.

None.

Maybe a shower, fresh clothes.

He was not snooping.

There were no towels in the bathroom, he went to look for one, they used to be in these drawers but Eli's family's cleaning service had recently moved them. He was not snooping, he was looking for towels and a drawer might have been opened along the way, one of the drawers they used when they stayed in the house, and there it was, her little diary, practically on top of the clothes, Maggie had been keeping this their whole time together, little flower-covered notebooks, lightly perfumed.

There it was, that little diary.

Oh there was hesitation, there was misgiving. He understood it was wrong, and even more that he shouldn't do it, for himself, for her, but then, somehow, by some chain of reasoning he could not later reproduce, he found himself thinking, it's okay, it's allowed, it's been three years, I have a right to know, I'll trust myself, I'll trust myself, and he reached toward it.

This wasn't such an offense, was it? Maggie herself had read him passages at times. Like about the music box, last January when he left for Florence, that was a grand slam, *Way to fucking devastate me* she had written in her room after returning from the airport, having already listened to that little music box play "The Beginning" for her a dozen times and crying her eyes out. That was good, wasn't it? Great, even? There would be more of that in there, wouldn't there? It would be good for them, for him, for her.

His hand was on the little flowered cover.

Those key junctures, those decision points that determine future trajectories, those flaps or don't flaps, are actually a dime a dozen. That conversation on the beach, sure, but did you have to storm into the house afterward? Did you have to open this drawer which you knew, didn't you, wasn't a towel drawer? Later on are you going to wonder what might have been if you had not picked up the little diary? If you had not chosen to say *it doesn't get any better than this*? If she had not put her lips on yours on that Halloween almost three years earlier ...

Was this one of those moments?

Maybe stop now, El Jefe, J.-man, J.?

Jeff Jeff Jeff Jeff Jeff.

Were they any branches out of this trajectory?

Maggie had those eensy-weensy abandonment issues he suddenly remembered. He had abandoned her for a semester in Italy, you know she had always trusted him, he had always honored that trust, and no, he was not going to abandon her now.

He looked at the unopened diary.

He buried it back in the drawer.

He closed the drawer, and exhaled deeply.

That would have been an awful trajectory, he thought.

It already was.

"What more do you want, man?" Black asked after a *very* long phone conversation the next day.

"I want to rewind," Jeff answered. "I want to redo that conversation. I want to undo it. I want it never to have happened."

"Good luck with that. But in the meanwhile, man, remember. You got a treasure there. Don't blow it. Repeat after me: 'Don't blow it.'"

"Don't blow it."

"Don't blow it. Move on. Don't say a word. Swallow it, J. Keep it inside you, even if it eats you from the inside. I tell you this: There is no future trajectory, as you like to put it, that includes your continuing that conversation and comes out happily."

Jeff, to his credit, kept it in over the next few days, including through the move-in to launch their senior year. Less to his credit he couldn't stop ruminating constantly, so he was grumpy, irritable. Maggie tried to talk to him about it at one point and he snapped at her.

"What the hell," she recoiled, irritated at his lingering foul mood.

"I'm sorry," he regrouped, thinking quickly, doing his best. "It's just that Black is going crazy about Jesse Jackson possibly running for president and it's driving *me* crazy. He's calling me a racist because I didn't want to sign up for his anti-Jackson campaign. Just trying to follow his logic is enough to wreck your brain."

But you couldn't keep it inside you, could you, J.?

Being eaten up from the inside feels so bad you convince yourself to let it out, even if you know that doing so will be worse.

And so you let it out.

And so, as these things tend to go, this thing went.

On the first day of classes Maggie dumped Jeff.

=====

3.

watch and learn, chickadees

It was the best of times, it was the worst of times.

Or maybe just the worst of times.

Tayvon, persuaded by Ren to do his senior thesis on "The Long-Winded Writer," was himself long-winded on this subject.

"You think it was an accident that Dickens, Proust, Joyce, all died young?" he said at dinner in the dining hall the first week back. "They produced so many words so fast they ran out of things to say. Then, kaput."

"What is 'young'?" Swill asked.

"Proust was fifty-one, Dickens and Joyce both fifty-eight."

A collective snort arose from the table.

"I think I speak for everyone here," Iggy said, who would think differently when his early time came, "when I note that that counts as fucking ancient."

Tayvon ignored him. "The genius in that opening line comes, first of all, in the apparent contradiction. 'Best' and 'worst' are opposites, so a certain time couldn't be both. But of course something can be the best in one respect and the worst in another, so the sentence demands immediate clarification, and therefore sucks the reader right in. Dickens continues: 'It was the age of wisdom, it was the age of foolishness, it was the epoch of belief, and incredulity,' and so on. Further ambiguation that sucks you in. There may be many who value 'enlightenment' and *also* many who value religion. All these people living together yet experiencing the world differently, in one sense we live in the same world and in another we live in our separate universes. And furthermore ..."

"It is going to be a long year," Jude whispered to Thorn who was arriving to the meal on crutches, both legs in casts.

Jude knew better than to discuss his own pending thesis. Too bad, because it was interesting stuff. After some long talks with Jeff—including the poor fellow pouring his heart out over Maggie—he was going to study the chemical properties and synthesis of 3-[2-(Dimethylamino)ethyl]-1H-indol-4-yl dihydrogen phosphate, which involved—right, not going to discuss it. To be honest, anyway, he was just as excited about his promotion to Dining Hall Manager, though he also knew better than to discuss that with these meatheads either, who simply could not be brought to understand how central to the mission of the university, and therefore of civilization, was the post.

"It's going to be a long year," more than one Piersonite said when informed that the year's menus would become increasingly vegetarian.

It was going to be a long year—and a big year, this best of times, the senior year of the bright college years. They had theses to write, natural phenomena to decipher, goals to score, memories to make, graduate school and employment applications to submit, and future careers to provide foundations for. Most of all, as seniors most of them would be living in the Lower Courtyard. This separate small courtyard was essentially a commune, a kibbutz, minus the socialism. Come Christmastime they—Croc—would decorate the whole space with lights and set up a tree in the little alcove. It was also home to the Tuesday Night Club room and its hosts for the year, Jeff and Beamie, having snagged it in the spring lottery during much happier times, at least for Jeff.

Speaking of which, the first TNC of the year was always a big one.

"You've got to come see this, people!" Ignacio burst into Rudy's to collect his friends who weren't planning to head over until after 11:00. "There's a new kid in town, I'm afraid. We're going to have to up our game this year."

TNC was packed. Crowds had formed around the center of the room, where the Ezra Stiles freshman had already vanquished several upperclassmen in Tending the Teat and was now preparing to send several more to worship the porcelain god in a match of Beer Hunter.

"Watch and learn, chickadees," the young fellow said then offered a veritable master class in getting other people to blow chunks. "All right, then," he said when said chunks began blowing, "any of you clowns around here man enough for some Slush Fund—variation Boot Factor *Six*?"

"Who *are* you?" Jude said, who rarely came to TNC but had come to see for himself.

"Name's Brett," the freshman answered, clearly disappointed as one of Croc's teammates, a 250-pound offensive lineman nicknamed "Death," passed out. "Just call me the Kavster. Damn, you clowns are lightweights," he added—as Thorn, who had borne the nickname Keg-Killer since he was twelve, collapsed on top of Death—then muttered, "Mother was right. I should have gone to Harvard."

Croc was as busy trying to resurrect Death as he would be this season trying to resurrect his team, in both cases without success. Death slept it off on the TNC floor and the football team was about to embark on a 1-9 campaign that would have Croc envying Death many times before it was over.

Zar was lying on the floor before the fireplace, tending the fire, gazing at it. He had a senior thesis to write, and every moment counted. His work on liquidity last year was largely successful, the model was nearly perfect though again there was that little piece that didn't quite fit. But this was the big year, the year of modeling fire, the problem he had started with freshman year, and he was either going to solve it this year, or—hm, he couldn't think of any other option—he was going to solve it.

Sitting beside Zar on the floor was Jasmine, watching him watch the fire and thinking that Zar's eyes reflecting the flickering flames were the most beautiful she had ever seen.

For those keeping score, Jeff was on the sofa in the corner, looking miserable. If you're wondering why someone so miserable would bother being at the party, remember that this was his room.

And no, Maggie was not there.

It was going to be a long year.

=====

4.
the age after aquarius

Tayvon and Lisa also called it quits, early in the new year.

"Honestly, Lis," Tayvon said, his arm around her on his sofa, "I just don't think I can pursue both the relationship and my thesis and give each one the love and attention they clearly deserve."

"Tay, that's one of the things I love about you," Lisa said, snuggling into him. "We're just like so on the same page. I was literally going to say the same thing to you tonight."

"You're the best, Lis. Best friends?"

"Forever, Tay."

Two mature adults making mature decisions, nothing to see here folks.

More dramatic was the response across campus as word spread, among the women, of Tayvon's availability. Almost as dramatic as the subsequent despair when it began to sink in that the man was serious. "I just need to work some things out, to work on myself," he would say to yet another co-ed come calling when the breakup news made it her way. "I want to focus on my studies right now, and on being comfortable with being alone. But thanks so much for dropping by."

More dramatic still was the response when the Masters decreed that Tang should go the way of Bladderball. "Who died and made *them* Masters?" an outraged Samilla said at dinner, caring less about the drinking than the principle of elites oppressing others.

"It's not about dying," Fregoli volunteered, never one for figurative language. "There's a committee that appoints them."

"Right-o," Ig said, thinking he may have liked Fregoli better when the guy was off his meds. "But maybe it's time for the slaves to revolt, people. Who's with me?"

"Ig," Maggie put her hand on his arm. "Maybe it's a good thing. We can live without Tang."

"Whoa whoa whoa," Tayvon interjected. "Who are you, and what have you done with 'Muffin Man Maggie'?"

"Maybe," Maggie answered, ready to shed the drinking game nickname she'd earned freshman year, "now that we're seniors I've evolved a little, unlike you Cro-Magnon meatheads."

"Fun fact," Jude, standing next to Maggie on a quick break from dining hall managing, offered, "Cro-Magnon man and Neanderthals inter—"

"*Guh-huh!*" Beamie ejaculated and when absolutely no one responded got up and headed back to the library which, frankly, he never should have left.

"Anyway," Samilla continued, "there's a bigger picture here. Tang today, TNC tomorrow."

"You like never even go to TNC," Maggie said, well aware that she herself was not going any time soon and only sitting at the dinner table now because Jeff wasn't there.

"It's the principle. That should be my choice, not a choice made for me by power-hungry elites."

"That is ridiculous in so many ways," Black said, arriving at the table. He had no idea what Samilla had just said but that didn't deter him from weighing in.

"Save your foreplay for later, you little hatebirds," Swill said. "Samilla's right. The writing is on the wall." He held up the copy of the *New Haven Register* that had launched this particular conversation, reporting that the Connecticut drinking age was to rise to twenty come October 1. "Already Mory's has announced they won't admit underage members. I'd say The Man is drunk with power, if he weren't cracking down on drinking."

It was the worst of times.

A bomb brought down a plane in the United Arab Emirates, killing 117. Suicide truck-bombings attacked the French Army and the U.S. Marines in Beirut, killing nearly 300. And of course AIDS was underway, though its significance was not yet appreciated. In times such as these you could understand why Reagan's announcement that the Orwellian technology called the Global Positioning System would now be made available for civilian use—thus revealing the government was already using it on its citizens—barely registered.

"You're wrong," Swill insisted one fall afternoon in the courtyard, playing bocce. "These are the best of fucking times."

"Yeah right," Jeff muttered, having joined the game after first ensuring that Maggie was not there. This wasn't much but at least he was speaking.

"How so, Swill?" Maya asked with a perfect throw knocking Swill's ball away from the jack.

"Two words," Swill nodded approvingly at Maya's throw. "*Homo technologicus.*"

"How about a few more words, Swill?" Ren suggested, writing everything down.

"Technology," Swill continued, "We are at the highest point of civilization ever and a glorious future awaits us. Last month six men walked underwater across Sydney Harbor. A few weeks ago some dude set the new land speed record of over 600 mph in an act of engineering so sophisticated it makes even Zar look like, I don't know—" he looked around, wanting to avoid having any of his bones broken, "Thorn. Just last week they made a telephone call with a mobile unit. Meaning no fucking wires. It's fucking science fiction. And Ronny's Global Positioning System alone is going to revolutionize everything, especially once it's connected to mobile telephones. Whatever fucking age comes after Aquarius, people, we are entering it. I submit to you: these are the best of fucking times." He concluded with a nearly perfect throw knocking Maya's ball directly next to the jack.

"Even when that same technology produces suicide truck bombs?" Lisa asked, knocking Swill's ball further away.

"Especially when," Swill said.

"I'm sure that's amusing, but it makes my own point. It's not about the technology, it's about the politics. And, weirdly, I agree with you, on that front: these are the best of times."

"Yeah right," Jeff muttered again, whose throw was apparently aimed toward some invisible jack that no one else was aware of.

"How so, Lis?" Maya asked.

Talk to a senior about any topic whatever and within five minutes they'll be talking about their senior thesis. In this case that included her refutation of now star sophomore Anne Applebaum's recent ideas about the future trajectory of that "Evil Empire," as the President had recently put it —take *that*, Anne! And of course the larger point was that human beings had finally figured out, in the liberal democracy, the best form of government and it was just a matter of time before it was universal. (Take *that*, Fukuyama, she would later argue in her successful plagiarism case against the eminent political scientist.)

You know maybe these *were* pretty good times.

"You gotta emphasize the positive, J.," Black urged Jeff later, having met him at the Buttery after angry sex with Samilla—her boneheaded views on trickle-down economics were hot—and after having first scouted the area to make sure Maggie wasn't there.

"Yeah right," Jeff muttered, staring at his untouched onion rings.

"At least the Guy is back."

"Yeah, right," Jeff muttered, though this *was* good news.

It turned out the Guy's father was a key player at a major Wall Street firm and key supporter of the Yale endowment, and so in this case, at least, The Man made the problem go away.

With a minor slap on the wrist the Guy was back, and back in business.

=====

5.
bad liver and broken heart

"Let's go, J., J., J.!" Ig came dashing down the steam tunnel and clapped Jeff on the shoulder. Jeff was at the Buttery—first sending Beamie to make sure Maggie wasn't there—drowning his sorrows in a chocolate shake. "Let's go! Rehearsal time!"

Now normally Ig was more of the "hard work is so hard" kind of guy—no, wait, that wasn't fair. That was how you pegged him freshman year: the sort for whom immediate gratification was too slow, for whom TOO MUCH was not enough, who lived by "seize the second" because you might be dead in another second and have missed out on *now*. And it's funny how the way you peg a person sticks, because now he was the sort who had spent two summers training and who, once Maya had incomprehensibly suggested he inflict his rasp at the Pierson Cabaret, intended to make it happen, rehearsals and all.

"Come on, let's do it," he had said to Jeff in Jeff's room around 2:30 AM that night, having wandered in there in search of weed and, seeing Jeff awake staring at the ceiling, ran the idea by him.

"Yeah, right," Jeff muttered, but this was the newer Ig, who persisted, even after he had found the weed in Jeff's drawer.

Much as Jeff dreaded the idea of listening to that voice, he realized it would be good for him, too, to get him out of this despair, cycling between classes he couldn't concentrate in to meals he could barely touch to his nonexistent senior thesis (on quantum chemistry) which so far consisted of a box of blank typewriter paper. Most of the time he would otherwise spend on classes and theses and med school applications he instead spent avoiding Maggie, which was particularly challenging given that her room was adjacent to the Lower Courtyard so his journeys to the dining hall or out of Pierson took him right past her first-floor window.

The first agenda item was deciding what songs to perform—beyond "Imagine," of course.

"What the fuck was that," Iggy asked, floored, never before having heard a song so anguishing at the same time as he literally had no idea what it was about.

"'Tom Traubert's Blues,'" Jeff said. "What do you think of this one?"

He turned the record over and played another.

"And that is?" Iggy asked, tears streaming down his face.

"'Bad Liver and a Broken Heart,'" Jeff answered, tears streaming from his.

"You're killing me here, man. Those are like the two most beautiful painful songs I have ever heard. But Jesus. Too much."

"I thought you liked 'too much.'"

"Yeah, when I inflict it on others. What else have you got?"

"All right. How about this?"

Jeff put another on the turntable.

"My God, when his voice cracks ..." Ig said, weeping, on hearing Tom's song, "Ruby's Arms." "But they're just too fucking painful, especially with your situation with—you know. You got anything other than breakup songs, pal?"

Jeff sighed, incapable right now of performing any other material. "Yeah," he nodded, grabbing another record. "How about this?"

Would it be an exaggeration to say that Ignacio ended curled up on the floor bawling, the tale not of a breakup but of an utterly heartbreaking love having stomped that big heart of his into many pieces?

Not by much.

"I know, right," Jeff wept on the floor next to him, the floor being where he usually ended up when he listened to "Kentucky Avenue," particularly that moment where the strings come in and you want to just throw yourself out the window, if it wasn't too soon to say that.

"I can't fucking do this, man," Ig said, wiping his eyes. He was a man of good cheer, at least with his secrets stuffed away, and if the only thing his potential accompanist could offer was the bleakness of the aching heart, then he was out.

Later, when the gang learned that Jeff had derailed Ig's Cabaret plan, even if unintentionally, he would be much lauded.

But first, now, there was Beamie standing in the doorway, weeping too, but at least holding himself upright. He had heard the music, the sobbing, coming from the bedroom and crept in to listen. As often as he had already been subjected to Jeff's dark music in recent weeks, he, in opposition to Ig, couldn't get enough.

Jeff looked up at Beamie through moist eyes and both knew.

"You in?" Jeff asked.

"I'll do it," Beamie said.

=====

6.
then the music began, and you sang

"I can't do it," Beamie said about three seconds later realizing he had *way* too quickly jumped into this.

"Of course you're fucking doing it," Ig said, who now that he was out was all in on Beamie.

"Oh my God, Beamie," Maggie said the next day, after Ig spread the word. "You've got to do it. You have the most beautiful voice. Everybody needs to hear it."

Beamie shook his head.

"You are so doing this, Beamie," Tayvon added. "Don't be a loser."

"Maybe we should try a different tack," Swill said, his arm around Maya. "Abandoning the loserness might be too much to ask."

"*Swill*," Maya said, squeezing his hand on her waist.

"Sorry," Swill squeezed back. "What I meant to say was yes,

Tayvon is right, Beamie. You've been wanting to shed the cooties since we met you. And you certainly have tried on the romantic front. But now, look, Tayvon is right, and if anyone knows about not being a loser, it's him. You have the opportunity to be a winner here. Opportunity is knocking, man. Open the door."

"Damn," Lisa said. "Who knew Swill could be so, I don't know, empathic?"

"I've been working on him," Maya whispered to her.

"I don't know," Beamie said. "I don't like—the center of attention."

You can't just change who you are, just like that, can you?

And especially with those romantic setbacks he found himself crippled with fear, of putting himself out there again. Sick to his stomach every time he thought of Isabela in particular, how he could have been so self-centered, so absorbed in his own personal needs that he was utterly inattentive to hers, he didn't think he would ever get over that, recover.

"It wasn't your fault," Maggie squeezed his arm, apparently reading his mind.

Beamie grimaced.

"And remember," she continued. "We've already heard you sing. Your friends. And we loved what we heard."

"I don't know," Beamie was a little thrown by Maggie's hand lingering on his arm, *your friends*.

"Just pretend we're the only ones there," Maggie squeezed again. "You can do this, Sam."

Well the arm squeeze and the use of his first name were an irresistible force, not to mention another demonstration of the magical powers of Maggie. Meanwhile Jeff somehow overcame his destruction by those same powers to play his own role in getting Beamie onto the stage.

"Let's go, J., J., J.!" Ig dashed into the Buttery and clapped Jeff on the shoulder. "Rehearsal time!" It was lovely how enthusiastic Ig was about getting Beamie onto that stage too.

A couple of weeks work and they had come along nicely. Beamie was able to do what Ig could not—besides actually sing—and managed to move Jeff away from performing Tom's heartbreak songs.

"I get it, Jeff," Beamie had said in their livingroom late one night after listening to Jeff lament again. "You're hurting. And there is nobody, but nobody, who expresses that pain as Tom Waits does. But you know, it's been like seven weeks now. There is still a whole senior year to have, and maybe it's time to start the healing. The healing process is knocking, man. Maybe open the door."

Jeff looked at him through watery eyes. He had already spent an hour earlier in the evening pouring his heart out to Jude and just didn't have any more fight left in him.

He nodded.

"Just no fucking Neil Diamond," he said.

"Deal."

It helped that the first song was easy, suggested by Beamie.

"I feel I owe it to him," Beamie said, having suggested they perform "Imagine" in honor of Iggy, whose role in moving this forward was immeasurable.

"That works," Jeff agreed, despite having heard Iggy butcher it so many times and having heard Black butcher its universalist political vision almost as often. Plus there was something touching about Beamie's support of Iggy who was supporting Beamie, given how utterly different the two were.

"That," Jeffrey mentioned to Debra years later, "was a moment where we were aware that if they hadn't been randomly thrown together into Lawrance Hall freshman year they never, ever, would have had anything to do with each other. It made you wonder who your friends would have been, your gang, had you been thrown into a different college. Not to mention—"

"Who you would have fallen in love with," Debra finished his thought.

Jeffrey gazed at her. "You know, there is a reason for you and me."

"It's not random?"

"It's not random."

"Is that clarity of vision?"

"That," he said, "is clarity of vision."

And once Beamie and Jeff had adopted a John song it was clear there should also be a Paul song, and then maybe a Harry Nilsson song too, given the latter's connection to John. The setlist settled, they settled down to rehearse.

Jeff would later capture that special evening in his own song at the end of the year:

Bring the lights down low, everybody feeling dreamy
Let's all welcome Pierson's own, resident entertainer you know Beamie
And then you came on stage, you looked afraid
But then the music began, and you sang ...

In the misery that was poor Jeff during those months, there was this one small respite, when the lights finally came down low on the stage set up in the Pierson Dining Hall.

Beamie and Jeff stepped onto the stage, Beamie to the mike, Jeff to the piano. Jeff began noodling, variations on the intro to the Nilsson song "Maybe," waiting for Beamie to start singing. Beamie, facing down who knows what internal demons, arrived on the stage with an unlit cigarette on his lips for some reason, and rather than begin singing he started talking.

"You know some good friends convinced me to do this," he said, the cigarette dangling on his lips, sweat glistening on his forehead. "I don't usually do this in front of people, I usually just do it in the shower, you know, alone," that got some nervous laughs in the audience, "along with a lot of other things." Wait, was that funny, or just awkward? "I'm kind of nervous up here," he continued, "Maybe you can tell. I don't even smoke." That got a nice-sized laugh, what with the now soggy cigarette dangling from his mouth. "Just started today."

At the piano Jeff laughed. "Running out of ideas here, Beamie," he called out in encouragement.

Beamie looked out into the audience, bathed in the lights from the stage. Opportunity was knocking, he thought—or maybe just his own pounding frightened heart.

It wasn't clear who started it—the first person he heard was Thorn or maybe Croc, but what he didn't know was that Ig had just given the pre-prepared signal—these three fellows who should never have been his friends began the chant and soon they were all in.

"Bea-mer! Bea-mer! Bea-mer!"

The room was rocking.

Beamie—Beamer—realized he really didn't like the diminutive that had followed him since freshman year and he really loved hearing his actual last name being chanted like that, by his friends, and these other whoever they weres packing the dining hall. Slowly he broke into the famous smile that motivated the nickname in the first place.

"Beamer!" the room rocked.

"Yeah," Beamer smiled at the audience, with a nod to Jeff at the piano, "maybe you can tell I'm a little nervous. Maybe you'll be really nice to me and give me a listen. Maybe I'll sing." He took a long fake drag on the unlit cigarette, "'Maybe,'" he said, and launched into the Nilsson song as if that whole introductory bit had been rehearsed.

And *nailed* it.

The whole gang was there.

Jeff glanced into the crowd while Beamer was singing, his friends all there, and—Maggie there, smiling, snapping photos of Beamer with the Nikon Isabela had left her. She was not looking at him so he could steal glances at her, while playing. Nearly two months in, this was the first time they had been in the same space at the same time. But there she was, her face bathed in the light from the stage, loving Beamer, she was snapping photos, dozens of photos because that was how you got the best one, the right one, the one that captured the moment as it was, as you wanted to remember it, you know, she looked happy, why wouldn't she, this was a happy moment, but could it be, could it really be, that she was so entirely over him just like that …

That was Jeff's world but everyone else was in a different room, loving it as the performers segued smoothly into "The Long and Winding Road." Beamer had a lovely way of doing the song, with a bit of humor—so unlike him, the humor, the *successful* humor—exaggerating the British accent at key spots, there he was on stage singing in a voice almost as pure as the original about that woman who had abandoned him to idling *he-yah* … Big laugh, big applause, he nailed it, Jeff stole a glance and Maggie was beaming, at Beamer, at Beamer.

"And now," Beamer was saying as Jeff segued into the familiar opening chords, "I'd like to do a song for a good friend. You know him as Naked Guy on a Hog at 3:06 AM," big laugh, Beamer was killing it, "But I just know him as Ignacio, so this one is for you, good friend."

My goodness how Beamer could channel John. Envisioning that there was no spiritual paradise, perhaps, except that there was, and he was in it, and when he sang you were in it with him. True, there had been much debate about Lennon's vision, yeah yeah harmony, affection, mutual comprehension, but was a world without religion, borders, differences really a good thing etc? But all of that was irrelevant because when Beamer sang your heart sang with him and you all indeed were as one ...

Ig was in the front row bawling, for the now departed Lennon, for the very much present Beamer, and for all the betterness to be found in the depths of the human heart. Not to mention that now he knew he had what he needed to score that goddamn goal and after the gang celebrated tonight he was going to hit the rink tomorrow at 9:00 fucking A.M. sharp and get to work.

"Bea-mer! Bea-mer!" they chanted when it was over, it was over and the applause was deafening and Beamer came down into the audience surrounded by his friends, hugs, high fives, tears of joy, Maggie snapping photos and hugging him, Ignacio pounding him on the back, *they like me*, he was thinking, somehow channeling Sally Field of the near future, *right now they like me* and all the rest of it well it just didn't matter because now he had everything.

Come the morning he would ask the gang to stop calling him "Beamie."

Jeff meanwhile had slipped away from the stage and departed alone through the rear door of the dining hall.

It was the best of times, it was the worst of times.

=====

7.
you have hidden strengths

No, it was only the worst of times.

The football team—don't even go there. The season was a bust from the first quarter of the first game, which they lost to Brown. Loss after loss after loss, by scores such as 38-12, 42-7, 17-0. The only thing left to hope for was Harvard; a win against them at the end of the season—especially since it was the 100th anniversary of The Game—would at least take some of the misery away.

The gang still went to the games, of course. "Yes but you're *our* stinky team," Maggie would say, if she were there. She wasn't, having ceded the games to Jeff, who mostly sat through them muttering about the worst of times and barely touching his beer.

At least he got football, and Tuesday Night Club, he consoled himself in the corner of the sofa while TNCers partied around him. "That's a damn good deal, J.," Black assured him early in the semester. "I've heard of a lot worse divorce agreements, man. Like my dad's. My mom got the house, the boat, and the nice car."

"What did he get?"

"The kids."

"Sheesh."

"Tell me about it. I'm telling you, J., you gotta dwell on the good things you have, rather than the things you don't."

"Easy for you to say. Like everything's going great for you right now."

"You think?"

"Yeah. Like your thesis, for example."

"True dat," Black rubbed his chin. "But shit, man, Sowell—" on whose work he was writing—"makes it so easy, it practically writes itself."

"Exactly. And your world was like made complete with *Thriller* last year. You're on, what, your third copy of the record?"

"Fourth, my brother."

"There you go. Plus you're getting laid every night."

"That shit's insane, man. She's insatiable."

"I rest my case."

Maggie, in this divorce, also more or less got the kids.

The breakup didn't just affect the two of them, but everybody. They had been together since early freshman year and thus had the same friends. Since Maggie and Jeff could not be in the same space that meant their friends had to navigate everything. Any activity, any outing, had to be calculated: go out for a meal, or for drinks, or a movie—which one to invite? Who liked that activity more? Who might be more hurt by not being invited? (At least bowling was a no-brainer; Maggie never saw the appeal.)

When *The Big Chill* came out they obviously had to see it, since it was kind of about them: a group of college friends coming together after the death of one of the gang. And how could they exclude either Jeff or Maggie from this important group bonding event? Well, Maggie couldn't be excluded because she had one of the cars they needed. The solution was to go twice, one night with Maggie and the next with Jeff, but not let either know about the other night. The logistics were hard but they pulled it off, including borrowing Maggie's car on the night they took Jeff.

Credit to them, even if their subterfuge turned out maybe unnecessary.

"Guys," Maggie said, feeling moved after the movie, "you really should go again with Jeff."

"Guys," Jeff said, feeling moved after the movie, "you really should go again with Maggie."

To be sure, they tried hard, really hard, to live up to "everybody in," and they mostly managed to keep both of their friends in their Venns. But ineluctably, the ineluctable (Tayvon had a whole chapter on Joyce's use of that word). Maggie, in time, was in, and Jeff was, well—out.

He had TNC and football because Maggie yielded those to him.

But she had everything, and everybody, else.

Well, maybe not everybody.

Beamer was there.

Well he had to be there, as they were suitemates.

But Beamer *was* also pretty devoted to Maggie, and, anyway, Beamer was Beamer, even after the spectacular Cabaret performance. Who Beamer was definitely *not* devoted to, however, was really the only other meathead who went largely Jeff's way.

"I wouldn't trust him," Beamer said to Jeff one evening.

"Oh, he's all right," Jeff said, grateful for any support.

"Fun fact," Jude was saying in their livingroom—no, Beamer wasn't spying but he couldn't help overhearing, from his bedroom, what was ostensibly a biochem study session but actually consisted of Jude explaining the material to Jeff, whose body had been attending classes while his mind was elsewhere. And there was also this principle: speak to someone recently dumped about any topic and within five minutes they will be talking about the relationship. So what began as a monologue with words such as phospholipids, ATP, and the Krebs Cycle soon segued into a recount of the *New York Times* article that Jude had recently read. "The national divorce rate has broken all sorts of records through the past two decades. In 1981 there were 5.3 divorces for every 1,000 people, which means that, at that rate, something like 50% of first marriages are going to end in divorce."

"Why are you telling me this," Jeff muttered.

"I am trying to comfort you, man. Even if she had not dumped you now, there was a fifty-fifty chance she would have dumped you later."

"I'm not sure that's comforting."

"You have to look at the big picture. Most relationships do not last. You are wallowing in your misery right now as if the whole universe has targeted you for suffering. But half of all marriages are ending in divorce. You are hardly alone."

"And how is that comforting?"

"Misery loves company?"

"If that's what you consider comforting then maybe I should study alone."

Jude shook his head. "Listen, meathead. Right now you are awash in subjectivity. You are experiencing the world through your feelings and you have lost all perspective. You have material comfort and plenty that most humans in most ages could not even dream of. You are studying at one of the most elite institutions in the history of civilization. You live in a country which, despite its warts, is perhaps the freest and most prosperous country in history. You have all your limbs and you are basically healthy despite the pollutants you ingest. The fact is, the objective fact is, that you are better off than 99% of all human beings who have ever lived."

"Yeah," Jeff muttered, "but worse off than the 1% I actually compare myself to."

"That is not unfunny. But I cannot tell. Are you agreeing with me or disagreeing?"

"Both."

"Well that is illuminating, little Jeff-Jeff."

"Fine. Agree. Things could be worse, for me, for humanity. So I should appreciate what I have."

"And?"

"Disagree. The fact that things could be worse doesn't make things any better. In fact it makes them worse. Because in addition to things being lousy I have to worry that they might become even lousier. Not to mention worry about everybody else's suffering, in those rare moments I can escape from my own."

"I think I liked it better when you agreed."

"OK. Agree. The fact that things could be worse gives me reason to be glad that they are not. And who could deny it? I'm really glad I'm not some medieval peasant wallowing in the mud dying from plague."

"Or Beamer, for that matter."

"Hey!" Beamer yelled from his bedroom, from where he was not spying.

Jeff nodded. "But disagree. Things could be worse for me, but things could also be better. So I've got just as good reason to wallow in misery and resentment and rage that they are not."

"True," Jude affirmed. "You could be me. In which case you would not have missed my point entirely."

"Which is?"

"Forget the comparison to other people. I only mentioned that as a propaedeutic. The real point—"

"A propa-what?"

"What?"

"I don't know what that word means."

"'Propaedeutic'?"

"That's the one."

Jude narrowed his eyes at Jeff. "Are you sure you were admitted here?"

"Fuck you. What does it mean?"

"So I have to give you a propaedeutic to the word 'propaedeutic'?"

"Do I have to say fuck you again? What does it mean?"

"Does not matter." Jude was enjoying this; you could tell. "The point is this. You are not actually suffering. You only think you are. But you are the master of your thoughts. So stop suffering."

"Just like that?"

"Just like that."

Jeff sighed. "So basically I do have to say fuck you again."

"Man, I am just trying to help you, little Jeff-Jeff."

"Then make sense. Suffering is no less real because it's subjective. And same with happiness. And objectively I have lost the primary source of my subjective happiness. So I think I am pretty entitled to wallow in my misery and resentment and rage."

"You have more power than you think, Jeff-Jeff. You have hidden strengths."

Well if Jeff had hidden strengths they were pretty damn well hidden, he thought, as the semester creeped on. What wasn't hidden was his misery. He'd go for hot dogs at Wawa and the clerk would take one look at him and throw in an extra. He'd walk past one of the churches on the New Haven Green—near where Jude installed a commemorative plaque for Brother John, whose fate he had been unable to determine—and the clergyman would glance at him and start crossing himself.

"I didn't even have to say anything," Jeff told Black over a slice at Naples on one of their rare hangouts. "I just went to check out a book and the woman at the desk looked at me and started crying."

"You think the fact that you were already crying yourself tipped her off, J.?"

"Not impossible."

"Was she cute, man? Maybe go for the sympathy lay?"

"Seriously. I'm even thinking of getting some dating pointers from Beamer."

Black laughed. "I'm working it, J. I even asked Samilla if she might, you know, help a brother out."

"I'm sorry? You asked your girlfriend if she would provide me a sympathy lay?"

"Damn, man, you say it like it's a bad thing."

"If I weren't so desperate, I would explain to you why it is," Jeff shook his head. "Well?"

"What?"

"What did she say?"

"Yeah. Didn't take too kindly to it, man."

Talking to Black did somehow help ease some of Jeff's suffering, unlike Jude, who was more likely to exacerbate it. But Black was not much available, also unlike Jude, who seemed to have stuck with Jeff. Black did feel loyalty to his former roommate but it wasn't so easy for him to abandon his Magdalena and, damn it, he couldn't be in two places at once. And, damn it, Samilla consumed just so much of his oxygen. Most recently it was in spats over Reagan's retarded move (you could use that word then), his capitulation, to declaring yet *another* federal holiday—lazy people make any excuse not to work—this one for Martin Luther King, Jr. Black admired MLK himself, his commitment to color-blindness as a social ideal. But there were *so* many reasons not to create another federal holiday, and all of this was happening at the same time as their squabbles about Jesse Jackson's campaign. He and Samilla had broken up like seven times already on just this one issue and great as get-back-together sex was, it was all so damn exhausting.

Best of times, worst of times.

=====

8.
jammed in that juncture

Maggie's strengths, in contrast to Jeff's, were right up on the surface. When the other inevitable would happen—Jeff would cross paths with her, he'd see her across the courtyard, okay maybe he would glance in her open livingroom window—she was always smiling surrounded by friends, including friends from other colleges, when had she acquired that entourage? He didn't recognize all those people. Wasn't he with her all the time during those years? Was she having a secret life that whole time, under his nose?

Maggie was indefatigable, no question. But you shouldn't take the utterly subjective perspective of a clinically depressed raving madman as gospel in your conception of her. The first sign that something was off for Maggie too was the amount of ice cream she was consuming. Fit, lean, athletic, committed to soccer, normally she allowed herself ice cream only to mark the end of the soccer season. But the first weeks of this semester, her senior year, found her in a regular rotation of Ashley's, Aloha, and Barron. Yes she always had friends with her but anyone who knew her could see that, despite her smiles and hugs, she was suffering. Maybe not in the way that Jeff was, or the way Ig (with his secrets) or Isabela (with her breakdown) or F. Scott (with her desire to be seen) or Thorn (with his need to destroy anything close to him) were, but she was suffering *for Maggie*.

"Happy people are all alike," Tayvon might say if he were there, paraphrasing another long-winded novel, "but suffering people each suffer in their own way."

But Tayvon wasn't there, too busy working on his thesis about said novels.

"It's tragic, is what it is," Jasmine said to Maggie over scoops at Ashley's.

"Criminal, even," Lisa added.

"I mean why shouldn't you be allowed to go to Tuesday Night Club? And football games?" Jasmine continued. "They're as much yours as his."

"I don't know," Lisa said. "There are worse divorce agreements. Like my dad's. He only got the house, the boat, and the nice car."

"What did your mom get?" Maggie asked, feeling the rush of sugar in her veins along with the remorse.

"The kids, of course."

Jasmine and Maggie shook their heads. "Poor guy," they both said.

"But still," Jasmine continued, "I think you should fight for them."

"It's all right," Maggie said. "TNC is great, but you know, I do fine the other six days of the week. And football, well. The other five days of the week. And the season is short. I'm fine. And really, Jeff—"

"What?" Lisa asked.

"Let him have them."

Jasmine and Lisa both saw the sad look in Maggie's eyes.

"And 'The Game'?" Jasmine asked.

The 100th anniversary of The Game this year called for something special. Maggie was not superhuman—was she? To miss out even on this?

"To be determined," she answered.

It was nice, Maggie thought, getting closer lately to Jasmine and Lisa. But was she close enough with either of them to *really* share—well, it was more their closeness to everyone else—this was a family and people talked and if it ever got out, she just couldn't bear it.

"Are you shitting me, Magdamazing?" Mairav exclaimed. "Why am I just now hearing of it?"

They were sitting in Mairav's livingroom in her dorm at Penn, eating the gallon of Baskin-Robbins Pralines & Cream that substituted for dinner. Maggie's off-weekend in the soccer schedule had allowed her to visit her friend and catch her up on the relationship saga.

"I don't know, it's all been so crazy, I'm sorry," Maggie said, spooning out of the carton. "I was mad at him, you know he was always a little jealous, a little suspicious, I sometimes thought he was snooping on me. One of his letters from Italy, there was this innuendo, like I was cheating on him. I mean I know it came from his insecurity, and we had our issues, but I was basically pining away for him and he goes and writes me that letter. So I thought all right, I'll test him when he gets back, I'll see if he is snooping."

"So you left your diary out."

"Yeah, more or less. I stopped hiding it. Left it on the top of the clothes drawer we used at our friend's house."

"And he read it."

"We had this stupid fight on the beach about this little joke I made. When I went back in later I saw the diary had been moved beneath my clothes."

"Oh," Mairav grimaced. "Was there anything, you know, bad in there?"

"Nothing. Nothing but love. Pining for him, while he was away."

"Wait. I don't get it. If there was nothing bad in there what's the problem?"

"He read my diary, Mairav."

"I know, but I mean, didn't you, you know, sort of entrap him?"

"Tested. Not entrapped."

"Did you talk to him about it?"

Maggie shook her head. "It was too late."

"Magdamazing," Mairav said gently, after a moment, "I don't know how to say this, but are you sure you don't want to, I don't know, undo this? Rewind it or something?"

"Mairav," Maggie said, the tears falling into the ice cream, "It's broken. We can't go back."

So yes Maggie was suffering, but you couldn't just say, no, it didn't happen, what mattered was the trust, not what she wrote in her diary but the reading of the diary. Okay it was maybe entrapment, she left it on top of that drawer—but even so what mattered was what *led* to her entrapping. And you know, she loved this guy, but the trust, the incomplete trust, how does one navigate that? Sure they meshed well but that trust thing was a snag, a tiny gap between them, the gap that he then sensed, that made him insecure, that made him jealous, that made her question the trust, and by then the pebble was a snowball was a boulder hurtling down the mountain.

Did he drive her to it, the whole thing, was it all his fault?

"It's banal, and so deep, how hindsight can clarify what's obscure at the time," Jeffrey said to Debra years later. "At the moment of a breakup you are still so close. Your lives are entwined, in those last seconds before the one says 'We need to talk' you are still together and then boom, the next second, you are not. But in those first seconds after the fissure you still feel close, so damn close, you're just seconds away from when everything was okay and you feel that it is still there, you can reach it if you just try, you're just jammed in that juncture and unable to extricate."

"Nice touch," Debra nodded, his singing of that last phrase having referred to one of her favorite songs.

Jeffrey smiled. "But it turns out the closeness is an illusion. The fork, the break, is absolute even if it still feels reversible in the moment. I imagine drawing an angle, the branching point, you've got the vertex and the two rays coming out from it. Make it a small angle, say two degrees, make the x-axis be time. When the break first occurs the two rays are oh-so-close to each other, you can reach over the little gap and touch the other side, you feel you can grab it and pull it back. But as time goes on they get further apart and then you get to later, where the gulf is vast, unbridgeable, ungrabbable, no illusion thereof. But the key thing is this."

"Drum roll?" Debra asked.

"Please."

She obliged.

"The key thing is that it's always the same angle. That two-degree difference is two degrees at the break and two degrees forty years later. Time just gives you the clarity to see how far apart you actually were even in the first moments of the break. Or maybe—"

"Or maybe—" Debra hesitated, to let him say it.

"Or maybe," Jeffrey continued softly, "to see that there had actually always been a gap there, all along, even before the break."

And so poor Maggie was suffering too, suffering from the loss, from the hurt she had inflicted on someone she loved, the hurt she had been driven to inflict, and suffering because it was a lousy thing even if it was the right thing, or maybe it wasn't, it was such a fine line, how can you know? Suffering that not even Ashley's—though mitigating it a great deal—could relieve.

And no—Jeffrey never did learn that Maggie thought he had read her diary, at least not until this writing.

"Fun fact," Jude might say with raised index finger. "The truth can hurt."

=====

9.
you and me, man

Speaking of, as Maggie got closer to Jasmine and Lisa, Jeff, in parallel, got closer to Jude.

"Gosh, you're spending a lot of time with him lately," Beamer observed some time in November in their room.

"Who? Jude? Is that a problem?"

"No. It's just—"

"I know, you wouldn't trust him."

"Exactly."

"Man, what is with you and Jude already? Are you like, I don't know, jealous?"

"What? No! Fuck," Beamer said quickly. "I've got to get back to the library to work on my thesis. You know, you should consider the same."

"Yeah, right," Jeff said as Beamer ran off.

"Women like that," Jude was saying, "You know, she really was not worthy of you."

They were sitting in the red sunset maple in the Pierson courtyard, late that Saturday night.

There was this perfect spot toward the top of the tree, about even with the third floor of the dorm, just room for two people in the little nook up there. Still a few leaves left on the tree, and between the elevation and what leaf cover there was you really felt secluded. There was much buzz in the air, what with Senator Gary Hart's fundraiser at the Master's House last night and his address at the Law School this afternoon. Jeff, whose personal problems were at the moment far more significant to him than the country's, didn't participate. Jude, with a keen sense of those problems but keener sense of the uselessness of politicians, had spent last night and today working on his thesis—Jeff really should get going on his—and now climbed up into this little space to continue working on consoling his friend.

"How do you figure," Jeff asked, enjoying the crisp clear night. He'd taken a few days off from smoking weed, felt a little clearer-headed, maybe there was something to this clarity of vision nonsense.

"Do not get me wrong. I mean Maggie is all right. But her need to be around people all the time. Constantly needing to be validated. All those friends, like she is afraid to be on her own for even two minutes. It is very superficial."

"Yeah, it's true."

"Same thing with the boyfriends. Always had one in high school, you said. Then all that time with you. It is like she just cannot stand to be alone."

"Are you saying—" Jeff's stomach sank. "Is she—?"

"No, no, she is not dating anyone," Jude assured him. He had been continuing to "keep an eye on her," had seen her a couple of times with—you know—Burt the Turt—but apparently she was just in another class with the asswipe. "But you know, women like that. She will be dating someone soon enough, because she needs to be. It is really pretty shallow, in the end."

Jeff nodded, not liking to think about the Turt or any future iterations thereof. But he did like thinking that what to many was a great asset—everybody loved Maggie—was somehow a fault.

"You and me," Jude continued, "to be honest, we are operating on a different plane from most of these meatheads, including her. You, even with your drug-addled brain, at least grasp the mysteriousness of it all. Even Zar, he sees how the pieces fit together but misses the mysteriousness, the fact *that* the pieces do fit together. But once you have had that glimpse, what need do you have for all those friends, boyfriends, girlfriends, that superficial version of what meatheads call 'happiness'?"

Speaking of meathead happiness some shrieks emanated from Black's room. What a few days it had been—Reagan's federal holiday, Jesse Jackson's candidacy, Senator Hart on campus—Black and Samilla were like hyenas in heat.

Jude snorted. "That is some job."

"Dating Samilla, or dating Black?"

"Both."

Jeff laughed, for a moment. But wow was that weird, to laugh. But then he felt the despair coming over him again. Black and Samilla were hardly the aspirational couple, but you know sometimes a guy could use some meathead happiness.

"You know what fucking kills me?" Jeff said, revealing how little of Jude's monologue had sunk in. "The Princeton game is next weekend and we had this thing, the sofas, every Ivy League campus so far. Except fucking Princeton. And now I have to go down there by myself."

"I know. That is upsetting," Jude concurred. Sick as they all were of Maggie's and Jeff's sofa project, it violated his own sense of order to hit only seven out of eight.

"A fucking tragedy is what it is."

Jude nodded. "I tell you what."

"What?"

"I will go to Princeton with you."

"You'll what?"

"I will go with you."

"What? You like never go to the away games. Are you propositioning me?"

"Do you want me to be propositioning you?"

"Now you're fucking with me. Are you fucking with me?"

"Fucking with you by proposing fucking with you, you mean?"

"In a word."

"Are you *sure* you were admitted here?" Jude narrowed his eyes as if to examine him. "Oh, I have an idea. Is it too late for me to fuck with you on every Ivy League campus?"

"Ah!" Jeff exclaimed. "That seals it."

"What?"

"You are officially the most annoying person in the—"

Just then the light flicked on in the third-floor window directly facing them.

"Shh," Jude shh'd.

Their classmate Magina had entered her bedroom.

"The light shineth forth," Jude whispered as the glow from her window bathed them. The whisper was both to conceal their presence and because speaking of her must be done in a reverential manner.

"She's too beautiful," Jeff whispered. "Not of this world."

"Not worthy, no mere mortal male," Jude whispered.

Aphrodite, Venus, Diotima, Sophia. Helen of the 1,000 ships. The Lady of the Lake, Vivianne. Marilyn. Raquel. Bo. Just a few of the terms by which they referred to her, mostly supplied by Tayvon, because it was too unbearable to use the name Magina whose similarity to vagina could not for one moment be put from mind. They had finally settled on Nirva when the polyonymosity became too confusing.

She was looking at herself in her mirror next to the window, so she almost seemed to be looking at them. Her face wore a beatific expression—in fact it was sadness, at the end of yet another long day in which almost no one had spoken to her—but on her the sadness only enhanced her sublimity.

"Nirva we bow before thee," Jeff whispered.

"Hail Nirva full of grace the Lord is with thee," Jude whispered.

"But you don't believe in God."

"God, no. Goddess, yes."

And then the inconceivable started to happen.

Magina took off her sweater.

Just like that, facing them, she pulled it over her head and paused again to look in the mirror.

Both Jude and Jeff took such sharp intakes of breath that they simultaneously grabbed each other's arms and shushed each other.

And then Magina unbuttoned her blouse.

The top button, and the next and the next.

And then she removed it.

Magina was standing there in front of them wearing only her bra, her sublime ample bosom separated from their sight by one very thin layer of fabric.

If you looked closely you could maybe see the protruding outlines of her—

If they had looked up they would have seen, through the

remaining leaves, the heavens, the stars, it was a clear night and the whole cosmos was on display. If they had looked down they would have seen a couple of people walking at this late hour through the courtyard, back to their rooms. If they had looked at each other they would have seen eyeballs propped open as wide as those of the villain in *A Clockwork Orange*, which most of the gang had seen at a midnight Film Society showing stoned out of their minds and never really recovered from.

But why on earth would they look anywhere other than where their open eyeballs were looking?

"This is not happening," one of them said.

"Pinch me," the other said.

"I *am* pinching you."

"Actually fucking stop pinching me. If this is a dream I do not want it to end."

"It is not possibly going to go further is—"

Magina, still facing them, reached her arms behind her back to unclasp her bra.

Jeff, as part of his quest to glimpse the mysteriousness of it all, had taken a couple of religion classes and was always intrigued by the idea, in Judaism, that God, though omnipresent, was *especially* present in the innermost sanctuary of the ancient Temple, the Holy of Holies.

They were about to see the very Holies themselves.

"Avert your gaze!" Jeff whispered. "Turn away!"

"What? Are you out of your fucking mind?"

"No man can see them and live!"

Jude pondered this a millisecond. "I will take my chances."

And then there they were, like warm orbs of love light beckoning sailors to safe harbor on a dark and stormy night, shining on this darkest of dark nights.

"There *is* a God," Jeff whispered.

"Two," Jude whispered back.

"The mysteriousness of it all."

"The sublimity of it all."

"The ineluctable modality of the visible."

"What?"

"The ineluctable modality of the visible."

"No, what does that mean?"

Jeff turned to Jude. "Are you sure you were admitted here?"

"Fuck you," Jude whispered, turning to him. "I have heard Tayvon's monologues enough to know that you are quoting Proust. I am just asking how you are applying it here."

"Fun fact: it's not Proust, it's Dickens."

Tayvon would have fallen out of the tree at that point, if he were there.

"Fine, Dickens. But how are you applying it here?"

"So basically you are asking for a propaedeutic literature lesson?"

"Fun fact," Jude whispered. "You are annoying when you pretend to be me. But do not even try, Jeff-Jeff. You could not be me if—oh damn, man."

He had turned back to the window and discovered the shade was closed.

They'd been so distracted they had completely failed to see Magina pull her thin silk sleepshirt over those beautiful breasts and then her perturbed expression when she heard something outside her window and then her rush to close her shade.

The light clicked off behind the shade.

There was a long silence in the tree, a long silence, under the stars.

"Did that really just happen?" Jeff finally whispered.

"Hail Nirva full of grace," Jude whispered back.

"I'll never wash my brain again."

"You and me both, man," Jude whispered, still whispering.

"We have seen what no man has seen before," Jeff whispered back.

"And lived," Jude touched his arms and legs to make sure all the parts were there.

"You and me, man." Jeff extended his hand to Jude, hand up, palm to Jude, who put his own palm against Jeff's.

"You and me, man," he whispered.

=====

10.

you cannot really trust *anybody*

"Seven out of eight is not bad," Jude said on the train to Princeton the following Friday afternoon.

"Ninety-nine out of a hundred isn't bad, either," Jeff said, "except that that last one, that dangler, remains unresolved forever, defying you, taunting you."

"Letting you know you are not the boss of it. An open file."

"Exactly. Fucking forever."

"Seven out of eight," Jude relented, "is pretty bad."

They rode on in silence awhile.

That was preferable to the first half hour of the trip, which Jeff had spent lamenting. The rest of the gang was driving down. Unspoken was the fact that, according to Jude's report, Maggie was coming to the game. It would be unfair to expect her to miss their last Princeton game, and anyway for an away game it was easier to steer clear of each other. Also unspoken was the additional agony imposed by the fact that both of them would be there on the campus, maybe there would be extreme drinking and they would cross paths and maybe for the sofas, for the sofas ...

"The chance of that happening is 999 out of 1000, against," Jude said, seeing the look on Jeff's face.

"So there is a chance?" Jeff said hopefully. Funny how here that little dangler was a sliver of solace whereas earlier it was a dagger of despair.

"Not a chance," Jeff had said earlier, when Beamer tried to persuade him not to go with Jude.

"Come on, roomie," Beamer said. "Hang back here. We'll have a blast."

"What, working on our theses side by side in the library?"

"No?"

No. Jeff wanted to hang with his new best pal Jude, who had clarified in the week since they had glimpsed eternity in the courtyard that he was happy to hang with Jeff at Princeton but there would be absolutely no hanky-panky on a sofa. "You and me, man," Jude said firmly, "has limits."

Jeff and Jude made it to Princeton but would not make it to the game.

That was unfortunate, because the season's penultimate game turned out to be the first game that Yale actually won that season. It was further unfortunate because they also missed Croc enjoying what might be the greatest moment of his life. Late in the game, the score tied, the Princeton quarterback's pass got tipped in the air. One enormous defender managed to grab the ball and lumber it twenty-seven yards, bawling like the oversized baby that he was, into the end zone for the winning score. Croc was so excited that he didn't even mind the unsportsmanlike conduct penalty for subsequently running the ball a lap around the stadium then pulling down his pants to enormously moon the Princeton cheerleaders.

Jeff and Jude would be elsewhere—literally and figuratively.

"A woman like that," Jude was saying on the train once past New York. You have to credit his patience, having yet another installment of the conversation. "You really cannot trust her. The whole keeping secrets thing, the diary."

"I know, right," Jeff concurred.

"And you know, you did not even read the thing. Who knows what you did *not* learn about? You do not know what you do not know. For all you know, you know—the Turt."

"Fuck," Jeff had almost managed to stop thinking about that possibility. But then his heart stopped and he gazed at Jude. "Wait. Do you know something?"

"What does that mean?"

"Are you just speculating or do you know something?"

Jude had been spending some time with Maggie, "keeping an eye on her," maybe she had told him something, let something slip?

"No, man," Jude demurred. "You and me, man. I would tell you if there was anything. Just speculating. But you know, I mean, how well do you really know her?"

"What do you mean? We were together three years. I know her family, all her friends. I'd say I know her really well."

"Yeah, of course. But I mean, you cannot ever *really* know another person. What they are on the inside, what they are thinking, what they are feeling. We all live in our little private universes. The whole secret diary, the secrets it contains. And what does that show you, Jeff?"

"That I can't really trust her."

"That you cannot really trust *any*body."

This depressing conversation was interrupted by their arrival at Princeton Junction. The ten-minute walk to Jude's friend's dorm wasn't encumbered by luggage as they had brought only tooth-brushes. They found the new Rockefeller College—Princeton was just establishing its own residential college system— and arrived, happily, in time for a home-cooked Indian dinner.

"Hey, nice to see you again," Jeff said, entering the suite where Jude's friend Vijay lived with another Indian fellow, and where they were immediately hit with some powerful unfamiliar aromas. It was a nice place, with communal kitchen and laundry, apparently the college of choice for most international students.

"Hey Jeff," Vijay extended his hand.

"Rohan," his suitemate said, extending his own hand.

"Howard Gordon," a third fellow said, a strikingly handsome classmate of theirs who had stopped by to drop something off.

Someone worthy of Nirva, Jeff thought on seeing him. He looked over at Jude.

"Nirva?" Jude said, thinking the same way.

"Yah," Vijay said, "Howard is writing a brilliant novel for his senior thesis. I tell you, he is going places. He comes by every Friday afternoon to deliver the next installment."

"And to grab a samosa," Howard said with a smile. "You're too generous, Vijay."

"And you are too modest, Howard. *Fine-Tuning the Universe.* Isn't that a brilliant title?"

"Great title," Jeff concurred then looked at Jude, who had come up with that phrase last year on his own and now used it often in his rants.

"Very interesting," Jude nodded at yet another data point that there were no coincidences.

"Well, nice to meet you," Howard waved. "Enjoy your dinner."

"Speaking of, Vijay my friend," Jude said once Howard had gone, "What *is* for dinner?"

It may have been better not to ask.

"Try it," Vijay said once they were seated at the table. "You just may like it."

"I thought Indians were vegetarians," Jeff said, not trying the dish before him.

"Many. Not all," Vijay said. "And fewer would be, if they would just try this. Go on."

Jeff was staring at the fried calf-brain quivering on his plate.

"What do you suppose it is thinking about?" Jude asked, not helping matters. His own vegetarianism had the added benefit, besides promoting clarity of vision, of freeing him from trying the thing himself.

"Put me out of my misery?" Jeff said, ambiguous between his or that of the quivering brain.

"Look at the way it quivers," Jude observed, realizing as he spoke that *Quivers* would be the perfect name for his assorted rants.

"It's a specialty from Vijay's state, Telangala," Rohan said. "It's made with an oil that is only produced there."

"Telangala is a shithole," Vijay added, "but our fried calf's brains are delectable."

"You're not going to eat that, are you?" Rohan said, pointing at Jeff's plate.

Jeff shook his head.

"Mind?"

"Help yourself," Jeff shook his head again.

"Speaking of brains," Rohan added, scooping them onto his own plate. "I believe Vijay here has something else for you."

"These are also from my state. Even harder to get," Vijay pulled a baggy from his pocket. "Shrooms, boys. You in?"

Well *that* was a fine howdy-do.

"Jude?" Jeff said, having already decided, after no brains for dinner, that it would be a no-brainer to say yes here. Maggie had tried several times to convince him to do shrooms, but now, well, he had little to lose—abandoned, depressed, not getting any work done anyway—and maybe this would be a good way to get past this, to move into the next phase of his life?

"Really?" Jude said, and offered his usual talking points: he didn't need drugs to appreciate the world, drugs are an escape from reality whereas he preferred reality, head-on, full frontal, clarity of vision, blah-blah-blah. "And also," he concluded at the end of this, his first official Quiver, "I cannot stand the taste of mushrooms."

"Have it your way, buddy," Vijay said, having not only finished his brains but swallowed down his portion of the shrooms while Jude was Quivering. "We're out of here."

"You sure?" Jeff said when they had gone.

=====

11.

there is that

The next day, an hour before game time, the same baggy was on the coffee table before them in Vijay's livingroom. Jude had taken the sofa, *the* sofa; Jeff borrowed a sleeping bag on the floor. Vijay and Rohan had been out all night, never come back, no doubt communing with their many gods.

"You want to go to the game?" Jeff said wearily from the floor.

"Honestly," Jude answered wearily from the sofa, "I can think of little less interesting than watching large sacks of meat piling on top of each other. And besides, do they not suck this year?"

At 0-8, yes, they did suck this year.

"Yeah but they're *our* sucky team," Jeff echoed weakly.

"Cut that shit out."

"Well there's that," Jeff nodded toward the baggy on the table.

"There *is* that," Jude said.

"I mean, you don't know what you don't know, do you?"

Jude nodded. "I guess you do not."

"I mean, if we're not going to the game...?"

And Vijay and Rohan had gone out and never come back, and didn't that sound appealing, to go out, to get out, and never come back?

Jude was giving the baggy a long hard look.

What was Jude thinking, during that long hard look?

No, he did not need it. And yes, he was committed to clarity of vision, but really, what harm could a few hours of obscured vision do? And given that he was a scientist—an honors chemistry student doing a directly relevant thesis on neurochemistry—well a scientist needs data, and here was some data waiting to be collected, and there was his poor friend little Jeff-Jeff suffering so who wanted him to do this, and bare minimum it would surely be better than watching his alcoholic friends get blotto watching meaty pile-ons.

There was nothing to lose, nothing to be afraid of, right?

For science?

"All right," Jude finally said, to Jeff's pleasant surprise, "I shall trust myself."

No, he did not know that Brother John, long gone, never come back, had used the same words in deciding to go off his meds, though he did know there were no coincidences.

"You," Jeff said getting out of the sleeping bag, "Are. The. Man."

"I do however hereby register my general disapproval of the acts being undertaken here today," Jude announced solemnly a few minutes later as he swallowed the chunks of dried mushroom mixed with the double chocolate ice cream they found in the communal freezer to disguise the horrible taste.

=====

12.
stop look think

If only … if only …

Years later, when Jeffrey was being interrogated about the grisly murder—the gnarly jagged knife, the detective actually used the word *gnarly*, was apparently from Jude's own large collection—he had this to say about the five or so hours that followed, with his lawyer's permission.

"We headed over to the Institute for Advanced Study. To stride where Einstein strode, Von Neumann, Gödel, maybe could inspire even mediocre minds like ours. Beautiful buildings, gorgeous grounds, lawns, stunning trees, the leaves were past peak colors and starting to fall but they were still stunning. Almost immediately we came upon this cat wandering around the rim of the pond. We probably spent half an hour staring at this cat, who just stared back at us. It was a perfect moment, early afternoon, cool air but warm sunshine, everything absolutely still, and this cat who lived *in* the moment, an ongoing present, now, and now, and now, no thoughts of past, no anticipation of future, it existed only in that moment with us. After a while I looked over at Jude and he was staring at one of the trees, all Halloween orange and chimney red, you know he always loved trees, he could tell you every little fun fact about them. At some point he closed his eyes, kept them closed, for a long time. I didn't mind, I had plenty to look at myself, plenty to think about, even after the cat wandered away on its aimless trajectory through life. After a while, forever, ten minutes, it was impossible to tell, I looked back at Jude and he was there, now lying on his back, eyes closed, his arms spread out, absolutely still, the sun, now dropping in the sky, it was mid or late afternoon by this point, the sun was just above the canopies

and most of the area was shaded but from where I was standing you could see the rays directly illuminating Jude's upper body
lying there, in my mind the whole area was dark and he was illuminated, his face, his chest, like on a stage. I had this moment
when I thought I loved this guy more than any other human being
I had ever loved, I mean that was a little crazy, we were just pals,
but you know he had really been there for me during the hardest
time of my life, I had literally cried in his arms, and you and me,
man, we had this thing, this bond, and there we were."

"You need a moment?" his lawyer inquired, studying him closely.

"No, I'm fine." Jeffrey rubbed his eyes and continued. "So I'm
staring at him all illuminated, still, and just then I had the thought
that maybe he was dead, like how long had he been lying there
not moving, eyes closed. I panicked a little, I poked him, to wake
him up. But he was not dead, not even sleeping. He opened his
eyes slowly, looked at me. His eyes were full of tears. I said are
you all right."

"And what did he say?" the detective asked.

"Just one sentence: 'Clarity of vision.'"

"What did that mean?"

Jeffrey sighed. "It's a long story. But he talked about it in one of
his last Quivers."

It was a Quiver viewed 30,000 times on Youtube before the
murder and double as many in the weeks after. In that Quiver
Jude drew a straight line from that afternoon in lush, fall-colored
Princeton to that afternoon in a dessicated Arizona desert some
thirty-six years and 2,400 miles away.

There he was strolling through the dehydrated brush, speaking fast into his phone camera as he strode, "I was lying there
looking at the insides of my own eyelids, the swirls of lights on
the insides of my eyelids, and they were a gateway to some other
place, beckoning me in. So in I went, into this new space, and
it was a magnificent space, a vast ocean, teeming with life, there
were rainbow streamers, kelp fronds, giant kelp fronds, *Macro-
cystis pyrifera*, the fastest growing plant on Earth, hidden in the
depths of the oceans like a submarine forest. Streams of sunlight
streaming down through the green water, through the fronds, I
was underwater, breathing underwater, and then a huge beautiful

tuna swam by, looked at me with those huge tuna eyes, looked at me looking at him, what was that expression on his face, it was loving, it was accepting, or was it judgmental, was it harsh, were we, I suddenly thought, not living up to some existential code? And then the tuna vanished and everything vanished and it was dark, bitter dark, and I was utterly alone. I understood that I was dying, that this was death, it was black, empty, cold, I was sinking, sinking. This was it. I understood that at every moment, every instant, I am just one instant away from this annihilation, this inconceivably thin veneer separates my being from my non-being, and I understood the power of it all, the power of being, of *a* pure being that could annihilate me any instant, just being in its presence would make me an absence, it was that powerful … nobody could be directly in its presence and live … "

Jude stopped the Quiver for a moment, he kept on recording himself in the silence, his eyes casting around, taking in the deserted arid landscape, before he resumed.

"And then, just then, a tiny little tropical fish, all gold and yellow and green, swam by out of the darkness, he swam around me, he circled me, this little rainbow gleam in the dark abyss, and then he swam away for just a second, he was going for his friends, and he came back and there were more, dozens of them, hundreds of them, these swimming rainbows swirling around me, there were thousands and the kaleidoscope light was so brilliant, swarming me, supporting my arms, lifting me, and I understood, I understood, that I was always on the edge of this abyss but that that same being that would annihilate me by its mere presence in fact sustains me, these rainbows were its messengers, they were sustaining me in their world, elevating me. No man can experience this being and live and yet it was letting me live, it was personal, this being *wanted* me to live, *me*, to live, *it wanted me to live*."

Another pause in the Quiver, Jude had stopped walking on the dry trail, the scorching sun above him, the shriveled growth around him, the desire to return to those depths within him.

"I emerged," he continued slowly, "I came back out into my eyelids again, the sun was burning down on my face, I was aware that its light was penetrating my closed lids, and then I saw the patterns, they were the blood vessels in my eyelids of course.

Kaleidescopic patterns like those tropical fish, circles of bright lines against the dark background, they would swell, and contract, and as they swelled I would see that the larger patterns were made up of smaller patterns, each filament of a circular line would swell and the filament was composed of smaller circular lines, and these would swell and were composed of still smaller circular lines, circles made of circles made of circles, all the way down. It was a fractal pattern, self-similarity on different scales. I had been studying fractals, in math and in chemistry and especially in biology, they were everywhere and then there they were inside me, *inside my own eyelids*, they had been there all along literally in front of my eyes and I had not seen them. It became as clear as day that this was no accident, that there was a pattern to the cosmos and I was beginning to unravel it, these patterns inside my own eyelids were meaningful, they were a message, the being was addressing me, *me,* and it was telling me that *I was on the right track* ... It was the most beautiful moment of my life. I started crying, like a newborn, because it was just that, a new life. It was clarity of vision, clearer than I had ever seen before."

Jude took his penultimate pause, in this, his penultimate Quiver, and looked into his camera. "It was my brother who was trying to reach me, to tell me, a long time ago. About the beings that surround us all the time, outside us and in, we do not see them because we do not know how to, we need to learn how to tune in, then boom! there they are, they were there all along, and we, we are just visitors in their world. If we are good to them they are good to us, but if we are not good, whoa boy, watch out. It is intimate, it is personal, they know who you are, where you are, where you are at. Demetrius—friend and foe, lover and annihilator, wrapped into one. Pay heed, man. Stop. Look. Think on it."

The last pause.

Then in a final look that was so unbearably lonesome, so unbearably sad, he said, "Jude here, with another Quiver, signing off," and the video ended.

Oddly, in one of those non-coincidences that happen all the time yet nobody notices, Jude was experiencing that most beautiful moment of his life at exactly the same moment that Croc was enjoying *his*, as he began his thunderous journey into the great end zone of life.

In another one of those same non-coincidences, a few days after they returned to New Haven, a prospective freshman visited campus and happened to be standing in line at Durfee's Sweet Shoppe in front of Jeff, who was making his nearly daily run, those days. She was loading up on Skittles, recently the rage, on her way to visit the math department. Jeff didn't notice her. Why would he? He was busy dithering over whether to get Jelly Bellies—which he loved but were tainted by the President's fondness for them—or Tootsie Rolls, which were his new favorite along with Jude, as they had discovered a stash of them on returning to Vijay's and Rohan's room late last Saturday night. "You and me, man," was all they said to each other as they munched that evening, and really for the next several days.

So no, Jeff did not notice his future sister-in-law when he was as close as he would ever come to actually meeting her.

=====

13.
game time

Who had time to notice prospective freshmen when there was much planning to do, on, oh, maybe the greatest prank in the history of all humanity? After the Princeton victory put a lift in everyone's step and restored that smidgeon of hope that they might prevail against their nemesis—in the 100th anniversary of The Game a week later at the Yale Bowl—it was clear they had to do something themselves, to mark the occasion and make the memory.

Everybody was in, and they were going to be ready.

"Piglets, people, piglets," Swill had been urging since freshman year, and now, at last, was his time to shine, with Maya by his side.

"I'm putting the women on the uniforms," Maya barked at the operations meeting Tuesday night in Ig's room, after TNC. It wasn't safe to do the planning in public; the fewer in the know, the better. And Ig's room, speaking of piglets, well, no one would wander into that pigsty unless they absolutely had to. "Jasmine, Samilla, you're in charge there."

"I don't know, isn't that kind of sexist?" Samilla vaguely protested, having failed to identify a racist angle in the project. "Like women, clothes?"

"It's just maximizing competence," Lisa answered. Jasmine's music connections included members of the Yale Precision Marching Band, the not entirely serious ensemble that made funny noises during Yale sporting events. They needed to obtain four YPMB uniforms, hopefully by tomorrow so they would have time for tailoring, if necessary.

Ig guffawed.

"What?" Lisa asked. "What'd I say?"

"Nothing. I just love this whole thing *so much*."

Lisa smiled at him. Hm, Maggie wondered, was there something developing over there?

"Lisa," Maya barked, "You interview the Drum Major. Find out what you can about the planned routine."

"On it."

"Thorn, Swill, Black."

"Yes Ma'am," the former answered while Swill stood proudly beside Maya watching his long dreamed of plan unfold and Black just grumbled, thinking this was all ridiculous.

"We have an appointment at the farm for Saturday, 7:00 AM. That's you three."

"Affirmative, Ma'am," Thorn said. "And the vehicle, Ma'am?"

"You will coordinate with Maggie about the vehicle."

"Mmm," Maggie objected. "I have to be honest. I'm not really keen on using my Spirit for this."

"It's okay, Ma'am, I got you," Thorn turned to her. "I picked up drop cloths this afternoon. You have my Scout's Honor the vehicle will be returned in its original condition."

"Guaranteed shit-free," Ig guffawed.

"Tayvon, Eli, Jasmine," Maya continued. "Rehearsals tomorrow at the Bowl but after that we have learned there will be extra security. Thursday and Friday, we'll rehearse at the cemetery."

"Aye aye, Cap'n," Tayvon said, who was working on his Melville chapter and very into things nautical lately.

"Oh, and Jude," she turned to him, whose role was essential: he would provide the lard from the dining hall and, most importantly, had agreed not to mercilessly mock the thing, a major concession given his strong line on animal rights. But you know, post-Princeton he was just so mellow, amenable, saying "you and me, man" to Jeff all the time, and telling most everyone else that he loved them. "Tell Jeff that he and F. Scott are responsible for the beer."

Needless to say, since Maggie was there, Jeff was not.

"Aye aye, Cap'n," Jude echoed Tayvon, then turned to him and said, "I love you, man."

"Permission to speak, Ma'am," Swill's chest was swelling with pride.

"Granted," Maya said.

"I think we should get Zar involved. He seems a little untethered lately."

"How can you tell? He barely speaks."

"I don't know. Maybe it's the days he's spending in his room at the fireplace, burning every piece of shit he can get his hands on."

"He's got like no furniture left," Tayvon noted.

"He burned our entire sofa," Jude confirmed, "I love that guy."

"I think it's for his thesis," Maggie offered.

"Okay, Tayvon, Eli, Jasmine," Maya made the decision. "Bring Zar to rehearsals. Let's rope him in."

"Maybe Zar can roast the piglets afterward!" Beamer tossed out.

Everyone looked at him, but except for Jude—who mouthed, "I love you, man" to him—they immediately looked away and carried on the deliberations. You know the guy could sing like an angel but he was still Beamer.

And then it was time.

The early morning trip to the farm—check. The meeting at Ig's room, the pigsty, for the preparations—check. The supply of lard—check. Bagging up in a few of Ig's extra hockey equipment bags—check. Uniforms—check.

Off to the Yale Bowl—check.

It was game time, and time to get their game on.

=====

14.

a radically new, and much worse, trajectory

The 100th playing of The Game, Yale leading the series 53-37, with nine ties along the way.

Ladies and Gentlemen, welcome to THE GAME! blared the loudspeaker, that deep male voice that seemed to be the announcer of all sporting events. "I love that guy," Jude commented, sitting next to Jeff, because of course he was sitting next to Jeff—you and me, man.

"Who wants a beer?" Beamer called out, having brought the booze upon being delegated to by Jeff.

The conditions could not have been more favorable for a mid-November Saturday afternoon: fifty degrees, fair skies, 70,000 fans in the Yale Bowl. Harvard was favored to be sure, with a 5-2-2 record, but Yale had the momentum of last week's Princeton win and of course the home field.

But seriously now, who could pay attention to the game when you were sitting with your friends and about to do possibly the greatest thing you would ever do? Jeff was sitting as close to Maggie as he had been since the breakup—at the entirely opposite end of their group—and—this was strange—it was not entirely horrible, merely somewhat painful. But now who could get worked up about some private agony when glory was imminent?

A scoreless first quarter—a definite moral victory, and testament to the pure grit of Croc and his fellow defenders. It was after all the last game of his college career and, therefore, the last game of his football career—he already had a consulting job lined up after college and last he had checked McKinsey did not have a football team. At one point early in the second quarter he threw down three offensive linemen and nailed the Harvard fullback for a seven-yard loss, the greatest moment of his life since last week's interception. The home crowd roared, but his section of the crowd—the meatheads—were on their feet roaring above them, for him, and roared all the more when he looked up to their section and pointed at them, then pounded his heart. It was a wonderful moment, one to be cherished, because the very next Crimson play began a 9-play sequence producing 57 yards and the first touchdown of the game.

Down only 7-0 at the half?

Another moral victory!

It was showtime.

A few minutes before the end of the half the Yale Precision Marching Band moved down from the stand into the area behind the Yale end zone. A few minutes before that, Tayvon, Eli, Jasmine, and Zar, dressed as YPMB members, made their way over to mingle in with the band. Oh, some members of the band were confused: they didn't recognize these four people, and it was odd that instead of instruments they were carrying hockey bags, and—what *was* that smell? But there was no time to think about this because it was now time for them to put on their meticulously rehearsed half-time show. So out they began marching onto the field, in their formation, the four impostors marching with them, and Jesus, what the hell *was* that smell?

Well one of those YPMB losers—that trombone player with the angel wings on his suit jacket—alerted the Drum Major, who somehow managed to keep his composure and the beat while casting *very* disapproving glances towards the meatheads among them. But he must also have signaled for muscle, because they weren't even out past the thirty-yard line when two security men began hurrying toward them.

"Now?" Tayvon asked, his heart pounding like that of a literature major opening his first long-winded 19th-century novel.

"The plan was wait until midfield," Jasmine said, her heart pounding as it did lately whenever she was near Zar.

"Maybe we should abort," Eli said in a rare moment of insecurity, it occurring to him only now that his father's having appointed him Executive Vice President of McKinsey effective on graduation might actually be jeopardized by these drunken shenanigans.

"Fuck this," Zar said, fulfilling his verbiage quota for the afternoon and unzipping his hockey bag. When the rest saw what he had done—it was ineluctable now—there was nothing to do but follow suit.

The four squealing greased piglets covered as much in their shit as in lard were released at the thirty-four-yard line and there was much wonderful mayhem.

YPMB members were freaking out, completely breaking formation despite the Drum Major's apoplectic screams of "Stay in formation! Stay in formation!" The two security men aborted their effort to tackle the meatheads and instead went after the piglets. You've got to give them credit: they were making $3.35 an hour, expecting to stand by the end zone all day ogling co-eds, and here they were stepping up to tackle some shit-covered greased piglets.

The crowd meanwhile was loving it, thinking it was all part of the performance. That Yale Precision Marching Band pulling off yet another badass halftime routine!

In fact that was the one flaw in the plan, Maya argued later, debriefing: the band got the credit (or discredit, depending on your perspective) when it was over, which the Drum Major was smart enough to embrace at the press conference. ("Yes we rehearsed that all week," the douchebag told the reporters.) Meanwhile in all the mayhem—it took almost twenty minutes for all four piglets to be captured—Tayvon, Eli, Jasmine, and Zar managed to escape from the field, remove their fake uniforms, and make their way back to their friends, where Maggie took that classic photo of them, arms around each other and up in the air, laughing, smiling, enjoying that perfect moment. It's even not impossible that, amidst the celebrating, Maggie and Jeff might have locked eyes and it wasn't absolutely totally horrible.

"Ten to one, pork chops for dinner tonight," Jude said to Jeff when it was over, and Jeff laughed, but then saw that Jude was *not* laughing.

"Oh," Jeff said, realizing another flaw in the plan: nobody had thought about the fate of the piglets.

"You know," Jeffrey said to Debra years later, "I was sitting next to Jude because we were attached at the hip in those days, you and me, man, we've seen what no man has ever seen, yadda yadda. But when he said that I realized we had overlooked the piglets. At the time it was hilarious, it was a bonding experience for us, I mean, I don't think I regret it. But I simply cannot believe we could do such a thing. It seems unspeakably cruel today. I realized in Jude's remark that he was aware of that all along and while he went along for the gang I think he was suffering from it. Completely over my head." Jeff made a whistling noise and moved his hand over his head. "I honestly don't recognize that person who could be oblivious to such a thing. How is it possible that I am somehow related to that guy?"

As for the rest of the game?

Who cared!

Yale managed a touchdown in the third quarter, to tie the game. The crowd roared but the meatheads barely heard, celebrating among themselves. Tied 7-7 at the end of three quarters—"Valiant," President Bart said afterwards of the effort by his team, a fancy word for "losers"—but the dam finally broke in the fourth quarter and Harvard did what everyone knew they would do and who even remembers the final score. The meatheads were the real winners of the day, and they were so busy celebrating their victory with drinking, with guffaws, that they barely noticed the game was ending, barely noticed the crowds swarming onto the fields, nor did they notice when some fans pulled the goal post right down on the head of an eighteen-year-old Harvard freshman, whose life was at that moment diverted onto a radically new, and much worse, trajectory ever after.

The Yale team ended the season at 1-9, the longest worst season in its history despite these being the shortest gladdest years of life.

Oh well, couldn't let it get them down.

The hockey season started in a few days and hopes were high, not just for a good season but that Iggy would finally score his damn goal.

part 5
senior year
spring

=====

1.

if that isn't life

A Calhoun senior was found dead in his room during finals at the end of the fall semester. A history major specializing in things Byzantine, he went to sleep one night and didn't wake up. Went from a trajectory that included graduate school, professorship, and a partner and two children to no trajectory whatsoever, overnight. Ig knew him, had hung out with him, a good guy, and man that weighed heavy on him as the hockey season began. Maybe that accounted, partly, for the dreadful start to the season, for Ig and the team, losing ten of their first twelve games.

Not that you had to know the guy for it to weigh heavily: there but for the grace of God go I, you know. Just when you think you are immortal, or even just significant, off you go. Death occurs to you while you're distracted formulating alternative arrangements.

Things stayed heavy as they transitioned to their final semester.

A divinity school student had been missing since New Year's Eve in New York City. His was the first missing person report of New York's brand-new Orwellian year of 1984.

"At least that's special," Swill said at the dining hall one evening the first week back. "If you're going to go missing might as well be the first one of the year."

Nobody found that "special," not least Maggie and F. Scott, both of whom had volunteered with the search efforts.

"Stop. Look," Jude said to Swill, and when Swill turned to look at him mouthed, "I love you, man," still riding that wave of wonder.

Speaking of wonders, Jude had established such efficient systems that the dining hall practically ran on its own now. That left him more time for his thesis, as well as his new work for Doc. He was taking a final class with the man, "Humour and Pus," ostensibly about the literary applications of the ancient doctrine of the four humours but really about the strange idea that the world should be intelligible at all. "Irony is the fundamental tone of the universe," was the first thing Doc said the first day of class, really resonating with Jude who, since Princeton, had become fixated on the very intelligibility of intelligibility itself.

"So sorry, my brother," Jude might say to Jeff when Jude couldn't listen to him lament, "but I have got some work for Doc. Helping him develop an elixir to advance his theories. I will be back by eleven."

The dining hall efficiency also allowed him to spend more time at the dining table. Better able to "keep that eye" on Maggie during meals, he assured Jeff, who had himself resolved, this last semester of their college years, to achieve some sort of betterness out of the debacle.

But that pesky Death—the Grim Reaper, not Croc's teammate—remained in the air. Yale prof and literary theorist Paul de Man had also checked out over the break. For those unfamiliar with his work, consider yourself lucky. Moreover Jude had been decreasing the meat on the dining hall menu, which led to another debate about vegetarianism; he himself briefly considered becoming a pescatarian instead of vegetarian, on the grounds that fish were at least free to lead decent fishy lives until they were yanked from the sea and slowly suffocated with thousands of their kin flapping helplessly on the deck of some ship.

"If that isn't life," Jeff observed, putting the nail in the pescatarian coffin.

One more bit of death, more aspirational than actual: word came through that Maggie had had a relationship over Christmas break.

"What kind of relationship?" Jeff asked urgently, already testing his resolve to make this semester one of betterness.

"I cannot exactly say," Jude answered.

"Is it still ongoing?"

"I am not entirely sure."

"What is your source? How do you know?"

"Jeff," Jude said gently, "you can trust me. You and me, man."

What was known was that it was some other asswipe in Timothy Dwight—T.D. was like a cesspool of asswipes—who apparently was everything Jeff was not: a preppy wealthy pre-law type who insisted on going by 'Reginald' and who was also captain of the crew team.

"*I hate him so much,*" Jeff seethed in his livingroom, where Jude was conveying the news.

I hate him so much, Beamer was also thinking, listening in from his bedroom, referring both to the asswipe and to Jude.

Jeff's fists were clenched. "I mean, like what does 'Reginald' have that I don't?"

"Everything?" Jude offered. "But stop, look, Jeff-Jeff. It is not about wealth and power and athletic prowess, or good looks. It is about what is in your heart, man, and if anybody knows about that, it is me, you and me, man." Jude himself did not have it in his own heart to tell him that apparently Reginald was also a really good guy.

"You and me, man," Jeff echoed weakly.

You know, he had made such great strides in getting over Maggie—no, "over" wasn't the word—dealing with her? Living with her, meaning along with all their friends? Or living *without* her, among their friends? This was a setback, to be sure, but frankly—it helped that "Reginald" was such an obvious asswipe, and anyway, at least he was relieved it wasn't with the Turt, whom Jeff had murdered many times in his thoughts.

And the reality was, he was really grateful for his friendship with Jude.

Nothing but betterness was coming of it all, when you thought about it.

He'd lost Maggie, but let's face it, Maggie was never for forever. Jude had made that case repeatedly, and now the Reginald thing confirmed it, he pointed out: if she could like that kind of guy, then she really wasn't the woman Jeff thought she was and wasn't for him. And meanwhile, he and Jude, that was real, sprouting like a mushroom on the decaying remains of the Maggie relationship. When word also came—again from Jude, just a few days later—that Maggie's fling had ended as quickly as it began, that didn't really change a thing, other than meaning that he could dispense with the murder-murder-suicide plan he had been drafting.

Death was in the air, but with the beginning of classes, the start of this, their last semester at Yale, things were ready to come to life.

=====

2.
alpha, two o'clock

You could feel the intellectual energy.

Black was particularly excited and returned to campus ready to "roll with Sowell." First, he had all his records put into storage over break and came back without them.

"I just realized, man, it was me or Michael," he explained at the first Sunday brunch back. "That video really drove home the point, man. Michael was fucking haunting me." He had at one point watched the "Thriller" video that had debuted on MTV the month before for seven hours straight.

More importantly, Black and Samilla reached the end of the line. Really, how many times can you think that your partner's politics are reprehensible before you think maybe they shouldn't be your partner? Or is it not necessary to share political views with your partner? Can't you love and respect somebody you disagree with, even about fundamental things? Many a conversation on that topic when neither Black nor Samilla were present, easy in the latter case because Samilla yielded the meatheads to Black and within days found some other Black man to date in Berkeley.

"You're dumping me because you are a racist against White people!" was Samilla's final yell at him in their final fight, an accusation that rang fairly hollow given the number of White women Black would eventually go on to marry.

And finally Black was just on fire with excitement when his good friend, his brilliant brother in Calhoun, Roosevelt Thompson—a triple major, Phi Beta Kappa, football starter, volunteer for New Haven projects and tutoring in the public schools—only won himself a little thing called a Rhodes Scholarship. Oh people made a big deal that he won as an African-American, "But that's bullshit, man," Black said, "we gotta stop labeling people by their race and ethnicity. What matters is that my brother Rosey is da man, not that he is *a* brother."

"Have to be honest," Jeff said—they were in the CCL snack area, taking breaks from their theses, "I don't entirely love that you have other friends besides us."

"I know, man," Black laughed and started humming "Jealous Guy," having lived through his share of the Maggie saga and invoking the Lennon song to show some solidarity, "but look, my brother, you got your own thing going on, with the devil-man."

"Man, you still don't trust him, do you?"

"I would trust him with my life," Black said, "if I were suicidal. Otherwise, I'm not even comfortable being alone with him, man."

"You know, he's really—well, softened."

"Yeah, well, he's just setting you up for when he's ready to thrust his scaly hand into your torso, rip out your heart and eat it with that little forked tongue. All right, I'm out of here." He stood up, pulled on his coat. "Heading over to celebrate my man."

"The most amazing part of that," Jeffrey said to Debra years later, "was that Black had himself applied for the Rhodes and didn't even get interviewed. But he was 100% elated that his friend made it."

"It's the opposite of that Oscar Wilde line you like so much," Debra noted.

"Right. It's not enough that you should succeed—"

"Your friends must also fail."

"Exactly. But not for Black. It came first out of his politics. You have no reason to resent someone else's success, he thought, because it's better for everyone, for the whole society, when the best people rise, even if you don't."

"First?"

"Yeah, but it was also personal. He was just happy for the people he cared about. Your success was his success, even if it came at his expense. Pretty nice, for an angry guy."

Meanwhile the frost between Maggie and Jeff began to thaw, at least around the edges.

The passage of time played its role, that thing with Reggie—for that's how Jeff thought of that asswipe who had slept with his girlfriend when imagining his brutal death by "accidental" causes—well that was painful but it also produced some emotional distance, and his bromance with Jude, to use that word, well, it all helped, and Jeff was if not entirely ready then not absolutely opposed when Maggie unexpectedly showed up for Croc's Super Bowl party.

From her perspective, we should note, the frost was one way: she was hurting too and it only hurt her all the more that Jeff had frozen her out.

"I mean," she might say to Maya or Jasmine or Lisa, "how do you share so much with someone for so long, then just, what, never speak to them again?"

It killed her how much Jeff was obviously suffering, and killed her more that he was obviously avoiding her. She missed him, she did, she sometimes spoke to him in her mind, her auditor … And that Reggie thing (for that was how she thought of him), what an asswipe that guy was. Thank God she didn't sleep with him.

She would have liked to make fun of him with Jeff, she realized, sadly.

Enough, she thought.

Why shouldn't one be able to be friends with one's exes? You don't stop loving a person, much less liking them, just because you're not compatible as partners, do you? Or if a friendship was not on the table then it was at least time to be able to be in the same room.

So there she was, showing up at Croc's room, arriving halfway through the first quarter. *Enough*, she thought, seeing Jeff on the other side of the room and heading in his direction.

Jude saw her first.

"Whoa, there, big fella," he whispered to Jeff, whose eyes were on the game. "Alpha, two o'clock."

Jeff looked up and saw her and time, and his heart, stopped.

"I think I'm having a heart attack," he whispered.

"Probably just the nachos. Play it cool. I am right here if you need backup. You and me, man."

"Hi," Maggie said, standing closer to him than she had in, oh, 157 days.

"Are you addressing *me*?" Jude, thinking now was a good time for humor, parodied DeNiro as Jeff had dragged him to their classmate's film *Taxi Driver* just the other night.

"Hi," Maggie said again, looking at Jeff with those beautiful dark eyes.

"Hi," Jeff said, willing himself to hold her gaze.

Weird how here was someone you talked so much with for so many years, and now you can't think of a single thing to say. The awkward silence was replaced by racket when the Raiders' punt returner muffed a catch, giving the Redskins one of their best chances of the game, but—like Jeff at this moment—Theismann and team couldn't do much with the opportunity.

"Well, just wanted to say hi," Maggie said and turned on her heels and left the room.

The ice broken, her mission accomplished, let him have the game in peace with their friends. Anyway, she herself had a thesis date in the library with the artist Georgia O'Keeffe, whose major paintings' resemblance to vaginas could not for one moment be put from mind.

During the first half the Raiders would score on offense, defense, and special teams, on the way to a 38-9 thrashing. But don't ask Jeff about those details, whose attention was very much elsewhere.

"Do you think she wants to get back together?" Jeff asked Jude.

"I do not."

"I definitely think she at least wants me."

"I do not think so."

"She obviously wants to at least hang out."

"Stop. Look, my brother," Jude said as he put his hand on his brother's arm. "I think you need to have another beer and try to get your shit together."

Fun fact: The truth hurts, but deluding yourself with false-hoods can hurt even more.

"Holy fuck, did you see that," Swill said during the third quarter when the Apple Macintosh ad appeared. That question was rhetorical because absolutely everybody had seen it, including Jeff and Jude who were finally distracted from that repetitive conversation.

"My eyes," Ig cried dramatically, "they burn!"

"Fucking Orwell would be proud," Tayvon muttered. "This is the end of the world."

"Good fucking riddance, I say," Swill said. "I'm getting me one."

"My father already ordered one for me," Lisa said.

"Mine, too," Eli concurred modestly, not mentioning that his father had also got him a stake in the company.

Zar was looking forward to dismantling the thing and burning its components. Jasmine was looking forward to gazing at him as he did it.

"Seriously," Tayvon asked, "why would anybody need their own computer? We've already got the two in the steam tunnel and I don't even see the point of those." Pierson had recently installed two Wordstar machines in an auxiliary room down there. You could sign up for two-hour blocks if you wanted to type up your thesis on them, but so far there had been few takers.

"Jude," Jeff said, turning back to him.

"Yes, my brother?"

"You think she wants to get back together?"

=====

3.

could tristan avoid his isolde

How *do* you interpret another person's behavior?

Maggie began being in his presence again.

She popped by Tuesday Night Club. She was at the dining hall table sometimes when he was. She came to some home hockey games, to cheer on Ig. But it's not like she was coming after him. She smiled at him, she said hi. Of course these were also her friends, so maybe she was just hanging out with her friends in her final semester of senior year, and it had nothing to do with him. But how could it have nothing to do with him? She was smiling at him!

"Hard to interpret, my brother," Jude reported back, who had been spending more time around her in the search for clues. "She does sort of smile at everyone."

"Yeah but there's something about the *way* she smiles at me."

Of course you could just ask her directly.

"Are you and Jeff like getting back together?" Lisa asked as they walked back from Beinecke Plaza.

Maggie smiled softly. "Who wants to know?"

"All of us, pretty much. Can't help but notice you're hanging around him a little more lately."

"Yeah, I know."

"So, is that meaningful?"

"You know, you don't necessarily stop loving someone just because you break up with them."

"I do. When I started dating Tay I was in mad love with him, and when we broke up I was done."

"I don't know, I find that strange. I can't bear not remaining connected, even if we're no longer dating."

"I find *that* strange. When I dump a guy I pretty much never want to see his ass again."

Maggie laughed. "Well you've failed miserably in that department with Tayvon."

"Family," Lisa smiled. "But you know, we just moved on."

"Speaking of," Maggie said as they crossed Elm Street, "You and Iggy?"

"Yeah, well that's a mystery."

"Yeah?"

"Yeah. We really click, but he seems to, I don't know, keep his distance. Like I'm threatening him somehow."

"Hmm."

"Is that all you have to say?"

"Yep."

"Okay. Well, I'll keep working on him. But meanwhile I also notice you didn't answer my original question. Are you and Jeff getting back together?"

"Let's just say," Maggie said as they turned up Pierson Gateway, "that I would like to remain connected to him."

All right, so asking her directly didn't clarify either. People are hard to interpret, even when you ask them directly.

Another person who was hard to interpret was Ignacio, speaking of.

That was about as opposite as you could expect, given that freshman year he was pegged as a person with no inhibitions, who truly gave meaning to the expression "let it all hang out," starting with his sac. Well lately the man with everything hanging out had started keeping it all stuffed in. It wasn't just his cageyness around Lisa and her advances. He was the first of them to stop coming to TNC, just as Maggie started coming again.

"What is up with this, Ignacio?" she confronted him as he was exiting TNC early, "Are you avoiding me now?"

Ig guffawed. "Could Tristan avoid his Isolde? Abelard his Heloise? Descartes his Helena?"

"What? Who *are* you?"

Ig, having been grilling Tayvon about literary romances, guffawed. "On second thought scratch the last one," he answered. "Descartes dumped his Helena. Sort of."

"You know I have no idea what you are talking about."

"I know. Isn't it fantastic? Maggie, my love," and here he embraced her in his arms, made more powerful by the long hours in the weight room, "fear nothing. You remain Beatrice to my Dante. I just have things to do, weights to lift, and theses to write."

With that he was off, leaving Maggie to realize, on entering the party, that TNC wasn't as much fun when Iggy wasn't there.

In fact it wasn't long before most of them stopped going.

With spring break approaching the end of semester came into sight, and with that their thesis deadlines. The week before spring break only two meatheads attended TNC: Maggie, who popped in for a study break, and Jude, who popped in to keep an eye on Maggie and left a few minutes after she did. Not even Jeff popped in, whose room it was. He was in the library working on his own thesis while his room partied on without him.

There were still the hockey games of course.

Also coming back to life was the hockey team.

After their dreadful start where they looked like little girls starting figure-skating lessons—"Sorry if that offends you, Maya," F. Scott said at lunch, "but it's true. And if anyone knows the difference between boys and girls I think it would be me"—something kicked into gear and they started to look like boys in hockey skates and then, frankly, like men. One theory traced the initial problem with the team to Blithe, the knock-down gorgeous Davenport freshman who had apparently made it her own first-year project to get knocked-up by a hockey player.

"She *is* awfully lithe," Tayvon observed, in putting forth this theory.

"Happy to give her my tithes," Black added, wondering if it was too late for him, as a twenty-one-year-old whose main athletic accomplishment was to have pretended to be a basketball player, to join the hockey team.

"Would love to make her writhe," Swill concurred.

"She's definitely blithe about having sex," Beamer said.

Everyone looked at him.

"What? I was following the pattern."

Unanimous head shaking up and down the table.

"That doesn't even make sense," Jeff said, stealing a glance at Maggie at the other end of the table. "The girl was jumping every guy on the team. That is hardly being blithe about having sex."

"Wait, what does 'blithe' mean?" several asked.

"Doesn't it mean indifferent?" Maggie said, briefly glancing at Jeff before getting up to return to Georgia O'Keeffe's vaginas.

"I believe it also means happy or joyous," Jude got up to bus his tray as well.

"So, what," Swill said, "the word has basically opposite meanings? That's bonkers."

Jeff watched Jude leave too while the gang explored other words with two opposite meanings, but you know lunch was long, and different people came in waves, and even after three-plus years there was still so damn much to talk about. Yet despite the digression the main point was not lost: that like Ig last year Blithe had picked up some crabs somewhere, which meant the hockey team was dealing with crabs at season's start, but now that they were finished with the crabs—and with Blithe—the wins started coming. After the bad start they were to win eight of their next eleven.

Iggy, meanwhile, was apparently one of the few on the team who had not writhed with Blithe, so you couldn't blame the travails on him. Just the contrary: despite his own heavy heart at the start he was the one bright spot during that stretch, earning assists on many of his team's goals, though the magic goal itself still eluded him. He was in the weight room daily; he stopped going to TNC, stopped drinking, and he was working with the team's nutritionist to stop stuffing garbage into his belly. He also started going to bed at a reasonable hour, at least for college students, by midnight. Plus beyond all that he was studious in a new way. "Sound mind and sound body," he would say, breaking from the weight room to work on his thesis, "as inseparable as Henry II and Rosamund Clifford." Inspired, his teammates were motivated to keep pace, in the weight room, the dining room, and with their studies. Ig became a leader both on and off the ice, and once the crabs were conquered the team caught fire.

Ig was going to get that goal.

=====

4.

the bottom of that pile

But they were running out of time.

It was already mid-February. There were only four games left in the season, and with their hot streak they were neck-in-neck with Harvard for the Ivy title—and Harvard was in town for the biggest game of the year.

That would be a good time for the goal, Iggy.

Every meathead was inside the Whale, along with an above-capacity crowd. The Elis were on fire and Ig was a sight to behold, earning the assist on the key Yale goal. The only problem was that the Crimson were also on fire and the game ended in a thrilling 1-1 overtime tie—not without the excitement of Ig's slapshot with nine seconds left that had "game-winning-life-altering goal" written all over it until it somehow ended up in the tip of the Harvard goalie's glove.

"*I hate them so much,*" Jeff muttered to the gang—including Maggie—as they trudged back down Prospect Street after the game, referring to the Harvard men's hockey team, football team, and anyone affiliated with the school.

The loss at Cornell three days later was also hard to take—a shootout that ended 7-6 in the Big Red's favor, a loss that stung only slightly less because how stupid a mascot name is "Big Red"? The sting was also lessened when the Big Red also beat the Crimson (stupid name!) a few days later, keeping Yale's Ivy championship hopes alive. Meanwhile Ig got assists on three of his team's goals and hit the crossbar on two shots—man, Ig's fans were wondering, who does a guy have to blow around here to finally sink one in the net?

Today such a remark would be considered "homophobic," but for the record, none of them was offended when that question was expressed at the dinner table. "You find the guy," F. Scott openly volunteered, "and I'll do the honors."

"Team player," Jasmine said.

Or just anyone, F. Scott thought but did not say.

And so it all came down to the final game of the season, that Saturday night, against Brown at the Whale—whether they'd win the Ivy title, advance to the playoffs, and Ig would conclude his college career with the dubious Ivy League record for most career assists with zero goals.

The place was abuzz with energy normally reserved for Harvard games, packed, loud. Brown, ever the color of shit, was a shitty team that year, which made it all the more frustrating that the score remained knotted at one late into the third period.

But the energy didn't wane—the meatheads didn't even bring alcohol to the game, and were clear-headed as they cheered on their team, and their brother, Ig—who looked great out there, managing an assist on the goal and several shots, none of which penetrated that shitty Brown goalie's defense.

"Shit, fuck, and damn!" meatheads exclaimed when the goalie made the saves.

Jude would later produce several Quivers on the topic of subjectivity, explaining how we all perceive and evaluate the world through our own subjective lens. "So basically," he might say, "you think the world is an awful place because it is not going as well for you as you would like. But stop. Look. Really look. When you do you will realize that that is like an ant looking up at the heavens and saying, 'Goddamn it, why did I have to be the ant?' There is so much order and beauty in the diversity of living things, even if that means some things have to be the ants. It is not about you, even if, being human, all too human—like being an ant, all too ant—you see things that way. Know this: You have the power to see differently. And when you find the right frequency you *will* know this."

Not yet having found that frequency—whatever the hell Jude was talking about—Ig and the gang were perhaps not to be blamed for feeling that it *was* all about them: that if this world were a good world, and surely if it were the best of all possible worlds, then it must include Ig scoring that long coveted goal. Here it was nearly four seasons into his career, just twenty-three seconds left in that career—and you would like to say it all had a happy ending and Ig scored that goddamn goal, would you not?

There it was, in slow motion because that is how all of them would remember it.

Ig was in the slot, to the goalie's left. He muscled off the defender checking him, that extra weight room time providing that extra ounce of muscle that was the difference between losing the puck and not. He was slightly off balance from the effort but was so clearheaded, all those beers he hadn't drunk in recent weeks now absent from his system, he could maintain his center of gravity. He reached inward for that extra calorie of energy, all those cheesesteaks not eaten failing to slog him down. His left wrist bent, ever so slightly—in slow motion he had all the time in the world—he had this insight for his thesis, about how Hegel's philosophy of history illuminated Bismarck's unification of Germany, all that time focusing on his studies had focused his mind, and then his wrist was flicking, the puck was accelerating toward the goal, lifting upwards. At just that instant another defender hit him and he lost his footing but the puck was launched, and as he fell sideways to the ice he could see the puck hurtling—slowly—toward that open spot just above the goalie's right shoulder, that shoulder that was—slowly—moving upwards to block that spot, and it was at exactly the instant his own shoulder hit the ice that he saw the puck make it just over that other shoulder, landing in the upper back corner of the net, scoring his goal, winning this game, winning the Ivy title, and basically completing his entire life's purpose.

The roar in the building, it was said, made the catenary arched timber roof tremble, and had the building been designed by anyone other than Eero Saarinen would probably have made Ignacio the Samson to the Temple of Dagon. Another miracle was that Ig survived the ensuing pile-on—his entire team was on top of him in seconds—not to mention some Brown players because who wasn't game for a good old-fashioned pile-on?

And damn, how the hell did Tayvon and Black and Jeff and Swill and Maya and Jude (who could not care less but hey, a pile-on) and oh goodness even Thorn was there too—after all that hostility he was the first non-player on the pile—how the hell did all of them get down there on the ice so quickly, on top of that pile?

And there was Maggie, on the ice with Isabela's Nikon, snapping that pile-on, snapping that incredible shot of Ig's face at the bottom of the pile with that smile, the widest most happy-making smile to ever adorn a human face, she got herself a shot of that grin before jumping on top herself.

And okay it's not impossible that Jeff's hand brushed Maggie's arm when she joined the pile but for just one minute anyway the story was not about him. Thank God, they all said afterward, that Croc had at the last second decided not to pile on too, or that might have been the end of them.

Okay, so Harvard (they learned later) destroyed Princeton that same night and then beat Brown three days later to actually win the Ivy title and advance to the playoffs, but why let a snarky little fact or two get in the way of the narrative?

Ig, at the bottom of that pile was enjoying the highest moment not merely of his four years in college, but, as it would turn out, his life.

Let him have it.

=====

5.
two and a half out of three

Things could get a little rough both inside and outside The Bubble.

It was announced that the term bill would hit the unimaginable sum of $14,000 the following year. The U. S. Marines withdrew from Lebanon with their tails between their legs and the body parts of many comrades in tow. And there was the McMartin Pre-school affair, which produced many dining hall conversations about just what was more impossible to believe: that preschool teachers performed Satanic abuse on little tykes or that the whole thing was a mass hysteria that boded ill for the future of America.

But as spring break approached it could not be denied: the world might be turbulent around Jeff but there was an island of serenity inside of him, inside his own bubble. He and Maggie had been speaking again, nothing deep, but something; his thesis was finally gaining traction, his you-and-me-man thing with Jude was great even if something seemed to be bugging Jude lately, Ig had scored his damn goal.

And the song he had started writing over Christmas break—

"What we had," Jeffrey said to Debra years later, "this group, was special. We were thrown together freshman year and boom! this thing emerged, the meatheads, us. Not just lifetime friends but it shaped who we were, what we became. There was no short-age of material but—what?"

Debra had laughed. "'No shortage of material'?"

"What?"

"Understatement of the year."

"Is that a good thing?"

"It's 'fantabulous,' you idiot," she touched his arm and smiled.

"Whew. Good. Anyway, plenty of material, but, you know, as

Ig liked to put it, sometimes it's good to make your memories, too. So—"

"—that's why you wrote the song."

"Yeah. The alma mater put it well: 'bright college years,' 'the friendships formed at Yale,' that sort of thing. It captured the universal but it didn't have *our* story, *our* particular friendships. So yes, that's why I wrote 'Life's Great These Days.' To try to capture this thing that was flying by, disappearing before our eyes, to try to hold onto it a little longer, maybe forever."

"And the title?"

"I know."

"You know what I'm going to say?"

"Of course I do," Jeffrey smiled. "First, that it expresses an optimism you don't normally associate with me. And second, even more impressive—if you don't say so yourself—that it reflects a remarkable sense of perspective, especially for a twenty-one-year-old going through some really difficult stuff at the time. And third, you would probably observe that it reveals a deeply attractive soul whose three children you are proud to have borne and for whom you would consider it a privilege to cook dinner for the rest of your life."

"Two and a half out of three," Debra laughed, "not bad."

Well the song was nearly finished.

The plan was to stay behind for spring break, to work on his thesis and to finish the song and record it on the baby grand in the common room. The target date was the first Monday back from break, March 26, 1984, when he would gather the gang in his and Beamer's livingroom and play the recording. *What a day, open up my eyes and say, I think the time is here,* he had written on the pad for the lyrics. *Can you believe how the years have drifted by, it's the spring of senior year* ... Talk about a time warp, how about the one where you enter college then blink your eyes and you are a senior barreling toward the end? Spring break was two short weeks, then just five more weeks of classes ...

The big question was whether he should invite Maggie to the gathering.

On the one hand of course he should. As part of the gang she obviously belonged there. And they were getting along better now; getting along, period, compared to before. And to be honest, although he maybe knew better he still had that little hint of an inkling of a spark of a hope, that maybe that spark would lead to a rekindling …

"You and me, man," Jude said with just the hint of an inkling of hesitation in his voice, the Thursday night before break. "You know I love you, man."

"Why does that sound like the preamble to something bad?"

"It is not bad, it is just …" again that hesitation, "I am not sure you should invite Maggie."

"Not invite her? But there might be the hint of an inkling—"

"Yeah, yeah, I know. But I do not think so. No."

"You say that with such confidence." Although there was that hesitation, was it a lack of confidence, was it something else?

"Look, you and me, man," Jude answered. "But I just do not want to see you get hurt. You have these high hopes. I am not convinced they are real."

"A boy can dream, no?"

"Nightmares are dreams too."

"Nightmare? Really?"

"What else do you call it when dreams are shattered against the rocks of reality?"

"A tired metaphor? Man," Jeff shook his head, "aren't *you* a little ray of pitch black."

"I just call it as I see it, Jeff-Jeff. And what I am afraid I see here, my friend," Jude shook his head, "is some pitch black."

"So, what, just not invite her? Wouldn't that be cruel?" Jeff tried another tack.

"Was it not cruel of her to dump you?"

Jeff hesitated as Jude repeated back to him one of the many lines from his litany of lamentations over the preceding several months. Something seemed different, suddenly, between him and Jude. Jude often would affirm his complaints, of course, but here he was advocating for something extreme, even cruel—and no, Maggie was not "cruel" in dumping him, his litany notwithstanding. Maybe the passage of time allowed him to think that now. And anyway it's not like he thought it was a done deal or anything but he did have this inkling of a wisp of hope, you know—

"You and me, man," Jeff said calmly, peacefully, "but I've got to invite her. Wherever she stands on me, I think I owe her that much."

"All right then," Jude said quietly.

"Hey, are you all right?" Jeff looked closely at him.

"Yeah. Why?"

"Nothing," Jeff said uneasily.

=====

6.
f-cking holy f-ck

Spring break!

Maggie was gone. Jude was gone. Zar was good for a "'Morning" at breakfast but not much more, Tayvon might chat a bit longer but then was off to work on his thesis, and Black's bromance with Sowell was now a full-time affair because Jeff saw his former roommate only once the whole break.

It was a little odd how Jude disappeared before break, Jeff thought, and he would have appreciated some final feedback on his song before recording it. Well, whatever, Jeff was overall pretty pleased with it, and it now had its title, too: "Life's Great These Days." Not what you'd expect from the pathological pessimist, perhaps, but he had to admit, even with the persistent ache around Maggie, that, as a senior soon to graduate with his many brothers and sisters, life was pretty damn great those days.

He borrowed some recording equipment, set himself up in the common room at the baby grand, and knocked off the thirty-minute masterpiece in a single take onto a master cassette. He typed up the lyrics—eight single-spaced typed pages—no shortage of material—on the Wordstar machine, and dropped it off at Kinko's to be xeroxed.

If the *magnum opus* turned out to be a *magnum stercus*—"big piece of shit" per the library's old Latin dictionary—at least it would be memorable. "Sometimes," he quoted Ig in remarks at the start of the recording, "you have to make your memories."

Even, possibly, the bad ones.

Jeff had bumped into Jude earlier that afternoon, the last day of break, didn't know he was already back. "How was your break?" Jeff asked.

"Fantabulous," Jude said, didn't seem to have the energy to come up with some new witticism, was strangely vague about how he had spent the break, but accepted the spontaneous invitation to see the new film *Koyaanisqatsi* at the York Square Cinema. "Life out of balance, apparently," Jeff explained the title. Weird as things were feeling between them, Jeff thought, Jude was the only one likely to appreciate the mind-blowing what-the-fuck-was-that film about which critics were using such words as ethereal and sublime.

"What the fuck was that," Jeff said as he and Jude exited the theater.

"Fucking holy fuck," Jude concurred.

"We should come see it again."

"Yeah. We should."

"Maybe tomor—oh wait."

"What?"

"Tomorrow night is my song."

"Ah, right," Jude nodded.

"Tuesday night?" Jeff proposed.

Jude hesitated, then said, "Without fail."

They failed.

=====

7.
then he pressed play

And then it was time.

Everyone was there, piled into Beamer's and Jeff's livingroom after break, the beginning of the home stretch, just five more weeks of classes then reading period then finals then the end of the year and of their college careers and, it sort of felt, their lives.

"They call it 'Commencement,'" Tayvon observed wistfully at dinner that evening, "like from the French, to begin. I get it, I do, The Bubble is ending, the real world, our real lives are about to begin. So why does it feel more like an ending?"

"Yeah," Swill agreed. "They should call it *la fin* instead. *La terminaison.*"

"How about the Endment?" Maya said.

"Or how about just," Ig proposed, "'The End'?"

Some eight weeks until The End.

You know they had so much to be grateful for, but who knew, at the time, how lucky they also were for the primitive state of communication in those days? "I mean we weren't sending smoke signals from hilltops," Jeffrey said to Debra years later, "but somehow we hadn't yet heard the tragic news."

That tragic news was that their brilliant classmate, and Black's friend, Rosey, had been killed a few days earlier in a collision on the Jersey Turnpike returning from spring break to campus. A truck swerved to avoid a tire in the road and that was *his* end. The news only really hit Yale, and Black, the day after their gathering in Jeff's room, so for one night, at least, the gang could believe that Life Was Great Those Days without being confronted with the unpleasant reality that maybe it was not.

The lights were low, there were drinks, there were snacks, Jeff said a few words, glancing around the room, not lingering his glance on Maggie, Jude was in the corner in the ratty comfy chair, the sweat-and-beer-and-a-little-vomit-soaked comfy chair, no one believing *how the years have drifted by, it's the spring of senior year ...*

"I couldn't write it from everyone's point of view, obviously," Jeff was saying, "so I wrote it from my own. But, you know, everybody is everybody, and while my experience has some particulars it also reflects everyone else's in various ways. The particular, we sometimes forget, just *is* the universal. So there's enough here you should be able to relate to, and also maybe give you a little more insight into some of the things that have been going on."

And then he pressed play.

=====

8.
the truth can hurt

The piano intro, getting the acceptance letter to Yale, *those first weeks September* of freshman year *what a memory*. Trying to pick up their freshman dean's wife. The parties, the Dens of Sin and Iniquity. Sophomore year Jude's failed attempt to rehabilitate Brother John, Fregoli freaking out playing Polybius, *Black moved out*, Ig's tragic affair with Erich Segal. Junior year's *hullay* and *habba-do gaggedy*, and *all relationships at Yale have their ups and downs*, and Isabela, that was a sad part of the song, the song was getting heavier because life got heavier as they moved deeper into their time there, including the going away party they threw for him, then *she drove me to the airport ...*

Jeff glanced around the room, most people looking down, Maggie looking down, he couldn't read her, it was maybe uncomfortable for everyone, but how could it be otherwise? The song was about their relationships, their ups and downs, and you know he had gotten back to slogging through Proust, it was slow going but it was really incredible, and the painful uncomfortable parts were essential because how could any art be meaningful unless it dealt with truth head on, full frontal truth, truth in the raw. Life itself could not be truly great unless it confronted truth and that was what the song was about. Of course there would be some positive uplifting material at the end but the heaviest part was yet to come. Like the blow-off-steam tunnels you descend into the dark depths in order to appreciate the subsequent ascent into the light …

Jeff glanced at Jude in the corner, he was curled up in the comfy chair, Jeff had recently read about the use of MRIs to image the fetus in the womb and that was what he was reminded of seeing Jude. The heaviest part was starting, and that was when Jude had shone, you and me, man, when most of the gang left with her …

The break-up, last fall, Jeff treated that lightly at the start, oh they were expecting the worst you could see it in the way they sat, uncomfortable, but he started with humor, mocking himself, the logistics of avoiding each other, weaving in Beamer's fantastic Cabaret, his own failed quest to ask some women out, mocking himself as a Beamer driving women to lesbianism, he glanced at Beamer who was smiling, always smiling, you know Beamer also stuck with him, he had to admit he loved that guy, then the Reggie thing, his brutal "accidental" death, uncomfortable laughter … Another glance at Maggie, her head down, couldn't read her at all, and then a glance at Jude so dreadfully contorted in that little ball like he was trying to crawl inside his own body and hide.

And then *the saddest part of the whole story now …*

"The song had to be authentic," Jeffrey told Debra many years later in an uncomfortable moment in their conversation as well, "and baring my soul would make everyone uncomfortable but it had to be there, each of us was part of each of our experiences and most of them had had their own relationships, their own ups and downs, their own breakups, they had gone through it too—I remember glancing at Black, and at Samilla, at Tayvon, and at Lisa, and at Maya and Swill—their heads were all down too, in their private worlds within this collective space, we were many but we were also one. It wasn't about me and Maggie it was about *all* of us, it was about *every* relationship, *every* breakup, about all of our experience, the human experience, if nothing else Proust had taught me that."

"It can be hard for me to listen to, too," Debra said quietly.

"I know, I get it. I probably listened to 'Jealous Guy' a thousand times back in the day. I cannot stand the fact that there were any men in your life before me and frankly I do not accept that there were. But—"

"Way to deal with 'full frontal truth,' Mr. 'Listened to 'Jealous Guy.'""

"Thank you. But even if it's hard for me to hear about your past it's essential, because your past is part of who you are, who you were is part of who you are, and it is you, the whole package, who you were and who you are and who you will be, that I love and will always love."

"Aren't you the poet."

"I'm trying to be. Are you upset?"

"'Fun fact,'" Debra quoted. "'The truth can hurt.'"

"Okay," Jeffrey hesitated. "Is this banter or bicker?"

"Neither. Both? But I do have a question for you."

"Yes?"

"How do *you* feel when you drag this all back up?"

"Well," Jeffrey said after a moment, "let's find out."

There it was, the melody of his first song for her, "The Beginning," but he had taken that melody and transposed it into the minor key, the happy now made sad, the auspicious made inauspicious, "The Beginning" now pointing to The End. Maggie had always wanted her name in a song, it was a running joke because there were no good rhymes for "Maggie." Well, he had finally solved the problem: don't rhyme the name, just sing it. He had it all mapped out, the slow-down, the dramatic pause, then drop from the relative minor to that heart-rending major-seventh designed to just level you as he sang her name—but as he was recording it and he approached that moment he suddenly understood, and instead of singing her name he left it silent, a blank, a space, an absence, an open file, there was always that dangler, it was incomplete, unfinished, because that was it … it was unfinished, because—*it was finished* … it was finished … *if that isn't life* … that void in the song the silence that said more than a word ever could …

There wasn't a dry eye in the room, except for Jeff's, having cried himself out over the past months, stealing glances at Maggie, she was crying, thank God she was crying. Glances around, everyone was crying, he had nailed it, his truth, their truth, the truth, even Jude, look at him, sobbing in that chair, contorted into the chair, but who had time to think about that because the song, having speared everyone through the heart, promptly pulled out and up and ascended into the final segment, *Let's get everyone in the picture and the song … Old Beamer the stud got lucky, but through the hole in the shade so did we*, and *Zar the keeper of the flame*, and *Croc you will always be Mr. Christmas for me*, and *even Thorn's pretty lovable as long as you don't pay him too much mind*, and Ig, Ig, that goal, all of you, *you made my day, and I've got to say, hullay hullay, life's great these days* … and a final slow-down, coming to the end, the Cabaret again, and the line to Beamer but really to all of them, every single one of them, *And I'll never know*, he sang, *just how this came to be*, via the random processes that flung them together, *but your friendship was very important to me, then, Beamer* …

And then the very final bit, from the alma mater, *time will naught avail*, he sang, *to break the friendships we have formed or leave behind the time we've shared at Yale* … and ending, the end, with a rousing rendition of the Yale fight song, *Bulldog*, that they had sung so many times during the past four years.

It was over.

They were hugging, crying, laughing, the song was a hit, he had made a memory, was this to be perhaps the greatest moment of *his* life? They milled about in his livingroom, they hugged him, they hugged each other. They began filing out, they were heading to Rudy's to continue the moment, oh tomorrow they'd buckle down again on those theses but tonight was tonight, a night to remember, to remember.

Black approached Jeff and stood before him.

"What?" Jeff asked after a moment of silence.

Black placed his palms together in front of his chest and bowed his head for a moment before him before giving him a crushing man-hug and heading out to Rudy's.

Thorn approached. It occurred to Jeff that he had probably only spoken directly to Thorn a handful of times and yet the man was as much a part of his circle here as any of the rest of them.

"I'm not a bad guy, right?" Thorn said, looking him over. "That's what you're saying. 'Pretty lovable'? I'm not a bad guy, right?"

"Not a bad guy," Jeff smiled, and received Thorn's salute before the man headed out to Rudy's.

Ignacio approached.

"I loved that, asshole," he said, "and I love you, man, as much as I love a double cheesesteak. And you know how much that is." He then gave Jeff a wet kiss on the cheek and headed out to Rudy's.

And then Maggie came toward him, she lingered, did she want to hug him too, she lifted her head briefly to make eye contact, to feel him out maybe, her eyes were moist, everyone's eyes were moist but *her* eyes were moist, he held her gaze the briefest of moments an eternity and how could you summarize everything in that gaze, it was so much it was too much and he found himself looking away, he looked away. In his heart he hoped she wouldn't give up, she would reach over and touch him, she would speak to him, she lingered, she hesitated, but then she quickly touched his arm and filed out with the rest of them and was gone.

Jeff realized that Jude had disappeared, after that sobbing fit and all they had been through together you'd figure he'd stick around, but he had slipped away.

Out they all went, Jeff decided not to follow, he had had his moment, now he needed to withdraw, maybe lick a wound or two. Beamer stayed behind with him, Beamer was a good friend. They cleaned up a bit, talked about the song, Jeff was feeling spent, numb, they drank a couple of beers, when Beamer finally went to bed Jeff thought about smoking a doob, decided not to, had barely smoked lately, just enjoying that, what, clarity of vision.

He was about to turn in himself, around 1:30 AM, when there was a knock at the door.

=====

9.

really, really sorry

Maggie?

Could it be?

He hesitated to open the door, to leave that trajectory alive as long as possible.

The knock came again.

The ineluctable ...

He took a deep breath and pulled open the door.

It was Jude.

One look at his face and Jeff understood.

How quickly one's trajectory can change.

Just ask Rosey Thompson.

Was it too late to close the door?

To have never opened it?

They stood there and both stared at the ground.

Jeff delayed, preferring this excruciating moment to the more excruciating moments that were surely coming next.

"Can I come in," Jude said without raising his gaze.

Jeff exhaled, and gestured him inside. "Do you want the chair that Iggy vomited in, or the one that Tayvon did?"

Jude returned to the comfy chair he had been sobbing in earlier, the Tayvon one.

Jeff sat in the Iggy one.

They did not look at each other.

The guy famous for staring without blinking suddenly couldn't make eye contact.

"I do not know how to tell you this," Jude finally said softly, sounding different, somehow, like someone Jeff didn't know.

Then don't, Jeff thought. Like reading the diary—STOP NOW.

Let the trajectory end here.

"What?" he said weakly.

"Jeff," Jude started to say, then began to break down.

"What?" Jeff repeated weakly.

"I have been … Maggie and I … I am so sorry," Jude was crying again.

Just how deep can a knife blade go, Jeff thought, his stomach turning.

"How long," he said weakly.

"A … while," Jude choked out between sobs.

Deeper, Jeff thought.

"You were—sobbing, during the song," Jeff said.

Jude nodded. "I am so sorry. I felt so awful. Listening to you. And then—"

"What?"

"I thought she was maybe going to want to stay with *you* when it was over."

Oh … Jeff thought.

Had there really been a chance? Was there a moment when that crossed Maggie's mind? Could she have zigged, instead of zagged, right then? She had lingered on the way out, hesitated, right at that juncture, but the butterfly didn't flap, he had broken the gaze, he had turned away … *It's your fault, you made me do it*, she had said to him when she dumped him, your suspicions, your insecurities, the demand for affirmation, they had had quibbles all these years but they never raised their voices at each other but now she was so upset, *I couldn't live like that* she said, feeling accused, *and then when you read my diary* she thought but did *not* say, did not say so that Jeff could not respond, *How could you do this to me*, he responded instead, he was so upset, *I didn't do it*, you *did it*, she said, it was horrible, *you made me do it* … It was impossible to recover from that rupture, they couldn't go back, could they, maybe it wasn't impossible, is that what Jude was saying, maybe that was why she had lingered at the door, that other trajectory right there just reach out to grasp it and then he had turned away …

Jeff felt sick, reliving it here with Jude in this moment, it was all coming back, rushing back, every moment contained every other moment.

She had left, had walked out that door, hadn't come back.

"You all right?" Debra said to Jeffrey years later.

Jeffrey slowly nodded.

"It's part of who you are," Debra observed quietly, "and you can't truly be who you are, or who you will be, unless you affirm who you were."

"That," Jeffrey said as quietly, "is very wise."

"I have a good teacher."

"Smart?"

"Very."

"Kind?"

"The kindest."

"Compassionate?"

"The compassionatest."

"Father of the year material?"

"Of the decade. The century."

Jeffrey hesitated. "Good looking too?"

"*Very.*"

"You know," Jeffrey said after a moment, with a gentle smile, "I love you for that."

"For what?"

"All of it."

"And I," Debra said back, taking his hand, "you."

"Do you think..." Jeff squeaked out, squirming in his chair, "is it ... serious ... you know ... Like is it a fling, or do you think ... it will last?"

Jeff didn't know why he asked this, did it matter, no it didn't, but somehow it was the most important question in the world.

He glanced at Jude.

"Jude?" he asked.

"I think it is serious," Jude said still looking at the floor, and it *was* serious, though perhaps not as serious as its implication in his murder would be some several decades later.

"What happened to 'superficial'?" Jeff asked in really what was about the most pathetic Hail Mary you could imagine. "'Women like that'? 'Can never really trust her'?" Jeff hesitated, then closed his eyes and launched that really deep bomb to the very back corner of the end zone, "'You and me, man'?"

Jude looked up at him, gazing, moist eyes, then raised his hands, helpless. "I—I cannot explain, Jeff. Everything makes sense, except—this." He stood up slowly, looked at Jeff with such pain in his face. "I am really sorry, Jeff, really," he said, then walked out the door of the suite.

He would never set foot in this room again, ever.

There was a quiet creak as the other bedroom door opened.

Beamer emerged, no beaming smile, his eyes, too, moist and red. "I'm really really sorry, too," he said softly, "roomie."

=====

10.

aren't *you* a little ray of blinding light

The next night Senator Gary Hart won the Connecticut Democratic primary for U. S. President, but who had time to think about that? There were classes to wrap up, theses to finish, and the shortest gladdest years of life to conclude.

But first, at midnight three days before theses were due, there was a gathering of strangely dressed men—by this point such midnight gatherings were not noteworthy—but this group gathered at Harkness Tower then marched around campus, college to college, tap tap tapping on very select doors, informing their newly tapped members of their being tapped, who then donned similar strange costumes to join the group to the next college, the next door, the next tap, tap tap ...

Beamer and Jeff were in their rooms, tap tap tapping at their typewriters, when the tapping came to their own suite door.

Jude? Jeff thought to himself, then shook the thought away.

"I'll get it," he called and went to the door as Beamer emerged from his bedroom.

There was a group of strangely dressed men at the door.

"I hope it's for you," Jeff called back to Beamer.

"We summon Samuel J. Beamer," the group chanted as one, "to step out and receive the tap."

"Oh my God, oh my God," Beamer was crying, his hands on his face, coming outside where he was surrounded by and disappeared into the strangely dressed throng.

"What the hell is this?" Jeff asked as others emerged from their rooms to see what was going on.

"Oh my God, oh my God," Beamer was weeping as he emerged wearing his own strange costume and then came right to Jeff and gave him an enormous hug. "I made it! I made it!"

"What?" Jeff asked.

"It's the fucking Whiffenpoofs, man," Iggy guffawed as he came out his door across the way, clapping Beamer on the back as he launched into his rasp of "'*To the tables down at Mory's…*'"

"Beamer! My boy!" Croc said, standing there beaming like Beamer.

"Oh my God," Jeff said, realized he was weeping too—for once not about himself. "I don't understand."

"I auditioned in secret. I didn't think I had a chance. I just can't—oh my God. Gotta go!" and with that he was swirled away to tap on some other lucky fellow's door.

There were details to be worked out, Beamer would explain later, he would defer his graduation, not participate in The End this year, so he could sing with the group next year, a small price to pay for the experience of a lifetime, not to mention, the validation, the validation …

If you rolled back the calendar to freshman year, glimpsed this group at any random moment, you would reasonably have predicted that most of them would end up sleeping on the street alongside Sister Susan. And yet here they were, some three-plus years later, and every last one of them got their thesis in by the deadline and even, in some cases, smashed it out of the park.

It was really kind of neat, they would reflect over a meal, how they each addressed their own little piece of the puzzle that was everything, yet all those little pieces somehow meshed, everybody's thesis ultimately connected to everybody else's, the way the whole thing hung together.

Tayvon who had neither removed his shirt in public nor had sex in private since the start of the year not only wrote the longest thesis ever submitted to the English department, on "The Long-Winded Writer," but managed to squeeze a chapter on Beckett in there and make it relevant.

"Just typing that thing," Jeff whistled when Tayvon brought the behemoth to the table.

Tayvon simply nodded, not mentioning that Eli had paid the hefty fee for the typist.

Eli's money also went to one of his father's senior lackeys, who wrote Eli's senior thesis, "On the Principles of An International Economy," which would later underly many of those Russian dealings of Eli's on which Lisa would report.

"You're sure you don't want to write it yourself, honey?" one of his father's senior mistresses asked him early in the academic year.

"They are my ideas," Eli answered, not untruthfully. "Gorby will merely work out the details."

Speaking of Lisa, her thesis had fine-tuned her earlier prediction of the demise of the Soviet Union to "by Christmas of 1991." Credit to the equal prescience of the Yale Political Science Department, which awarded her thesis its top prize that year.

Speaking of prizes, Zar's transdisciplinary thesis earned top prizes in all four departments that considered it. He had finally cracked fire. What he had failed to understand during his first attempt, freshman year, was that fire could not be cracked independently of the other elements. It was only when—with Jude's urging, Jude reminded him—he synthesized his separate models of earth, air, and water—each of which was left with a dangler, you'll recall—together and with fire that he could crack the whole thing. All that deep thinking outside the box ended up inside a very large box, containing three hundred pages densely filled with symbols—Eli paid for the specialty typist, too—and a very little bit of quite elegant prose.

Ren, who had filled *many* notebooks with his observations, whose vision of the world was both panoramic and encyclopedic, wrote a high-honors-winning "nonfiction novel," as he described it, called *bright college years*. More precisely, he carved out an excerpt from the larger ongoing project that would constitute his

life's work. Though focusing on their particulars (and with a special nod to Jeff) its theme was that the whole is contained in the
part, that every thing contains and therefore reflects every other
thing, that every moment contains and therefore reflects every
other moment, that nothing is actually random and that, therefore, you have to understand *everything* in order to understand
anything. Thus, as the *New York Times* would put it in its glowing
review when the non-novel was published the following year, it
was a book that virtually contained all other books.

You wouldn't think one could write such a book, but you
would be wrong. Just ask Doc, who had guided Ren through the
endeavor, and then ask Charlie Kaufman, the brilliant screen-
writer who would be influenced by Ren's work just as Doc had
anticipated, who would in turn influence another brilliant writer
named Andrew Postman (Pierson '83), who would write a masterpiece novel called *This Is Not (a) Test* featuring a character named
Ren, in honor of Ren.

The little fellow would do all right.

Also doing all right would be F. Scott.

Jeff, in that dark place, had gone to her last semester to apologize.

"I'm terribly, terribly, sorry," he said, arriving at her door, weeping.

"Honey, what is it?" F. Scott said, "Do you want to come in?"

Jeff crossed the portal to her livingroom, which, now that she
was in a single, she had decorated to her fullest capacity.

"What is it, honey?" F. Scott repeated.

"Freshman year," Jeff spoke slowly, the tears stopping as his
eyes began to absorb the sculptures installed around the room.

"Honey?"

"Sorry," he turned to her. F. Scott really had lovely blue eyes, he
realized, never having looked that closely before. "A couple of times
you invited me back to your room. Freshman year, at the Den of
Sin. Sophomore year, Croc's Christmas party. Do you remember?"

"I do, honey."

"You wanted to show me something."

"Mm-hm, I did."

"I don't think I was very nice to you. I just was a little—I don't
know." Jeff was weeping again. "I'm really sorry. I'm here now."

F. Scott touched his arm. "Oh, honey, I'm sorry for what you've gone through. And I would still love to show you—these. I always had the sense that you would appreciate them. Something about your—spirit."

She was gesturing to her sculptures.

She was right.

Jeff managed to sneak into her room shortly afterward, take half-decent photos with his little crappy Kodak and show them to the Fine Arts Department, then convince F. Scott—after arguing that the truest art is the most personal and then just pleading with her to reveal her damn talent to the world—to meet with them, who unanimously awarded her not only highest honors for her senior work in sculpture but a three-year fellowship to pursue sculpting at the Royal College of Art.

There was another tap tap tapping on Jeffrey's and Beamer's suite door.

It was F. Scott.

"Do you want to come in?" Jeff asked on opening the door, seeing *her* there weeping.

"No," she said softly. "I just wanted to thank you. For making me do this. You have no idea, literally no idea, how much that means to me."

Jeff smiled, starting to weep for her, then gave her an enormous hug that was promptly joined by Beamer weeping, a lovely group hug right there in the doorway.

For the record it was Eli who eventually purchased her entire collection and established a permanent exhibition of her work at the Museum of Modern Art in New York, shortly before his first stint in prison.

Even Ignacio.

The man spent the final weeks in the semester as the weather warmed sitting outside in the courtyard, shirtless and in shorts, drinking soft drinks, running an extension cord out to his Smith Corona typewriter where he was working out that insight he'd had when scoring his goal and tapping out his thesis on 19th-century German history. Ignacio's thesis earned him "Recognition" by the History Department and, for once in his life, it was recognition in a *good* way.

Fuck you, Erich, he thought to himself on learning of the award, and for once in his life, thought something without saying it aloud.

Jude won the chemistry prize (obviously).

And maybe most impressive of all, Jeff simply got his thesis done—*you* try finishing a thesis when your ex-best-friend and ex-girlfriend are ...

At one point he did go to Dean Christa, feeling overwhelmed.

"What do you mean, an extension?" she asked in that harsh German accent.

"*You* try writing a thesis when your ex-best-friend—" Jeff started to explain.

"*Nein*," she answered, having heard enough.

"God, I hated her in that moment," Jeffrey told Debra years later, "and I hated her every minute of the hours I then had to go spend in the library. I brought like a bag of apples and at one point I think I was in the library for seventy hours straight. But you know, in the end, maybe she was right. I got it done. It may not have been my best work, but that train had already left the station anyway. I got it done."

Debra's eyes were moist. "These stories you're telling me, Jeffrey. My heart goes out to you. I can't imagine how you got through all that."

"I know. But you know, I think I always knew."

"What?"

"I need to warn you that—"

"Forewarned."

"Right. It's the Nietzsche's demon thing I told you about. The moment that makes all the rest of it worthwhile. Enough so that you would live it all over, all the darkness, all the pain, an infinite number of times even, just to have that one moment again. I understood then, even as it was happening, that it was all part of one package. That all that crap, all that bleakness—"

"Are you going to start weeping again?"

"Not at all," Jeffrey smiled. "I was grateful for every moment I had with her even though that made it so painful to lose her. And Jude too, and losing him. You know by that point it was really about him more than her. But then I was ultimately grateful for that pain because I knew it was shaping me, it was producing the person who loves you the way I love you today, the person who is loved by you, this gorgeous thing you and I have, this very conversation, this very moment. Now that I am here I see so clearly that the conclusion *was* implicit in the premises as the premises are manifest in the conclusion. I would gladly live it all over, an infinite number of times, all that pain and misery again and again, just so that I could land right here, again, with *you*."

"And you knew all that at the time, even though you didn't know me yet?"

"Maybe not in those words. But yes."

"Well aren't *you* a little ray of blinding light."

"Exactly, my baby."

"And so when I feel a little, I don't know, uncomfortable, maybe even jealous, when you tell me about Maggie, what you're saying is …"

"Right. Please don't be jealous, even if, for a moment, I seem to be back there forty years ago reliving it. Because that was then, and that is what produced me now. The new me. The new, much better me."

"The one who barely recognizes the earlier one to whom he is somehow related."

"The one who now says—"

"You're about to quote Proust again."

Jeffrey smiled. "Paraphrase, but yes: To think of how I suffered, back then, for a woman who, in retrospect, from who I am now, doesn't even appeal to me, who—" he hesitated, then continued—"wasn't even my type."

"Wow. And yet without that old you—"

"—no matter how little I relate to him now, or to his feelings—"

"—there would be no new, much better you."

"Exactly."

"So what you're saying is, basically…"

"No Maggie, no J. Jeffrey."

"No Maggie, no you. So if I love you—and I do—"

"You must also love Maggie. Don't be jealous of her. Be grateful to her."

"Wow." By this point Debra had laid her head against Jeffrey's shoulder. "I really *would* like to subscribe to your newsletter."

"For you, my baby," Jeffrey said, kissing her head, "no charge."

=====

11.
if ever

American scientists announced the discovery of the AIDS virus the same day that the Grateful Dead came to the New Haven Coliseum for two shows. Jeff went to both shows alone. True, most of his friends were also there, including Maggie and Jude who suddenly was willing to see the Deceased, but he didn't hang out with them and surely did not glance in their direction during the concerts.

"You sure you don't want to come?" Beamer asked him the next day, referring to the Blow Off Steam run.

"I've already blown off whatever steam I had," Jeff answered, feeling so drained from recent days, weeks, months.

"Fine, I'll meet you at Abe's birthday," and off Beamer went to emit some steam, of which he had plenty thanks to the fantastic Whiffenpoof news he'd be riding well into next year.

Jeff made an appearance at Abe's birthday on that last day of classes, attending alone, if by alone we mean surrounded by all of his friends including Maggie and Jude and most other Piersonites. But he was alone, he reflected, gazing at the glowing bonfire as dusk finally descended in the courtyard, thinking about how profound loneliness can be in the middle of a crowd.

It was all happening so fast.

Four years seems like an eternity when you're a freshman, and then, impossibly, it's hurtling toward the end. Classes were over, check—theses submitted, check—steam blown off, Abe's birthday, check, check, now it was reading period again, the last reading period. The Buttery was open every night but now when they called "last call" at 1:00 AM it really was, really could be, the very last last call. Most of the gang was there that last night, having that last cheeseburger, those last onion rings.

"This," Jeff said to Beamer, bittersweetly, "is the last Buttery French fry I will ever eat." And then after two bites, "and this is the last bite of the last Buttery French fry I will ever eat." And then a moment later, with mouth full, "my last Buttery French fry swallow." And then another moment later, "my last Buttery belch."

And there was the last Tuesday Night Club.

It was low-key, there were so many lasts to experience, but the highlight of this one was that it featured the return of everybody's favorite sex twins, Temperance and Chastity, eager to end their college years as they began, with a little romp with everybody's favorite demigod.

"I'm good," Tayvon answered when they sidled up to him and asked how he was doing.

"I'm good," he also said a few minutes later, declining their invitation to join them back in their room where, by the way, their younger sister Patience was also waiting and anything but.

"Oh … my … God," Swill, Iggy, Thorn, even F. Scott crowded around him after the twins left in a huff, "how in the world did you decline that opportunity?"

"I really *am* good," Tayvon said, holding the last Tall Boy of his Tuesday Night Club career, "and I really just want to be with the people I love."

While everyone was distracted by that encounter another encounter went under the radar.

Magina, who used to come to TNC sometimes but got tired of standing alone all night there, had dropped by for one last evening of being ignored.

Ren, who had enjoyed unrequited love affairs in his head with every female member of every class he had taken at Yale, decided he was tired of being rejected in his mind and was ready to actually be rejected in person.

He approached Magina and looked up into her eyes (she was several inches taller) and said, "Hi, I'm Ren. Hey," he added when he saw her response, "Why are you crying?"

The final, final exams.

Who knew one could get emotional about final exams?

No, nobody could believe it, that they were now in their last couple of weeks together, with Commencement—The End—two weeks from the first day of finals. It was hard to study, true, but with theses behind and vast open futures ahead, final exams seemed the last bit of normalcy, and they were, well, not relished, but relished. Lisa made this observation at lunch the day before exams began, which reminded Jasmine they were out of relish on the salad bar, which reminded Iggy that Jude had really been slacking lately, which reminded Maya that Maggie had not been around much the past few weeks, which reminded Swill choking up a little that they only had a few more dining hall meals before their last meal together, which reminded Tayvon that he was really impressed with the emotional progress Swill had made because who even knew that Swill had emotions, which reminded Iggy to emit one of his famous belches at the table—would it be the last one?—because wasn't belching also an emotion he asked, to much guffawing?

Guffawing, too, because one day earlier the very worst song in the history of the world had won the Eurovision Contest, surpassing even the "Making Your Mind Up" phantasmagory owning that title since freshman year. But like rubberneckers at a grisly traffic accident the gang couldn't get "Diggi-loo Diggi-ley" out of their minds ... The only redeeming feature of it was that it was so eminently mockable.

"Worth the investment," Eli said, who had sprung for the three sets of matching white slacks, black leather belts, gold foil boots, and the bright red, blue-purple, and aqua short-sleeve button-down shirts that Tayvon did not remove in public.

"I think I've retired that pulling the shirt off thing," he answered when Swill inquired.

Tayvon, Ig, and Black scored a video of the winning performance by the brothers Herrey and spent many hours nailing the Swedish and English lyrics and lame dancing routine. Those hours may perhaps have been better spent studying for finals, but as Ig put it, "Priorities, people, priorities!" They did the performance in the common room, toward the end of finals, to a full house: cleared the furniture, set up some lights, and after debating whether to lip sync or sing along to the Betamax, hit on the really genius idea of doing it a cappella.

"Haunting," Swill observed, their almost disembodied voices making those sounds while their bodies were moving so queerly without the music.

"Chilling," Jasmine said, snuggling with Zar.

There was Maggie snapping photos, Maggie probably actually loved the song, she had that thing for cheesy Euroculture, but then how could Jude tolerate it, he had depth, maybe taste, and do you think it's really coherent to simultaneously like a person but dislike everything they like?

Well Jude seemed to be tolerating it just fine, Jeff observed, watching them on the other side of the impromptu bonfire the gang made in the courtyard after the performance. It was maybe 1:00 AM and no they were definitely not allowed to be doing this, the Abe's birthday bonfire had had a special permit, a fire pit, they definitely weren't allowed to just dig a hole in the courtyard and fill it with broken wood—wait, where did the wood come from?— and light the thing on fire.

"It's allowed," Ig had insisted with a guffaw, and really, what harm could come of it? From a few inebriated young adults dous- ing broken furniture with lighter fluid and sitting back to admire the huge sparkling fire with glistening embers floating upward? Who would even notice that they built it under the branches of a very flammable tree?

A red sunset maple tree, by the way, a famous tree at least in the minds of Jeff and Jude, the you-and-me-man tree, though of course nobody else knew that, unless he had told Maggie, but he wouldn't have done that, would he?

And anyway, what were they going to do, kick them out? What would be the point? Tomorrow was the end of finals, then a few days of Senior Week, then Commencement, no, The End, they were all being kicked out soon enough.

Well eventually it was determined that Ig was responsible for the bonfire, for the broken furniture and the lighting fluid and for bringing the match to the doused pile. He thus got rusticated for the remainder of the week, which meant that he was not per- mitted on campus again until the coming Sunday night, the night before The End.

"Totally worth it," Ig said, guffawing, when he received the sen- tence the next day, though to be honest the timing of it was a blow for the gang, to be deprived of him in their last week.

Better timing was had by Thorn who, it turns out, had also

been making emotional progress. Around 2:00 AM of the bonfire night, most of them still there, Thorn turned his speakers out the window of his room and began blasting into the courtyard the song that would become their anthem for this last week.

Time, flowing like a river
Time, beckoning me

The Alan Parsons Project tune had been out a couple years already but holy cow what a punch that packed in a 2:00 AM courtyard to a bunch of people approaching the end of everything. The piano, the synthesizer, the strings, the half-diminished chord that reaches into your chest and squeezes your heart, the lushness and the melancholy and the words,

Goodbye my love, maybe for forever
Who knows when we shall meet again,
If ever

They were silent, letting the song wash over them, embrace them, thinking about their last moments together, *maybe for forever*, who *does* know when we shall meet again, that little *if ever*, that way you don't always know when it's the last time, the last time you speak to a person because they move away or the relationship withers or they are murdered by a gnarly jagged knife, every time could be the last time, the last time ...

But time keeps flowing like a river (on and on)
'Til it's gone forever

"Fucking Thorn," Croc said with tears streaming down his face when it was over and replaced by the utter silent stillness of a 2:05 A.M. courtyard.

"Who fucking knew he had a soul," Lisa said, tears streaming down her face.

"Just ... plain ... fuck," Ren moaned, tears on his face, he who had spent years chronicling pretty much everything summed up what everyone was thinking, though they weren't also thinking

317

about how they were going to be meeting up with Magina when the meathead gathering was done.

Well that little emotional bomb did its work—the party had to dissipate after that, everyone returning to their respective rooms either alone or in dating pairs to mourn their pending losses in private. No one thought to ask what Thorn was doing while he was in his room blasting that song at them, but suffice to say that the tears streaming down his face were not (he would insist) those of a woman and the sobs he was choking back were not those of a little girl.

=====

12.
the end of the dynasty

It all began to blur as they slipped from final exams through the bonfire into Senior Week. Along the way the place had been emptying out, as underclassmen finished their finals and departed for the summer. That left the seniors alone on campus, the place theirs for one last hurrah, a blur lasting through the weekend, though it was cut short for the gang since they had their own thing planned, a final Penzance Party at Eli's house for the weekend. They piled into cars for the three-hour journey to the Cape, to beach, to sun, the last day or two of sun because rain was called for Monday's End.

Staying behind, Jeff.

He just couldn't bring himself to go. Too painful, too—close. There were other activities on campus for the weekend, there were other people to hang out with, share those precious last seventy-two hours with.

Beamer stayed back with him.

"Who else am I supposed to watch the game with?" Beamer explained to his fellow Islanders fan. That would be game five of the Stanley Cup Finals, where their New York Islanders were on the cusp of ending one of the greatest modern sports dynasties. "*I hate him so much*," Beamer muttered for at least the dozenth time since the finals had begun, referring of course to the Oilers' young phenom already known as The Great One.

Is a meathead by himself just a meatball? Jeff wondered more than once that weekend, trying not to think about not being with his friends at Penzance. Then *My God I've been spending so much time with Beamer lately that I'm starting to sound like him.*

Jeff didn't participate in any activities that weekend, didn't hang out with any of those other people, and basically only emerged from his room for last meals in the dining hall with Beamer and to watch the end of the dynasty with him at Rudy's. Jeff did not say anything other than his customary "Have a good night" to Leo the bartender when he walked out of Rudy's for the last time of his college career and for the last time of his life.

Beamer straggled along behind him back to their room, feeling awfully dejected for someone whose team had won four straight Stanley Cups and made it to the finals of a fifth.

"*I hate him so much*," he muttered for at least the dozenth time that evening.

=====

13.
were you dreaming of lost bananas

And then it was the day before The End.

Slept late.

Quiet.

Their rainy Yale felt just so empty. Only seniors were left, and many of these were away for the weekend, doing their own last hurrahs with their own meatheads at their own Penzances. Funny to think there were parallel groups of meatheads in the other colleges, that other people had had their own entirely different experiences at this place. Was there some other poor sap in one of the other colleges right now, sleeping late, his friends away, not having joined them because it was just too much to expect him to spend forty-eight hours near *them*? The last brunch at the dining hall, it was gray and drizzly outside so he took the steam tunnel, straggled in around 12:30—almost no one there, Jeff sat alone after oh so many meals as opposite of alone as one could be.

He sat long but didn't talk much.

Beamer eventually dragged in from bed and joined him, minutes before the 1:00 PM close of brunch.

"I hate him so much," Beamer said but a lot of the anger had gone from his voice.

"Next year."

"Next year," Beamer sipped his coffee. "What do you want to do today?"

"Dunno."

"Well, when are they coming back?"

"Dunno that either."

There was literally nothing they had to do. The rooms were packed up, posters removed from walls, the Tuesday Night Club gear (beer posters, signs, drinking game book) in storage for next year's seniors.

One of the dining hall workers came over to retrieve their trays, an annoyed look on her face. Then again she always seemed annoyed with Beamer, tracing back to sophomore year when they began eating in Pierson. "I don't know what your problem is," Jeff said to Beamer some time junior year, "Florence is always perfectly nice to me." Indeed she was, always good for a smile when Jeff appeared on the serving line, always giving a little extra helping of the meatloaf, and then when Beamer came along—often right behind him—the smile would disappear and the portions would shrink. "Maybe she just has a good loser detector," Jeff proffered by way of explanation once, to Beamer's irritation.

"How are you today, Florence?" Jeff asked as she appeared at their table.

She smiled. "Feeling more and more better every day. Tomorrow big day, yes?"

"Yeah," Jeff nodded. "We'll miss you. Always that smile."

"Hey," Beamer asked as she reached for his tray, "may I go get one more cup before you take that?"

"No," Florence said and was gone, never again to have any roles in their stories.

"I know, I know," Beamer said. "Good loser detector."

"You know," Jeff said, gazing at his friend, "not really. You're all right."

"What?"

"Don't make me repeat it."

"Wow," Beamer said, "that is the nicest thing you have ever said to me."

"I guess the bar is low."

"Yeah. You all right?"

"Hmm."

"Listen, I had an idea. I thought maybe we could do a roomie last tour of campus, you know, last time here, last time there. Maybe drag up a memory or two, reflect on the meaning of it all, before The End. What do you think of a little walk down memory lane?"

"That sounds like an awful idea."

"I didn't say it was a good idea. Do you have any better ones?"

Really, no. Their lives were packed up, their future not yet begun. There was just the day, the hour, the moment. And you know, so what, a few tough memories. Memories don't have to be good; maybe difficult memories are the most meaningful, and if there were anything they should do today, waiting for the gang to return, it should be something meaningful.

Jeff shrugged. "Memory lane it is."

"Great! Listen, I invited Francis to come along. That all right?"

Francis was a junior sticking around to work at Commencement. Jeff wasn't entirely inclined to include her—it felt a little intrusive—but then again Beamer had something of a crush on her, he really had come through for Jeff by skipping Penzance with him, and anyway Francis had a cheerful personality and was pretty cute.

She smelled nice too.

Might take the edge off.

"Sure," Jeff said.

"Sorry I'm late guys, had to shower before coming over," Francis blew through the door into their room, their denuded room filled with boxes to be carted away tomorrow. "What a beautiful day!"

"It's raining," Jeff observed with the same degree of gloom as the weather.

"That's what I mean. I love May rains. Everything is green and moist and alive."

"And that's good?"

"No, it's great. Don't you think?" She shook her head, spraying some drops of rainwater or shower water or both. "God I love it. And the smell in the air, it's lilac I think. Sam, thank you so much for letting me hang out with you guys!"

Jeff pulled out a sweatshirt and grabbed the umbrella and they headed out into the rain. It was a pretty awesome umbrella: Eli's people at the National Weather Service had alerted Eli to the likelihood of rain for The End, so he had custom-ordered umbrellas for the gang, large transparent bubble umbrellas with Pierson black and yellow trim. "Lower the conoidal dome of noiselessness," Jude had parodied *Get Smart* when Eli distributed them a few nights back, lowering his slowly over his and Maggie's heads. Francis's own little rainbow umbrella stood out against the overcast sky as they headed across the courtyard and under the Pierson Tower and out the Gateway.

"I need to pop in here a sec," Francis said as they passed Wawa's, and wandered off for some hand cream with Beamer in tow while Jeff contemplated getting one last hot dog at the counter. All was quiet today, just a few lonely hot dogs spinning endlessly on their rollers with no one to consume them, including Jeff, who just wasn't hungry.

If that's not life, he thought.

Jeff went in search of Francis and Beamer, walking past the rack for the *New Haven Register* that, forty-eight hours later, he would see bearing the headline: YALE'S 283rd COMMENCEMENT IN THE RAIN. Beneath the headline would be a photo of Jeff and Iggy in their graduation garb, underneath their bubble umbrella, having made the front page. That look on their faces, a mix of elation and inebriation and exhaustion and confusion, having been up the whole previous night celebrating, having spent most of the morning, the procession, and the ceremony under their umbrellas, pretending they were fish in a tank, making fish-mouths, or announcing, in the voices of somewhat disabled people (it seemed profound and hilarious at the time), "Hello, people! We are *Special* People! Special *Bubble* People!" They *were* Special People, were they not? Special Bubble People? Jeff, the very last of the friends to finally move out, would stare at this photo for a long time, all alone in the store, and then buy two copies, one for himself and one to give to Iggy the next time he saw him, whenever that would be—a visit, a wedding, a reunion?

A funeral?

If ever?

"Come on, let's get out of here," Jeff whispered to Francis and Beamer at the register where she had just paid for the hand cream.

They came to the intersection of York, Elm, and Broadway, the light drizzle no longer worthy of the umbrella. The hours they had spent around this busy corner, seeing people go the different directions, a hundred different destinations, at once. Townies, businesspeople, tourists, professors, students, prospectives, each with their own trajectories, overlapping, criss-crossing; the street people, this corner was Brother John's favorite, he'd hang out here chatting with somebody, anybody, he who wandered those avenues day and night "just lookin' out for my brothers," who could talk you into giving him your shiny new bubble umbrella but then settle for thirty cents for a cup of coffee. Jeff wondered what had become of him, so weird that after being so involved in his affairs, via Jude, the man just disappeared. Today this normally frenetic corner was almost empty, quiet, too.

So weird too, Maggie, Jude, gone, disappeared.

But he wasn't going to think about that.

The drizzle was more of a mist as they walked down Elm Street, turned left on High. A last look at Sterling Library, and the underground Cross Campus Library, you could not count the number of hours in those places. They passed by that majestic elm on the Cross Campus courtyard that Jeff had stared at Jude staring at, Jude firmly persuaded that trees were the key to understanding everything. Weird how that tree, and the red sunset maple in

Pierson, ended up playing such roles in Jeff's life.

"Anyone up for a last Naples slice?" Beamer suggested.

"We already had our last slice there," Jeff pointed out, "last week."

"So how about a last last slice?"

"But then we would have to get a last last last slice."

"You all right, roomie?" Beamer peered at him. "Since when do you decline pizza?"

"You guys are too much," Francis stamped in a puddle. "Forget Naples. Follow me."

The rain was starting again as they followed her back through the Old Campus—The End would occur there tomorrow—then left on York Street. Fran was talking about next year's football team and stamping her feet in every third puddle for emphasis. She quieted as they passed the dark facade of the Art and Architecture building. No pause there, the day was gray enough without those memories. Her apartment was just across Chapel Street, where she'd been living this past semester. It was an old building that had been completely renovated except for the tiny, rickety elevator that took them to her fourth floor. A little creepy in there, they were all squeezed in, Beamer being very quiet, and hey Francis did smell nice. Then the contrast, as they entered the renovated space, between the old and the new, was jarring.

"Like us," Beamer said quietly as Francis disappeared into her bedroom.

"What?"

"Like, Yale is ancient, and we are new."

"Now you're a philosopher."

"Now I'm a philosopher."

Francis had retrieved her cassette player, they were once again descending. For a second Jeff felt himself gripped with anxiety. *Edgar waking at night to feel the hot breath of* the thing *on his face.* What, and now he was quoting Poe in his head, he thought, remembering Tayvon doing that reading in the common room a couple Halloweens ago. The women had decorated the place like a Victorian drawing room, the lights were replaced by candelabras, and Maya somehow managed to borrow a black cat for the evening as well.

Beamer suggested going to Harkness Tower—Jeff had resisted

returning his key—but for some reason going back to Pierson seemed more appealing to Jeff at the moment.

"Sure let's go back to your room a bit," Francis bubbled. "We can smoke a joint and listen to music. You won't believe this weed my roommate scored. I think it's laced with something."

"Seriously?" Beamer asked. "You're not worried it's not safe?"

"Gotta live a little, Sam! And not seriously, silly. I was kidding about it being laced."

"Ah, okay," Beamer said, relieved.

"Actually I wasn't kidding about it being laced," Francis whispered to Jeff a little later when Beamer stepped out to use the bathroom. "Sam is so cute when he's worried, isn't he? Anyway we smoked some last night and I'm still here, right?"

"Looks that way," Jeff answered.

"You're in, right?"

Jeff thought a moment, then answered, "I'll trust myself."

Back in Pierson, back in their suite, they piled into Beamer's emptied bedroom. They set up the tape player, they left the lights off, it was dark gray outside and dark gray in there, deepening into black. Jeff selected Pink Floyd, they sat on the floor, their back against the bare wall, Francis between them, facing the tape player, in the dark. The equalizer lights began to flicker. Francis brought out and lit the doob, took a hit, and passed it over.

She smelled nice in the darkness.

It had been a very long while since he had smoked.

The party again, all of them there, in costume, drinking too much, Jude was in charge of the bar, didn't drink himself but liked others to drink, kept insisting Jeff drink 'von die Franken-Stein.' The music was loud, always loud, and everyone laughing as Maggie tried on the perfume, the 'bewitching' scent he'd bought her, a drop on a delicate pink finger placed gently behind each ear, God he loved her in that perfume. But then she disappeared, for an hour, or two, like before, he couldn't find her, and then they were continuing the fight, The Fight, later, afterwards, in the dark, in the bedroom, she smelled all clean and fresh from the perfume and that infuriated him because she wasn't supposed to wear it when he wasn't there, *I can do what I want*, she said, *I want you to want what I want* he said, she was angry, of course she was, and then she was gone, and then that nightmare, he'd had it so many times, it was night and Maggie was running through the street she was so athletic so fast her long black hair trailing behind her, she was running because she was being chased there was a man behind her running after her, Jeff screamed at her to warn her but she didn't hear, but then he realized that she did hear but it didn't matter because it was all staged, the man was precisely five minutes behind her and she was leading him somewhere, that couldn't possibly be, that couldn't be ...

RRRING! RRRING! The album pierced his reverie. Beamer was looking at him intently. Jeff closed his eyes again.

Alone, alone, at a movie, a film, a gray drizzly night on the Gothic campus, Maya had dragged him to the European Intellectual Film Society showing of something heavy and pendulous, trying to make him feel better that was nice of her but then she disappeared and he was watching this cerebrous thing—was *cerebrous* a word?—a tortured young fellow in anguish over his lady friend, she is not what she seems, he grows suspicious, the anguish growing like a tumor, he becomes incensed if she is late, he starts examining her clothing, possessions, her letters, her diary, calling her at random hours and hanging up like Swann knocking at windows in the dead hollow night saying *I will catch you yet, I will catch you* ... She is innocent, she is innocent, she tells him, he doesn't believe her, what do you want me to say, she says, I want you to say you love me, he says, and she says you are driving me to this, she says you have driven me to this, she says YOU MADE ME DO IT, something snaps and he slaps her, he *slaps* her, in a little cozy bar in a dark European city on a gray drizzly night and she is gone, gone, out the door, running away, and he is alone, he is lost, in a vast strange city and it's dark it's windy it's night ...

The album pierced his reverie again, his heart pounding, he was thinking, it's dark, it's dark, it's all so dark.

The three of them sat on for a moment in silence.

"That was *great*," Francis exhales.

Jeff looked at her.

"For a minute during the music," Beamer said to him, smiling, "I thought you looked like a monkey. But not a very happy little chimp. Were you dreaming of lost bananas?"

Oh God, Jeff thought. "Can we—get out of here," he said, standing.

In the courtyard the early evening sky was lit by a deep orange haze, with a thin mist. Francis splashed in some puddles, she would probably stop to build a castle out of the mud if Jeff weren't hurrying them toward the Pierson Tower, the Gateway.

"Hey, where you guys going?" Charlayne called out.

Fellow Pierson senior, really nice woman, a theater person who hadn't been interested in joining their circle, but feeling the mood herself—the desolate campus, having just emerged from the last supper at the dining hall (which Jeff realized they had missed), the looming End—was eager to make small talk with her acquaintances.

Now there's a question, Jeff thought, only in a space for big talk, not small. "Out," he said, pausing a few polite minutes while Beamer and Francis chatted with her, then leading them under the Tower and out the Gateway and into the next phase of their evening.

The mist had begun to thicken, it felt almost like 19th-century London, walking home late one night through alleys and old buildings and fog while Big Ben tolled the hour. No, Whitechapel, Jeff thought, thinking *I have been here before,* "Imagine," he said, leading the way through the mist, "wandering streets like these, on nights like these, returning home from the theatre—" *thee-ah-ter*—"your cloak pulled tight, when suddenly Jack the Ripper leaps out and stabs you in the heart! If that isn't life in a nutshell," Jeff concluded triumphantly, "then what is?"

"Actually," Beamer said, "I think he cut his victims' throats."

"Can't you just be happy?" Francis objected.

Right, Jeff thought as they arrived at the Branford gate.

They went through, found the thick wooden door, and began their ascent of Harkness.

Up the internal stairs, the winding stone steps, to the iron door, to the platform, standing beneath the huge structure containing the carillon. It hung by steel cables from the columns of stone rising from each corner of the platform, columns that now con-stituted the entire external structure of the Tower. That was it, no more. They were essentially outdoors. A medieval wind began to blow as they looked up the circular metal staircase that wound fully exposed to the elements alongside the carillon to another platform some sixty feet above.

Francis paused to coo at two pigeons who had found a comfortable little niche. They then started to climb, the wind gaining with the elevation. The final twelve steps straightened through the square opening onto the flat, circular summit.

"Well, here we are," Jeff said.

"It's *amazing* up here," Francis whispered.

It was a perfect night for reminiscing.

Yale was spread beneath them in every direction.

Memories beneath them, in every direction.

They stood at the railing on the eastern side, looking down to the Old Campus.

Where it all began.

Freshman year, Jeff started telling Francis, "I was always attracted to the bells, I would be studying in my room on the fifth floor in Lawrance when they rang every evening and would open my window to listen. The medieval clanging brought this whole place to life, I'd think, feeling its ancientness, feeling a part of this long chain. Okay, fine, the place is only three hundred years old but it's modeled on the medieval universities, it felt like centuries were passing and finally producing me, I had arrived...

"That was the kind of freshman I was, Francis." Jeff shook his head, realizing that he *was* that kind of freshman, and many other kinds of freshman at the same time.

"And then I joined the Carillon Guild, and when I played I controlled the life blood of the campus, *I* created the atmosphere, the soundtrack to *all* this. From my perch up here I felt like I owned the place, I was its master, and from anywhere on campus I could look up at the Tower and say, 'See that? Mine.'" Jeff paused, reflected. "One night I brought Iggy up during a storm, I hardly knew him then, but you know," he didn't have the energy for the whole story, including Ig arriving to the platform to see Jeff doing that Yoga pose under the lightning-bolt sky, "anyway, that's the night we became friends in our own right.

"So look, Francis," he said instead, pointing down, "just yesterday there we are arriving as freshmen. Moving in, there, on the stairs, bumping into a girl named Maggie, meeting the others in Lawrance Hall, having our parties, and there, back there by Phelps

Gate, there I am with Maggie loading her car on the last day of freshman year and driving off toward that first summer break.

"And by turning south," which they did, "we change the channel, there I am on the screen as a sophomore, spending the winter at Ashley's Ice Cream just over there where Maggie thought I had a crush on the counter girl but it was only on Oreo Crunch, and mostly just slumping around without direction, and without a major. But we can flick the dial again to the north, where we find me in that physical chemistry lab all fall junior year, having found a footing in pre-med, see me plowing through the snow, heading home to Pierson on dark December afternoons after lab, home for a quick dinner—as if we ever did meals quickly here—then to the library for marathon study sessions to prepare for the MCAT. This picture's gray so let's flick the dial to the west, to our Pierson College, to senior year, color brought to you by the now set sun, the last sliver of orange in the sky, wondering, wondering, where our friends are, when will they come back ..."

"Yeah, where are they," Beamer echoed. "I guess they're having a good time."

"Of course they're having a good time," Jeff said, "but let's finish the picture, turn back one more time to the east, to the Old Campus, where tomorrow it will all end under ominous skies. See, they already have the chairs set up down there, they set it up, they celebrate us for an hour then they kick us out, then pack it all up again and September rolls around again and our replacements arrive, who will take our classes and live in our rooms and begin their own adventures. This place takes us in, transforms us, then vomits us out when it's all over. We come and go, but the institution abides."

Beamer was listening intently even though he'd heard this rant many times in the past few weeks. Francis had been silent, taking in the spectacular view.

The lights from below gleamed off her pretty face.

"Time to go home," Jeff said.

Jeff and Francis descended quickly, down the winding circular stairs. Beamer, in no hurry to come down, lingered a while longer. Jeff got to the bottom just before Francis and scribbled with his finger, in the mud on the floor, "Help I'm trapped in the mud." Francis plopped off the last step beside him and read the message now addressed to any who might one day happen by that way.

"You think cool thoughts," she said, stabbing him in the heart.

Though the two pigeons, sitting in at home on this quiet Sunday evening, one of a long series of indistinguishable evenings, seemed unimpressed.

On the way down Jeff rang a few notes on the carillon for their benefit, the last notes he would ever play on a carillon. For a millisecond he contemplated playing "The Beginning," but then instead played a half-dozen random notes with a hint of dissonance among them. They fluttered emptily over the deserted campus, down the vacant streets, between those abandoned buildings where few human ears now remained to receive them.

At the very bottom Jeff locked the door to the Tower. The fog was beginning to lift but there was still a 19th-century London feel to the vaguely familiar courtyard. A man in a raincoat was standing with his back to them, beside a little dog. When the Tower door closed he turned around and hailed them.

"Buds, what is up with that," he said as rapidly as Jeff had ever heard anyone speak. "Really? It's like the middle of the night. You're playing the bells? What are you thinking?"

It was the new Master of Branford, a history professor Ig had raved about who had replaced the previous Master last year.

Same old, same old, Jeff thought, making their apologies. Jeff was not the first to play these bells at impermissible hours and would not be the last. It had all happened before and would happen again, as if it were all planned out. Here, now, tomorrow, Yale, the world, all carefully constructed to whoever made the effort to unravel their mysteries.

Jeff and Sam walked Francis back to her apartment. She spoke of summer plans, how they'd all stay in touch and how Jeff would come back to visit her and Sam next year. Outside her door Sam kissed her. Good for Sam. Jeff hugged her. She smelled nice.

Jeff and Sam headed back down York Street.

"I'll catch up with you in a bit," Sam said at the base of the Gateway.

"What? Where are you going?"

"I don't know. I could use a little more air. Heavy night."

"Okay. I'll see you back in the room."

Jeff started walking down the Gateway, though looked back and noted that Sam had turned in the direction of Francis's apartment.

Good for him, Jeff smiled.

Sam was a good friend.

Jeff turned back, glanced up at the clock on the Pierson Tower as he went through the gate. It read 3:06. That was odd, Jeff thought, looking at his watch to see it was 9:00 PM. The clock had never been broken before.

The courtyard was empty, desolate, still. The rain was done, the mist was done, the skies had cleared revealing a million stars above, the calm before tomorrow's storm.

This place had been so full and loud for so long and now it was empty empty empty.

He made his way to the red sunset maple, you and me, man. He stood adjacent to it, looked up at the stars above, then moved directly under it.

Who knows the exact sequence of thoughts, probably starting with the reminiscing on Harkness, but he found himself thinking of that Yoga class freshman year Maggie had dragged him to a few times, it really wasn't his thing but they would get stoned before they went and there was something pretty hot about stretching next to each other in sweats. And of course there was that pose he liked, The Butterfly, Jeff tried to remember it, he lifted his arms straight to his sides, hands to the level of his shoulders, did a dip, a 'v,' at the elbows, hands above his shoulders bent sharply down at the wrist, fingers pointing to the ground, was it something like that? He had his legs crossed, his right foot over his left foot, no that wasn't right, with his arms elevated like that it felt more like a crucifixion, didn't Jesus have his legs crossed like that on the cross. He uncrossed the legs, hesitated a moment, then remembered, lifted his right leg, bent at the knee, standing on one foot. That was it, he found the sweet spot, just balanced, maybe he could even try it with his eyes closed.

There he was, dark, silent, emptying himself out, feeling like it was the end of the world, all alone at the end of the world, he had never felt so alone like this.

That is where he was, he was in the zone, so focused his eyes closed almost like a sensory deprivation chamber, he didn't hear the rustling around him, he was thinking about nothing or was that the same as not thinking, there was a gentle clamoring around him he did not hear, he was just becoming aware of the ache, the ache of keeping one's arms elevated, the deep ache within, was wondering how much longer he could keep it up he didn't want to come out of the zone when he felt a body sliding in beside him, under his right arm, his right arm now resting on a shoulder, and he felt another body sliding in under his left arm, his left arm now resting on a shoulder, he didn't open his eyes as he felt arms now resting on *his* shoulders, he felt the jostling, he began to hear the clamor, there were more bodies, they were forming a circle, arms on shoulders under arms, and he opened his eyes and next to him on the left was Black and next to him on the right was Iggy, and next to them were Tayvon and Swill and Jasmine and Lisa and Thorn and Samilla and Croc and Maya and Eli and Ren and Fregoli and F. Scott and Zar and Sam and Francis and even Charlayne you know he should have gotten to know her better, they had all dropped their enormous bubble umbrellas in a pile and joined on in, and just then there was a jostle under his right arm and Jude pushed his way in, his arm on Jeffrey's shoulder, and there was a jostle under his left arm and Maggie pushed her way in, her arm on Jeffrey's shoulder, and then Sam started to sing, with that velvet voice, *Time, flowing like a river*, Sam began to sing, *Time, beckoning me*, they all joined in because of course, *Goodbye my love, maybe for forever,* they pushed in together, the circle was collapsing, a group huddle, a hug, a scrum, Thorn was right at home in a scrum but here he was weeping like a little girl, *Who knows when we shall meet again,* then that line that stomps on your throat, *If ever,* if ever, once Thorn broke down that was it for the rest of them, *But time keeps flowing like a river*, flowing on, flowing through and in and over them, the circle collapsed, they were weeping, *'Til it's gone forever*, they were weeping, *Gone forever*, twelve hours before The End, *Gone forever*, they were in on each other and in the middle of the scrum was Maggie, and Jude, and right in the middle Jeffrey, right before the final *forever*, Iggy, who had spent his rustication finally nailing the ability to do so on command, let loose a wet fart so magnificent it deserved its own Guinness entry and then just as suddenly as they had started weeping they were laughing, they were laughing, they were all laughing.

BRIGHT COLLEGE YEARS (OR, IF THAT'S NOT LIFE)

in after years, should troubles rise
to cloud the blue of sunny skies,
how bright will seem, through mem'ry's haze
those happy, golden, bygone days!
oh, let us strive that ever we
may let these words our watch-cry be,
where'er upon life's sea we sail:
"for God, for country, and for Yale!"

—Yale alma mater, second stanza

Made in the USA
Las Vegas, NV
25 January 2024

84868922R00204